THE
DRIFTERS

A Christian Historical Novel about the
Melungeon Shantyboat People

OTHER BOOKS OF INTEREST FROM MARQUETTE BOOKS

Ron E. Goetz, *The Kid: A Novel About Billy the Kid's Early Years* (2005).
ISBN: 0-922993-20-3

David Demers, *Dictionary of Mass Communication and Media Research* (2005).
ISBN: 0-922993-25-4

John C. Merrill, Ralph D. Berenger and Charles J. Merrill, *Media Musings: Interviews with Great Thinkers* (2004).
ISBN: 0-922993-15-7

Ralph D. Berenger (ed.), *Global Media Go to War: Role of Entertainment and News During the 2003 Iraq War* (2004).
ISBN: 0-922993-10-6

C. W. Burbank, *Beyond Zenke's Gate* (2004).
ISBN: 0-922993-14-9

David Demers, *China Girl: One Man's Adoption Story* (2004).
ISBN: 0-922993-08-4

Larry Whitesitt, *Northern Flight of Dreams: Flying Adventures in British Columbia, Yukon, NW Territories and Alaska* (2004).
ISBN: 0-922993-09-2

Melvin L. DeFleur and Margaret H. DeFleur, *Learning to Hate Americans: How U.S. Media Shape Negative Attitudes Among Teenagers in Twelve Countries* (2003).
ISBN: 0-922993-05-X

David Demers (ed.), *Terrorism, Globalization and Mass Communication: Papers Presented at the 2002 Center for Global Media Studies Conference* (2003).
ISBN: 0-922993-04-1

THE DRIFTERS

A Christian Historical Novel about the
Melungeon Shantyboat People

Tonya Holmes Shook

MARQUETTE
BOOKS SPOKANE, WA

Printed in the United States of America

Library of Congress Cataloging-in-Publication Data

Shook, Tonya Holmes, 1935-
   The drifters : a Christian historical novel about the Melungeon shantyboat
people / Tonya Holmes Shook.
   p. cm.
   ISBN 0-922993-19-X (pbk. : alk. paper)
   1. Melungeons--Fiction. 2. Women--Kentucky--Fiction. 3. Shantyboats
and shantyboaters--Fiction. 4. Kentucky--Fiction. I. Title.
PS3619.H653D75 2005
813'.6--dc28
                                                2004022665

MARQUETTE BOOKS
3107 E. 62nd Avenue
Spokane, WA 99223
509-443-7057
books@marquettebooks.org
www.MarquetteBooks.org

CONTENTS

PREFACE

Before the settlement of Jamestown there lived a people in America who built houses and had a complex social order, but history books have little record of them. They trace their ancestry to Portugal, Spain, North Africa, Turkey and Greece and to Native Americans, with whom they intermingled. According to old Mediterranean library records, their ancestors were once slaves of the Vikings, who used them to help colonize the new world. But they eventually were abandoned, left to survive as best they could in a foreign land. As the generations passed, these people acquired certain physical and cultural characteristics that distinguished them from European ancestors. They were called Melungeons.

Dr. N. Brent Kennedy, author of *The Melungeons, The Resurrection of a Proud People: An Untold Story of Ethnic Cleansing in America,* has researched the genetic and cultural peculiarities known to this people. Like African American slaves and Native American peoples, the Melungeons were treated unfairly by the European settlers, who forced them off their land. They were tagged as "free people of color" and at one time were prohibited from owning land, attending school, and marrying outside of their "own kind," except in Kentucky.

The ill treatment of the Melungeon people helped create a distinctive and clannish folk that had low self-esteem and peculiar ways. A mixture of Mediterranean and Indian bloodlines, they developed a race that clung to its own tried and proven traditions, trusting no one outside of family.

This novel tells the story of one Melungeon family. It is based on word of mouth stories from descendants of Harriett Riddle Holmes, my great-great grandmother, who began her married life on a houseboat during the same year as the Trail of Tears. She survived through the dire times of the Civil War, experienced heartaches relating to her sons William and Jasper, and relocated after the war to Texas, where some of her sons participated in cattle drives.

This story begins in the southeastern Cumberland area of Kentucky in 1837. The main character also is named Harriett Holmes, but she has no history, or none that is readily traceable, a phenomenon common to Melungeon people. Many, like my great-great grandmother, tried to assimilate into the dominant society, but rejection caused them to be more clannish than ever. They had few friends outside of the kinship clan. This social isolation contributed to the development of a unique culture, one that the reader will vicariously explore in this book.

This book is basically a fictionalized biography. The names and story line are factual, but the glue cementing accounts together comes from my imagination. I hope the reader finds this book enjoyable and educational.

ACKNOWLEDGMENTS

I owe a debt of gratitude to many distant relatives who validated the word of mouth stories I received from my own family. It was wonderful to hear familiar stories from people who once were strangers.

I also thank Dr. N. Brent Kennedy, an expert on the Melungeon people, who became known to me after publication of my documentary, *Displaced Cherokee: Come Home, Come Home.* Discoveries from his writings shed new light on a 56-year search for my lost heritage. Dr. Kennedy has been my mentor, encouraging me for about ten years while I worked on this book. He continued to have faith in me even when times were difficult. One of Dr. Kennedy's uncles was named "Holmes" Mayo, and he told me the name "Canady" (a character in this book) was the early spelling for "Kennedy." He and I may even be related.

My good friends and voracious readers, Jo Ann Rowan and her husband, Red, have given me valuable information about their state of Tennessee. It was with their help and encouragement that I received bits and pieces of information to fortify the historical facts in this book. Also, their natural talent to nit-pick my work— a worthy talent—proved a tremendous boon to help me keep on track. I was further encouraged by their excitement after reading my material.

I wish to thank my distant relative, Virginia Edwards, whom I have never met but who, by some divine intervention, called to tell me what she had learned about the shantyboat people who once lived in her area on the Ohio River, not far from where the characters in my story passed. She obtained from a friend and sent to me a photograph of the shantyboat people (see page 9).

Thanks to Shera Isler, Faye Hamilton, and Nicki Green for giving me feedback on earlier drafts. I also need to thank my patient husband, who "lost" his wife to a computer for days on end for more than two decades. And I also thank the publisher, David Demers, who found this lost history worthy of print.

Every day while writing, I thanked God for the ability to persevere. He fits into this big time and has orchestrated it all.

Tonya Holmes Shook
Hastings, Oklahoma   November 2004

Shantyboat people, circa 1910

There are many plans in a man's heart;
nevertheless the Lord's counsel, that will stand.

Proverbs 19:21

Chapter 1
TRANSITIONS

Harriett fumbled her way in toward Canady's lumpy bed. Her feet unsteadily inched along the plank floors until her hands touched the bed claiming a corner of the houseboat. It was not the feather bed she and her cousin, Elizabeth, had shared back in her Kentucky holler. Carefully, she sat down on the straw mattress. Stirrings inside her belly connived with the movement of the plank floor as if competing for her attention in this strange, new place.

Harriett swallowed hard, and pulled her woven shawl tighter around her shoulders. December cold made her numb. She tried to decipher her surroundings veiled by darkness, but was unable to see anything. Unsettled mysteries compounded her depression. She knew the houseboat, secured to a riverbank in Kentucky, was Canady's home, but that was of little comfort. Knowing they hadn't left Kentucky made no difference either. It wasn't home.

How could Canady stand it? Unidentified odors coming from the dark spaces spun her imagination out of control. These reeking smells conveyed it would be a difficult transition. She could not see the boarded, stretched hides piled across the roof and sides of the boat but their musky presence didn't require sight. Recollections of another time and place, not connected to this houseboat, came flooding back. The stench floating throughout the cabin reminded her of a fierce morning sickness she had suffered only a few months earlier. Darkness prevented any visual distractions, birthing a dread that odor could provoke more than thought. Harriett knew she could deal with the known; it was the unknown that terrified her the most.

Tired and disoriented, the pregnant, teen-bride associated her surroundings with that of a formidable foe, instead of a Beulah Land of hope with her new husband. She had an immediate and intense desire to return to her aunt and uncle's house. Before reacting to feelings, reason returned instead and ruined her fantasy. It wasn't that simple to go back. Planted firmly on the bed, Harriett struggled to replace panic with reason. She had made a promise. In fact, she had happily made a promise that very morning to Canady, even if the celebration had a smudge of regret tainting it. Her uncle had not been too sad to see her go either, considering her circumstances. There was no other option than the one she had taken. She rearranged her shawl closer and tucked her hands under the fringed edges.

The cabin swayed with a gentle bump each time her husband came on deck with an armload of things from the wagon. Creaking planks announcing Canady's steps were sounds of comfort in some ways, but still voiced reminders of homesickness refusing to lose a grasp on her. Nothing seemed to work to dispel her resistance to the offensive place to which she had been brought. For this occupant in the gently moving houseboat feelings alone dominated, not reason, as every reality she knew took flight and vaporized. She'd had fifteen years of living. Granted, it was a short life, but enough time to formulate some plans for a good future. What spirit had led her to this misdirection and then impishly abandoned her?

Canady came in with another armload of goods, after roping the team between the houseboat and the borrowed wagon. He was completely familiar with this cabin and could find anything he wanted in the dark, but he knew Harriett would be disadvantaged. It would be better to introduce his worldly fare, or lack of it, to his bride with his presence. So, until the time was right and the wagon was unloaded, he prolonged the introduction to his home. *Best she sit there 'til I get this done,* he thought to himself.

"Well, I fed them mules," he said after several more trips. He set the lantern down on the table. "Here, let me light this here lamp and it will make things a might easier to get around," he said. "I had a hard time findin' the lamp. It was next to the sideboard and your trunk, Harriett. That's why it took me so long."

Harriett noticed how lightly he walked toward the table when he sat the lamp down. Canady had stealth-like movements that came naturally from trapping and hunting, but she sensed the boat reacted no matter how lightly he stepped. Her resourceful trapper husband of one day had traded for the lamp at the trading post before bringing the preacher back to say the marriage words over them.

Harriett had deliberately put the new lamp between her trunk and the wagon sideboard after it tumbled over when the wagon had pulled out of the Riddle yard that morning. Instinctively, she had grabbed it when it rolled by as she lay on the cot Canady had fixed for her to travel on. Heavy with child, she felt clumsy enough without proving inept to care for the one new thing they had purchased: their oil-lamp. Greatly relieved it hadn't broken, she had then securely wedged it behind her trunk.

Harriett watched Canady adjust the elevation of the wick. Glimmers of light broke through the cabin's darkness replacing her imaginary monsters with undeniable facts. She saw the scarred table the lamp was sitting on. Its burns and nicks reflected lack of care. Obviously the table had been an abandoned orphan for many years. Her throat grew tighter as she viewed the scene surrounding her. Two iron skillets, a cast iron pot with a handle, a wash pan, and clothes piled atop clothes hanging from pegs decorated the rustic plank walls. The weathered walls were interrupted by a square boxed window covered over with a shutter and burlap curtain. Across from the bed was a small iron stove used for heating and cooking. Not too far from that, near the door, was a pie safe and dirty washstand bearing a bucket with a dipper handle hooked over the pail. Tears welled up and fell down her face, tattle-telling on the youthful disappointment she was so desperate to hide from her new husband. Unable to speak, she attempted to digest the shack. *I never seen such empty nothin'!,* she thought.

After Canady had moved the lamp to the middle of the small table, he quickly stuffed some kindling into the iron stove he had taken from the corner wood box. Puffs of smoke gave way to crackles of fire eating the kindling, then orange and blue flames grew from the logs he added.

What she had only guessed at before gravitated to something worse when she could see by lamplight. A simple solution to such visual dismay would be to retreat under the bed covers and pull them over her head so she didn't have to see anymore. *Maybe I could forget 'til mornin',* she thought. Only problem with that idea was that the reality of her surroundings was no longer a mystery. It wouldn't do any good to cover her head and go to sleep. The picture was still there, shouting in her mind, eyes shut, head covered or not. Too late! Forgetting wasn't an option for her either.

Can't go back, can't forget, she admitted to herself. The fifteen year old reached for a handkerchief in her apron pocket and tried to wipe away the evidence of her disappointment. *I can't cry neither. Uncle Will is let down enough. I can't go and do that to Canady.*

"There, now, it'll be warm in no time," Canady said then sat down on the bed next to Harriett.

Because of their marriage yesterday the trapping dandy's months long absence was somewhat forgiven. She forgave more readily than her uncle. Will Riddle harbored more than misgivings about Harriett's selection. The holler people considered boat people as intruders. Upon Canady's return to ask for Harriett's hand in marriage, unbeknown to Canady, he had averted his own disaster.

Tempers were hot in the holler. Harriett had been a prize sought after, hoped for, and lost. Worst of all, she had been lost to a river-man. Prospective suitors had still had hopes, regardless of Harriett's circumstance, but their hopes disintegrated yesterday morning. This silver-tongued interloper was due retaliation that mountain people with long memories were quite apt to give. Any excuse for Canady Holmes' demise could still possibly open up future opportunity. Beside, none of the mountain people liked Canady anyway, for other reasons. Boat people don't mess with their holler women!

Harriett's uncle let good sense control his first inclination when Canady declared his intentions toward Harriett. She watched their initial encounter in abject fear while hiding around a corner of the Riddle cabin. After seeing all Canady's furs, and hearing reasons for his long absence, Will said, "It's a tolerable reason, I reckon," lowering his shotgun and relaxing his taut jaw line. Will's temper cooled somewhat with Canady's explanation, but Canady didn't want to take any chances of riling it up again either.

Now that they were married and the situation rectified, there was a good chance Will would do his best to overlook all the rumors he knew to be circulating. Canady overheard Will tell his wife, "He at least took away a tad of the smudge, Nancy." Nancy shushed her husband for fear Canady would hear as the couple left the Riddle yard in their borrowed wagon the next morning.

Canady's lifestyle was one unique to trappers and traders because of his ability to maneuver. It gave nomadic rise to many opportunities for dalliances.

Rumor had it there was seemingly endless feminine hospitality lined up and down the rivers and throughout the hollers for this charmer. However, to his surprise, Canady had run into the unexpected when he met Harriett. His granite resolve with women was usurped to sandstone at his first glimpse of her. Instantaneously he was blinded to his normal passion for variety when he peeked through the cover of a thicket at this little Melungeon-Cherokee beauty picking mushrooms. "Gol'durn!" he whispered under his breath when he spied her in the clearing. She was the jewel he had been traipsing the world to find! *You knowed it when you knowed it,* he told himself.

From that secretive beginning Harriett became the challenge he least expected. Immediate thoughts of pursuing her were so strong that Canady's vacillating habits were, for the most part, forgotten. Maybe it was her freshness, her youth? In all his twenty-seven years he had managed to escape any permanent alliances but this fifteen year old woman-child was different. Nagging ideas as to how to pursue her began to formulate from the onset. He understood only one way.

When Canady Holmes came back for Harriett, his promiscuous life became secure only after he assured her uncle of his intentions. Canady had planned to marry her after trapping season anyway and sold Harriett on that notion before he broke her resolve. Satisfied after his claim was staked, he believed he had eliminated all other suitors vying for her attention and left with that confidence to finish out the trapping season. He soon discovered trapping wasn't as gratifying as it usually was because his affections grew and he pined for Harriett during their separation, an unusual distraction for Canady Holmes. Coming back to a pregnant sweetheart was not what he expected. Obviously, if he valued his life, he had to follow through with honor. Like all mountain men, Will Riddle was a good shot and he had no qualms about doing the duty. The trapper knew it.

Since Canady had to borrow Will's wagon to barter for supplies from

Smith's Trading Post, he hospitably asked the uncle to go with him. Will gladly accepted the invitation but would have gone with Canady anyway to guarantee the honor-ability of his intent and the safe return of his wagon. He wanted to believe this trapper meant what he said, but Will Riddle was no man's fool either.

Harriett's uncle made sure Reverend Goins, the Methodist minister, was sought after the bartering was completed. The willowy and meek little preacher followed Will and Canady on their return trip to perform the necessary ceremony to restore Harriett's honor and secure Canady's life.

Either from being closest to the fireplace or, from being nervous about the fact the wedding was uniting not only a bride from the holler to a boat man, but a very obvious mother-to-be, caused the squeaky voiced man of God to get the vows said in a hurry. Harriett's Aunt Nancy fought tears as did her children, fourteen year old Elizabeth and seventeen year old, William, named after his Papa. It was during the ceremony when Reverend Goins said, "Do you Canady," that Harriett took a peek around the edge of her blue-checkered bonnet to see Canady's face. He was more quiet and pale than she had ever seen him and he only said what was expected of him, "I do."

After all the months of anxiously waiting for Canady to come back and clinging to his promise to marry her, Harriett experienced unbelieving numbness when it was actually happening. It was as if she were hallucinating rather than being married. Somehow, she had always thought getting married was supposed to be different. Their courtship had come and gone so fast, with passions surging like hot lightning flashes striking the earth and disappearing before the forest fire began. Something seemed to be missing.

After the ceremony a relieved Will offered the Riddle hospitality to the new couple. Canady learned what it felt like to sleep on a fine feather bed. Will wanted that memory to come to visit him from time to time. He wanted to egg Canady on to provide something decent for Harriett since he knew she was going to call a houseboat her home. A disgruntled Elizabeth, not at all happy about giving up her bed, had to sleep on a pallet near the fireplace, but not without protest.

Early the next morning Canady told Harriett to say her goodbyes from Mr. Tucker's wagon. Will's neighbor, Fred Tucker, always called Tucker for short, had offered to loan his mules and wagon as a wedding gift. This same man had been ready to assist Will in using shot on Canady earlier, but things change quickly in the holler. Tucker would send his boys to retrieve his mules and wagon in a few weeks.

Excitement over a wonderful future and new life fueled the trip for the teen bride but now that the weary ride was over, any stamina she had left suddenly retreated to resignation.

Harriett's apprehension was distracted when she heard Canady's voice. "By the time I get the wagon unloaded, maybe this place will be warm e'nuf for you to fix us a bite to eat? I'll be a'bringin' in the slab bacon your Aunt Nancy sent.

It'll taste pretty good, don't you think?"

The lamp sputtered, the new wick was reluctant to fire up. After some more readjustments, Canady managed to get a maximum glow into the recoiling dark corners of the cabin. He slipped out the cabin door for another load of supplies before she could answer him about fixing supper. He needed to muster more courage and stalled for a little more time before he faced his bride. All too well Canady knew that Harriett had discovered the houseboat bed had straw for a mattress. The ways of the river would be different for his bride, and he knew it. He hoped pining for holler ways wouldn't muddy her new life with him. It was no secret there were plenty of women who would love to be sharing his straw mattress. But, for some reason, Harriett was the only one who ever showed reservations. It worked like a flame to a moth.

Light from the kerosene lamp ceased its sputtering and grew Harriett's shadow on the bare plank cabin walls. Bravely she tried another appraisal of her surroundings when she heard him coming back. Nothing had improved since the last look.

"There, now, it will be warm in no time," he said laying the bacon on the table next to the lamp. Canady came to the bed, sat down and coaxed Harriett to lie back with him on the lumpy plane. Reaching around her growing belly, he pulled her close and kissed her cheeks.

"By the time you get through with this here cabin, it'll be the coziest spot on this good earth." Holding her face between his large hands, he kissed her again. Canady's lips discovered what she had been trying to hide. His mouth moved from her wet cheeks to a passionate kiss on her lips, although he was careful not to squeeze her too tight. His tenderness elicited tears she couldn't stop. Words wouldn't come to answer him about fixing up the place so she nodded instead and turned away hoping her bonnet could save face.

The baby moved inside Harriett. At least the baby's world hadn't changed. Not yet, anyway. Welcoming a chance to think about something else, she reached for Canady's hand and placed it on her moving stomach.

"The Injuns are moving tonight, ain't they?" he asked trying to break the seriousness of the moment.

Harriett knew he would have to be a fool not to notice her wet cheeks. The teen bride was beginning to learn Canady was a lot of things, but a fool wasn't one of them.

Maybe now more'n ever Canady sees the differences of our years. Here I am blubbering like a baby and afixin' to have one! Harriett scolded herself. *Then, again, he might ne'er remember where I come from and to what I'se brought.*

A lump rotated inside her belly under Canady's hand. Both of them broke out in laughter, relieved to have something of mutual concern. Lack of life's creature comforts didn't alter some things. The baby kicked again. Laughing eased the tension, making surroundings inside the houseboat not appear so important. Beside, when you laugh hard, tears come from laughing. *Maybe he'll forget them salty tattle-tales,* she wishfully thought.

Canady turned over on the bed and gave her a warm embrace, the kind that comforts. His act of tenderness began a diluting process much needed for bitter disappointments. A soft yellow glow from the oil lamp lit up his handsome face, magnetically drawing her to look. His hypnotic brown eyes held her captive as if some compelling spell gave her no other choice. Seven months earlier she had learned about such mysteries. His eyes could still create excitement, causing Harriett to toss caution aside. Tonight would be the ultimate test for Canady. Never one to be timid, he always felt up to a challenge, even in the worst of circumstances. There was nothing he couldn't handle when it came to women, he was certain, but special skills were required tonight with his young bride. Even a rogue could appreciate that. Their once-shared past now belonged to his present. But, this time they were in Canady's territory, on the March River and on his straw mattress where he could dictate the terms. As exquisite as their first passion was, so it was again. Locked in each other's arms, two independent people became united in body. More importantly, bonds of partnership began this night in a definitive way inside Harriett, a new life connection in spirit. The something missing during their wedding ceremony was becoming found.

Savoring the closeness and warmth of their bodies—moments of security and comfort—Harriett kissed Canady's neck and whispered in his ear.

"Things is goin' to be fine, Canady, everythings goin' to be fine as silk," she said out loud, reassuring herself as much as her husband. She turned aside to view her new home once again. This time more bravely.

It ain't Aunt Nancy's kitchen but it'll do, I s'pose, she reluctantly admitted to herself. Kissing Canady's neck, she snuggled closer to him. New spiritual stamina returned in the comfort of his arms. Suddenly, she freed herself and sat on the edge of the bed.

I'll make better smells come from that old cook stove. It'll cover up that musky. That'll be the first thing that'll make a difference. "I need to fix us a bite," she told her happy husband. With determination she took the hanging skillet from the peg next to the hot cook stove. It was time to fry slab bacon and make gravy. It was time to feed her man.

Harriett Holmes

Chapter 2
MEMORIES BAKED IN CLAY

Homesickness and empty feelings that once consumed Harriett were becoming less worrisome. With dogged determination, she had made mental adjustments to living on a houseboat during the past two weeks. She had time to accept her life's direction made from personal choices already set. For those choices, there was precious little anything could be done about it now. She looked forward to having her baby to love. But, there were unnamed forces involved in determining their lifestyles too. Harriett had to endure choices forced upon her that were real and threatening interferences and she was aware of a tightening noose since it had already affected her Grandpa. His Cherokee plight to leave on his own or be forcibly removed could also be hers if it weren't for Will Riddle.

Her Uncle Riddle might be Melungeon folk, shunned for the most part by the people driving buggies rather than mules and wagons, but he didn't have removal threats made upon him or his family. If it weren't for Canady, it still might be her plight, or at least she feared the possibility. Two weeks to cogitate about such things, after she got rid of the musky smells distracting her, was enough time to give her a better acceptance for river changes.

This morning Harriett lit the lamp from a piece of burning kindling then moved the oil lamp to the back of the scarred table for biscuit-making room.

She slipped into her smock and put the hand-me-down apron around her before smoothing her hair up in a bun. The cabin was already warm since Canady had made a fire in the cook stove before he left. Harriett pulled the knob on the flour bin in the small pie safe. Everything was smaller in the cabin than what Harriett was used to: the stove, pie safe, table and bed. She knew Canady would be hungry after checking his traps and resetting them. If she got busy, the biscuits should be about ready when he got home. After cupping some flour into a big wooden mixing bowl, she reached for the salt crock and threw a pinch in before adding some soda and a little grease from the grease tin. Canady didn't have a cow. There was no way to make buttermilk biscuits. They didn't have milk, let alone buttermilk. Harriett dipped water from the pail on the washstand in place of buttermilk. *The biscuits will taste tolerable.* Before her grandpa, Chief Whitehorse, had to leave, Harriett used to make buttermilk biscuits when she visited him at the Indian village. She cut the biscuits out and put them in the oven box.

Slicing and frying bacon was done by rote after doing it so often in Aunt Nancy's kitchen. Her hands knew what to do without her mind informing them. This morning her hands did the work while her mind drifted to her grandpa. The holler people always knew him as Silas Choat. Silas had told his daughter, Nancy, and her family that his stay at the village was getting short. They were leaving. Most of the people in the Indian compound had agreed to move west. This decision had finally come after they swore it would never happen. Their actual decision to leave was made on January 1, 1837, to be exact. The chief knew he could stay and lose everything, or he could move early and possibly salvage some of his possessions. Certainly he had a better chance to keep his freedom if he left before any actual threat of removal took place. He had a fine house at the compound ,but not as fine as Will Riddle's in the holler.

Them Kentucky mountainsides talked back a plenty from all those teams of horses pullin' packed wagons. Everything Cherokee in the compound has packed up and left, all but the Walkingsticks. How well I know. I seen it done.

Wagons had every nook and cranny filled the day they pulled out. Leaving wouldn't be a trip to a nearby meadow for a pick-nick or an outing to gather wild blackberries this time. This leaving had permanent severance to it. White man's demands continued tightening the stranglehold on Indian land. Before he got squished in the closing door shutting Indian people out of a civilized world, Chief Whitehorse left and took most of Harriett's family and friends with him.

Any unpacked pot or kettle would be gone forever from pillagers ransackin' the compound after the family left it, she thought. The last moments played on Harriett's mind.

"Come'er, Tip. Hurry up, come on here!" Pierce Bluerain called to his hound. Tip wanted no part of the wagon but he succumbed to the stern, no nonsense command of his master's voice.

"Jesse, hold on to that dog now, hear me? He'll jump out of the wagon if you don't hold on to him. Stop your cryin', son. Pay attention and hold on to that dog!" Jesse tried hard to mind his papa. *No more 'n five, he's small for his years,* Harriett recalled.

"Harriett, can you give me a hand with this churn?" Pierce had said before turning back to give his empty house a final check.

As he handed Harriett the crockery, not breaking stride for the house, Pierce made excuses for his wife. "Suley is about past doin'. I just pray she don't start her time early. It'll be close e'nuf as it is for her to hold out another month." Pierce was busy taking care of packing out by himself. Suley wasn't much help to him because he and Suley had lost their second child not quite two years ago.

It would be touch and go even if they didn't have to make this trip. But, they did.

The old yard gate, hanging by one hinge, was pushed back against the fence once more. Repeated swinging movements had dug furrows in the ground each time it was opened. Suley sat silently on a big walnut stump inside the fenced yard. She always knew her husband had good intentions to burn out the stump and fix the gate. He passed by both with nary a notion of such plans now.

"It's time, Suley," Pierce snapped on his way out of the emptied house. Wagons were already on the move passing them by and Pierce was antsy. All the commotion broke up the sun-baked ground and stirred up dust.

Suley brushed at her dress before climbing up next to Pierce.

After loading Suley's butter churn, Harriett saw her Grandpa atop his big white stallion riding toward her. Somehow, she had managed to ignore these past weeks before this last goodbye. It was her habit to play hide and seek (without any intention of seeking) when life had hard spots. Harriett didn't want to think about it. The day she had dreaded most had come. This was one of those choices determined for her and certainly not one made by any free will.

"Time's come, Harriett," he said reigning his fidgety horse to a stop. Chief White Horse stared at Harriett for a few moments without speaking or dismounting. Silently, he drank in the image that stood before him.

All too soon memory would become distorted like reflections in stirred waters and he knew it. Finely, after clearing his voice, he said in measured words, "Make your own path in life, my granddaughter. Never forget your worth no matter where your path leads or what some may say. Bake our memories in clay and don't let them fade. You are from the loins of Chief White Horse! Remember that! Remember me!"

After speaking, he reined his horse to spin away from his dead daughter's child before his grit could be tested anymore.

"Grandpa, I ain't never gonna fergetcha!" Without a final touch from her grandpa, she watched him ride off. He gave no indication he had heard Harriett but she knew he could not stand any more gut -wrenching goodbyes. The chief's stallion had jumped to a gallop, abruptly terminating their conversation along with other known earthly ties. Through blurry images she struggled to watch the backside of the white stallion gallop toward the lead wagon until she could no longer see him. The first crater in Harriett's heart was etched that day from this monumental heartbreak.

Shaken, she climbed into the Bluerain's wagon and gave Jesse, Suley and Pierce a tearful and final hug goodbye. Tip was nervously whining until Harriett got out of the wagon, then he began barking. Jesse's little knuckles looked bleached holding onto the rope around Tip's neck.

"Suley. Jesse. Don't give way to no tears now. It ain't time for it. We ain't whipped and don't you let nobody get a notion we are," She had heard Pierce say these words through clenched teeth. She watched him fiercely crack the horse's reins and the Bluerain wagon moved out.

The hollers are silent. There ain't no laughter com'n from Indian children playin'. The flute's song a'callin' Indian meetin's has died. My memories of it is goin' to wash out in time, I'm a'feared. Harriett set the platter of sliced slab bacon on the scarred table. *The die's done cast, it's final,* the nagging voice inside her scolded. Feelings of emptiness took up residence every time she reminisced and without exception triggered the formation of tearful puddles. Harriett dusted flour off her apron before grabbing it to wipe her face when she heard Canady step on the deck. She safely hid the tears, but the apron left flour traces where tears once resided.

"Traps was empty, Harriett! I ain't gonna put up with no poachin'. Them Tuckers ought to be here in a day or two. We're movin' on when they come. Ain't gonna put up with this any longer'n I half to. If you weren't here, I know what I'd do. Handlin' it my way ain't a safe thing for you when I'm off a'trappin' and you are here by yourself," he said while rubbing his hands and face with wash water. Canady was a determined man. He grabbed a grayed cotton towel, wiped his face and sat at the table.

Harriett had come to know her husband well enough that there must be more to it than what he said. Canady never let any poached traps bother him before from what she'd heard.

"Where we a'goin,' Canady? We are too far from home as it is when my time comes," she said wiping her hands and trying to keep her voice from trembling.

"Down the river a ways, to the Cumberland."

Canady began scoffing down biscuits, gravy and bacon. She helped herself after he had already begun to devour his breakfast. Really too worried to eat much, she sipped coffee from a tin cup after toying with her food. There were too many unknowns in the future and it loomed even heavier after hearing Canady's intention to move on. *What was he thinkin'?*

After a gulp of coffee to wash down his breakfast, he tried to inform his wife he was taking good care of her. It was important for Canady's manhood to be ready to defend his home and to care for his woman. He didn't want her to doubt that he was capable of such. The life offered to his bride, a disgrace only boat people knew, had to be countered by his own ability to fight the stigma.

"I have someone down river a bit who can help out when your time comes, Harriett," he finally said, sensing what Harriett wasn't saying. Her silence was deafening.

Canady finished his meal quickly. He reached for the metal box on the shelf above the washstand and took out extra shot. After sticking the shot into his pouch, he sprang out the door and off the deck. Harriett was puzzled. *Maybe Canady had changed his mind about takin' things into his own hands?*

Reaching for the metal dipper, she poured several dips of water from the bucket into the dishpan. Canady's plate, fork, and knife got an extra hard scrubbing. Unsolved issues and no foreseeable way to remedy them perplexed Harriett the most. She noticed each day seemed to grow more challenges. Canady was good at formatting conflict with no apparent solution. The river had its own problems for inhabitants like them. Birth of a baby was one of them.

Conflicts owned by Canady Holmes weren't from intentional slights, but slights nevertheless. Canady accomplished what he felt needed to be done the only way he knew how. Before Harriett, it had been unnecessary to think of anyone but himself. Most of the time, from habit, he kept his plans to himself, leaving his young wife to guess. He saw no need to make any change of habit in this matter since such patterns had worked for years. *Harriett will come to know my ways by and by,* he thought feeling justified.

Furs had been heavy and bountiful for trade this year and they were ready for barter whenever the opportunity came around. Canady continued to add to the pile of furs when his traps weren't poached. A trapper's tried and proven habits were still vague but maybe his wife expected too much for two weeks? Maybe things would get better when she got to know his ways more? He was counting on it.

The teakettle with the blackened, wooden handle whistled. It must have been on fire once. Harriett rinsed the dishes and dried them noting that cooking seemed to help ease her mind. Busy work took away nagging misunderstandings. Keeping her hands busy was the best solution for unknowns and certainly this life with her new husband fit this category. She had little expectations in life other than a pushing reality growing inside her which would be another learning experience. This mornin's busy work produced two pecan pies. After pulling browned pies from the oven-box, she wiped the perspiration from her face. No matter the season, winter or not, the cook stove was hot.

"Anybody home? I say there! Is anybody home?" came a voice from the direction of the wagon.

Her heart quickened when she heard a stranger's voice. *Who in the world could that be?*

Harriett glanced at the empty gun rack on the wall. Canady had the guns! What was she to do? She gravitated toward the iron poker in a bucket near the stove. With her fingers tightly wrapped around the hard handle, she carefully peeked out the door.

Good smells coming from the cabin had drifted outside and found the noses of Wilber and Clyde Tucker. Even though Canady mentioned them at breakfast, she had forgotten about the Tucker brothers. Harriett was mentally unprepared for a holler twang interrupting the familiar sounds of squirrels barking and the chewink of the towhee.

Looking at the mules each day, feeding them, and sitting in the wagon had been a small pleasure. The team and wagon had brought a certain aura of peace and touches of her former home to the houseboat. Today, that connection had come to an end. Harriett recognized the Tucker boys. There was no danger. She stepped outside onto the deck about the same time Canady came into view.

"Howdy, boys," Canady said extending his handshake to well-known, past rivals. Canady had been an interloper in Smith Holler and his intrusion was never quite forgiven by the Tucker boys. It was especially galling to lose out to one of the boat people.

"Howdy Canady, Harriett," Wilber said, tipping his hat and showing a row of crooked teeth after shaking Canady's hand.

Clyde's handshake was accompanied only with a nod and a side-glance at Harriett. He smiled at Harriett but quickly erased it after looking at Canady.

"What news you hear from the holler?" Canady asked, trying to be hospitable. Before the Tuckers had a chance to reply, he interjected, "Ain't much happen' around these parts 'cept some fool is treadin' on thin ice messin' with my traps." Canady's words could be taken as a threat just in case the Tucker boys had a hand in it.

"They's puttin' up stockades all over, I hear," Wilber said. "Sorry state of affairs, Canady." He sidestepped the poached traps issue.

Both of the boys glanced at Harriett at the news Wilber shared about stockades.

"Seems Tony Walkingstick got himself near killed. Soldiers busted right in the door of their house. They manacled his parents first." Wilber shifted his feet before looking Canady in the eyes.

"I knew they ought ta go with grandpa," Harriett interrupted Wilber. "Tony told William they planned to take to the river if they needed to."

"I hear Tony's sister, Farina, ran out the door when they first come up on 'em," Wilber continued. "Soldiers chased right after 'er though."

"What happened to Farina? What happened to Tony?" Harriett butted in again.

"Well, no doubt about it, that girl was sceered to death. It didn't take them soldiers long to catch 'er to take advantage," Wilber said, tingeing red but not from the cold. "It was when Tony tried to knock the soldier off Farina when he got bayoneted. Oh, it ain't nothin' mortal, mind you," Wilber quickly added. "But he'll carry a scar to the grave, he will! Went right in his thigh."

Clyde finally spoke up, "It was a fool thing to do anyway, from what I hear. All of 'em got put in stockades but, from what the news is, they ain't in the same place. There's another one over at Creedo Gap beside the one outside the holler. I think Farina and Tony was put in one at Creedo Gap and their Ma and Pa was put in the one at Smith Holler."

Wilber and Clyde were asked to eat and to finish out the news telling. Without hesitation and fully expecting the hospitality, both Tuckers welcomed the invite. Canady's hunt after breakfast had provided welcomed extras for company:

a meal of squirrel, rice and gravy.

"I don't know which sounds the worst, the first cry you can hear a'comin' from those places or the echo bouncin' through the hollers," Wilber said, sampling Harriett's pecan pie at the end of their meal. He wiped the crumbs stuck on the side of his mouth with his sleeve.

"This shore was a fine meal, Harriett," he said. "I heard you was a fine cook and all. This was mighty tasty. We'se much obliged." Hopes of what he wished had been still put a twinkle in Wilber's eyes when he paid the compliment.

Canady bristled a bit. It was good Wilber realized Canady was a lucky man but it was time to subtly remind the Tucker boys, "Meal was et, pleasantries is said, guess it's time to hitch up the team."

Time's a wastin', he thought. *They best be on their way so I can do the same.* The river man had places to go and a person he needed to find.

Shelby Holmes

Chapter 3
REVELATIONS

Canady gathered his traps and stored them with the dried jerky, curing salt, and lye soaps in the outside store closet. His traps had to be packed in an orderly way to fit. If there was anything Canady took care of, it was first his guns, then his traps and he liked his trapping gear stored when they were moving.

It had been two weeks since the Tucker boys paid them a visit and took the mules and wagon home. Harriett knew the signs: when she saw him store his traps she knew they would be leaving. Shortly after that he began to pole out, describing his destination to his wife as, "We'se just goin' down the river a ways."

The more he worried, the more he climbed inside himself, forgetting the need for communication. This river man had been isolated from family life for a long time, but even he knew the baby's birthing time wasn't far off.

"You know, Harriett, I've been thinking about somethin'," he finally said, breaking the rhythmic swoosh made by poling. Precious little had been shared about where they needed to go before now. All she knew was the general vicinity was downstream away. Harriett was patient when he sometimes never finished sentences. She observed more and more of late that Canady retreated inward, chopping up his scarce words with some activity and keeping the rest of his conversation to himself. Packing his pipe this morning gave his hands something to do when his mind was searching for the right way to say something. She knew she would hear it eventually, but only in his time, so she patiently waited. Cogitatin', she perceived, was the reason for his speechifyin' troubles.

Canady carefully weighed his topic, chomping on his pipe stem and jabbing the pole systematically in the riverbed, taking care to formulate declarations. He didn't want to lessen his wife's evaluation of him. Saving face was of utmost importance as there was little else to save. He knew full well he didn't have any feather bed, no cow for milk, no company to socialize with, but he didn't want any either. There were serious times ahead, serious enough to be concerned without a cow or other ties restraining him.

"I think it's about time to get us a midwife to stay with you. I ain't no good at birthin time'," he finally said. "Leastwise, I don't figure I am."

Harriett had been patient for several bends in the river waiting for her handsome, muscular man to finish the conversation he had started. Hearing her husband's admission that he couldn't help her, in disbelief she answered out of frustration. "Well, Canady, why in the world are you movin' us away from the only help there is? It appears to me we ought to be a'goin' back the other way."

Canady looked up over his pipe in wide-eyed surprise. Little talk came from Harriett. Most things she thought were as much a mystery to him as his transient life was a mystery to her. Harriett never voiced complaints nor had she ever tried to impress her trapping dandy with superficial whims. She sensibly did what she knew to do. Aloofness was provocative to Canady. Most the women he had dealings with before were willing subjects and anything but mysterious. Harriett was spontaneous enough, but not clingy. She used her youthful ignorance artfully to draw attention from her terrestrial husband with feminine ways that came natural without having to ponder on them. She was as common and easy as a morning glory, but for Canady, she mystically transformed, when he least expected, into the most delicate of orchids. Harriett indeed was the rare, exotic flower hoped for by every male looking for a prized treasure. Canady couldn't believe his eyes when he first saw her.

Prior to their meeting, his conception about women's issues was one he grudgingly tolerated. Things that were important to women had their place, he supposed, but such was not nearly as important as manly concerns were. The past twenty-seven years taught him women were either pleasing to solicit, or were dreadful things a body best skirt. That is, until he met Harriett.

Staying busy helped Harriett deal with anxieties until exhaustion interfered, sometimes making her temper short with Canady. She had scrubbed on the old plank floors, walls and the window. The cook stove got scrubbed, as did the baby's cradle her cousin William made from a walnut tree. It had been polished until it glistened. She made flannel blankets and hemmed the edges with fancy stitches when other chores didn't demand her time. However, all the work hadn't brought her to one solution for the birthing process. Concern shadowed her face. Even more so after Canady's admission he wasn't going to be any help to her.

The trapper intended to continue to be the master of his own life even if his wife's pregnancy was a concern that made saving face and finding a solution very difficult. When the Tuckers came for the mules and wagon, Canady felt an uncomfortable stirring of competition. The best way to handle that kind of problem was to make himself scarce. Rivers could accommodate this inclination best, but old patterns of escape wouldn't work with Harriett. He had to solve this perplexing need for a midwife somehow.

"There's somebody I never told you about, Harriett. It's my Aunt Arimenta. Problem-solving had been weighing heavy on Canady's mind. He had to think about solutions, and rethink about them before he made his deductions known. "We ain't too far from their village and maybe they's the lucky ones. Leastways, I'm acountin' on it," he continued after taking a long draw from his pipe. Canady appeared much more confident than he really was. He was at the edge of a precipice. He always took things to the edge, but this one about finding a midwife was as far as he had ever gambled before. It was a long shot. Canady hoped his aunt's village hadn't been invaded yet and that she was available. He tried to discount the possibility that soldiers had already rounded up her village, but maybe not. Maybe she had escaped to the hills. If her village people had fled to the rivers like he had, then all hope would be lost, he was afraid. But, if he could find her (and it was not a case of "if" anymore, it was a "have to" case), then maybe Arimenta would take her chances on the houseboat with them.

"From what the Tuckers said, and what I heered at Smith's tradin' post, her comin' with us is sumthin' she more than likely will do, I figure. After all, we can help her out and she can help us," he argued out loud between draws on his pipe.

Satisfied he had found the solution for Harriett's conditional problem, he went back to poling, this time with more vigor.

Harriett looked at her puzzling husband. Tan skin and brown eyes did show signs of Indian blood. *Just how is it you ain't worried for yourself?*

She stepped closer to Canady seeking comfort without any comment. Both of them watched the towering sentinels lining the Sequatchie Riverbank stretching their bare branches over the water, passing one after the other. Those woody giants testified in whispers circulating through their treetops about an evil pouring from the hearts of ruling men. Owls heard the testimony, squirrels heard it, Indians sensed it, as did Harriett and Canady. It was as if the trees were clawing woody fingers into the open spaces above them like a warning, but the houseboat managed to slip through their leafless grasp.

"My Pa's name is Shelby Holmes," he said eventually after going yet further down the waterway. "He married right soon after Ma died," he suddenly blurted out without preparing Harriett which direction his conversation was headed. She listened intently to whatever he was going to divulge about his family while savoring the smell of tobacco smoke escaping between his words.

"Pa had us six kids to take care of. They tell me he was a good farmer, but he was terrible a'takin' care of kids. It was a woman's chore," he said tucking the pole under his armpit while packing his pipe again.

"Our new Ma was nice enough at the beginnin'. But the peacefulness lasted about as long as smooth water on a windy day. Their marryin' was one of necessity, you might say. It was Pa's necessity. It weren't no necessity of mine, I can tell you for sure. It weren't much a necessity for the younger ones either. Her name was Cleo. I ain't never gonna forget that name neither. She is the reason for my grit to go, you might say." His soft brown eyes grew steely at the mention of this woman's name.

Harriett had never heard Canady say so many words at one setting in his life. *I can't imagine why he's tellin' me this. Why is he tellin' about his family now?*

"Pa was glad to give her complete reign over us kids and she begrudgingly took it. Cleo Holmes wasn't too sure she wanted to be a stepma to some half-breed kids. We soon was made to feel it was best to make ourselves scarce, not be underfoot and all. As far as she was concerned, every last one of us kids was territory, a territory that used to belong to our Ma." Canady looked at Harriett's response to his family secrets. He couldn't read anything across her face other than intently absorbing eyes soaking up his revelations.

"It weren't to Cleo's likin' neither," he continued. "She was stuck with us, weren't nothin' else she could do. Ever chance she got, she used the razor strap expressin' her wishin' us gone. Maybe if we got beat 'nuf we'd grow in a hurry."

Harriett had never heard Canady talk about his family before. The evil woman he described explained the reason he had been on his own for so long.

"Cleo dug in by gettin' rid of Ma's memory in ever way she could. She was a'goin' to get rid of any notion there was Indian connection to us kids. That never bothered me none. I never looked back once. I was out on my own at thirteen."

"Canady, you've been tendin' to yourself since you was thirteen?"

"I reckon that's so, Harriett."

That's the reason he's a hard one to figure, Harriett thought. *He thinks of things with nary a word to me! He waits til the last minute. Til a time suits him. No wonder he does like he does, he's been a'doin' it a spell and already in the habit of it.*

Harriett listened and learned how and why Canady had weaned himself from his family and escaped the confinement of farm life. He wanted no part of any of it. Being away from kin suited him just fine since his Ma died

"It was when I turned fourteen I quit goin' around family anymore. "I ain't never pined for anything with Cleo in it. I never look back, Harriett. Ain't worth it. I just move on," he told her. "I learned boat people can do such as this."

Survival was second nature to Canady and he was certain he had a solution for the baby's birthing—his Cherokee aunt.

His mother's sister had been delivering babies all her grown life. She had been a frequent visitor before Cleo married his Pa, but Cleo had put a stop to visits soon after she and Shelby Holmes married.

Well, I don't figure this baby cares one whit about his pa's ramblings and why he's a restless soul, Harriett thought when the baby moved. *I get reminded every time this youngun' kicks, birthin' is bound to be soon. Might be better if I put the idee out of mind and think about it later,* she thought to herself. Unknown things were more tolerable if she didn't cogitate on them.

Two days after Canady declared his solutions for a midwife, he poled the boat into a riverbank on the Sequatchie River. Early February weather was surprisingly mild this year compared to last winter's blizzard, the notorious blizzard of 1837, the one Chief Whitehorse had traveled through. Canady expressed hope his aunt's village was still intact when he tied up their boat. If they were not there, he had every intention to find where they were. Rumors of stockades had set off alarms inside, making him keenly aware and in tune with his surroundings. He knew time was bound to be short for Indian habitation and soldiers could be just about anywhere to carry out routing orders.

There had been no boat people seen on the river, the banks were bare, and no news was heard. He was instinctively sure whatever was happening was not good. Canady had no other solutions in mind for Harriett. Necessity preceded his natural inclination to flee. He certainly didn't want to be the only person around when the baby started coming. Quickly filling his pouch with jerky and biscuits he headed for the cabin door to seek out his Aunt Arimenta.

"When will you be back, Canady? I can't use your gun even if you was to leave it. The kick is too much for me now." Harriett was having a strange tightening across her belly. Arimenta might be a necessity but she didn't like for Canady to be far from the houseboat. No matter how much she tabled troublesome thoughts, being alone and very pregnant was something she had to think about, want to or not. It was unnerving to be docked too. Probability for marauders placed her in jeopardy. These were desperate times when people were running away.

"Don't you worry none, sweetheart. I'll only be a day a'goin' and a day a'comin'. I've had trappin' spells for near that long and you did fine, remember? Now, that ain't too bad, is it?" he asked her, knowing full well this was the end of the discussion. His course was set.

"You can make it, I know you can," he added for good measure, bouncing onto a muddy bank without looking back. With long strides he was out of sight in a matter of minutes.

The two days Canady spoke of stretched to a third, then to a fourth, fifth and into the sixth day before she heard him calling out to her. She didn't answer him.

Canady quickened his pace, leaving Arimenta behind. "Hurry Arimenta," he called. "The baby ain't come yet but its bound to be here any minute," he said after hurrying inside the cabin and finding Harriett in the midst of heavy labor.

February winds refused to be tamed and returned with blasts of cold air. Burning wood crackling in the small wood stove forced a heated teakettle's song to sing with Harriett's cries of anguish mixed with Arimenta's words of encouragement.

"I can't do this! Make it stop!"

Canady took on every cry she made as if he were uttering it himself. With each pace back and forth on the plank deck he kept asking himself why she ever had to get pregnant in the first place.

"Push," Arimenta ordered sternly.

How could lovin' been so good with such pain connected to it? Canady
bemoaned to himself, pacing on the deck.

With another command to, "Push," Arimenta scooped up a slippery baby
with flailing arms and gasping sputters erupting into a wail.

Canady took giant steps from the deck into the cabin to Harriett's side in
time to see a wet and wiggling baby being laid next to her side. Arimenta cut the
cord and laid a small piece of it on the scarred table before she started to wash the
baby. It was Indian ways to save part of the cord.

"He's a fine baby," commented Arimenta. "Harriett you will be blessed with
many babies. Your time was easy."

While Arimenta busied herself with the baby, Canady squatted on the floor
next to Harriett and blubbered something about his aunt helping his own mama
bring him into the world. He further spouted something about she had delivered
all his Ma's kids, then added an illogical deduction that his Ma had died when he
was eleven, though one had nothing to do with the other. Memories of his own
upbringing during better times forced entry into his mind. His own baby's birth
gave him pause to reflect on past family. The heritage he had once ignored at age
fourteen came back full circle as he looked at his Indian princess who had just
born him an heir. An heir that was part Indian, just like himself as well as his
mama.

Today, Canady realized he became somebody's background, his newborn
son's background. This baby had two kinds of folks in his ancestry. Canady
acknowledged he only shared half, Cherokee and Melungeon. Harriett's ancestry
lived through the gift of life she gave to their child, also. They both looked at the
wiggly blend of love, a mishmash of a miracle. This new miracle was also given
another heritage in the making. A disreputable cloud of disgrace, belonging to the
lowly boat people, baptized him at birth.

Harriett could hardly believe her tired ears when she heard Arimenta's
comment concerning an easy birth! "How can you say such a thing about this
bein' easy? What do you mean an easy time of it? I can testify for sure, it ain't
so," she defiantly said.

Arimenta chuckled to herself. "You did just fine, missy. You will have many
more babies," she told the tired mother. She knew her nephew's nature. She also
knew from years of experience, children come easier for some than it does for
others. Harriett would have many more children.

"Harriett, let's name him for Pa." Canady had tears in his eyes and looked
with expectation at his wife. "He should be called Shelby, Shelby Holmes," he
repeated. She nodded. The silver-tongued dandy was speechless watching his tiny
son nestled to Harriett's breast making squeaking sounds.

"My raven-haired princess and my red-faced prince, this old houseboat
never seen the likes of this before! But, if Arimenta is right, it's bound to see it
again." Joy and love struck a cord never hit before in the heart of this trapping

boat man.

Harriett noticed there was something almost holy about it.

Canady got up from sitting on the floor next to Harriett. "Well, it looks to me like this papa best get out there and rustle up some more furs for barter. We are goin' to be needin' em. Pot's Holler ain't too far and we'll be there before you know it. I've been a tradin' there for many a year. We's in need of a good barter now, ain't we?"

Canady turned back to his wife in a state of relief and said, "I confess, I almost took out, Harriett. I couldn't stand no more and I almost took out. Oh, Harriett, I wouldn't have missed this for the world. I'm mighty proud I stood it out." He bent down and kissed her forehead, rubbing his finger across Shelby's satiny cheek.

The aroma of rabbit stew filled the cabin with good smells. Arimenta had tidied up the cabin while an exhausted new mother watched in slow motion before drifting off to sleep. At this point she was too tired to sort things out, but alert enough to know that life as it had been, would never be again. What used to be was becoming a fuzzy memory. Maybe Canady was right. *It ain't worth lookin' back. Best to look forward.* Harriett drifted off to a welcome sleep.

Water hadn't frozen up like it normally did this time of year, but Canady poled the houseboat downstream when the riverbed was too shallow until the banks got further apart. Ice had formed at the water's edge a time or two but never froze solid. In many ways, this cold was good. "Cold weather pelts are top barter," he always said.

Arimenta opened the door to throw out a dishpan of water when movement along the bank caught her eye. She saw people who looked familiar to her on the shoreline. While she was squinting to focus, one of the people waved at her. She returned the gesture.

Then, Arimenta saw more people gathering firewood further downstream. Fog meandered around tree stumps and mixed with smoke from their campfire. Apparently the fog was in no more hurry then the lazy wisps of campfire smoke this morning. Both hung in the air, apparently with no place to go, and white and Indian people moved slowly, following the example of the smoke and fog.

This tranquil scene was out of place for these uncertain times. Obviously, neighbors were busy building a new cabin for a Cherokee family as if denying Indian removal threats existed.

Arimenta came back inside and hung the pan on the wall next to the big water bucket on the washstand. "It's pretty cold to be buildin' this time of year," she said. "At least their cabin should be built in time for spring plantin'." Arimenta talked like she was trying to convince herself.

After changing Shelby for Harriett, she handed him over to nurse. Arimenta said, "It gets easier in time," when Harriett flinched. Harriett bit her lip exemplifying hope that she was right.

"They's a'wastin' their time," Canady finally said. "Harriett's grandpa didn't stick around to see what that wishy-washy Congress was a'goin' to do next. I hate to say it, but it's useless, just useless. They's all a bunch of lyin' skunks. They's such happenin's everywhere, treaty or not. One thing's for sure, them sorry smellers won't get us. Just let them try to find us!"

Canady removed the grate on the stove, reached in and pulled out a piece of burning kindling to light his pipe. "'Sides, I look like my Pa. Nobody's goin' to mess with this white man's son," he bragged.

Arimenta was visibly quiet. She tightened her lips to a thin line.

"We'll take you with us, Arimenta, if you've a mind to." Until now, she had kept her feelings to herself but Canady's boast had stung. He realized the offense afterward but it had been said and was too late to make a difference now. White men were causing her family to lose all they owned. Canady's brag didn't sit well. Unintentionally, Canady had challenged his own heritage. He had denied part of it and put down the other half of his biology.

Arimenta couldn't let it go without some comment. She said, "I haven't told this to anyone outside our village. None of us think our Chief Ross in Washington understands things right. Mr. Ross thinks he can talk their language but he can only talk one side of the white man's talk. He doesn't understand the other side. It is plain to see from what we are a'hearin'."

She turned to look out the window at the people along the bank once again. "Word's already sent out by runner. It's the family in Kentucky that don't pow wow. We sent word by your Uncle Tomah, Canady. He has become the spokesman for our family. We made us a plan because some of us are old and wont' be able to go fast when the time comes. There's a plan before it's too late," she said again. " We ain't' movin' off from sacred places and I am afraid for anyone without a plan to go. If we have to leave, it will be where we want to go, not where they want to take us," she said. Her voice echoed Chief Whitehorse's words of defiance.

Arimenta added in a firmer, more sure voice, "Some supplies are hid in a secret place. I can't tell the place, only when the time comes we will move to our campsite. Pine Mountains holds many secrets," she concluded.

Canady could tell his Aunt Arimenta had her mind set to stay with her people. He figured there was no need for any argument to convince her otherwise. As much as Harriett hated for Arimenta to go, she respected her convictions, relating it to her own grandpa's viewpoint.

A few days later, they said their goodbyes and Canady helped his aunt return to her village.

After Arimenta left, the days were full and busy establishing routines demanded by a baby. Daily chores stayed the same but all the months of anticipation waiting for the baby, preplanning the needs, had to be rethought. "Babies is a lot of work, Canady," Harriett told her husband when she hadn't baked him any pies. Lack of sleep soon became less of a problem. Shelby contentedly settled in and Harriett picked up her chores once more, adding baby care to her list of life's work.

Each day produced new vistas on the river. Lacy patterns formed by branches struggling to give new life and meaning to the season arched in every direction with outstretched arms for bird rests. Buds on woody stems were intent on escaping their bark prison, adding new shades of green. Each bush, sapling, and tree moved frantically in the breezes as if to find places for their branches, mimicking competition of people salivating for Indian land.

Canady never felt easy when the houseboat was docked. As soon as he got full traps he took his fare and moved on, not staying to reset and trap again. He seemed less restless and more at ease in the middle of the river.

The winter's trapping had been good for needed barter at nearby Pots Holler. Canady had used the trading post in Pots Holler long before he ever met Harriett. However, this trading trip he had more on his mind than he'd had at other times.

For no apparent reason Harriett could figure, he chose to blurt out before they arrived at Pots Holler, "Those hooligans' Tucker saved me from would be only too glad to turn some government soldier onto me!"

Harriett put Shelby back in his cradle and asked her husband, "What you talkin' about, Canady? You ain't gettin' feeble-minded on me, are you? What government soldier?"

Canady clenched his teeth and brooded but didn't answer her question. Arimenta's words about his stepmother had been eating on him ever since she left. Adding to Canady's mental war, Wilber and Clyde had told Canady about their Pa saving him from some wishful thinkers out to get him before he and Harriett married. The Goins cousins, related to the preacher who married them, lived near the Riddle place. They had spouted off about getting even after they learned Canady Holmes had beat them out. Canady, an outsider, had ruined their prospects with Harriett and they were out for revenge. The Goins cousins could deal with losing out from holler folks but not from outsiders. Beside that burr rubbing him wrong, news Arimenta had told him before they first got to the houseboat, about having to leave the village, and her final warning when she left was weighing heavy. He had to make a stop at Pot's Holler to barter. What or who would be waiting for him? That was the question. Past trades with the post owner in Pot's Holler guaranteed this boatman's safety to trade in town. He knew he couldn't ever take anything for granted no matter what the past had proven, however.

"Brother James never has been closed-mouthed about Mama, her bein' Cherokee and all. No doubt those ne'er do goods would love to get some sort of revenge. James and the Goins cousins used to go jiggin' together and if anyone in the holler would be out to get me, it would be them. Poachin' has been one of their tricks. That's why we left when we did back yonder. My traps was poached again and I think I knowed who done it. I have suspected they trailed my traps' just like a hound. At first I thought it might be the Tuckers, but after some figurin', I changed my mind."

"You think those Goins are emptyin' your traps? Canady, we are a long ways from home. They wouldn't come this far, would they?"

"Knowed it Harriett. They have bartered at Pot's Holler before too. Just goin' along behind me and takin' a chance to make a few easy pelts is what they's done before. It's what I 'spect they's a'doin. There's reason e'nuf, I reckon. Those Goins boys knowed all about us."

"James was thirteen when Mama died and Cleo could never turn his head or heart a'gin' Mama no matter how hard she tried. James talked about Mama all the time no matter what Cleo did, razor strap or no. I cared for my Ma 'nuf, but I moved on. James has a way of hangin' on to somethin' that just ain't no more. He told everybody about Ma and how he missed her, lickin' or not. Goins folk knows us well, I reckon," he told Harriett clenching his teeth against his pipe stem. "Tomorrow we'se makin' tracks ourself, my little princess."

Chapter 4
SHADOWS OF THE PAST

"I'll get to see them calicos and maybe some finery never seen before! Shelby, your Mama is a'goin' to show you the sights," she said as she put him back into his cradle. Quickly walking toward her trunk, Harriett pulled out her good dress and blue calico bonnet. "Steam a'comin' from my teakettle should pull some of them wrinkles right outta there," she said while unfolding her dress. Planning for a trip to Pot's Holler trading post was the most exciting thing to think about in months. The only contacts she'd had with people since she left her aunt and uncle's home were with the Tucker boys, Arimenta, Canady, and now her baby, Shelby. She had seen some other boat people but they kept to themselves and went about their own business. This morning's anticipation for a town visit forced her to face how isolated they had been from humanity. She had almost forgotten what it is like to see and talk with other people.

River life was different for Canady than it was for her. He had lived with a disdain, a caste system socially attached to boat people for a number of years. Canady was used to it. He still saw new scenery and had a variety of chores from setting and checking traps to skinning and tanning hides when he docked in remote places and came ashore. During such times he experienced walks into the woods, the open spaces, and had that independent freedom he had once explained to her as "the freest life there is."

Her work had become daily routine done in a very small, solitary space, expanding only when she washed clothes no further than the riverbank. Most of the time she had to scrub clothes from the deck. Without it being said in so many words, on a number of occasions, Canady had hinted they best not go near people. He had neglected to tell her the part about most town people not wanting to have the likes of them around. Revelations concerning life on the river had come only by periodic insinuations from her husband after they married. He failed to reveal any discouraging aspects of it when he was explaining to her about his free life.

Dreaming about seeing other people and an interest in the latest fashionable things the ladies wore in Pot's Holler gave her a new expectancy this morning. Disappointedly she had discovered her new life seemed to have a shame attached to it, but it was quickly forgotten by dreaming about a time in Smith Holler. It was easy to revert back to her life with her aunt and uncle. For Melungeon folk, they were treated fine enough. Sam Smith was happy to trade with her Uncle Riddle.

The shocking reality she didn't want to think about was the fact that boat people were less desirable than the Melungeon people in the holler. It was a double whammy to be both a Melungeon and one on the run. Her very background of Cherokee, Melungeon, and the new label—with Canady—of boat people, was more serious than she could fully grasp. True to form, she determined this troublesome thought was something she preferred to forget for the time being. Harriett dipped water into the teakettle with gusto.

"Oh, Canady, I can't hardly wait. How much longer do you s'pose it is afore we get to Pot's Holler?"

An ominous dark frown crossed Canady's face. She instinctively knew it was one of those times Canady was having trouble with words, but his difficulty didn't affect messages already being said with expression. Finally, he stammered, trying to uncover ways to break what he must to Harriett.

"I'm a'thinkin' you best you stay out of sight while I take care of business." His words were hardly audible enough for her to hear but she did hear it. What he expected and dreaded, he read immediately from the face of his shocked wife.

Canady had always been tolerated ashore due to the value of his furs. The post had done business with him for several years in Pots Holler, even if none of the boat people were welcome in the town. Canady had always been accountable and dependable and that counted with the post owner. There was only one other place outside the post he knew he had no worry about going to whenever he came to Pot's Holler. He hadn't told Harriett about that place.

Before a barrage of protests could come from Harriett, he started his explanation. "I figure the best way to not take chances the Goins cousins is up to no good is to get my business done over with in a hurry. I'm a'goin' to walk right up, bold like, and take care of business just like I always done before."

Determined, the river man tried to explain his situation as he saw it. He had married a strong-willed woman and the response about to come from Harriett gave him warning from the look on her face. Time had come to increase his volume with an air of unbridled authority. After his objections about her going into town, regardless of being advantaged by more years than she, he could lose ground.

"I have been there many a time, Harriett. They know me. We can't take no chance now for figurin' we'se Indian.

That was one major reason, but the other reason he couldn't bring himself to say. He knew too well boat people were not the most favorite guests to any town. It was best to use the threat of Indian removal reason. Harriett understood that one.

"With just me a'goin' in, it probably won't never come to mind," he said, mustering enough grit to look in her eyes. He tried to side-step the issue of her disappointment. Canady wasn't accustomed to making an accounting to anyone. This was one of the reasons he chose the river life.

Harriett couldn't believe what she'd heard him say. All her fancy plans, her fantasies she had dreamed about, the free life he had promised her, were dashed by his pronouncements. Confined, confused, angry and puzzled, she heard him spewing out more verbal dams blocking her town visit before she had a chance to plead her case.

"If the Goins is a'tradin' in Pot's Holler, who knows what talk is out, specially if they see me with an Indian woman? I ain't no fool, Harriett. Them Goins knowed we'se married and ain't too happy about it neither. They's more then biled over account of me messin' up their time with you. We ain't a'takin' no chances, Harriett. I ain't a'feered of 'em, just don't think now is the time for a stir."

If it had been only the boys from Harriett's old holler who was out to get him, she knew Canady could settle up with them. Obviously this was only part of the problem. She was discovering the world she lived in at Smith Holler had been more than sheltered and her circumstances were not the same with her river man. She wasn't ignorant about Indian removal talk, but she didn't understand about the lack of acceptance of boat people.

The danger he talked about went beyond a mere scuffle and Canady had far more to lose then he was willing to chance. He knew more about such than his wife, but didn't know how to share it. He thought it best not to.

Any further protests would have been to no avail. The disappointed Harriett had come to know Canady well enough by now to realize words in anger would not advance her cause one bit. His face was set in stone.

For the next two days she tried to cover up her disappointment. Going to that trading town had been the carrot telling her this confinement wasn't all that bad. After Canady's decision, the carrot had been caught and it had been eaten, but not by her. Thoughts about Pot's Holler had fertilized her dreams and she was expecting showers of adventurous exploration to nurture those dreams, but drought came instead.

The gray plank walls of their cabin amoeba-ed into a formidable foe that seemed to shrink inward. She had wanted to go into that trading town more than life. It was not to be. Canady's mind was made up. No more mention was made of it until he docked in Pot's Holler early the next morning.

Canady began getting ready to go to the post to trade. She watched him wash his face after shaving and knew she couldn't keep her disappointment to herself much longer.

Harriett gingerly sat on the straw mattress, unusually quiet while holding and nursing Shelby. She calculated   new approaches that might work to her advantage about going into town. Every move Canady made this morning—his taking extra pains for a closer shave and more effort to comb his unruly hair—infuriated her all the more. She watched knowing she was not going to share in the experience.

Canady's hair ain't straight like mine, she sullenly thought. *This white man's son probably took his stubborn hair after his Papa!* The more she watched, the angrier she became. While concentrating on his looks, he exemplified an air of cockiness. Harriett was momentarily impressed until reminders of her circumstances competed with his tapestry. Anger won.

"Canady, Shelby and me could go one way and you go another," she pleaded once more, introducing a solution to Canady's concerns. "Ain't nobody a'goin' to connect us up if we ain't together."

Canady didn't answer. It was useless conversation. He continued combing his hair. Harriett's resentment had no restraints. For the first time since she had met her trapper, dissatisfaction with him began growing bigger than the bundle of furs he had to trade.

"It's best you keep Shelby quiet and stay out of sight," he answered. He knew too well that the people there knew boat people. They also knew Indian people. He couldn't chance it.

Plainly, Canady didn't want to deal with rethinking his plan. His air of authority, white man's authority, stuck in her craw this morning even more so after that last comment. With a reckless air, he put the finishing touch to his morning's toiletries. The coup-de-gras followed.

"Besides, I ain't connected to nobody around here. Leastwise, that's the way they know me and best keep it that a'way."

Love connections holding their trust pulled the stretched links to the limit this morning. Harriett hated it. Since she had no history herself in Pot's Holler or any other reference to refute her husband's take on things, she felt trapped. Like it or not, she was trapped.

"It's the best thing, Harriett, the best thing. Trust me," he told her, walking out the door, stopping only long enough to heave the bundle of furs atop his shoulder. The conversation was over.

Harriett was watching through the window when he bounced off the deck. Resentment or not, she did what he said—stayed out of sight of the milling crowd—but she couldn't fight the temptation to peek out the window. Then, she saw his hoisted bundle of furs rotate a bit when he left the houseboat about the same time she heard giggles. The laughter came from two young women standing close to the water's edge. Blood rushed to her face when she witnessed the flirtation. Anger overtook caution. Harriett flung the tortoiseshell and boar-bristle hairbrush Canady had used to primp with earlier across the cabin. The brush made a loud pop when it bounced off the hanging wash pan. The noise startled Shelby and he began to cry. Angry or not, she remembered Canady's warning to keep Shelby quiet and quickly snuggled the baby under her chin to rock him back to sleep. A need to protect her baby put her temper in check momentarily.

Living in such confinement had taken a lot of getting used to at first. She had felt pretty confident she'd overcome her initial tendencies of claustrophobia. "'Stay out of sight,' he said," she repeated aloud. *This ain't the way it's supposed to be!* Suffocation of spirit once again raised an ugly head!

Wild imaginings tormented her after seeing those women giggle. Harriett put the sleeping baby back in his cradle then returned to the crude window and watched the freedom of movement people had in Pot's Holler. Her movement from inside a dark, plank-walled cabin was minuscule.

Harriett saw other boats docking, but only one other houseboat among them. People were spilling out of the vessels, adding to the already congested town. She observed that most of the people were headed in the direction Canady had gone.

Dogs barking, squeaks of wagon wheels, men's laughter and loudmouthed brags sifted back through the cabin window to Harriett's ears. She wiped an irritating tear from her cheek with her dress sleeve. Her wet cheek was cold. The weather seemed to be cool even for late February in Pot's Holler, Tennessee. Undoubtedly this crispness was responsible for the arriving people to escalate the momentum of this lazy, river town. Expectancy for the day's trade was exemplified in everyone's walk.

Canady had been here many times before and knew exactly where to go. He made his way through trunks and boxes being toted and pulled in the street. Part of the congestion was being moved about in carts and wagons while other wares were being hand-carried. A few early buyers carrying purchased commodities were returning to their boats against the tide of people moving crates and packages toward the trading post.

When he had left the deck this morning Canady slipped into an old habit. As if by rote and without thinking, he had winked at the whispering young women standing at the water's edge a few feet from the houseboat. Certain patterns in certain places were difficult to break for this river man. The women's flirtatious giggles gave him a surge of added energy and upon the second look, he winked. Visually, he thought the women were interesting, but not enough to break his stride for. Winks take no appreciable effort. He continued his way to the trading post porch without stopping to rest from his massive load of furs.

Canady deftly sidestepped some visiting traders congregated on the porch. Working his way past the spit and whittlers into the log building, he sat his furs on the dingy plank floor. No more had Canady taken relief from his load than another trader pushed past him, bumping his arm as he went by. Without excuses or pardons, the pushy intruder toted a large, heavy chest he apparently was anxious to deposit. Nimbly, he made his way past Canady to the counter at the back of the building. This newcomer's brash tactic caught the proprietor's attention because he had first seen Canady with his large bundle of furs enter his establishment.

Canady's furs had a significant reputation for quality already established with this owner. It was a known fact from Canady's previous trades he could count on top dollar for them from Boston furriers. Some buyers were already milling around in the store eyeing the huge bundle Canady had. Being hopeful Canady would show this year, he had been relieved to see him walk through his door. With profits assured from the river man's pelts, he was ill-prepared when this unknown trader pushed his way ahead of him.

Taking full advantage of the position he had artfully created, the brash trader promptly set his chest under the scrutiny of the post's owner's eyes. Ignoring any possibly established pecking order, the trader took out a key and unlocked his chest atop the counter before any other trader could push ahead of him. With great showmanship, he lifted the lid, revealing many glittery objects. Normally, Canady wouldn't take such rudeness without a retaliatory response. However, the wares inside the chest caught Canady's eye about the time the intruder began his sales pitch

Curiosity replaced injured pride. He moved closer to hear more. Canady picked up his furs and set them on the floor next to counter. Intently viewing the contents of the chest, he scrutinized a shiny silver tiara and matching concho belt. Without saying a word to this brash foreigner, he reached across the chest for the tiara to examine it more closely.

"Sir," Canady interrupted, "would you consider a silver fox pelt for your lady's crown?" Before the seller of trinkets could reply, Canady picked up another pelt to barter with for the matching belt. "These here furs are the best you can find in these parts," Canady assured the dealer of baubles and shiny things.

At this point, the irritated post owner was getting antsy over the barter being conducted right under his nose. A solid market for Canady's furs was already established, but the treasure chest full of ladies' trinkets was more gamble than fact.

Noticing the post owner's nervousness, the newcomer saw his opportunity. Eying Canady over, he thought, *from the looks of things, I could trade the pelt back to the owner if my merchandise takes low barter.* Value of his trinkets he knew had not been established at this post and apparently the fur market had been. The intruder quickly accepted Canady's deal and made the exchange immediately.

The owner's frown completely overshadowed his normal poker expression, allowing the pushy salesman to grasp a clue for possible infringement and advantage.

Roughly, the post owner pushed the foreigner aside, making a grunting noise as he reached down and lifted Canady's furs onto the counter. Red-faced from the exercise, it was plain to the owner he had better take care of Canady before the boatman got any more harebrained notions. Those valuable furs had a solid market just waiting for Boston traders. Out of the corner of the proprietor's eye, he had seen some buyers milling around and advance closer to eye Canady's furs. The owner realized money was being lost right under his nose and knew he best settle up with Canady Holmes while he still could.

Tucking the silver things into his pouch, Canady was all too glad to get the post owner's redirected attention. It more than made up for the abusive bad manners of the foreigner earlier. Barter was agreed upon and the accounting had a final tally after Canady selected supplies to restock their larder.

They needed more flour, lard, spices, dried beans, cornmeal and some lime for tanning. They also needed a big tin of soda, baking powder, a couple of tins of pipe tobacco, curing salt, and a jug of molasses, leaving a bit of coin after settling up.

The day was still young when his business had been completed. Canady picked up his supplies and left the trading post with a heavier load than the one he arrived with. He went to Frinelle's Saloon across the street from the post.

Pushing open the swinging doors, Canady dropped his burden in the corner of the saloon's dark room just inside the door. This gathering place had held a special attraction for Canady from past visits to Pot's Holler. A number of saloons were available up and down the main road of this river town, but Canady found Frinelle's was the place he liked the best. Outside news sifting into Pot's Holler usually came here first because visitors found Frinelle's draw as enticing as Canady did. Some of the brags heard on the street and at the post was repeated news picked up at Frinelle's. Most said stories coming from there were more reliable than the Boston fur trader's newspapers, if a body could read such. Not everyone in Pot's Holler could read a newspaper, but information grape vining throughout the hollers didn't depend on printing presses. Since Frinelle's was the first stop, gossip had less chance to be distorted from repetition. If you got it from Frinelle's, it was more reliable, they said. You went to Frinelle's to quench your thirst first, catch up on news second, and other things third. The locals and foreigners who visited other establishments after being to Frinelle's first, had a surer handle on any scuttlebutt. It only became gossip when it reached the competition down the street, the place where stories began to change shapes.

Like many others, Canady never had time to learn to read but never felt disadvantaged that he couldn't. He was too busy trapping and didn't like the confinement and ritualistic patterns of school anyway. He resorted to word of mouth information, as did most folks he knew.

"Well, hello there! It's been a long time since we've seen the likes of you in here!" The voice was familiar. It was dark inside compared to the bright outdoors. He looked toward the direction the voice was coming from but wasn't able to focus in the dimly lit room. Only after his eyes became accustomed to the inky colored spaces, did he see Prissy standing behind the tall, wooden bar. Encouraged by her vocal enticement, he straightened his tired shoulders still sympathetic to the heavy load he just sat down.

"Thunder, gal, how you be?" Canady asked, making his way toward the bar. "You sure is a sight for my sore eyes," he complimented Priscilla Green, a woman he'd had some history with. Canady never called her by any name other than Prissy. From the very first day he ever stepped foot in Pot's Holler, she had only one name, as far as he was concerned. For him there was no need to investigate Priscilla Green's heritage—the name Prissy would do for what he had in mind.

On the other hand, Canady had always been special to Priscilla Green. In her estimation he was a person worthy of special attention and stood out from all the rest even if he was a boatman. Frequent customers often joked about Canady's visits after Prissy would mention her hopes, usually after some abuse by another customer. She still held out for the impossible, no matter how much she was chided. *Maybe someday he might make good the promises said on a cold winter's night or whispered on a warm springtime evening?* She optimistically clung to the absurdity of it no matter how many disappointments she endured. Moments of heated passion meant one thing to Prissy and something else to Canady.

She was a pretty enough girl who had fallen on hard times. Like many others, her parents had died during a flu epidemic, leaving Prissy alone at fourteen to make her way in the world. She had no place to go, but found Joe Frinelle sympathetic enough to give her room and board for cleaning up the saloon. By the time she was sixteen she discovered she could make more money with a lot less effort by helping customers pass a few lonely hours in pleasure. Joe taught her how to work the bar. This was the setting where she first met Canady.

An empty saloon by midmorning was rare. The place was usually full of customers no matter what time of day they visited. Today, Frinelle's was empty, with the exception of a drunk sprawled atop one of the back tables. It appeared the customer had deposited himself across the table after his last drink hours ago and hadn't awakened since.

Canady noticed him after he got accustomed to the dark room when he sat his heavy load down. Burly Joe Frinelle was too compassionate a guy to throw his drunken customer out in the street this time of year. He let him sleep his whiskey off in the back of the room. Beside, his rooms above the saloon were totally occupied anyway. Joe figured his customer just needed to wile away the hours somewhere. Even if the drunk could afford a room, all the traders and foreigners wanting to be liberated from the paddle boats occupied every space in town. February was too cold a month to toss the derelict out.

For the past two years Canady had been off trapping, had found Harriett and had not been near Pot's Holler, let alone Frinelle's. He marveled how some things didn't change a bit, even the familiar voice he heard. The handsome boatman walked over to the bar and leaned up against it. His brown eyes twinkled.

Prissy could see in the darkly lit room all she needed to see. She took liberties by stretching her arms across the scarred oak surface toward Canady and pulled his face toward hers. Her actions were done in an intimate way, as if he was something she had a right to, as if she had just seen him a few weeks ago.

"I've missed you, babe," she said with a nonchalant air, too controlled to be believable. She knew Canady ran from clingy types.

There was one thing she didn't know, however. She didn't know he had found someone else who demanded his attention, but such a thing shouldn't be much of a surprise to her either. Prissy had come to know a lot about Canady. She knew he would always seek women's attentions, but she didn't know he was capable of the type of commitment he had given to Harriett. Prissy had been forced to face that he only gave so much—just whatever it took—but nothing more.

"It's been a cold winter and nobody can heat up my bed like you, Canady Holmes!" Her sultry voice was brazenly inviting. Prissy had never been slow when it came to Canady. She let him know right away what was on her mind. The temptress had always been easy, so easy the trapper knew there were lots of comforters coming to her aid in his absence.

Carnal territory with Prissy was a familiar one. As if time had stood still from his last encounter, he was sucked back into the habits of the past and felt her artfully draw all his thoughts toward her. Canady's temptation to taste the wares began causing any loyalties elsewhere to suddenly recede. Prissy was so capable of creating this well-known whirlpool.

Lack of intimacy, which had been interrupted by the birth of Shelby, made him even more susceptible and only fortified her poison working toward obliterating any marital attachments from his conscience. If not able to completely achieve that goal, he allowed Prissy to temporarily place his reservations some place else. Lovemaking, something hoped for but put on the back burner, was stretching for justifications in the confines of the moment. Arimenta's presence had presented a hindrance before Shelby was born, and healing time shouted a preponderances of excuses afterward. It had been a long time.

Canady swigged down the whiskey she set before him. His hand brushed her half-bared bosom when he set the shot glass down. The touch released a floodgate of hot, searing sensations into his stomach, setting off a tug of war between lust and love. Whiskey helped dull the higher ground and known obligations as he listened to a temptress' voice begin a chain reaction he knew all too well.

Seeing her opportunity, she continued refilling his glass.

Not saying a word for fear of quenching the coals of passion growing inside him, he was close enough to look into her eyes for permissions she had shown him in the past.

While sitting on the barstool with only an oak counter between them, a growing furnace radiated upward into Canady's neck, fueled by past episodes dancing in his head about one so delectable two years ago. Water to a thirsty man might look good no matter its purity, was the way he justified his numbed sensibilities drawn from the whiskey. His eyes traveled over Prissy's supple planes, enticing an acute hunger voracious enough to overlook good judgment.

He got off the stool and reached for Prissy across the bar. Grabbing her around the waist, Canady pulled her across the top, knocking over his shot glass. Her bottom smeared the puddle of whiskey as he slid her over the top and down the front of the bar. Smashed against the wooden surface, Prissy's legs embraced both sides of his buckskinned thighs. Canady refused to retreat and gave her little room in his vise-like hold. Any notion of propriety disappeared with the alcohol depleting his conscience. Passionately, he had his hungry mouth on hers with a type of kiss demanding more. Canady saw no objection coming from Prissy, but he never expected any objection either.

"How about a little service here, ma'am," said a gruff voice, followed by a chorus of snickers. "Sorry, fella, but we are damned near dry as dirt and would appreciate some liquid relief," a man said with a Boston accent. "Don't worry, son, me and the boys don't plan to hang around long and you can pick up where you leave off," he said, as more snickers came from his party.

Canady let Prissy go. She reluctantly went behind the bar, begrudging the intrusion of business. Determined to get them taken care of as fast as possible and with plans of her own formulating, she brazenly said, "Here you go, fellas. Have a ball!" Sitting down shot glasses and a bottle of Joe's cheaper whiskey, she called out, "This should turn some of that dirt to mud," then wheeled around to go back to Canady.

The bar stool was empty! Prissy shot looks throughout the room but Canady was not in the saloon. Running to the door, she scoured first one direction, then the other. The streets were still full with milling people, but nowhere in sight was the man she had given her heart to years ago. The love she had shared with this elusive man had spoiled her chances forever for finding happiness with anyone else. As it had always been, so it was once again. He was gone.

Sadly, his disappearance was not unlike another disappointment she'd had two years ago after accepting Canady's proposition to leave with him for a life on the river. The shared life wasn't a marriage proposal, but she accepted whatever he could offer. She began preparations to leave. They were to go to the river together as soon as he picked up supplies from the post. After eagerly packing her meager things, she said the final goodbyes and thanks to her boss for his help over the years. Then she waited on the porch of the saloon to accompany Canady to his houseboat. Time came and went. Prissy heard guffaws coming from her former customers at the bar when they asked Joe why Prissy was sitting on the porch of the saloon. When it became darker outside than inside, Prissy was seen by lamp light slumping back into the saloon and up the stairs to her room.

So, such was the history with Canady and Prissy. She was always willing. He was always calculating. When Canady got close to being confined to one woman, he picked up and went—until he found Harriett.

Chapter 5
BAUBLES AND TRINKETS

Protective, maternal reactions for her baby overrode an intense anger toward her flippantly arrogant husband this morning. Shelby had been startled by the loud bang of the tortoise shell brush popping off the wash pan. After gently rocking and calming her fretful baby, Harriett's emotions were sidetracked. Even anger didn't cover up the tender spot she had for him. "You'e one thing I can't rightly live without, Shelby. Sometimes that ain't so easy to say about your Pa," she whispered.

Harriett had been programmed with a new and compelling force after Shelby's birth. It was action easily taken without thought when it came to her baby. Looking at him, she tried to remember ties to people in her life that she could equate with this invisible cord attaching to them. There was none other that could equal it. She remembered no mother's love and her father was spoken of with disdain, leaving no parental yardstick to pattern after. Maybe not a mother's love, but some sort of love—a sense of obligation, even responsibility, had been conveyed from her aunt and uncle.

"Grandpa must have felt somethin' like this, youngun," she whispered, tucking a flannel quilt she had made around him. "Now, your Pa, that is somethin' else, it ain't like this, Shelby."

At times Canady left her puzzled with fleeting moments of emptiness. This had been one of those times. "He don't need no takin' care of the way you do. Besides, he's been hoofin' it since he's thirteen. Things ain't gonna change now."

Signs of the times and her husband's warning to stay out of sight increased a need for caution. She understood the Indian removal threat. Her husband had introduced her to another type of rejection as well, that of the boat people. She was coming to know that townspeople disliked boat people as much or more so than Cherokees. Harriett noted some of the boat people looked Indian. Maybe they were?

A need to protect her child from possible cruelty kept her senses alert. This fierce desire to protect her child was something she hadn't known she'd possessed. Harriett remembered seeing her Aunt Nancy's love connection toward her children. She had accepted it, maybe wished to have been more of a recipient herself, a little. Such connections were personally untested until she had given birth to Shelby. Now she knew no one could have explained a mother's bond to her beforehand either. This was something new.

Once this door to maturity had opened, nagging questions began to formulate about this new bond. *How could such a thing be without a spirit of some sort willin' it to be? How you s'pose such things start and who begin it?*

Life before she first met Canady had been too busy with frivolous and fanciful thoughts to consider such things, but since Shelby's birth she lived with a new reality in a new world. There were no answers to the troublesome question concerning who the Spirit was that planted these curious seeds in Harriett's heart. Nevertheless, ignorance of ownership couldn't discount they were rooted in. Maybe when they sprout more there could be other questions yet to be thought of? The only thing for certain at this point, she knew life's purposes had forever shifted. Untested passions—to fight to the death if need be—had become a part of her transformation. This was the part she understood. The other part, about who began it and made it so, would have to be thought about later.

She believed Canady had also been awakened to a new discovery when his son was born. She witnessed his transition at the time of their baby's birth and was sure of it. Wives just know such things. But this morning, her husband's behavior was not the image of that touched man and his indiscretion lit a bubbling cauldron of doubt, hurt, disappointment, and for the first time, resentment.

Those women standing near the water's edge, wearing heavy, long coats had showed more than a passing interest toward the influx of new faces in their town. More men were in the streets than women. But, it was these two who had caught Harriett's eye while hidden away observing from a houseboat window. When she saw the load Canady was carrying rotate in the direction of those women and heard the sounds of giggles, her resentment grew and triggered red flags of warning. The image caused a cauldron to glow from deep rage and refused to dim. For the first time, a realization concerning a new stigma attached to her personhood manifested about the unacceptability of some people. Harriett had grown up with talk all her life concerning the possibility of Indian removal. It was only talk. She had heard differences made about the holler people too. Melungeon people pretty much stayed together and didn't mingle with other holler people. She wasn't subjected to what she had come to know since living with Canady. Being considered as one of the boat people added more oppression. Harriett felt three strikes against her this morning.

Outside activity momentarily distracted thoughts of her husband and her circumstance. Some men on horseback and some driving teams of horses pulled packed wagons, while others walked ahead of carts or carried a load. She saw those giggling girls being greeted by several of those men when they passed by.

Festering disappointment escalated from her observance. Another troublesome acknowledgment about all the activity on the streets: there were no Indian people, just like Canady said. As many Indian people as white people traded at Sam's place back home in Smith's Holler. This morning the streets in Pot's Holler didn't have any Indians milling among the traders. Warnings Arimenta had made earlier rang in her head. *I'm wonderin' about you, Arimenta. I hope nothin's happened to you.*

She peeked out the window again. Canady was no place to be seen. Only wagons coming and going, making ruts upon ruts in the soft dirt street and loaded with sacks of flour, cornmeal, rice and beans, were visible. The supplies going past the docked houseboat reminded her how empty their storage closet was.

Being careful to dart back into the shadows inside the houseboat if anyone came too close, Harriett resigned herself to the futility of searching for Canady anymore. He had already been lost in the crowd. *Best see what I can because Canady ain't a'comin' back for a spell,* she consoled herself.

Scanning their surroundings took her mind off the twisted knot forming in her stomach. Other boats in the cove were visible on the windowed side of the cabin. The biggest was a paddle boat further down and it seemed to be the focal point that most of the wagons were coming from and going to. Harriett was mesmerized by the size of the paddle boat.

I 'magine there's some fancy ladies in that place with all sorts of fine dresses! Wish we had a nice white railin' on our boat. It's goin' to be a chore to keep Shelby away from the water when he gets to crawlin'. Many rooms in the paddle boat compared to their floating one-room quarters challenged her fantasies.

She could tell by the carts full of pelts going toward the boat that some of the Boston fur buyers had made purchases already and were returning to the boat. *That's probably why Canady took out so early,* she told herself as if this should calm down ruffled feathers. There's plenty more a'leavin so not all of them has traded yet, she figured.

People leaving the boat dressed in quaint clothes and tall beaver hats, blended in with those in buckskins toting pelts. They were obviously outsiders to these parts—Easterners. When they came close, she darted back in the shadows of the cabin but was still able to see them. She watched buyers shaking hands with others they must have known from past buying trips. *I ain't never seen such white skin! They's down right sickly appearin'. Even Melungeon clans in the holler is darker skinned then them furiners.* Straining to see and not be seen, her determination egged her to view all she could, regardless of the warning her husband had given her.

It was late in the afternoon when Canady got home. Shelby had been awake for several hours keeping Harriett from eavesdropping on the outside world. She had nursed him and put the sleeping child back to bed by the time his daddy stepped on the deck.

Taking care of his business, this freewheeling river man put freshly purchased supplies in the empty storage closet before he spoke to Harriett.

"Howdy, you 'bout ready to go on down river?" Canady didn't say much more. His quiet matched her mood and both shunned conversation. Certainly, he had no way knowing his wife had witnessed his indiscretion this morning. As far as Canady was concerned, she probably was still upset for having to stay out of sight.

Time had been a healer while he was gone, a cooling off period that had helped, but her husband's flirting when he left the houseboat resonated in Harriett's mind. She saw and heard those silly women giggling each time she looked at him.

After his salutations, he set the molasses, soda, and baking powder on the scarred table, expecting Harriett to put them where she wanted. As quickly as he came in, he turned to go outside and pole away from the bank. It wasn't long until the houseboat was in deeper water with the sights and sounds of the river town shrinking, becoming silent.

Slowly, scenery changed from a trading hubbub to that of a tranquil river. The river quiet, however, didn't offer any appreciable antiseptic for two kinds of turmoil, one known by Harriett, and another known by Canady. Poling did help to ease the tension for Canady, but he remained distant. The more he poled, the more Pot's Holler was slipping out of view. Harriett's turmoil, on the other hand, had no acceptable escape valve.

Good riddance! Harriett said under her breath. "I never want to see that place again," she said, loud enough in hopes Canady heard it, but not so loud to make him believe that was her intention. *Life on this here houseboat does have some profit to it,* she thought as she secured the newly purchased soda, baking powder, and molasses in the pie safe.

Day stretched into evening. Seeing Canady encased in moodiness turned her stormy disposition into loneliness. He was there, but he wasn't. She had never felt this detachment coming from him like this before. Harriett knew something was bothering her husband, causing more questions to develop about his solo trip into town.

She ventured out on the deck by the time Pot's Holler had completely disappeared, hoping her memory of it would do the same.

Shadows had become long, making their world kaleidoscope with each bend of the river. February cold gave Harriett reason to pull her shawl up around her shoulders as she walked toward her husband. They stood close to each other without saying anything. Harriett didn't know what to say, but after the uncomfortable silence she looked up at his face, into his eyes. Timidly, Canady returned the look. After meeting her visual survey, she saw him reach for her hand. Her first inclination was to pull back but his touch was received enough to grow hope that could ease her knotted stomach. Desperately she wanted to erase those suffocating feelings.

Harriett felt his gentle stroke on her arm, a tender touch with his large hands. They were warm against her skin on this cold winter's evening. With each slow caress, thoughts responsible for his far away gaze became less distracting for Harriett. Hope dared to trickle back.

Enjoying the closeness to each other, Harriett's bossy husband gave way to the little boy living inside himself. After caressing her hand and arm, he touched the smooth skin of her face looking for some familiar response coming from her. Asserting former rights, he bent down and kissed her petal-soft lips and whispered, "It's been a long time." A lover's search for the eye's message, took him deeper into the windows of her soul. "I'm a patient man, but it's been a long spell, Harriett. I need my woman."

Not waiting for her to say anything, he set his poling pole against the deck and put his arms around her waist. Canady pulled her to him and warmly kissed her lips only to release her to look again to see if she would react to his kiss. His hungry eyes continued their search into hers, leaving her no place to hide. With caresses, kisses, touches, to evoke familiar reactions from his young wife, the river man needed no words of assent from her. Canady took advantage of the moment for a deeper more passionate kiss while lowering his wife to the deck.

Winter's night air couldn't touch the pair. He had convinced Harriett and they felt nothing other than yearning for more. Like Solomon and his Shulamite bride, they delighted in the lover's table even if each held a morning's secret inside which threatened to spoil the course. Brown pools—enticing, compelling—gravitated like quicksand. Both were sucked into desire for the other, while each endured whitecaps of warning ominously looming in the background. The morning's memories wouldn't go away for either of them!

Suddenly, Harriett pushed against both Canady's shoulders to see who was reflected in her husband's eyes. Was it still she? Was she the only one he saw? His gaze never flinched from her challenge, but posed the same vulnerability coming from him. Cautiously satisfied, growing emotions gave permission to take the storms of passion into a deeper current racing more swiftly toward her lover. Responses from each kiss, each caress, coaxed submission. She gave without reservation to something holy and right.

There were no settlements along the Tennessee River. Canady had moved them out of civilization's watch. Earth making up the river's banks united itself to the opposite side by a river in common now belonging solely to these lovers. Their commitment to each other was in secrecy witnessed only by earthly creatures and the God who had made it all.

Carefully pinned hair came tumbling down, with a few black strands meandering across her cheek. Pushing wispy locks away, she moved her arms toward Canady's neck. Touching and kissing, importance was placed on satisfaction without fear of discovery or intrusion. This trapping dandy lit all-consuming fires, ones without boundaries, for his Indian princess as they relived past pleasures with deeper intensities. No moment had ever been sweeter, more passionate, more connected. Pulsating bodies gave way to disposed energies and eventually they lay silent in contentment. Moonlight's invitation for more reflected from the water, but intrusion from the cold night air encouraged their retreat into the cabin.

Canady lit the kerosene lamp, adjusted the wick and, after a long silence, blurted out, "Harriett, I found somethin' that belonged to you."

Taken back by his comment and not fully understanding, she became embarrassed and did her best not to giggle. Canady hadn't meant to be funny. He was never one to say the right things. He didn't know how to express his feelings to Harriett and in this awkward moment, he became more than tongue-tied. The trapper was a better lover than a talker, but Harriett's reaction loosed a tongue unaccustomed to chatter. He had to do something to rectify his own embarrassment from the concept conveyed, but not the one meant.

"When we's docked at Pot's Holler," he stammered, "I got somethin' for you." He pulled his bulging pouch toward the straw bed and sat down. Reaching inside his pouch, he disgorged the contents. Immediately, glow from the kerosene lamp reflected off the shiny objects Canady had bartered his first two silver fox pelts for. He handed the tiara and concho belt to her, his Indian princess.

Pangs of guilt for earlier hard feelings quickly flashed into Harriett's mind. Somehow, anger toward her husband became less important. She wanted to forget the memory and let it pass in the water a million bends away. His generosity had pushed her hurtful disappointment aside, but the memory would remain. *I don't want to cogitate on it,* she thought, looking at her new presents.

"Canady, where in the world did you ever find such fine things? These is the finest I ever seen." She touched the ornate silver objects. They felt cold and smooth to the touch. As if the act of touching became responsible for a practical concern, she blurted out without thinking, "Canady, where on this river could I wear these? If we ever head to land, where would I wear them to?"

Canady had to agree the question was a perfectly good one. He never thought of that when he bought them . After he had told her she couldn't be seen, let alone get off that boat when they were docked, where would she wear them?

She turned the fancy objects over in her hands, drinking in all the ornate scrolls and beads of silver adhered to both pieces. *So fine, and no place to wear them to.* Harriett was impressed, but saddened even more with the reality of their uselessness.

Canady wasn't expecting this turn of events. He never once thought about the practicality of such ornate baubles in the life of a homespun river woman. That was what he had caused an important Cherokee chief's granddaughter to become when he married her. Civilized society determined that boat people were life's refuse. Somehow, this cocky dandy trapping throughout the hollers, sampling feminine hospitality, never had cause for such notions before. He had told this rare jewel he found in the forest to stay out of sight when they came to the last civilization. Yes, indeed, the granddaughter of a famous Indian chief was the same woman he had convinced prior to their marriage about the free life on the river with him. Boat people's reputation had increasingly become that of the ill reputed.

She put the tiara on her loose black hair, then squinted into a hand mirror hanging from a nail on the wall. Canady watched every graceful move she made and with each movement he believed she validated the baubles belonged to her. Childbirth hadn't added new inches around her waist. She clasped the belt shut.

"Gol-durn, woman! If you ain't a sight! I'm a right lucky man, that's for certain. Even the Queen of England would have to take a back paddle to the likes of you!"

He couldn't help but make comparisons between the bar maid who had nearly sucked him in, to the woman standing before him. Her regal image left Canady in awe. The sight before him belonged to him alone and not every lonesome polecat up and down the river. He was the first. He had almost succumbed to something he'd live to regret the rest of his life.

She was embarrassed from his bragging, but loved it anyway. The notion of finding herself when she looked into his soft brown eyes earlier in the evening seemed unnecessary now.

I knowed he was a smooth talker. No doubt he's taken to many women before we come together, but I ain't afraid of it.

Canady acknowledged to himself that her attitude while trying on the tiara and concho was one of confidence, and that excited him even more. Harriett never had an easy spirit reduced to begging like Prissy had. She bore a proud countenance, a radiating serenity. He visually drank in his good fortune. It was time to put out the kerosene lamp.

She, his Indian princess, and he, her trapping dandy, locked in each other's arms once more, but this time on their majestic straw mattress. The straw mattress on their bed, in their houseboat, was on their river with all its sights being a part of their kingdom. What more could a man ask?

Chapter 6
TAPROOT OF SHAME

The river's stillness was shattered by a loud shriek coming from the shoreline. Canady sat upright. He slipped out of bed and into his buckskin pants and shirt. "That bobcat don't sound right," he whispered to Harriett, trying not to awaken Shelby. Harriett had fed him about an hour ago and put him back in his cradle. She roused slightly when he whispered and saw Shelby moving. It was beyond hope for him to go back to sleep now. Giving way to comforts of the warm bed, Harriett got up and put some wood into the stove and changed the baby.

They heard the scream of the strange-sounding bobcat again. "That ain't no bobcat, that's a woman," Canady said. Both looked out the window and tried to see through the early morning fog rising off the riverbed. There was nothing on the river. Then they heard voices of men amplified across the surface of the water. Male voices were mixed with a woman's scream.

Harriett looked at Canady to see what response he was going to take. There was a woman obviously in trouble and they both were aware of it. She thought it unlike her husband to ignore investigating, danger or not. It wasn't in Canady's nature to be cautious. She knew he wasn't a coward, even if he had run when those would-be suitors of hers were after him in the past. He played like a fox. This trapper wasn't a fool. His life had depended on outrunning those hopping mad boys and he lived to fight another day.

Tension concerning the activity on the shore began to mount. Puzzled by Canady's passive behavior, Harriett's protective curiosity and tempestuous youth got the better of her. She moved to get a better view from the cabin window. Morning sun struggled dully to pierce the foggy haze, making the scene a pinkish blur. A little Indian boy, about nine years old, was running frantically out of the bushes near the shoreline. Then, that's when she saw them, there they were! Close behind the frightened little boy were men wearing soldier's uniforms.

Kicking, and flailing his arms at his attackers, his screams chorused with protests from a woman, probably his mother. Laughter coming from the bushes joined the two soldiers' mirth on the riverbank after they collared the little boy.

"Canady, she's being attacked over yonder! Do somethin'!" she pleaded. Canady gently put his hand over her mouth.

The soldiers hadn't seen the houseboat. They were too occupied with their own pursuits to take notice. Having moored the boat to a hiding spot for the night had been a saving factor for them, but Canady knew it couldn't be counted on for long. A huge elm, leaning out over the water with many branches camouflaging the houseboat, offered only temporary security. Harriett had already fallen asleep when Canady decided to take further precautions last night in the brushy port. This morning he was congratulating himself for such astute maneuvers but the fog's cover was threatened by the intensifying pink from a rising sun. Preoccupation of the soldiers kept them from scouting out the area only for the moment, Canady was sure. Something had to be done soon.

Harriett felt her husband's hot breath in her ear and she struggled to remove his hand from her mouth.

"Be quiet, Harriett! There's nothin' we can do. There's too many of 'em."

Trusting he had hushed his wife, he released his hand. They heard more laughter mixed with a woman's cries of agony growing into sounds of rage, blind-angry rage! Instinctively, after freeing herself from Canady's grasp, Harriett ran across the cabin and grabbed the hunting rifle from off the wall. Strong hands clasped her wrists and removed the gun.

"Don't be a damned fool!" he spat out in a course whisper. "They don't know we are here yet. If they did, you'd be in the same fix as that girl and I would be helpless to do a thing! I'd probably be dead!" he told his angry wife.

Changes of circumstances this morning from those of last night transposed Harriett's lover to the unseemly position of coward. She sensed he was dead certain about something. Not knowing what, her mind raced to glean some reason without all the pieces to fully understand.

A lot of things had happened at Pot's Holler that Canady hadn't shared with his cooped-up wife. Living on the river required major adjustments for her as it was, but he had gathered news at Pot's Holler to stress her further.

Harriett had become somewhat adjusted to the separation from her grandpa, Chief Whitehorse—as adjusted as possible. He had no intention of stirring things up again unless he just had to. Alarming facts about his Indian heritage possibly being discovered caused more concern. Canady had pushed his luck to the limits camouflaging his own background, which could ultimately affect Harriett and Shelby if someone mentioned his Ma in these parts. The Goins boys hadn't been in Pot's Holler yet, according to the proprietor of the post, but he fully expected to see them. A stopover trade from them was past due. Canady knew full well he had better not tarry too long. The last people he cared to run into were the Goins boys.

Not intending to eavesdrop, he couldn't help but overhear some men talking as he was leaving the post.

"Naw, they ain't a'goin' to ketch 'em all. Them Redskins has been a hi-tailin' it for months now," one of the spit and whittlers said to two other mountain men scratching their scraggly beards and spitting off the porch.

"They's a buildin' more places to put 'em in down south a'ways, I hear. Maybe it's done built, now that I think on it," the second one added.

"Well, I guarantee ye, if they ain't outta here, them soldiers are thick as hops at Higgins Crossin'," the third man said, "and them redskins ain't gonna go no place now. It's done too late."

Canady needed little encouragement to tend to business, then head back after hearing what he did. He had one place yet to go to before leaving Pot's Holler for good.

That rumor apparently wasn't just a rumor anymore and obviously removal was taking place this morning. Canady had to put more credence to the news the Tucker boys told them about the Walkingsticks. Apparently, the Tuckers's story wasn't any isolated case.

"It ain't no rumor no more, Harriett." "Such talk as this has come and passed before. This time it's true. I have to tell it, Harriett. You have a right to know. "I know'd about this, I know'd it was a'comin'. Didn't think it was worth bother'n you about before."

"I knowed you'se perty unhappy not gettin' to go to the post with me. When I'se there and heard the news of them stockades and soldiers movin' in, I'se more then glad you didn't show. I hate to muddy the water anymore'n I already have, but you got to know," he confessed, trying to soothe his wife's disappointment about not getting to go ashore.

He looked for hints of her mind set. Morning's pastel light was sifting into the dark cabin and played across the planes of her beautiful, questioning face. Lack of understanding why such was happening on the bank flowed into another troublesome thought when he mentioned the post. She remembered two giggling women.

Canady had no reason to know his wife had seen his flirting indiscretion so naturally made. That recollection, further ignited by the screams heard from the riverbank, fueled more anger. He noted her set jaw and expected some retort, yet she said nothing.

"Times are a'gittin' bad, Harriett!" he pleaded. "It's done come. What they's talked about, it's done come," he said.

Canady left the cabin and went onto the deck to pole toward the middle of the river, away from the cover of the fallen tree. Fog was still somewhat benevolent, but it wouldn't be for long. Harriett followed after him.

"We've heard about this country movin' the Indians out before," he whispered. "Fact, we've heard it so often it ain't seemed a problem. Nobody believed it would happen. Sure 'nuf, it's done come," he repeated, as if convincing himself as much as Harriett.

"Look, Canady, look!" Distracted, Harriett grabbed his arm when she whispered the alarm. "Isn't that Arimenta?"

Soldiers were leading her, some in front and some behind. The ones in front had a rope around her neck, leading her like an animal, with her hands tied in back. One of Arimenta's braids had come undone and was flapping across her face by cold gusts of wind. Wild plum thickets snatched at the blanket partially covering her shoulders when she passed by. A stony expression replaced a face normally radiating kindness as if blankly tolerating her disheveled hair. All those self-assurances she had alluded to before leaving their boat for her village had been empty brags. Traces of hopelessness were evident as she succumbed to the unyielding force of soldiers dictating her life.

The soldiers and Arimenta had unexpectedly emerged from the sand plum thicket along the bank. Just as quickly, the thorny brush swallowed them up again.

"By the looks of things, that 'cryin' woman and the little boy must be from Arimenta's village," Harriett whispered to Canady. Harriett was petrified with fear. Now the bitterness she experienced in Pot's Holler lost some of its edge. After seeing Arimenta, she understood Canady's concern more clearly.

"Sons of bitches!" Canady swore under his breath. He felt helpless to defend his family member. It would be at the risk of Harriett and Shelby if he tried.

"I told you, it ain't safe. Keep real still, maybe we can make it out of here a'fore anyone can take notice." Canady began to pole with stronger moves, trying not to rustle the water any more than necessary.

The rising sun began to eat the pink fog and crisp up the riverbank, trees and bushes. Canady stayed the course, moving steadily toward the center of the river, letting the natural flow aid in their escape. Images of Arimenta and sounds of pitiful crying haunted each of them. They drifted past bend after bend, but the echo of the carnage remained in their heads and replayed anew with each turn of the river.

The young woman's cry from obvious rape tormented Harriett. Stories of her mother, White Dove, flash backed as if connecting the past to the distorted present and she being a witness to both. Harriett had formulated mental images from the stories the village people told about her mother and they were enduring enough to become actual accounts. Then, she did with the images what her Grandpa had instructed her to do. She had baked the memories in clay.

Because she knew the manner of her conception, she too experienced paralyzing fear when Canady initially came into her life. He had crept up undetected, much like that predator, her nameless father, had done.

Life needed sorting out. Harriett sought to find herself in all the segregation of human biology. Nothing made sense to her anymore. Who was she? Who was her father? Why weren't they able to live among other people?

Nestling the baby to her breast while sitting on the bed, she leaned against the cabin wall. *Just where in the world did the jigsaw begin? Them turnin' points, them crossroads, come about when I first seen him.*

"Don't be afraid," were the first words he said. "I mean you no harm. I heard you rakin' leaves on the ground and wondered if I was lucky enough to catch somethin' without trappin' this morning? You was so busy you didn't see me. I think these flowers might be better than a trap," said the cocky, handsome young man, grinning confidently as he handed Harriett a big bouquet of blue flowers. He shoved them in her face and she had no option but to take them so she could see who this intruder was.

I'm so glad I pressed them flowers, she thought, reaching for a box under their bed with her free hand to look at them once more.

Harriett remembered he had been an unusual talker that morning. She toyed with the dried flowers in her box and recalled how his chatter had lessened her defensive mood. *How could I have been so taken in?*

"Let me introduce myself, ma'am," he had said, keeping up conversation, grinning and showing off lots of white, straight teeth. *Oh, he was a handsome one, he was! He probably was the nicest lookin' fella in all the holler, but he still was a stranger,* she reminded herself while reflecting back. This newcomer must have opened a door to a discovery that morning. Harriett never remembered feeling a sense of power over a suitor before until she met Canady. Certainly, he had been spellbound enough even though she was barely fifteen, and he almost twenty-seven years. Harriett remembered toying with newfound powers over the male species.

The trapper hadn't tried to hide the fact that he was immediately afflicted by Harriett's beauty. Sensing her influence over him, she remembered giving herself permission to explore this happenstance a bit more. Springtime invited new things. She felt new things herself on the morning that a trapping dandy was responsible for bringing to life.

He was the only admirer who had been so bold that she could recall. Maybe his years added the boldness, she didn't' know. Canady gave her the opinion he was afraid of nothing.

He was special from the beginnin' but I was pert near the greenest persimmon they is. I've smarten'd up a right bit since this here bouquet of blue flowers, she thought, returning them to the box and sliding the box back under the bed. Dried flowers from the past, was just that, dead and dried. They had been alive once. Only daydreaming brought life back to them now.

"My name is Canady Holmes. I'm a trapper by trade," he had boasted. *Canady acted like he was the tradin' post owner,* she thought, remembering his cocky air.

"I can see you think I'm right smart at trappin', too, by that surprised look on your face, I might say," he laughed. "Iv'e a flat-bottom up the creek here a ways but it got too shaller to foller. I decided to step it off to see what I could see."

Canady stepped back after speaking to the kneeling girl with a basket of mushrooms. He saw black, loose hair hanging almost to her tiny waist. Her figure belied she was just barely fifteen. Canady hadn't seen many girls as mature for their age as Harriett and he had begun looking early in his life. His appraisal made, he subtly strutted and said, "Gol durn, I never spected to see such a sight as this!"

Even now, the thought of that first meeting brought a hot rush of excitement. She now knew he had begun spinning his web for her attentions right then and there. *That's when my sure foot lost a toehold. That spunky trapper had a way about him! Still does, I reckon.*

Tributaries connected to the Sequatchie bade farewell to the sojourners traveling its waters. More traffic from other houseboats was seen on the rivers than a year ago. Time spent fishing was confining for Canady, but it was too dangerous to do much trapping. Signs of the times were not conducive to boat people being on shore as they usually were. Fishing, but always staying to themselves, filled many days and made provisions but did little for the restlessness of a confined trapper. Canady was less antsy after nearly missing disaster. The occupants of the houseboat just ahead of them didn't fare so well when they reached shore. From out of nowhere, their houseboat was boarded and the occupants taken. Canady poled further out in the river.

Weeks passed. The rivers had more boat people on it than when Canady and Harriett first married, but each boat sought its own space. Only whispered communications were dared. They wanted to make sure their voices didn't carry across water to unknown ears waiting to do harm. Never once did they feel safe enough to dock, but remained a silent houseboat in the midst of the Sequatchie River. Dry land wasn't an option either of them was willing to take, no matter how inviting it looked. Temporary stockades holding human misery were only visible in some places, but the smell greeted them before the sight came into view. Stench from penned people carried across the river-water, as did their cries. Each day, more captured Indians were put in the holding pens before they could be transported in a mass exodus later.

"I think the Indian fix will be more tolerable down south a'ways," Canady said. Further south seemed a likely destination. Other boat people seemed to share the same idea and set their course cautiously on tributaries flowing south.

Chapter 7
CREATING CLANNISH WAYS

Shifting sand, lumped in the middle of the Sequatchie River, were targets for a secure anchor drop the next three weeks. The Sequatchie was larger and safer than staying on the March River, but it was smaller and more houseboat-friendly than the Cumberland when the shoreline was unattainable. Each day they moved away from the past gave them a breath of encouragement, a hope all fleeing boat people sought. In passing, occupants on other houseboats gave no more than a nod of acknowledgment to each other, if that. No trust dared go outside the confines of each little nucleus. Isolation set the standard for everyone. Messages sent from river activity appeared to pose a common question: could the nightmare be less threatening further south?

Indians were no longer visible along the riverbanks. Most of the stockades were out of sight, but the ones that had been near the shore were empty. Only stench remained from their confinement giving off clues about human agony and disgrace. For a short period of time, when the wind carried odors floating out across land and water alike, eager settlers and soldiers would be reminded about tainted titles to Indian farms. It was as if a special Spirit had the last word to the convergence, making them sensually privy to aromatic disgrace without a word being spoken.

For sure, cries once heard coming from the stockades had been silenced. Perpetually lasting and mournful protests following those tears shed from some of God's creation had not been silenced completely, however. Disgrace had left an imprint time would have difficulty in erasing.

Harriett and Canady's spirits continued to hear the outpourings of absent people, if only in their minds. The vacuous void further solidified and instilled a continuing need for personal attitude changes because of it. Cutting ties to heritage had come. Ties to thoughts of home had to be put aside or displaced people would live with torment from the memory of it. Hard facts to chew on and digest was that the land occupied for centuries by Native Americans no longer possessed touches of home for any of them. No familiar territory, house, or tepee would ever be in place because their fleeing occupants lived in a world out of sync. Like the abandoned grave of White Dove, Harriett's ancestral cemeteries were deserted forever. History, homes, and lives were to be whitewashed, to appear as if they never had been. No matter how much the inevitable had been put out of Harriett's mind, the time had come for a permanent farewell. It was time to say goodbye. She could no longer table the pain of being lost because a hole was etched inside her heart. Such a puncture refused to be silenced.

Seclusion on a river didn't lessen the   boat peoples' suffering after the damning peril of forced removal. Quite the contrary. Most had relatives among the displaced. If it hadn't been for the river, more than likely many of them too would have been on that deadly trail. Harriett and Canady didn't have to personally make a trip with them to know about the old, the sick, the newborn infant, and sometimes the birth mother. Undoubtedly, many would be buried in unholy ground along the way. The same, no doubt, could be said for some of the feebleminded people having problems with broken earthly ties. Perhaps for some lacking mental stability, insanity might offer a form of escape.

Keenly wounded in other ways, boat people resorted to thievery, hopelessness, suspicion, and all forms of depravity in their desperation. Only the sympathetic owners of cabins along the river offered well water to the meanderers when they came to shore. Many shantyboat people had given up once decent and respected reputations in their struggle for survival, to enter a status perceived as vermin by those not afflicted by prejudice. Being in like circumstance, Canady and Harriett wore the same cloak with the rest of the boat people and trusted in no one.

Canady grabbed his rifle and gave warning to a boat moving closer to them. The young boatman hollered when he saw Canady take aim.

"Hey, mistah, don't shoot! It's my wife, Mistah. She's a'needin' some help."

"Sorry, fella, ain't nothin' we can do for 'er," Canady said, and lowered his rifle a bit when he heard a woman scream. It could be a ploy. Any sort of antics could be used to rob. Canady eyed him suspiciously.

"Mistah, she's been at it a long time and nothin's done happened." Then, as if howling winds had suddenly stopped, leaving a deafening silence, the sounds of water lapping against the boat could be heard without being masked by human wails. The woman was quiet inside the houseboat. The young man turned his back toward Canady and went inside.

Harriett had come on deck when she heard the commotion and the young man asking for assistance. Canady waved her back inside the cabin until the young man entered his own houseboat.

"What's all the ruckus about, Canady?"

"That fella asked for some kind of help. I think it's his woman."

Cries came from inside the young man's houseboat, but they were not the cries of a woman.

"Oh, God, no! No! Sophy, you can't die on me! Sophy!"

Harriett and Canady knew what had happened. It was happening a lot on the river. Soldiers suddenly appeared at the shoreline. They must have heard the cries and gave up their hiding place to investigate. Without knowing it, the boat people were being watched again by soldiers whose duty was to pick up escaping Indian strays. No one could go near shore for fear of being arrested or worse.

Grief consumed the young man. After an hour, he was convinced his pleading for Sophy not to die would not do any good. He came to the cabin door with Sophy in his arms and struggled to get out of the doorway. His dead wife's body still sheltered their unborn baby who had left this world with the mother. The young man couldn't go ashore to bury her and he couldn't bear to see her ashen face and staring eyes any more. A splash broke the river silence as he threw her overboard into the water. The only thing left of Sophy was her blood smeared on the young man's shirt and pants. With a contorted face, grimacing in unbelief, he looked at Canady.

"Mistah, my Sophy needed some help. Ain't nobody care." With that he crumpled on his deck and cried as if his soul had burst. Buzzards flying upstream and some landing near the water's edge waited for Sophy.

The river swallowed up its secrets and became unusually quiet as the boat people suddenly lost their voice. No more chatter floated across the water from women fussing at kids, or men barking orders. Eyes were open and mouths were closed. Those in uniform on the shoreline and those in shabby attire on the houseboats witnessed a stillness even birds dared not break. Then the soldiers were seen leaving, retreating into secrecy to wait until a later time. No one was coming ashore.

Boats made their way further downstream, away from known danger. One thing for sure, water kept soldier and boat people apart. They kept moving.

Ever since human bondage had snaked its way to the west, when the river was quiet Harriett thought she could hear a lament whispering through the trees from time to time. When they passed another empty stockade, she softly said, "Listen! Can you hear it, Canady? Them river voices cry out through them woods like they's a'ridin' the winds. Maybe some of that is from Sophy, you reckon?" The houseboat glided by in silent respect. Nature's memorial dirge played throughout the boughs of woody blackgum and eastern red bud trees growing along the riverbank, honoring Sophy and her dead baby.

Each person shared the loss of a civilized time they had once enjoyed. Boat people faced dangerous threats if they wished to bury their dead on shore, making the loss of family members the most difficult burden of all to bear. Many others had met their end like Sophy. Some had died of old age and some of disease. In mourning, their bodies were kept on the boats for as long as possible until putrefaction was paramount, forcing the mourners to toss loved ones into the river.

"Best not look Harriett," Canady warned. "It ain't right, I tell you, it ain't right."

Time refused to stand still and in some ways that was good. In other ways it was bad. Harriett believed memories baked in clay had chips beginning to form around the edges.

A year of isolation had refined social withdrawal, making Melungeon ways even more peculiar if they were runaways on a river. Melungeon traditions begat austerity well enough, but the vilification of race went yet a step further with the removal of Native Americans. Because of the ethnic cleansing of Indians bonded with the Melungeon mixture, a biological tie to both ethnicities, many of them escaped to the rivers and grew peculiarities so strong that oddities would extend into future generations. Boat people's existence continued to remain in peril after the Indian removal, as soldiers scooped up runaways and vagabonds carelessly docked on shore. Whenever the river narrowed, Harriett didn't have to be told to stay out of sight as this action came automatically by now. She had seen with her own eyes what happened to people who had black hair and tanned skin. Only when necessity outweighed risk would Canady take the chance to dock at a trading post.

On his last stop Canady had overheard gossip about the Indian people's outcome. The news validated the voice Harriett heard while passing the emptied stockade. His barter was expected to be done quickly for a few necessities, but he cut his stopover even shorter when he saw military scouts ride into town. As deftly as tracking game, he slipped out of the post into the surrounding forest and onto the boat. Not until he had poled to the middle of the river did he share the news he had learned at the post with Harriett.

"Harriett, because of this here drought, most of them creeks is dried up all over, I hear. From what they say, the plans was to take the Indians on the rivers a ways but no boat could make it in some places. They had to go overland. It was bad, Harriett, it was bad! From what they tell me, the more they went west, the worser it got."

Harriett remembered Chief Whitehorse's words about making memories like bird tracks baked in clay. Those words took on more meaning after hearing the trading post gossip from her husband.

"Grandpa was might neer smart to leave when he did," she told Canady. She had a sense of relief mixed with sorrow. Harriett looked at Shelby and knew she would never be able to show him where he was born or show him his ancestry. He'd never see the village compound nor hear the flute's song. He wouldn't get to play with Jesse Bluerain, or Jesse's little baby brother or sister, if the baby lived. He'd probably never would know what a feather bed is.

"It's best Shelby never knowed any of it the way it was, Canady," she replied to his report. "He ain't gonna miss what he never knowed."

Grandpa told me to remember him, to not forget from where I come. That's somethin' you will know, Shelby. Ain't much else I can give to you. You ain't never goin' to know the love of cousins and kin, she thought, vowing to keep disgrace from her offspring. *Canady has made it plain, he ain't never goin' back into Kentucky again. Oh, my youngun, life's jig's done changed too much. You'll never know the steps,* she wistfully thought. *Life's changed as many times as bends in this here river. What will it be when you is growed?*

Both she and Canady had lived with the unspoken priority to stay out of reach and away from people for over a year now. Docking was becoming more of a concern since trading towns were leery of boat people. Many desperate and fleeing souls resorted to committing crimes to exist and put any conscience aside to accomplish their survival. Loneliness graduated to a circumstance boat people accepted. However, keen awareness of those who had been shackled and forced to leave helped dispel their discontented solitude. Harriett understood that those forced on that death march would have easily swapped places with the boat people. *Could be they's more soldiers lookin' for the likes of me?* With this possibility, assurances about being lonely were easier to tolerate. Harriett knew Shelby would grow up without any kin, but at least he would be free.

"It'll play itself out," Canady told her, trying to assure himself as much as his wife. He was not one to be confined by anyone's rules but his own, and then they changed from time to time. This life was difficult.

"They's only one way to make it. Can't see no chance of changes soon. Yes, sir, they's only one way to make it and, we are a'doin' it." He packed his pipe, and poled deeper.

Verbal comments were easier said than kept. The months of forced isolation grew lines of discontent on Canady's face. Not only did he view this as a place of no return, he realized his own rebellion had made him further alienated by becoming one of the boat people. With a few rare exceptions, he and Harriett were treated like plague coming to visit the townspeople each time they tried to dock.

Canady gave authorship to his stepmother as the cornerstone for his ancestral denial. His life had been lived where he purposefully acted as if there were no background and no connection to anyone because of her. It had seemed the best solution then, but he was beginning to realize this course was not unlike a Pandora's box.

As time passed, both Canady and Harriett felt doomed to removal in a different way. Initial meandering was due to trapping prospects, but trapping became less important when survival and freedom became an issue. Boat people had become as captive on the water as the Indian in the stockade. The only difference was boat people had more space in their watery confinement. Life on the river presented more problems than the initially sought-after solution. Solitary river confinement had to do. *"It'll do. At least for now,* he thought.

"We's gonna take a chance on shore down river aways," Canady finally said, after months more drifting and poling the river. Intense visual scouring of shorelines for strange movements had become a natural habit. Canady studied tired riverbanks concluding each bend suffered exhaustion from extricated inhabitants. Empty banks were bleak and desolate of humanity. So, cautiously poling through sundown's filtered softness, he glided inward.

Apprehensively, all three stretched their legs on land. Harriett picked up her youngster with one arm after he stooped down to dig in the dirt. Clutching her basket handle, she made her way toward poke salad leaves pushing up through the ground along the riverbanks. Green and tender poke would be a welcome change from winter's menu and it made their mouths water to think of eating something fresh. Canady began to cut poke leaves growing along the shore and stuffed them into a sling pouch. Harriett left the poke for her husband to pick and moved into the bushes further up the bank. Blackberry thickets growing along the upper bank had caught her eye. They didn't speak, nor did Shelby make any noise as they worked. Dirt's texture became a learning experience for Shelby. He continued to sift dirt through his little fingers while his daddy picked poke and his mama gathered berries, until it became too dark to see any more.

After sitting her full basket of blackberries on the table, Harriett put Shelby in his cradle, trying to soothe his tired cries. Washing his dirty face and hands before lighting the lamp proved challenging. Shelby was becoming more vocal the older he got and wanted no part of being left in that cradle, or the washrag. Crying outbursts from the toddler were still a worry for both his parents at times. Canady lit the lamp for Harriett since she was having difficulty tending to her tired and hungry child.

"Come 'er, son," he said, taking his fussy son out of the cradle to relieve Harriett

Harriett dipped water into the wash pan, saying, "My hands got so many stickers I can hardly handle this here dipper." Some of the pesky stickers were elusively embedded under her skin. More apparent injuries from full-grown thorns became evident with the lamplight.

"Careful bout gettin' poke juice on you for a bit", Canady warned. "It can make you perty sick. I can remember Ma gettin' pisoned by poke 'afore. Her hands swelled up big. It's sumpthin' else, ain't it, Harriett, how sumpthin' that's so good when it's cooked can be so bad 'afore it's cooked? Fact is, I have thought on this some about many a thing lately. That is, how somethin' good can be bad too."

Harriett nodded in agreement. "When I's a youngun, we saw a neighbor at Smith Holler with her hands all swelled up. Poke pison got into her blood and made her mighty sick," she acknowledged. "I knowed all about watchin' for this."

After trying to deposit Shelby in his cradle once more, Shelby let out a shriek. Canady retrieved him and bounced him on his knee to keep the noise level down, whether it was necessary or not. Harriett put a juicy blackberry into the hungry toddler's mouth, averting an aria competition with screech owls.

"There's a time when I never gave a whit about noise on the river," Canady said. "But, when I was a tadpole most holler folks lived in cabins, not houseboats," he reasoned, bumping his toddler up and down. Even Canady had to recognize many houseboats he had seen lately carried families. His houseboat had filled a need in his youth for escape from a troublesome stepmother, but his houseboat had carried a solitary occupant.

"Maybe most of them folks out here started out different too. What was once so good now's bad. There ain't no choice 'bout it now. Not anymore, there ain't," he said. Canady had become one of the boat people. He would be imprinted with an increasingly hated title the rest of his life. The die' was cast. No welcome mat was put out for boat people on any shore. Quite the contrary, there was no welcome mat put out anywhere for boat people. They were only tolerated at best.

In the beginning, Harriett hadn't given into resignation about houseboats, but she had succumbed to it since she was now part of a river man's life. It wasn't home. It was Canady who had been content to call the houseboat his home, not her. With the latest turn of events, even his contentedness had changed to feelings of entrapment. For this former handsome dandy, a lowly reputation attached to his fleeing lifestyle was not what he had envisioned for himself when he left home at fourteen.

Trying to keep Shelby quiet over the past year took too much of Harriett's time to suit her. He strained to see all the other boats, clapping his hands and screeching at them. Harriett scolded him once in a while for reaching out to strangers. He learned not to do it after a time. Becoming wary of others nearby was a lesson Shelby had to learn. From time to time a new concern about the possibility of her child drowning was added to the mix.

This ain't home. It ain't suppose to be this a'way. Younguns should be a'playin' in the dirt, runnin' around and chasin' chickens and such.

Since her husband had decided not to be a farmer, it was far too late to change his mind now. The river had to be home, like it or not. There were no other choices for any of them. During the deepest moments of pining for family she gained consolation by remembering the death march some of her family and friends were forced to make. This was the lesser of two evils.

To make matters worse, Harriett had a problem she couldn't put off thinking about much longer, as was her custom. She didn't want to worry Canady about it. Actually, she was afraid to tell him. Tell him or not, the obvious would be evident before much longer. Who would help her out this time? No Arimenta to count on. Now, what? *Best not to ponder on it.* She mentally sidestepped this issue again and put cleaned berries in a pan. Dipping more water into a pot, she sat the first cook water on the stove for the poke.

Chapter 8
ALABAMA PROSPECTS

"We are a'needin' to do somethin' pretty soon, Canady. This youngun ain't gonna wait much longer," she warned her husband. Harriett remembered poor Sophy. She didn't want to end up like her and, no matter what Arimenta said, something could always go wrong. Canady was the last person she wanted to attend to her. *My brave man ain't so brave when it comes to havin' babies. He best be a figurin' on somethin' soon!*

Canady stopped playing his juice harp for a bit to listen to his wife. After the removal threat had somewhat subsided, as long as they were careful about docking, he began to play in the evenings once more. Soldiers were still out there, but they had no intention of clearing out the rivers. Music had become a part of river life. It was the one thing that added something instead of taking it away.

Part of Canady's courting appeal for Harriett came from his playing a juice harp or mandolin, but both had to be put aside when concern for discovery threatened them. Passage of time had eased the threat a bit, but hatred for the numerous river travelers had increased. Canady believed the biggest danger concerning the necessity to stay quiet was behind them, however, giving rise for renditions on his mandolin or harp. Often he was accompanied by a fellow boatman's contribution. A melodious concert buoyed the souls of listeners along the muddy Sequatchie. Playing each evening soothed the restless soul of one who wanted to be tied to nothing other than the woman of his choice. Tonight she wasn't as receptive to his music as she once was.

He began to play his instrument again without responding to Harriett's concerns.

"I can only imagine what it's gonna be like chasin' after two of them younguns," Harriett fretfully continued. Her slender fingers tucked in wisps of black hair escaping from a coiled bun. With her long hair in place, she turned back to her husband, waiting for him to make some comment about her concerns. Canady remained quiet.

"What do you s'pose we should be a'doin?" she asked again, since he hadn't said a word concerning her question. He quit playing to look off across the water toward the post oak and sweetgum trees growing along the bank. Canady was lost in a world of his own tonight.

"How I wish Arimenta were here," Harriett finally told her muted husband. *Maybe a mention of his own kin might get some answer?* Soon Harriett heard a plaintive sound coming from the harp once more without any acknowledgment to her concerns.

He'll be a puzzlement til' I die, she thought to herself after he didn't answer.

Two days later and a little further downstream, Canady broached the subject she had prodded him about several days earlier.

"'Fore we left Kentucky, your Uncle Will and I got to talkin' about what we would be a'doin' and where we'd be a'livin'. I had to say the way it is after he told me, 'all the clan sticks together'."

Canady had experienced some indignation when Will Riddle pushed him to commit to a more grounded life. He felt he had to put Harriett's uncle straight.

"I know'd he meant well, and all, when he wanted me to meet up with the flurosbar bossman of his. Not then or now, I ain't a'goin' to have no part of minin' no more'n I'se goin' to have any part of my Pa's farmin'. Harriett, I don't reckon that set too well with your uncle. I told him, 'I ain't gonna be stuck in one place and be looked down on neither and that's it!' Didn't mean no disrespect to 'em. It might be fine for him to stick to livin' like that. So be it. It ain't my way."

Canady overlooked the sad turn of events their life had taken since then. How was he to know the river would get filled up with people escaping from one thing or another?

"There's a reason for me a'tellin' this now," he said, grabbing his pipe and tamping tobacco in the bowl.

Harriett didn't say a word, but listened to his delayed answer to a very progressive problem she faced. She thought if he didn't verbalize something pretty soon, she probably would have to interrupt and ask him to help her deliver their next child.

"When Will asked what idée I had in mind after refusin' his offer, I could tell he weren't too happy about it. I told him we'se a'goin' to find us a way that's different, but I hadn't got it figured out yet. Then I says to him, 'It'll come to me by-and-by, but until such a time come, I'll be a'trappin for a spell.'"

"Canady, why in the world are you tellin' me this now? What does that have to do with havin' another baby and the need for somebody to help me get it here?" Completely exasperated with her husband, Harriett's emotions gave way to tears welling up. She feared Sophy's fate was hers waiting to happen.

"Harriett, did you know your Uncle Will has kin not too far off from us now?"

"Never heard of such in my life. How do you know?"

"He said somethin' about a brother of his, Robert Riddle, and told me where he lived, the last he heard. Your Uncle Will didn't think he would be a'movin' off of the old home place. That's where they live," he said. "Will said he wouldn't be bothered to move any more than they would be bothered to move from Smith Holler with this routin' of the Indians and all."

Harriett was completely taken back by Canady's solution for the birth of the baby. She didn't know these people! But, she never knew Arimenta before either. At seventeen, she had come to know her husband was not like holler folk, nor was he like the relatives who once lived at her grandpa's village. Canady's problem-solving belonged uniquely to him, no matter if it hadn't been tried and proven. He was satisfied it would work.

"Well, now ain't that a fine howdy do! You ain't never been in these parts, how you 'spect to find him? You ain't been trappin enough to do much barterin' neither."

"I figure I can trap and put meat on Robert's table, help around the place some, cut wood and all, in payment for midwifin'. From what your uncle told me, his brother has a pretty big family. When you said we'se havin' another, I decided it best to keep a'goin' toward the old Riddle homestead he told me about. I figured there has to be somebody to midwife if you have a batch of younguns. That ought to take care of things, don't you think?"

Before Harriett had time to answer his question, he added, "Besides, it will be good for Shelby to see some of his kin and get use to some other folks since he ain't had much chance at it." Canady tugged again at his pipe and released a trickle of smoke from his lips, smugly approving of his innovative liquefaction.

Poling and drifting, the houseboat was purposefully moved, bend after bend, seeking an unknown destination. Canady's resolve to find Robert Riddle's cabin wouldn't waver. His fear of helping at birthing time was a great motivator to finding Will's brother and the need to find kin was a race against time. Harriett tried not to think about what lay ahead if Canady wasn't right about Will's kinfolk. She sensed the encouragement he tried to give her could be on shaky ground by his obviously worried look and deflated countenance, bend after non-descriptive bend. She went back into the cabin and gave Shelby a hard biscuit to pacify his fussing before putting him to bed. When Canady came to bed he was unusually quiet. That was the way he dealt with uncomfortable, unsolved situations.

"There she is!" he yelled the next day after searching until noon. Water gushing around a paddle wheel was pushed into a trough built from the river to a cabin just as Will had described it to Canady. That was the landmark he was looking for.

As soon as the houseboat came into sight, playing children next to the cabin rushed toward the pier. Watching from the deck, Harriett pulled Shelby from behind her skirt after he darted back there after he saw the noisy children coming toward him. Canady tied off the houseboat and made salutations to an approaching man carrying a rifle. The third time Harriett pulled Shelby from behind her backside, he began to cry.

Robert Riddle walked toward the pier with a frown on his face. Not used to company— intruders, they called the boat people—he was wary of anyone coming toward his pier, especially people in a houseboat with furs piled on top. As exciting as it was for the children, the sight suggested something else for Robert Riddle. He was prepared to stand his ground and see to it the intruders left.

"Here, you youngun's get back to the house," he ordered.

With a big grin on his face, Canady reached out his hand, introducing himself, Harriett, and their whining son. Only after explaining they were kin from Kentucky, bringing news about Will and the family, did Robert's uneasiness leave. He called for his wife, Ruth, to come outside the cabin. Robert introduced his wife and all the children surrounding her, whose names neither Canady nor Harriett could remember.

After greeting one another at the river, Ruth grabbed Harriett's arm, leaving Canady and Robert at the pier in deep conversation. When she turned Harriett toward the direction and hospitality of their home, both the women heard orders coming from Robert, "You younguns get away from there, leave that boat alone!" Kids converged on the houseboat, all eleven of them!

The two women walked up the worn path. A matronly Ruth gave Harriett a knowing smile and said, "It looks like you're pert near ready, ain't you, Harriett?" Harriett realized if anyone should know about such things it would be Ruth. Looking at the number of curious children overwhelming their papa at the boat pier was the clue Harriett relied upon. She counted squirming and giggling children scurrying everywhere, and if what she saw was right, there was a bulge under Ruth's apron. Number twelve was on the way.

Shelby wasn't happy walking with his Mama and the strange lady toward the cabin. His fusses grew to louder tantrums. With each squeal he boomeranged back into her skirt every time she pulled him out. Finally, Harriett picked the shy and protesting toddler up in her arms so she could move without stumbling over him. Straining to pick him up was all it took. That's when it happened!

Harriett raised back up with Shelby in her arms and didn't move. "I don't know when I've ever been so red faced!" she told Ruth. Ruth saw Harriett's wide eyes struggling to communicate something.

Canady thinks he has it all figured out and it's me that's havin' babies, not him, she thought to herself, in her moment of desperation placing anger on her husband for something he didn't know a thing about.

"Aunt Ruth, I'm afeered my water done broke! Wouldn't you think this baby would wait a bit, at least until we had our first howdy said?" Harriett was near tears. The mother of eleven kids understood women didn't get a chance to pick and choose the most opportune time for birthing. A baby was on the way and that was that. She told Harriett everything would be 'just fine as silk, and that she need not worry.

This time, waves of pressure started quicker than they had with Shelby. *Arimenta told me it would be so. How did she know so much?* Strong pains had already begun after she reached the two-room cabin.

There's a might more room in here than the houseboat! She nostalgically looked around at all the space resting on a non-moveable surface. At first glance, pangs of homesickness for Uncle Will and Aunt Nancy's home, the feather bed, and her pretty handmade furniture flooded back. She had done her best to put such memories in places where they wouldn't be so painful.

All Ruth and Robert's children slept in the big room where the big cook stove and fireplace were. Ruth and Robert had a new addition, a room just for them. The new add on was colder in the wintertime, but it also was private. When Harriett saw the added room, she was relieved. Ruth brewed some hot tea and fried some sugar-cured ham and cooked eggs in the grease. She already had a number of loaves of bread baked so she didn't bother to fix any biscuits for the guests and their own ravenous brood. Harriett sat at the table, at Ruth's insistence, during the preparation of the meal.

"Well, Robert, I tell ya, things is bad at home," Canady said. "Your brother, Will, says he don't have much to worry about as far as he's concerned. His woman is pretty tore up since her Pa, Chief Whitehorse, had to leave."

Robert was eager to hear any news about his brother who had left Tennessee to live in Kentucky years ago so he wouldn't be hampered about marrying. He knew he would be free in Kentucky to marry whomever he wanted, but Tennessee still held to Melungeon laws. They couldn't marry outside their own kind. Will Riddle wanted his own options, not ones that were forced upon him.

Robert Riddle took in all the news Canady was telling, mulling it over in his mind. "I know that Will is a stubborn one for striking out on his own. He probably married a perty woman since he was so particular. Judging from Harriett, if she looks anything like Nancy Riddle, she is a right nice looker, that's for sure," Robert told Canady.

Canady soaked up Robert's flattery. "Oh, I can guarantee ya that, Robert," he laughed smugly. "Nancy is a right smart looker, that's for sure."

"You ever hear anything about a Mason Riddle?" Robert asked as they walked into the house. Robert tried not to appear too interested but in an offhanded way sought information. He pulled two cane-bottomed chairs toward the fireplace. Mason Riddle was the black sheep of the Riddle family. No one had heard much about either of the Riddle brothers after they left. News of Will was sought and welcomed, but information about Mason would have to come in through the backdoor.

Robert's brother had learned years ago there were fewer legal problems in Kentucky. With the exception of the other brother, Mason, he was more independent than the rest. The family exception had gone to Kentucky too, but he was not talked about much. There was some idea about Mason having a connection to some kin of Will's wife, but nobody quite understood what it was. But, then again, no one really cared either.

Both men lit up pipes and stretched their legs in front of their chairs toward the open fire. The rock hearth was substantial, well-built with a fire crackling from fresh logs. Ruth had a pot of beans cooking in it.

"If I hadn't already been a married man with a family, I might have tried for a change myself, Canady. Ruth is my third cousin. We courted for about a year before the folks allowed us to marry."

Only with kin should one tell of one's history. Since Canady was sort of kin, it was permissible.

"Did you see any of the removal, Canady?"

"You'd be plumb dumfounded how fast them stockades went up after Whitehorse left, Robert. They must have had timber cut for some time for that to happen so quick. They's put up for a holdin' place so's they could move them to the main place down south later. Harriett and I seen evidence of them smaller ones a'comin' down the river. Why, lands! Sometime you could smell 'em a'fore you ever saw 'em. It was somethin' awful!"

Robert contributed to the information telling, "We kept to ourselves and was passed by while all this was a'goin' on. Ruth has some Indian, but our Pa wasn't no Indian. Our Ma was," he said, thinking they were lucky they didn't have to go. "We didn't want to chance it, but nobody bothered us."

"Well, smellin' them places was bad enough, but that ain't all," Canady continued. His mind was stuck on the atrocities they had personally seen. "There's a time or two, we heard cries a'comin' from the stockade direction. It was pure sounds of misery, if you ask me," Canady confessed. Your brother's wife, Nancy, would be in worse shape than she was when we last seen her if she seen what we seen. It was hard enough on her to tell her Pa goodbye, but seein' this would have added that much more worry. Whitehorse is still alive, I figure, but might as well be dead, as far as she's concerned. She'll never see'em again."

Canady watched Ruth preparing food to serve their kin, a rarity for the Robert Riddle family. No one noticed nature's process taking place with Harriett yet. This confidence was kept between Harriett and Ruth for the time being.

Just as Canady was isolated on the rivers and trapping in the woods, so was the Robert Riddle family isolated. They were tucked among trees crowding a bay on the Sequatchie River and left pretty much alone. Robert was constantly on guard to protect his place from marauding boat people brazen enough to sneak into the countryside looking for anything of value. By necessity, their family grew to trust no one outside of family. Kinship of-a-sorts, opened up a new reason for the clannish people to visit with a little more confidence.

"Brother Will never did get back home," Robert said, after sitting in silence for a minute to soak up all Canady had told him. "When Mama died, she called out for him a number of times." He shared this delicate information through an unoccupied corner of his mouth since his burl knot pipe rested in the other corner. "She never forgot Will. Now, Mason is another thing," he confessed. "He done broke Mama's heart."

Canady listened intently, remembering leaving home himself at a very early age.

"He ran off a'fore he was barely sprouted and no one has heard from him since. We don't know if he's dead or alive."

Canady relit his pipe automatically, deeply lost in thought. He was uncomfortable hearing about likenesses much like his own past history connected to that of a scoundrel. Robert knew nothing about Canady's background and as far as the river man was concerned, it was going to stay that way.

Canady remembered rumors had circulated several years ago, in hushed tones, about a brother of Will Riddle being the father of Harriett. *This ain't a time to tell it though,* he thought to himself.

Robert continued to tell his shirttail relative about Harriett's uncle. "Seein' Will weren't here when Mama died, though his leavin' was honorable, I might add, Mama and Papa knew they'd never see the likes of him again. So, when the time came, this here place was left to me."

Robert purposefully used silence to enhance the significance of his words, then blew smoke lazily into the room. Mesmerized by self-reflected importance, he shifted and drew his feet in closer to the chair legs to ponder his assets. Since they already had a number of offspring at the time of his inheritance, he had to build an extra room to accommodate his growing family.

"Mama! Mama! Mama!" Shelby screamed. Ruth had Shelby in her arms walking toward Canady. The men were so involved in their conversation they didn't notice Harriett had gone to that extra room off the big room. Ruth had to pry the protesting child from Harriett's legs before leaving the bedroom to put him on his daddy's lap. Red-faced, Shelby continued to sniffle in his daddy's arms. Ruth easily ignored the crying toddler because from her own brood she had garnered many references to different cries. This cry wasn't one to be alarmed about.

"It's time to eat. Supper's on the table," she said after giving Shelby to Canady. "You younguns, wash up. Canady, you can sit right here, if you like," she said pointing to her normal place at their table. "We have business to attend to. Harriett will be busy for a spell," she said before going back into the bedroom. Familiar signs written across Harriett's face said labor had begun.

It was much faster this time than when Shelby was born. She watched Ruth pull back the counterpane to the foot of the bed taking great care to not get it soiled. Ruth proudly told Harriett that she had spent an entire winter embroidering her counterpane.

"I assure you, I have been midwifin' for a quite a spell for permanent folks along the river," she told the worried young mother. "They always come for me when times are close," she said trying to encourage Harriett. As far as Harriett could remember, she didn't see any houses along the river. *They must be hid.*

Related to Ruth or not, this was not what Harriett had hoped for. She wanted Arimenta, but such hankering was impossible. She had already reached a birthing stage where questions become superfluous and the luxury of fanciful wishes must give way to reality. The baby was coming, ready or not. Ruth was the midwife, wanted or not. Harriett counted the good fortune she had, was relieved it wasn't Canady, and accepted the offer gratefully.

The side room was a welcome place to hide her embarrassment. Since having Shelby, she had something to relate this experience to and didn't want to make a spectacle of herself to these strangers, shirttail relatives though they be.

Ruth shut the heavy hewn door to the bedroom when her pains got harder.

Harriett tried to mentally prepare herself to have at least a full day of agony, but her baby had plans of his own. Maybe this was an omen? They say each child is different, she informed herself, beginning to realize things weren't the same. He entered the world in a little more than two hours after the shut door stood sentry to protect Harriett's dignity. It was as Arimenta had predicted. *I reckon I am goin' to have a passel of younguns. Uncle Robert and Aunt Ruth could say the same about havin' babies too, it peers to me,* she thought looking at the newborn cradled in her arms.

"Jasper Newton Holmes," she whispered in a tired voice to Ruth. "That's what I'm gonna name him. Canady never come up with a name and this is the name I am a'givin' him."

She told Canady what she wanted to call their newest son when he came in the add on room. He remarked, "That's a right handy name, no idée of Indian to him at all." This time Canady didn't appear as worried as he was with Shelby. He left the women and returned to the table.

"After all we seen, it's best not to put any more troubles on our new son than he can rake up for himself," he told Robert. "Jasper Newton Holmes, it is."

Their second son, Jasper Newton, was born a year after the stockades were emptied. Nobody felt safe yet since rumor had it soldiers were out there looking because there was bounty on run aways.

"The whole notion of gettin' rid of Indians must have come from too much whiskey drinkin'in Washington," Canady had always said. "That fool idee of takin' away their property has ruint us all. It took holt and tore folks apart, either from dyin' on the way or from leavin' family behind," he told Robert, justifying the new name of his son. "Any Indian still living in Tennessee don't feel easy even if they is hid," he said. "Jasper Newton Holmes sounds just right. This river man's son don't have no problems with a name like that."

Both the men pulled their chairs back in front of the big fireplace after eating. Canady told Robert about the beautiful farm and compound Chief Whitehorse had lost. Being a wanderer himself, he had owned no such property to make brags about, but used Chief Whitehorse's past position to validate his importance to Robert.

"Nobody has a right to own another fella," he said, taking a long draw on his pipe. Visions of his own aunt being led away by a rope to a high fenced stockade gave more reason for elevating his self worth in Robert's eyes. The memory was all the more reason for satisfaction about his new son's name.

"We don't know what to 'spect yet. No one can rightly say for sure," he added.

The next week, Canady made good his promise to work out their stay and keep. He had split several stacks of firewood after shooting a buck to salt down into jerky in the smokehouse. As soon as he mended the corral, Robert insisted he had more than paid his way.

"We's mighty glad to get the news about Will and do feel condolences for his wife," Robert said, when it appeared the visit was coming to a close.

Canady thanked Robert for his hospitality and said time had come they needed to leave. Confinement was eating at Canady and this cabin was becoming smaller with both families staying there, even if he and Shelby stayed in the houseboat at night.

Moving from place to place was once unnatural for Harriett, but after two years of mobile life it had become part of her normal expectations too. She was uncomfortable when her husband exhibited restlessness and without understanding, she tuned in to his need to move. Without ever realizing when this transition had begun, Harriett too was at the place where she was ready to leave.

"You know, Canady, if I was you, I wouldn't be in such a hurry to put in just anywheres yet," Robert warned. "I don't look for any more uprisin' but you can't tell anymore. Them soldiers is still a'lookin," Robert said, as they boarded their river home.

Easy birthing was a blessing given to this wanderer. Her visit had been a good break from the river routine and it was good for Shelby to see other people, even if he still remained shy with adults. He had gravitated toward cousins, youngsters the trading post people called half-breeds. His new playmates taught him how to build dirt mountains.

Shelby fussed going back onto the boat. He left his newfound friends in the same manner he met them a week earlier, in fits of temper tantrums. Shelby was plainly not happy.

River life had required adjustments stretching Harriett's patience at first, but time had been a silent teacher implanting comfortable aspects of this watery territory. The waterways went on forever and Harriett felt a sense of ownership. She could easily pretend it all belonged to them and looked forward to her own open spaces even if confined to a houseboat. The houseboat belonged to them, and she believed the river did too. Besides, there were too many people at the

Robert Riddle cabin to suit her.

As sure as the sun would be coming up tomorrow, she knew midwife needs would prove a problem again, *but Canady's done it twice, he can do it again*, she assured herself, when they poled out into the current of the Sequatchie. Even knowing there would be more times ahead for the need of a midwife, she left with a little more confidence about the unknown. It ain't the same for us women a'livin' on the river. But regardless of its hardships, she was ready to return to this adopted lifestyle. *Maybe they's more kin yet Canady ain't talked about? I ain't goin' to think about it. I'll think on it later,* she told herself after waving goodbye to her benefactors.

"River life is a far cry from what I knew as a girl, Canady," she told him after they had gone several miles downstream. "But, I might say, I'm right content to leave, to be back on the river again. They's something disturbin' I heard Robert say. I don't know what I hate the worst: to hear my kin bein' called half-breeds or Melungeons."

"Their younguns knows how to do the writin', Canady," she informed her husband, as if this attribute canceled out a label of Melungeon or Indian attached to them.

Ours won't never have a chance to do no readin' and writin'. But, she countered to herself, we've made it just fine without no schoolin'. I need not fret about this none. It's plain for me to see you ain't gonna be stickin' around too long anywhere for our babies to get schoolin', are you Canady? I can see no signs of change a'comin. Not for now at least, she thought to herself, as the houseboat once again moved down the Sequatchie toward the Tennessee River. Harriett felt the breeze off the water flow across her face.

Her husband had his tanned hand to the pole, getting them closer to a moving current. His skin was as tanned as hers from staying on the deck and taking risks to work along the riverbanks. Mother Nature's gifts of poke, nuts and berries were part of the river benefits, but reminders of the sun's exposure was left on the smooth, darkened complexions defining both of the river people.

Chapter 9
CORNERED TRAPPER

Before the houseboat entered the Tennessee River, Harriett washed clothes on a scrub board at the Sequatchie shoreline. Rainwater from the barrel on deck had gotten too low. They were in desperate need of a rain. She hung the clothes on bushes around pawcohiccora trees and gathered hickory nuts while the clothes were drying. Many times she searched the timber when Canady was trapping to look for slippery elm and sweetgum trees so she could scrape bark and extract resin to replenish their supplies for poultice and cough syrup medicines. Harriett remembered the technique to bleed sap to make syrup when she found a rock maple. Many times she had watched Chief Whitehorse bleed a maple, never thinking it would become her chore someday. This long and tedious process began as soon as Canady left the houseboat to hunt and trap, or there wouldn't be enough time to let enough sap drip to do any good.

So the days passed. Harriett gathered, washed clothes and tended to little ones while Canady trapped. From Canady's complaints, she knew hunting around the Sequatchie River was a challenge for her husband. He had complained that his traps were either poached or empty due to lack of supply. Game was becoming scarce and was not as bountiful as Canady had told her back in Kentucky.

"I figure there's been too much a'goin' on this way and probably same things' happin' clear onto Ross Landin' ," Canady admitted to Harriett. "They ain't no good trappin' from all the movin' about in these parts, I'll wager. At least for the last two years I see trappin' is playin' out'." Canady told Harriett he was ready to pull up stakes and move toward Sale Creek with prospects of trapping along the Tennessee River formulating in the back of his mind.

The move proved to be more of the same. Trapping with no satisfaction from one site to another, they pushed into the Tennessee River and trapped the surrounding woods to discover the same conditions. Nature's bounty had been a sustaining necessity. Heavy with child again, Harriett was hampered gathering nuts from the forest floor. Foraging was an important factor for survival and had to be done whether she was encumbered by the weight of another child or not.

Always, fear for the need of another midwife loomed in Harriett's mind. Her concern was well founded on the river near Cleveland, Tennessee. The family grew from two sons to a third son on the 17th of August, only this time, Harriett didn't get help. There was no kin to be found in those parts. Panic gripped her when the baby's birthing began because Canady had to do what he had told Harriett he dreaded the most. After the baby came, Harriett heard her husband award his own valiant effort, "This 'un needs to be named after his Pa, John Canady," he said smugly, after catching the baby. John Canady it was. Harriett herself had to tie John's umbilical cord.

Forever the optimist, Canady believed the trapping was bound to be better in Alabama after an explosion of white settlers had come to occupy Indian farms in Tennessee. More and more disgruntled and protective new settlers put up a fuss when boat people came near their places. It was their farms, and they figured their game.

Soldiers had discontinued their search from hunting runaways. The remaining Indians lived peaceably among the old white settlers and the steady influx of people coming from the east grew. Confident the mayhem was over, many Indian farmers returned to known populations and owned slaves to work their own farms like the white man did. Harriett saw Indian cotton farmers up and down the rivers with black field hands like those of the white plantation owner. So, blind eyes to human depravity had formed in both, the formerly hunted and hunter alike. Controlling other people's lives became a sin known to the Indian as well as the white man. *It's a disgrace, all right, it's a disgrace,* she lamented every time she witnessed such.

Permissive attitudes toward the remaining Indian population throughout the south came too late for Harriett and Canady, however. Habits of seclusion had already become a part of daily living for far too long for many changes to take place in their lives now. Too much had happened, too much loss had taken place over the years. No matter how unseen, the brand of racial denial had been deeply burned and refused to be extricated now. Lack of trust put up unspoken barriers, ingrained by a repetitious pattern blocking social interaction with land dwelling people. The boat people were genuinely feared.

After leaving Ross Landing—a place renamed Chattanooga since the removal—they docked close to Fort Deposit. Cotton patches were commonplace lining the Tennessee River. Harriett and Canady saw white fields peppered with slaves dragging cotton sacks when they tied up near lofty soft elm trees skirted by stunted dogwoods. Cicada's courting hum was interrupted by the whine of mosquitoes. The cabin was too hot to stay in and Harriett sat on the deck and chanced the mosquitoes. It was hot in the shade, but hotter in the cotton fields, full of cotton pullers.

A commotion in the cotton fields got her attention. People were talking about a small black child who apparently had found relief from the heat by playing in the warm water at the river's edge. Harriett hadn't noticed the child until she heard the warnings coming from the field hands.

"Angie, do you see your youngin over yonder? Chile, you git yoreself back here, ya hear me?" Rufus yelled. "Angie, look over yonder! Them's boat people, Angie! You better get yore youngin," the black field hand called to the child's mother.

"What chew talkin' 'bout, Rufus?" Angie asked. "I don't see nuthin.'"

"Look over yonder, behind that dogwood. If that ain't a houseboat, I ain't black!"

"O Lordy, you is right, Rufus! Railen, get chur self over here, get away from that water. You hear me, son? I mean get yoreself right chere."

The little boy threw a handful of mud into the water before moving back to the hot cotton patch where his mother was.

"You stay right behind me Railen, you can't go to the water now," Angie told her little three year old.

Harriett had overheard the excited Rufus warn Angie about her child. She knew the feeling of protection mothers had when it came to their children, but it saddened her to think she could be considered an obstacle worthy of fear.

Canady had put the ramp down to go ashore early when he and Shelby had gone fishing. It looked like a good place to fish and stretch their legs. He heard from some of the river people that they were buying fish at Fort Deposit. They aimed to sell a few stringers of catfish. Harriett led her two toddlers and carried baby John off the houseboat. As soon as they touched the bank, Shelby headed straight for the place along the shore where Railen had played. Jasper toddled close behind him. Jasper left his finger marks next to Railen's, then threw his wad of mud into the water too.

Fishing and hunting, even finding work in the same cotton patch where Angie and Rufus picked, helped subsidize them until they decided their welcome had expired. Canady received his coin at the end of each day's work and Harriett showed him the fish she had caught when he came in. After cotton season came to an end and the fresh fish sold at Fort Deposit, he moved the family further south to trap.

Steam ships used the Tennessee's deeper water while houseboats rimmed the edges of the river close to settlements. If the shoreline could be considered a host carcass, the occupants appeared as something constantly working, always coming while others were going. Trapping here and there, moving about when trapping was poor, kept the families moving. So it was for Canady and Harriett until they came to the Decatur in Limestone County.

Their family once again grew while in this congested commercial port where steamboats brought products to be to delivered by railway near Muscle Shoals. Harriett had help with the birth of son number four, James Madison, from another woman whose family was docked next to them. And so it was—more children, more mouths to feed, and more river congestion began the push back to where they came from, back to Tennessee, but not before another son, William, was born. It had been bad in Tennessee, but it was worse in Alabama.

James Madison and William were both born in Alabama because their father believed opportunity had to be better in Alabama for a river man. Two sons later he once again had to face the fact that he was lost and mistaken. It was a losing effort trying to compete with a loaded steamboat. Nobody wanted to deal with a little river man when there was quantity.

"It's done trapped out, Harriett. I can't feed these younguns where there's nothin' to trap," he fussed. It was cause enough to pole back to Cleveland, Tennessee. William, a native son, was going to be transplanted in Tennessee.

Cleveland was a disappointment. It wasn't the place Canady had aspired to institute some new formula to achieve livelihood. Until he was able to support his family through these changing times becoming more evident everywhere, he had hoped furs would barter better in Tennessee than they did in Alabama, but that too had became a disappointment.

Canady had a plan formulating to do something drastically different, but it required him to get the most financial gain he could from his pelts. Competition didn't allow this to happen in Alabama and, sadly, it was proving to be true in Tennessee.

Thoughts about a conversation once had years ago with Harriett's uncle encouraged disparaging feelings. "I don't rightly know what it is I want to do, but I figure on trappin' until such a time it comes to me," he had said. That concept had been enough to fuel a stubborn will to keep going even in light of failure in order to discover himself somewhere. He wanted the old self back now. Somewhere along the way, the man Canady once was got swallowed up.

In the meantime, the cocky dandy Harriett had been so enamored with became edgy and sharp. Trapping was supposed to be the means of support for only a period of time until he discovered that permanent occupation which he believed would come along. This notion had become lofty thoughts of the impossible. Each year transcended into another and he had to readjust to the fact that he was a river man and trapper, and no amount of previous speculation would resort to anything else. It would have to do, like it or not. Pressure mounted to find support from nature. The barter system, which worked well at one time, had become worrisome by the late 1840s. More and more the ports and trades places were dealing in coin, a confusing solution to the river man. He understood barter well. He didn't understand coinage value.

Canady took thirteen year old Shelby to hunt with him again after they docked in a place he insisted on calling Ross Landing, a place now renamed Chattanooga since the removal. Making life changes, even names of familiar places, was difficult. Between the two hunters, with Jasper and John doing their part fishing, Harriett tending to clothing needs, childcare, and foraging when not cooking, they barely got by. The houseboat was crowded and if it weren't for being able to get off the boat to hunt, Shelby might have decided to do what Canady did when he was Shelby's age—run away. Suppertime was the only time that Harriett saw much of Shelby and Canady.

Very pregnant again by 1849, Harriett thought about Canady. *He is either poling down a river somewhere or in my bed a'pesterin' me, trying to make more mouths to feed!* Any dreams she once dared to dream in her young life were replaced with resentments building up due to everyone's expectations of her. Expectations were hampered by the inconveniences of river life, lack of creature comforts, social interactions, and the constant needs of growing children—not to forget her own aches and pains. She put her own concerns on a back burner. *I dreamed once of a fancy life jiggin' with Canady and all the girls would be jealous when they watched us. I must have been a woman whose good sense got up and left!*

Harriett pulled open the drawer in the washstand to look at her tiara and concho belt Canady had given her so very long ago. *These have been tucked away a right smart bit,* she wistfully thought. *I'm a'wonderin' what might a takin' place if we was a'livin' some other time? But, Canady, you said to me, 'It's the freest life there is Harriett!' I wonder? Free for who, Mistah Canady?*

The houseboat needed repair. Canady hardly finished patching one thing when something else begged to be worked on. With five boys, trying to keep them from tearing up more than Canady could fix up or keeping them from rummaging around other docked boat people, stresses fermented. Her solution was to bog each youngster down with chores so she could keep tabs on them. Fishing was one chore all of them liked. Chores had become the blessed answer for a full houseboat and lots of family needs.

Harriett taught her boys how to gather sassafras bark when they could find it. It was used for ailments as a soothing tea. Instead of Harriett's sassafras, Canady used whisky for his ailments when he could barter for moonshine. He could see no reason he should not try his luck at making it, so Canady and Shelby hid a still for their soothing, but bitter, whiskey elixir in the woods. Harriett had to be very sick before she succumbed to anything but sassafras for her ailments. Canady became more receptive to the notion that he didn't need an extra infirmity to medicate from time to time.

One day out of frustration, Canady made a decision. Medication or not, nothing sufficed his desire to be his own person. "Just too many people a'livin' here to suit me, Harriett," Canady complained. "Our family is a'growin' out of this place and there ain't a thing I can do about it! It's plain to see, we'se goin' to be a'needin' somethin' different. I been a'hearin' land is real cheap out west. Maybe we ought to give it a try a'fore we get too old to get a start." "What do you think?"

For sure, Canady hadn't found the satisfaction he had been looking for ever since they got back to Tennessee from Alabama. It had been bad in Alabama. After leaving, he kept telling himself it had to be better where they had come from. But it wasn't. There were more and more settlers moving in and the trapping had changed. Canady complained about everything being trapped out. When he was successful finding game to trap, he discovered some poacher had gotten to them before he did. Thoughts of more opportunity out west played on his mind.

"What you suppose happened to your grandpa, Harriett? Reckon, he still be alive? Maybe if he ain't, there's some of your kin out there. Reckon we ought to give it a try ourselves?"

Canady saw she wasn't fussing with him about moving further away from spots along the rivers they had called home these past years, so he took advantage of the situation. "And, trappin' is bound to be better where there's fewer people," he said, as if to top off his argument in a more positive light.

Thinking about the possibility of different frontiers quickened her insides. The thought was hopeful and gave new reason to tired daily drudgery. Once again, she opened the washstand drawer and pulled out her tiara and concho belt. The silver had tarnished over the years, but it was still beautiful with the passage of time and additional patina. Harriett wet the end of a rag, dipped it into the soda crock and began to rub against the highest elevations of the ornamented tiara without answering Canady. She had to give his questions some thought. Bright and shiny silver peeked past the black stain. Amused, Canady's grouchy attitude softened.

"I want you to have your picture took, Harriett. You need a likeness, you in your belt and crown for our grand babies someday. Ain't a better time to get it done neither. There's a picture man in Ridgeside. At least he was there oncet and I bet he still is," he said. "You'se goin' to get it done, and that's it. We've plenty of barter for it." Canady still had a little coin he could pay the photographer. The matter was decided. "It's time to get your good dress out," he said. It had been packed away for some time. Canady saw her eyes sparkle with amusement when he suggested pampering herself to make preparations for a tintype.

"I hope my dress still fits," she replied, seriously toying with her husband's idea.

All week Harriett fussed with her black dress, getting it clean and shaking and steaming the wrinkles out. Amazingly, the fit was good, but it had been a little large for her years ago. Aunt Nancy's fancy needlework along the pin tucks on each side of the bodice had not frayed any, but the white crocheted lace about the neck had become a little yellow with age. Harriett agreed it really didn't look bad since it had darkened evenly. When the brooch once belonging to Nancy was polished up and fastened to the front of the lace collar, she thought the results were spectacular.

More people of late were having pictures made for their loved ones before leaving out west. An extra photograph usually was made to carry along to use for posterity's sake some day. Canady wanted his wife to have this too, but he didn't feel a need to have his picture taken. He thought that having Harriett's likeness made might make up for some of those imagined fancy places she never got to go to. He speculated that she had dreams with no fulfillment after he had given her those special gifts from Pots Holler.

"Here's the place I was telling you about, Harriett," Canady said after making their way from the houseboat to a converted blacksmith shop. It wasn't much larger than their houseboat. After leaving Harriett outside with the children, he went inside and talked to the photographer. When Canady came out of the photographer's studio, he said to Harriett, "Get it took," then he walked off with baby William and the rest of the boys.

Canady had made good his brag with the photographer for a picture of his wife. The little town of Ridgeside had been a good place for this picture man to become prosperous from settlers passing through en route to the west. The photographer willingly accepted Canady's coin.

Warily, Harriett walked inside. She heard a man's voice saying, "Come over here, madam, and sit on the stool." Then he said, "Madam, where is your bonnet?"

"Ain't got no need fur a bonnet. I'm a'wearin' what I aim to have my picture took in," she informed him. Harriett could see a frown spread across his face before he ducked under a black cloth and he asked in a muffled voice if she would like to straighten the tiara a bit. He came back out from under the black cloth and said, "Madam, you need to smile."

She informed him it wasn't a thing she did without a reason. *Well, the idée of him askin' me about a bonnet! Don't rightly feel like smilin'.* A bright flash of light blinded her eyes. Harriett thought he was as rude as the bright light forcing temporary spots to blur her vision. She was sure he was ignorant and couldn't begin to appreciate the finery she was adorned with. *He has no background fur it,* she thought. *I am certain of it. A body don't see just every day such finery as Canady got me. I'm right proud to have it and for certain, I'll not pay him no never mind!* She was more than eager to leave the photography studio in the makeshift blacksmith's shop.

Shelby had to tend to Jasper, John and James fishing the next morning, instead of getting to go with Canady into Ridgeside to get Harriett's tintype. He went alone, professing, "One trip'll do with them younguns." He refused to change his mind even after they made promises to be good.

A little more respect fleetingly sped through Harriett's mind concerning the skills of the photographer after seeing results of the rude man's work. Harriett was pleased with her likeness. The woman looking back at her from the tintype had grown older by a few years, but Harriett's frame and smooth skin had changed little with the passage of time and childbirth. When women were dying from giving birth to babies, Harriett grew a radiance of womanhood.

One change had taken place since she and Canady left Kentucky but it wasn't her looks. It was confinement to the cabin and to areas near the boat. She couldn't go hunting with her husband anymore. There were too many children.

Problems began to pile up in Ridgeside: washing in the river when there wasn't enough rainwater, cooking for their large brood, making food stretch, and one ailment after another. During difficult and frustrating times, Harriett took time to sneak a quick look at the tintype.

"Just a'lookin' at my likeness a'lookin back at me, makes me feel a might better," she decided. "Specially after bein' up all night with one of the younguns retchin' from eatin' somethin' he outta not et," she told Canady when he saw her holding her photograph. It was during those busy times in Ridgeside that the thought, *I wonder if they's any end to it*, came to mind, and it haunted her.

Canady was a determined man, but he too had come to the point of wondering if there were any end to life's complexities. Poached traps and empty traps from lack of game, no markets for his pelts, and the change in the barter system added to his frustration beyond patience.

"We'se goin' to look for your family out west," Canady said, red-faced after he and Shelby came in from checking his traps only to discover they had been tripped and not one of them had anything in them. Canady could see fresh blood. The traps had been poached again!

"I speculate land will be cheaper and I aim to try my luck with a bit of farmin' to fill in for bad trappin' times," he said, still fuming about his lost income. "That's what my Pa did, you know, farmin'. Never cared much for it myself, but maybe there's some purpose to it now, I reckon."

Harriett realized her husband was dead set on leaving this time. There was no misunderstanding about it. He wasn't just talking, he meant it!

"How, we goin' to do this, Canady?"

"Goin' by water on our houseboat," he told Harriett "There ain't no other way."

Dreaming about the possibilities for relief to demands from life on a houseboat, Harriett realized Canady hadn't said when they would be leaving, but the leaving part was a certainty. She knew he could be counted on for that much. Canady always kept his word.

"Oh, we can have chickens, and fresh eggs, and we can grow us a bit of corn, some squash," she was saying, when Canady interrupted her.

"Now, hold on woman. You just remember one thing. If we do this, I ain't a'goin' to give up my trappin'!"

She could see the thoughts about being behind a plow suffocated Canady just thinking about it, even before actual dust could cut off his breath.

Harriett endured his increasing quick temper flashes more and more from pressures of family responsibility. Agitated from not being able to meet his family's needs, since the way he knew to do didn't work anymore, he found his release on the boys when they least expected. The youngsters walked the straight and narrow when Canady was home.

Harriett saw lines beginning to rut her handsome river man's face. With each passing year, parts of Canady seemed to vanish. He lost one part after another. After the birth of the sixth son, Augustus Burton, born at Riversedge in 1849, he told Harriett, "It's time to go," and began to put his plans in motion to leave the banks of Tennessee.

Chapter 10
LOOKING FOR BEULAH LAND

"Shelby, fetch the ramp. We'se movin' out to Fort Deposit," Canady told his son. Their stay wouldn't be long in Chattanooga, just long enough to get their business taken care of, then they would move on. Fish caught between Riversedge and Chattanooga would be sold at the main pier before they left en route to Fort Deposit.

"Son, we got some serious fishin' to do." He increased the excitement about moving to the west by telling Shelby they were apt to see a steamship on their way to Fort Deposit, the first leg of the journey. The twelve year old pulled the heavy ramp onto the deck and pushed the side edge up against the outside cabin wall. He struggled to turn the wooden hinge to secure the ramp. Raising and lowering the ramp had become 13-year-old Shelby's job.

Fresh water from a down burst had filled the rain barrel. Harriett had taken advantage of the fresh water, washing their worn clothes and shampooing heads of hair. When another shower hit, she had to rush to retrieve the dried laundry still stretched across wild plum bushes.

Canady guaranteed his decision to go to the west by filling their larder with extras. He had stocked their pantry full of smoked and salted fish and a bit of fatback swapped out for labor at nearby farms. Pay for cutting wood from one landowner had been a sack of dried beans and five pounds of grits. Shelby did his part by stacking enough fresh cut wood on deck for his Mama to cook with. His pile of wood would have to do until the next stop at Fort Deposit because the houseboat could only handle so much. Time had finally come to set their sights for Chattanooga.

Canady maneuvered through other water vessels in Chattanooga's congested harbor where several brokers were on the main pier buying fish. The boat people docked at an empty shoreline closest to the broker with the least amount of customers.

"Mistah, I have a right nice batch of fresh catfish I am a'lookin' to sell,"

Canady called out.

"Let's take a look at what you've got there, sir," the broker acknowledged, reaching for the four stringers Canady had lifted out of the water off the side of the boat. Shelby pulled the other two stringers out, followed after his daddy walking toward the pier, then handed them to the interested broker. The broker nodded at Canady, taking his catfish.

"That is a right nice batch, there, young man," he said to Shelby when he took the two stringers from him.

"Are you wanting barter or coin, sir?" the man asked.

"I'se a'lookin' for coin, I reckon," Canady said, squinting his eyes at the broker.

"The going rate is not much this morning, mister, but if you want to go this way, I can oblige you," he said, handing Canady seventy cents for seventy pounds of fish.

"I thank ye," Canady said, turning back to his houseboat. After boarding, he and Shelby stretched against their poles and pushed away from the shore with nothing more said between them. The other boys couldn't be contained. They were running excitedly around the railed deck, making noise and pointing to different boats and people. Shelby had to do a man's work. There was no time for foolishness. They were en route for Alabama.

Scenes along the river looked familiar. Everything was much the same since coming this way a year ago with one exception—more cabins near the water's edge. Houseboats inhabited spaces that were once vacant. Harriett's fantasy, believing the river belonged to them, had a hard time playing out now. The river was shared by many other boat people, who probably had the same dream, but the congestion resulted in shrunken dominions for all of them.

When he first spied the steamer Gorge at Fort Deposit, Shelby was so excited he nearly fell off the deck. After many stops, they had progressed slowly from Fort Deposit to Decatur, moving on to Florence, and finally docking at a place called Waterloo. The family larder was empty. With the few remaining furs Canady had left it was time to go ashore to barter for more supplies.

"I'm sick of this ole boat! Ain't nothin' but stayin' put. You and me needs to go a'huntin', Pa," Shelby complained. Shelby's attitude affected his brothers, who were grousing more than usual too. Everyone had been subjected to more confinement this time then ever experienced before. Their Pa was serious about going west. Waterloo didn't seem too likely a place to hunt. Canady agreed he could use a break, good hunting or not. Both Shelby and Canady stuffed some biscuits and jerky into their pouches and left with little conversation to the others. Shelby sure didn't want Jasper tagging along! He thought it best to get off this houseboat as quickly as possible and leave it all behind.

Harriett was tired from trying to soothe and relieve baby Gus of his colic misery. She had tried all sorts of methods—sassafras, and even willow-water with a dropper of Canady's medicinal remedy hoping to ease him. Nothing seemed to work. Tired eyes watched her only help step off the deck amidst protests from her remaining brood wanting to accompany their brother on a hunting excursion.

She knew it wasn't safe to let the two older boys, Jasper and John, off the boat while Shelby and Canady were gone. *No tellin' what they'd get into and I ain't up to chasin' after 'em.* It was decided the best solution would be to have them both fish off the deck.

"You'll never catch anything splashin' in the water that a'way," she told her disgruntled sons after taking James and William and her washed laundry to the shore. She hung wet clothes on a nearby brush thicket to dry. Harriett had no sooner gotten the words out of her mouth when the jabber between the unhappy Jasper and John escalated.

"Whatcha do that for, dumb head?" snapped Jasper, whiplashing his grasshopper bait into the water. He had spied the hapless insect attached to the side of the cabin wall at the time Shelby and Canady left. Faster than a frog could scoop up a fly, the nine year old had the insect caught and into his pocket until such time as he skewered it onto his fishing hook.

"You pushed me, stupid," growled John, staring beady-eyed at his older brother.

"Stay on your side cuz this here spot's mine," the seven year old challenged his older brother, daring him to wiggle any closer.

"Says who?" groused Jasper. Jasper never expected an intelligent answer from his red-faced younger brother, but truly looked forward to the possible invitation his question could initiate.

Harriett had hardly finished hanging wet laundry on nearby bushes when fists started swinging on the deck of the houseboat. The boys' raging screams echoed over the water. Harriett knew early on that it was going to be one of those days when her boys would probably be headed to a familiar corner inside the cabin. They hated to be confined this way, but evidently not enough to pass up any opportunity to establish territorial rights.

She grabbed James by the hand and picked up William from off a big rock to take them inside the cabin. Harriett told them to be quiet while she tended to their older brothers. Baby Gus, finally asleep in his cradle after crying from colic for a couple of hours, was becoming fretful again from all the commotion outside. The ruckus on the deck was in full bloom by the time James and William were deposited in the cabin.

Both irate contenders expressing insulting remarks to each other knew what would be waiting for them, but ignored their mother's warnings anyway. They exhibited the attitude: It's gonna happen anyway, so let's just make it worth while! Righteous retaliation was given an open throttle.

Vigorous swings were hardly hampered by their mother hanging on to each one's arm. Fists continued to flail at one another in front of Harriett and then behind her, depending on who was dodging whom. Momentum of the swings catapulted all three against the outside cabin wall before Harriett could direct them to the cabin door.

Gus' crying, mixed with other grunts, groans, and name-calling, had turned their quiet little cove into the likes it had never seen before. Even the usually noisy birds hushed their chatter to observe unknown territorial sounds coming from human creatures. By this time, Jasper had a puffy eye and John's nose was bloody, but neither gave into Harriett's demand to stop fighting. She found an ear belonging to each of her headstrong sons a vulnerable spot she could exercise her authority from. Both boys were crying with rage.

"John hit me first," Jasper bawled in self-defense. Jasper pleaded his case. Since John was the one who hit first, he had every right to hit him back, even if John were the younger brother.

"Mama, Jasper pushed me and I didn't do nothin' to him," John wailed. Large drops of blood fell to the worn plank floor from John's wounded nose. He took note of the ominous red spots and with renewed justification welling up, he bellowed, "I was sittin' there mindin' my own bisness and he pushed me real hard for nothin'!" Taking advantage of his injury, John screeched like a wounded cub.

Harriett swatted John on the backside and handed him a rag from the washstand while guiding him to an all too familiar corner of the cabin.

Next she checked Jasper's puffy eye. For a minute Jasper thought he was getting his point across about John being the instigator, but he found John's enticement to fight leading to his reciprocation earned him a spot in a hot, stuffy corner too!

With noses pointed toward a familiar, limited horizon, this isolation was tolerated only because a big switch would be next if the time wasn't done honorably. Both had determined cheating or sneaking a peek wouldn't be worth it at this point. They had pushed the limits past worthy risks already. Those corners held their noses like magnets.

After sifting weevils out of the flour again, Harriett put four pans of bread in the oven box to bake. She fed and changed Gus again. The weary baby drifted back to sleep while his two older brothers resembled wooden soldiers, and Harriett sank onto the straw mattress in exhaustion.

"All this time on the water and land right outside the door, and look where you boys are!" she scolded.

After her chores, she had planned to take the boys into the woods to hunt for sassafras. Not now. Harriett knew her boys well enough to believe each of them thought the other to be responsible for their predicament. *They's that much like their Pa. This account ain't settled between 'em yet and I knowed it. They's stayin' in that hot corner for a spell more.*

James and William played quietly inside the cabin, something unusual for them. Harriett knew James had been a bit sick to his stomach earlier, but thought it was only a minor complaint. *He more than likely will be fine when Canady and Shelby get back,* she thought, but just then she noticed something.

"Come here, son," she motioned to James. "You look like you could have gotten into some poison ivy, James. There's a red spot on your arm, a rash like. Does it itch any, James?"

She raised his shirt to check for more red places and found his stomach covered with a lot of little blisters. "This here's no poison ivy, James! You've got the chicken pox!" she gasped.

Jasper and John nudged closer into their corners away from James's direction. They didn't dare chance a look when they heard their mother declare William also had those little red splotches. Further investigation of the boys alleviated other concerns as no signs of the chicken pox had been seen on anyone else. Harriett knew it was a certainty the rest would probably get it, however.

By nightfall James and William had running noses and fever so Harriett sent them to their pallets early. After Jasper and John finished their corner duty, they realized they had escaped some severe corporal punishment and now, chicken pox. They were fortunate boys, indeed. Jasper and John gladly went outside on the riverbank to play peacefully. Their Mama was in no mood to give any more warnings. Harriett kept a keen eye for new troubles, but that cabin corner wasn't going to be revisited again by them today. Both boys made sure of it.

The little cove began to return to its normal serenity again with the exception of some mockingbirds. They began to sing their dueling songs, maybe after taking lessons from the human battle cries heard earlier in the day.

Canady and Shelby saw the reformed fishermen busy and unusually quiet when they got home. Canady had a buck across his shoulders and Shelby brought home five squirrels. When they got on deck, Jasper and John ran after them and pulled up a stringer of fish to show the hunters. Canady didn't miss seeing Jasper's puffy eye when he complimented their good work. He said nothing about the telltale signs until all the fish were cleaned and the gutted buck was skinned. Shelby helped Canady salt it down for smoking. After that, his Pa had time to talk to the other boys about their behavior.

Harriett put a meal together from bread baked earlier in the day, fresh poke greens, fried squirrel and gravy. The treat was a blackberry cobbler sweetened with honey.

After supper, when the boys were asleep, she helped Canady cut up the venison. She gathered some twigs to help him build a fire on the bank to dry and smoke venison, then she rubbed spices on the slabs of meat before it was stripped. Working in silence offered each a rare moment of solitude together. Tonight would be Canady's night to sleep out on the deck to keep predators, two legged or four, away from the curing jerky.

The day had been long. Work was over for the day and it was their evening time they claimed after all the tired warriors found sleep. Sitting on a bench next to each other, leaning back against the cabin wall, Canady and Harriett's spirits enjoyed still moments both of them needed for repair and regeneration. A closeness to the other, yet a freedom, belonged to each individual. Love for the other knitted bonding afresh in the evening air. It was during times like these that all the busy work to keep going seemed worth it. Canady finally broke the silence.

"You know, Harriett," he said, taking a long draw on his pipe. "When I was a kid we had a neighbor with eight kids and they all got the chicken pox."

Harriett thought his statement seemed a bit strange. She looked up at him in expectation, distracted from mending a torn place in Shelby's britches by the bright moonlight. After pondering the statement he made she informed him about something he should already know, "Canady, when you got six kids, I can't see that two more makes all that much difference about gettin' the chicken pox. I s'pose the rest of the younguns will get it. We will be shut of it and not have to bother about it anymore then," she said in resignation.

Harriett saw her husband get a bit of a grin in the corner of his mouth, then heard him say almost apologetically, "You don't understand, sweetheart." He took more draws from his pipe, pushing her patience to wait for the amusing history of his neighbor. "All the neighbor kids got the pox all right but, not all at oncet. Each youngun took their turn at the two week waitin' spell afore they got it. Not nary a one took the pox at the same time," he finished telling her after relighting his pipe.

The thought was sobering. She straightened upright as if to focus better on what she had just heard, trying to digest the prospects!

"You don't reckon the rest of the kids will take it one at a time, do you, Canady? That would be two months of chicken pox!" She got up off the bench with those disturbing thoughts and went to bed.

William fussed the most with his itchy spots the next day. Warnings were given to James and William about scratching the mean little sores, but Harriett's counsel fell on deaf ears. As the days passed, the older boys grew more confident that the childhood misery would pass them by.

"He's cuttin' teeth," Harriett told her family when she felt fever in Gus. "It's probably nothin' but new teeth. Probably the two of you younguns will be all they is gittin' pox."

Four days later, Gus broke out from head to toe with the little blemishes.

"Mama, I can help. I can put the socks on Gus' hands this time," John gleefully offered. Gus squealed in rage when John tried to wrestle his little baby brother and pin his arms down.

All this help is goin' to be the death of me, she thought, trying to loose Gus from John's grip. "Here, now, son. You better let me handle this." Too many troubles came with all the helpful offers.

Two weeks later, Shelby came down with the dreaded white blisters, followed by two more weeks of incubation period before John, then Jasper, got the pox two weeks after John. All took a full two-week period in sequence before the unsightly sores appeared on the subsequent brothers. Canady's neighbor had nothing on the Holmes boys, other than having two more to continue the course. Harriett had a new appreciation for being fewer in number, but that appreciation wasn't for long. She had to face the fact she was pregnant again.

Chapter 11

CHANGES

After months of river travel, the Holmes family came to where four major rivers converged: the Ohio River, the Cumberland River, and the Tennessee River, all funneled into the Mississippi River. Paducah, Kentucky, was the place where most of the boat people congregated. Many had come down the Ohio River from the north, some from the Cumberland River on the east, and many, like Canady and his family, from the Tennessee River to the south. Conditions were grotesque and stagnated at Paducah since boat people's very lives were threatened if they came ashore. They were hated, distrusted and ostracized. Until some kind landowner offered to share well water with the desperate river life, many had to drink the polluted water infested with the floating bodies of their dead. The river people had no place to bury their loved ones on land. The boat people couldn't come ashore and the river was the only place they could place their dead. Cholera resulted, leaving a wake of devastation.

Because of the dangerous circumstances, Canady did not linger in Paducah, but kept moving until they were on the Mississippi going south.

Their long ride after navigating down the big Mississippi River eventually took the family onto the Arkansas River. Weary of river travel, the Holmes family finally moved westward toward Shoal Creek, Arkansas, the place where "land's cheap and it's easy startin'," according to the captain of the shabby houseboat.

The closer they poled toward Shoal Creek, the noisier the river became. Paddle wheels, private houseboats, and small flat bottoms all clamored about the river tending to business like honeybees to a honey pot. River life wasn't as they expected. This place was not remote but was humming with activity. Population was in abundance.

Canady had a sinking feeling in the pit of his stomach. *Where's all the land that's cheap and easy to get?*

"Shelby, you see that?" Jasper poked his big brother to take a look at the big paddle boat coming in their direction. They watched, open mouthed, as the water-eating monster passed them by. "You'd need a mighty big pole to fish off that deck, Shelby!" Jasper said through a dropped jaw.

Giggles erupted from John when he viewed the big boat, but William ran behind Harriett's skirt. Only when he felt security from his very pregnant Mama did he dare venture a peek. Timid William was the sensitive one of the boys. Whether viewing from behind Harriett, or racing around the deck of the houseboat to get a better view, all her boys—in rare silence—stared with wide eyes transmitting messages to their brains about new things. People wore fancy clothes and promenaded around the big deck of the passing river boat. Such a big deck!

Harriett welcomed the mental diversion for her mischievous brood. This was one time they were so occupied seeing new things they had no interest inventing trouble.

Rapt attention diverted to these strange happenings had actually altered their nightly routine. Happenstances were not as they had always known. For years the Holmes family was accustomed to claiming their surroundings solitarily to themselves when they docked at night or for trapping stays. This new river bank was full of nighttime intrusions and night had lost its privacy for them. Plinking sounds of banjos, the wail of mouth harps and fiddles filled the air. Unusual interruptions replaced familiar night sounds and commuted auditory distractions well into the night. Harriett found the novelty entertaining enough, but it was disturbing too after being used to having private space and listening to quiet and the relaxing mating calls from frogs and toads for nightly sonatas. Sounds from the big boat conveyed excessive energy for the end of her long day.

Many lanterns were lit throughout the paddle boat's numerous rooms. In the dark of night their light emitted twinkling reflections like jewels bouncing off the still Arkansas River. Watching the display, and fueled by lively music, the boys were so excited it was difficult for them to go to sleep for fear they would miss something.

Boisterous laughter mixed with the night music dislodged a rivers normalcy, to boat people's way of thinking, even if it was amusing for a short while. The amusing part began to lose its intrigue by the wee hours of the morning.

"Times are a'changin' ain't they, Canady," she whispered to her river man after the boys were in bed. "Reckon we'se up to it?" she asked. She knew he had wrestled with that question long before they left Tennessee. Ready or not, change appeared to be forced upon them. Both would have chosen another way, one closer to home, if such opportunity ever existed.

"Tomorrow's the day, Harriett. We'se goin' to put in at Shoal Creek Landin'," Canady said. "We'll stay there a day or two, time for me to work for some supplies. Maybe some folks might know about some of your kin? We don't have to be quiet anymore about askin' around for 'em here," he told her.

"Gol durn, we won't know how to act, not havin' to worry about such as that!" Canady admitted in a raspy whisper.

"Could be somebody knows somethin' about your grandpa, if he's still alive. Maybe they's heard of him if he ain't. We might be lucky enough somebody has, you reckon?" This unusual chatter, coming from the poker faced Canady, tattled on his uneasiness about what he was to do next. The young boatman was sure enough years ago when he rejected Will Riddle's offer to work in the mines back in Kentucky. In cocky confidence he had made a statement about searching out that special something in life other than trapping. Time was sifting out without a clue to what that something was. Canady didn't know what to do next since the miraculous revelation he was counting on in his future didn't materialize.

Harriett heard her dandy say, just before sleep overtook her in the comfort of their bed, "We'se gonna dock serious like soon, my sweet Harriett. There ain't much time to dally and I ain't gonna go through this again like I had to with John's birthin'." The sound of his pipe "pop-popping" against a hard surface was the last thing she heard. A nudge to move over a bit on the shared straw mattress was the last thing she felt.

Morning came early for Canady. He was poling out from the riverbank before the boys were awake. Late stages of pregnancy made him nervous. He didn't want to be so far away from civilization, paddle boat nearby or not, if the baby started to come. There were plenty of people passing on the river, but little good that would do them. Shoal Creek Landing represented relief in many ways.

Harriett was slow moving this morning. She was tired of the bed, but didn't feel much like getting up either, but her hungry family needed feeding. Since all of them liked to eat as soon as their feet touched the plank floor, she started slicing slab bacon and making grits. *That should hold 'em til the middle of the day,* she thought, after frying the bacon up.

"Shelby, come on and get up. Help me this mornin', son." Harriett nudged her sleepy eldest out of bed. She needed him to take care of fourteen-month-old Gus. The toddler was the first of the boys to get up each morning. "Seems to me you youngest 'uns get up first and you oldest 'uns get up last," she told Shelby, patting him on his sleepy head.

After breakfast, Harriett worked to get the dishes washed and stacked away. She gave stern orders for Shelby to continue looking after Gus while his Papa was busy. Then, Harriett did something she never did. She lay back down on their bed all the while trying to convince herself she wasn't cramping. "It can't be! Not yet! Maybe it will pass and just be practicin' cramps," she said, loud enough for Shelby to hear. Those well-known beginning waves of labor were indeed pulsating, nothing false about it. Shelby had witnessed his Mama doing this before.

August's heat was sending emissaries of warmth inside the boat cabin by the time Canady poled in at Shoal Creek. It was mid-morning and Harriett didn't want to leave the bed. She kept the labor pains to herself. Canady had suspicious inflections in his voice when he asked, "Are you tired or just poorly today,

Harriett?"

"I think it might be right smart to see if any of the kin lives in Shoal Creek" she answered him back. "To answer your question, you could say I am a might both, tired and poorly." She saw Canady's face start to drain of color.

"If things go like the last time, I will have plenty of time 'fore things get serious, but you need to look for some help, I'm a'thinkin'. It takes a bit longer for me now. You can leave Gus and William, but you take the rest of the younguns with you," she said, then turned her head toward the cabin wall and bit her lip.

Canady was out the door in a hurry. Even before they were off the deck he questioned the wisdom of taking the boys with him. Jasper and John had already started fighting.

"You boys straighten up here or you are goin' to stay with your Ma," he barked, knowing his threat was empty. The boys too knew this time their Pa's words didn't have much meaning. All the while Canady was fussing at his lively sons, John was walking on the back of Jasper's heels. James watched, but kept his mouth shut or the bullying taking place could turn on him.

This early mornings confrontation didn't miss Harriett's ears and she breathed a sigh of relief that the older boys were with Canady right now. James usually was never into much, at least not as much as Jasper and John were capable of getting into. Houseboats were confining and she understood how it helped mushroom pent up frustration in growing boys. Today it would take their Papa to handle things.

The baby had dropped already. In spite of her advancing labor, Harriett did take a peek at her dueling sons to see how Canady managed to corral them. Pains came again and her own situation refused to be ignored. *Hurry, Canady.* She knew it was time to reason with herself again. Since marriage at fifteen to the present age, thirty-one, Harriett learned it was best to reason and not panic in order to calm festering fears growing inside. She knew no other solution. She wished for one. Another strong, hard push began to radiate across her belly.

For sure, I do know what to expect. I know what has to be done after the youngun gets here. Knowin' and takin' care of your predicament is two different things, I reckon. (Confidence often got slaughtered during internal arguments.) *This here baby is a'comin' and that's all there is to it. Docked here is more of a comfort than bein' on the river a'ways,* she thought, like a person whistling in the dark. *I have to look on the good side of things. That's it, the good side of things.* Then another pain hit. *I'm sure Canady is a'lookin' right now for somebody!*

Shelby pinched Jasper's ear. "Leave John alone, Jasper, or I'm gonna tell Pa." Shelby hadn't seen John stepping on Jasper's heels. He just saw the retaliation. Jasper knocked Shelby's hand off his throbbing ear and yelled at the top of his lungs, "You sorry blockhead!"

His unexpected scream startled a rider's horse, making it sidestep so quickly the saddled animal suddenly moved out from under the rider and he fell to the ground. Totally embarrassed, with little ado, he quickly remounted his horse and sped away. The fighting brothers, engrossed in their parley, never saw him get on his horse, nor did they realize they were responsible for him being spilled out in the middle of the street in the first place. They did note, momentarily, from the corner of their eyes, some grown man groveling in the dirt, but quickly lost interest by honing in on their own escalating agitations at hand.

"You're always pickin' on me, Shell! Why don't you tell John to stop it?" Jasper was screaming at higher decibels by this time. "John poked me first, can't cha' see, you dumbhead?"

Ah, yes, true. John had poked Jasper. He was excited when he saw his Papa go into a saloon to check on the family. That was what Canady told the boys he was going to do, then he left Shelby in charge before he left. Keeping one eye on his Papa and the other on Jasper, John saw Canady making a sweeping bow to a lady dressed up in fancy clothes. By the way she giggled, John knew in his heart she must have been some of the family. "Why's she so friendly if she ain't a part of the family?" he asked.

John had poked Jasper to take a look at what he perceived was a family member talking to their Pa. Instead of taking a look, Jasper took offense instead. Both boys threw fists and ended up on the powdery street, sending puffs of dust fogging over their disheveled clothes.

"Jasper, there ain't no corners for you guys to get stuffed into out here, but I am big enough to beat the livin' day lights out of you if you don't act decent!" Shelby's face had become crimson red when he delivered threats to his brothers. "I didn't want you stinkweeds to tag along no how. Pa's inside that place and can't see what's goin' on out here. I'd just as soon give you a licken' as not," he growled! "You sorry sowbellies, Pa won't never know the difference if your nose gets busted from me or from you bustin' each other. I ain't a'skeered to do it neither!" Both boys stopped their flailing fists knowing Shelby's fists would hurt more.

"But, Shelby," John blurted. "That lady must have been some of the family! I seen Pa make a bow to her! She had to be somebody he knowed!" John pleaded his case with conviction.

The boys heard some snickers coming from behind them and turned around to see who it was that thought John's words were so funny.

A grandfatherly voice said, "Hey there, young fellas, what's all the ruckus about?" A gray-headed man with his slightly plump wife attached to his arm spoke to the boys before an all-out war started. Wide-eyed, James let out a sigh of relief to see the gentle pair. John saw his moment for somebody to understand what he was trying to say. His brothers surely didn't take him seriously enough to suit him.

"Pa's a'lookin' for the family 'cause it's time again for Ma, and Pa ain't no good at it," John explained to the strangers.

The gentleman and his wife smiled and looked at each other with a knowing nod. "What's your family's name, young man? Who is your Papa looking for?" the woman asked.

John was stumped. "Well, I don't rightly know, ma'am," he stammered. With a perplexed expression on his face, he said, "I don't recollect what the family's name is." John's blank look after the inquiry identified something missing all along, a name. Nobody ever said a name that he could remember.

"What is the name, Shelby?" Shelby ducked his head and made no eye contact while he kicked the dirt and small pebbles with his toe and didn't bother to answer his little brother. The steam he had earlier propelling physical threats over his rivaling siblings had retreated. Shelby was noticeably quiet.

Finally John broke the awkward silence and said to the couple, "Some of the kin come here to start over where the land's cheap and easy gittin'," he said triumphantly, trying to smooth over a disturbing new thought about a missing family name the couple had introduced. Then he added, "My Mama needs them now. You know, it's time again. Ma says she hopes it's a girl this time since there's six of us boys," said the loose tongued, impish little orator.

Canady was not really prepared to see all his sons in an upright position on his return. Upright was so unnatural. When they were left alone, it had usually been his experience to find them somewhere in a dust wallow with fists flying upon his return. Obviously, the reason for this change must be the couple standing next to them. He introduced himself and claimed the four well-behaved boys in an upright position.

"We are the Falkners, Sarah and Virgel Falkner," Mr. Falkner said. "Your sons told us you were looking for some of your family here. What would the name of your kin be, Mr. Holmes?"

"Nice to make your acquaintance, sir," Canady said, shaking Mr. Falkner's hand and nodding to his wife, Sarah.

"Well," Canady scratched his head trying to figure out the best way to tell he was trying to track down Indians on the run. "We'se hopin' to find the wife's grandpappy," he began. "He may not be alive yet," he said, feeling foolish not knowing how to address information about a lost family. Finally he added after a minute of cogitating, "His name is Silas Shoat, but he goes by the name of Chief Whitehorse too." Canady glanced at their faces to read their reaction to this revelation.

"Some of the folks over yonder at that there saloon, Harry's Place, said they heered of him. It's been a spell though since they did. Could be I have a real hunt on my hands. It's nice meetin' up with you folks, but we'se best find us some kin. I need to be a'goin'," he said.

Mr. Falkner quickly interjected, "From what your boys told us, you folks may be needing a doctor for your wife pretty soon, is that right?"

"Well, Mr. Falkner, I ain't rightly sure about needin' a doctor, but the wife will be a'needin' a midwife real soon like. What they told me at Harry's is the doctor is out of town. He ain't here."

Unusually interested, Sarah Falkner joined in the conversation. "Mr. Holmes, just when do you suppose your wife will be needing a midwife? I help Dr. Gore out, I'm his assistant nurse."

Canady was about ready to leave, but thought better of it after Sarah Falkner questioned him.

"I can't rightly say, ma'am. She was feelin' poorly this mornin'. This here's our seventh and she has them perty fast like. I knowed I best not go back without somebody," he said starting to leave again, remembering the intensity of Harriett's predicament, but Mrs. Falkner caught hold of Canady's sleeve.

"Mr. Holmes, do you suppose your wife would mind if I paid her a call? I have helped many a baby come into this world and it sounds to me like she has need of someone soon. You might say I am a mid-wife "stand-in." When the doctor is out of town on a case, he has sent me to help with births many a time," she said.

Canady, desperate by now, digested the possible solution. "I'd be mighty obliged if you would ma'am, if it ain't too much trouble." "I don't rightly know how to barter with you fer it, though."

"I understand you have a houseboat? Is that correct, Mr. Holmes?"

Canady nodded, "Yessum, I do."

Smiling confidently, Mrs. Falkner made her idea known. "Mr. Holmes, you could be of great service to Mr. Falkner and myself. We need to go to Jenny Lind. I would be more than happy to assist your wife to pay for our way to Jenny Lind after she has the baby. Do you suppose you would be interested in something like that?" Mrs. Falkner asked.

"Oh, yessum I would. You have yourself a swap, Missus Falkner," Canady said, shaking her hand and turning immediately toward the riverbank and the houseboat. The Falkners followed Canady and his sons with renewed excitement pulsing through their mischievous little hearts.

Canady saw William peeking out the cabin door when he stepped on the deck. "Go get your Mama, William, and tell her we have company."

William began to stammer and finally got the words out, "I can't Pa. Mama don't feel good. She told me to see if you'se a'comin."

Canady hurried inside the houseboat to find Harriett still in the bed. A relieved look crossed through her eyes when she saw him. He saw she was deeply involved in having a baby when another pain hit.

"It's time, Canady! I'se afeered you weren't a'comin back in time." Another pain came. "You can do it, Canady, I need you to," Harriett pleaded. "I can't do this by myself."

Mrs. Falkner heard the conversation and pushed her way into the cabin.

"Don't fret yourself none, Mrs. Holmes, I am here to help you," she said after introducing herself.

Canady kissed Harriett on the forehead. "She works with the doctor in Shoal Creek, Harriett, and is come to help you out. Now, you know I wouldn't let you down, Harriett. Don't I always take good care of things?" Canady consoled her, feeling great relief himself. His old cocky nature was returning with Sarah Falkner standing beside him.

Sarah reached out her hand to pat Harriett on the shoulder. "Don't you worry now, everything is going to be just fine. I have helped Dr. Gore many a time and know what to do," she assured her. Sarah took a washcloth off the washstand and put several dippers of water into the pan sitting on it. "Your husband has been kind enough to offer us a way to Jenny Lind for my midwife services and you don't need to worry about payment. The trip is already agreed upon," she said wringing out the water and washing perspiration from Harriett's face.

Another pulsating pain got Harriett's mind off any need to pay for anything. Something else was demanding her full attention. Her time was at hand.

"You boys go on outside with your Pa and Mr. Falkner. I will take care of your Mama just fine," Mrs. Falkner ordered the wide-eyed brothers.

Happy to leave, Canady picked up Gus while William tagged along behind his heels toward a cot on their open deck. Canady sat Gus down on the cot and told him, "You stay put, you hear?" then poled out away from the bank. Canady didn't want the whole world to know what was happening inside his cabin. Drawing from past experiences, Canady knew Harriett wouldn't be able to control verbalizing her discomfort much longer. The boat continued to glide through the shallow edge of the Arkansas River until the last rays of sun threatened to drop out of sight. Canady poled toward the bank.

Chapter 12
DISILLUSIONMENT

Shadows of evening converged together as the sun sank out of sight. Observance of this occurrence came more readily for river people. Sunset had come once again, but supper didn't. The boys were getting hungry and more fussy than normal for this time of day. Harriett would have had the meal cooked and the table cleared by this time, but she was in no position to cook. Her moaning throughout the afternoon and evening added to everyone's anxiety. Mr. Falkner tried to divert the children's attention, but they remained on edge waiting for this ordeal to be over. Hunger caused more irritation.

To make matters worse, Canady didn't find the solitude he was looking for when he docked his houseboat. About twenty yards away was another houseboat tied to a tree trunk. Both Canady and their river neighbors had made it to shore just barely before nighttime and found themselves tied closer than any of them would have chosen if there had been more daylight.

A young woman and man sitting outside of their hot cabin sought comfort from some possible cool relief in an August evening. Breezes lazily wafting off the river flowed around the houseboats, fanning ardent competitors serenading in the night. Frogs and cicadas sang their escalating love songs, but were interrupted ever so often by Harriett's contributions.

Obvious commotion coming from the Holmes' houseboat, as well as Gus fussing no matter what Canady tried to do to appease him, invited eavesdropping, intended or not. Agitated, prickly brothers annoyed each other without any good reason. Everyone was cranky. The young man got up and left their deck after his wife whispered something in his ear.

"Look, Pa, that man's a'comin' over here!" Jasper tugged at Canady's sleeve and pointed to the young man from the nearby houseboat making his way through the brushy undergrowth.

"Howdy do, sir, my name is Thomas Grebs" the young man said when he reached the houseboat full of noisy children. "My wife, Julie, sent me over here to see if you would mind havin' a bite to eat with us? She says the children needs feedin' and you folks need to eat a bite yourself, so you'all come on over and have some supper with us. We'se goin' to be havin' us a youngun soon too," he said, trying to convey a message without actually saying he and his wife had heard Harriett in the throes of childbirth. The polite young husband didn't want to embarrass Canady anymore than he knew he already was.

Canady wasn't used to hospitality and if it weren't a pressing necessity to find relief for fussing children, he might have refused the invitation for fear of an imposition he and his family might cause. Tonight was different. Not knowing how to accept gracefully without feeling beholden, he bashfully accepted anyway and kept his mental reservations to himself. With Mr. Falkner's help, he herded the boys to the Grebs' flatbottom.

Julie Grebs introduced herself while taking Gus from Canady's arms and trying to sooth his fussing with a warm biscuit. Gus' little fingers tore the biscuit apart and he stuffed a piece into his mouth, chewing between receding sobs.

"This is right nice of you folks," Canady got out. "It won't be long now, a'fore this is all over with, I reckon," he stammered, not knowing exactly what to say about the commotion going on in their houseboat. "We'se usually et before this time, but Harriett is ah, she's ah, she's a might busy, you might say."

Virgil Falkner introduced himself during the gawky silence after Canady tried to explain away lost control of his domain. With a bit of pride, while still shaking Thomas Greb's hand, he told the young couple his own Sarah was the midwife next door. Virgil further added that his wife assisted Dr. Gore at Shoal Creek, "Delivering babies, that is," he corrected.

"I dare say she is as able as the good doctor himself when it comes to delivering babies," he continued. Virgil was most proud of his Sarah.

Hungry little bellies welcomed the hot biscuits and gravy from this sharing pair. Stuffing their mouths restored evening's respectability and ceased all the eruptions drowning out night sounds. Virgil interrupted the youngsters in the midst of chowing down and told the wide-eyed children to bow their heads. "You don't mind if we say grace do you, Mr. Grebs?" The young man blushed and said, "Oh, of course not," and Virgil bowed his head while the boys looked at him in astonishment.

"Oh, Lord," he said, "Please bless this little family who has provided food out of the goodness of their hearts, and bless their gift to the nourishment of our bodies so we might serve You better. In Jesus' name, I pray. Amen."

William, James, Jasper, and Shelby stopped eating to look at Mr. Falkner. Their stares continued after the "amen" was said, showing bewilderment about the strange words spoken, all but John. John kept chewing and reached for another biscuit before his brothers regained normalcy. Mr. Falkner's strange speech hadn't registered any reason for John to ignore his number one priority to satisfy his empty stomach.

Thomas told his dinner guests they had family living in Shoal Creek. "We ain't got us a place yet, but will by 'n by," he said. It was obvious the young people would be in need of Sarah's or Dr. Gore's services for themselves in the near future.

Hungry little bellies were sated and temperaments grew mellow resulting from the hot biscuits and gravy shared by the young boat people. Because of their unselfishness, this illuminating kindness evoked a disturbing memory Canady had stored away from his past. Thoughts of a young man with his dead wife in his arms begging for anyone to help flashed in Canady's head. His emerging memory suddenly contrasted this benevolence to the withheld hospitality to another couple several years ago. That young family was in need. Canady had been in need too. A noted difference how needs had been met on two separate occasions rang in his ears, recalling the cry, "Mistah, my Sophy just needed some help." It was a disturbing concept—one Canady didn't relish remembering.

Cries from a newborn wailing in the night replaced a mother's moans and interfered with the mating frogs and cicadas. Tired little ears belonging to strangely quiet boys heard it, along with a very pensive father.

"Well, boys, it sounds to me like your Mama done got us another brother. No girl could caterwauler that loud," Canady said. The lusty wail put relief in his voice, with a slight detection of disappointment as well. "Soon as you boys finish up, we best go and check things out."

"Don't know how to thank you folks for the supper. I ain't much hand at cookin'. Probably can make out good 'enuf for myself, but it ain't easy takin' care of the boys. They are pretty used to their Mama doin' this sorta thing. We'se much obliged and will return the favor when Harriett's up and about," Canady said, shuffling his family off the neighbor's houseboat.

Thomas Grebs stuck out his hand and said, "It's nice meetin' you folks and it is a relief, I might say, to meet you too, Mr. Falkner. We'se goin' to be needin' help real soon too, I reckon."

Canady left before Mr. Falkner. Shelby ran ahead and pushed in front of his daddy before Canady got to the cabin. The newest member lay next to his very tired wife. John was close behind his Papa and blurted out, "Whatcha got, Mama? Is it another boy, or girl?"

"Well, you younguns got another brother," she said, motioning her children to come see him. "His name is Haden Leo, boys. You like that name?" This was the name Harriett and Canady had agreed on, but had kept to themselves because they might need a girl's name this time. Haden Leo, it was.

"You fellas take a peek and then it's off to bed with you. Your Mama's done tuckered out and so are you," their tired Papa said. Canady put Gus to bed next to William on their pallet and the rest fended for themselves. The truth of the matter was that after taking care of the boys, he was more than ready to see the bed. "Tomorrow's another day. We'se settin' out for Jenny Lind." He crawled over Harriett after bidding the Falkners goodnight. "We'se leavin' by sun up or a bit after," he had said when they were leaving.

As planned, Canady took the Falkners to the small river port near Jenny Lind, arriving later that day. Sarah had helped on the way in the care of baby Haden, giving Harriett a needed rest after the ordeal the day before. Age and childbirth had eroded her stamina, making recovery time more lengthy. With regret, Harriett had bid Sarah farewell and thanked her for her generous spirit.

Canady too had thanked Mr. Falkner generously as they were leaving. He was grateful to the Falkners for relieving worrisome pressures but, at the same time, Mr. Falkner had given Canady a revelation totally unexpected. He couldn't say it was a learning experience he was comfortable with, however. New thoughts concerning being "beholdin'" to someone for provisions such as food and lodging was a new one indeed. Unaccustomed to "speechifyin' a'fore you et" was a troublesome mystery he later told his wife. Also, the gentle spirit exhibited from both the Falkners and the Grebs was a puzzlement refusing to die. Canady wasn't comfortable with this new information. It was down right troubling.

When Canady came back into the cabin after the Falkners were out of sight, he was quieter than usual. Changes had been talked about briefly, but unspoken concerns were living monuments inside his soul. Farming was going to be the only answer for his family's keep that he knew of. *Where is the startin' spot? Harriett will be poorly for a spell. It's up to me to scout it out, but where? I'se got to get to it as soon as I can leave. Can't rightly do that just now,* he reasoned with himself.

Harriett's a'lookin for a place she can have chickens and a cow. She can plant her a garden if we can get the ground broke. There ain't room for another soul on this houseboat. The baby has no spot, the boys ain't goin' to get no easier in this crowded up place, I'se got to find it soon, wherever it might be. Ain't much time to wait.

The boys were sick of confinement. Harriett heard Shelby say, "When we get off this here houseboat, I ain't never goin' to go near the river again cept to fish off its bank!"

A week after docking near Jenny Lind, Canady told Harriett he was off to find them a place to move to. "I aim to see if I can make a swap of this old houseboat for a pair of mules to work the ground for farming. Maybe we can share crop for our house and you can make your garden. Who knows, Harriett, maybe the barter might get us a few layin' hens?" he said.

Evening came bringing Canady back home with no solution. Days turned into weeks before Canady found that place he could move his family to.

Mr. Floy Wilson and his wife, the former owners of the rundown cabin, had talked with Canady about his grandparents' old place when he ventured to knock on their door for information.

"It's in need of repair a might bit, I'd say, but if you are a mind to, you could make it inhabitable, I reckon," Floy had said. Mr. Wilson had scrutinized Canady with a keen eye. He couldn't help but feel a bit sorry for a man Canady's age making a new start in life with a growing family, the newest member being just a few weeks old.

The old homestead wasn't much to look at, but it did have two rooms and he shared the news with Harriett. Her response was one of joy if for no other reason than those two rooms wouldn't rock and sway like the houseboat did every time there was a strong wind. At least she wouldn't have to worry about any of her youngsters falling into the water and drowning.

Disappointment and resignation displayed across Canady's face when he brought his family to the worn out farm and house. Harriett, with a broom in one hand, put her other arm around his waist and squeezed gently, telling him, "It's a might better to be here than on the water, Canady."

Cracks between the rugged, horizontal timbers let daylight in and no doubt would welcome October's cold to chill the inside as much as the outside when a norther hit.

"We could chink the cracks with somethin'," Harriett said, giving reassurances to her husband when he examined the gaping crevices. *It sure ain't like the house I lived in as a girl but I'm too tuckered out to care. It's somethin' we can work on fixin' up.*

Canady took the four oldest boys back to the houseboat to load up their meager possessions into Floy Wilson's borrowed wagon. Harriett tended to William, Gus and the baby, straightening up and knocking down some cobwebs with her broom. The place had been used to store some old worn out furniture in need of repair that Floy never got around to repairing. While Harriett was examining possibilities for use of the broken furniture, Mrs. Wilson walked up with an armfull of old newspapers she and her husband had saved for kindling to help start her wood stove.

"Mrs. Holmes, hello, Mrs. Holmes," she called out.

When Harriett came to the door, Nelda Floy introduced herself and said, "I figured you folks could use these here papers to help chink up a few of those drafty spots. We figured you have more need of them than we do.

For some reason, Harriett right away noticed Nelda Floy had a similar spirit about her that Sarah Falkner had. It was notable without verbal description, a most unusual phenomenon.

"Well, howdy," Harriett responded. "You bet we could use them there papers. That would be right kindly of you, and appreciated I'm sure. Won't you come in?"

"Maybe for a bit, but I have a number of chores waitin' for me when I get back. If you can use any of that stuff stored in here, feel free to use it," Nelda added, rather embarrassed that people would inhabit something from them in such condition. "You suppose there's anything else I could help you with?" Nelda asked. I have some extra flour I could spare until you can replace it," she said, feeling terrible about leaving such poor people in such destitute conditions.

Harriett had dark circles under her tired eyes that expressed sincere gratitude for any benevolence. "I s'pose I could rightly use a bit of flour if you have it to spare right now," she said with a lump in her throat. *Yes, indeed, Nelda had a same type spirit as Sarah. They ain't kin, how you s'pose this could be?*

Nelda left and returned with a ten pound sack of flour, keeping her stay shorter on this second visit.

Before Canady and the boys came back with their personal belongings from the houseboat, Harriett had chinked some of the crevices and pasted newspaper over the chinked places with paste made from some of the flour, after drawing water from the old well. Instead of rope holding the long dipper, a chain held it. Harriett had let the dipper down, pulled it back up, then released the rusty spring on the bottom. Water flowed out into a dented wash pan she found stuck in one of the corners of the two-room house. She could tell an improvement already from the pasted barrier blocking wind blowing through the cracks forcing dust to change positions.

Surprising enough to Harriett, when Canady came home she saw two mules and a young heifer tied to the back of the borrowed wagon. The boys were excited to show off their new mules and had to be warned about getting behind them when they went to untie the heifer. Canady had traded for two sacks of flour, along with several sacks of corn, to tide the mules over while pasturing them on cured growth until the guinea grass came up in the spring.

"How'd you talk them owners out of tack, Canady?" Harriett asked in amazement. Sandwiched in between a miniature pie safe, scarred table, chairs, straw mattress, bedstead, worn out baby cradle, and the old washstand, was some tack for the mules. *My trappin' dandy still has it in 'em, he's a talker when it suits him!* Canady also had enough pelts left to swap for a turning plow now tied to the side of the wagon. Harriett saw her husband's trampled ego resurrected by making headway in providing for his family, even if it wasn't the magic revelation he had been seeking all their married life.

"You get that wash pan off the wagon, James," Shelby ordered. "Here, Jasper, help me with this here table. You take one of them chairs, William. You kids watch it! Don't go near them mules, ya hear?" Shelby's brotherly authority directing chore assignments for younger brothers was a new assertion.

Canady untied the mules and led them to the broken down corral where they would remain tethered all night until he repaired it. Thirsty mules drank water dumped in a trough from the long well bucket Harriett had discovered earlier in the day. He moved the mules into the stalls of a lean-to, putting corn in a dilapidated square trough.

After much hard work, the solution Canady thought he had found for his family needs proved to be more complex than he anticipated. The ground would require a lot of grubbing to remove all the embedded rocks. He couldn't plow ground when he had to search for dirt to plow. The boys helped him remove enough stones for a spring garden. When Harriett finished tending to the baby and he'd dropped off to sleep in his cradle, she joined the effort. Planting feed for the mules and heifer would have to wait until next year. Canady's back would only take so many hours of grubbing stones. At times, even after several years fussing about confinement in their houseboat, Canady heard comments from one of the boys about going back to the river where life was easier. There was no going back. It was too late for that.

Breaking ground for a garden and plugging drafty holes in the log house were first on the list of things to do. A broken old woodstove the owners had left stored had to be repaired because when Canady sold the houseboat, the buyer insisted the boat's stove remain in it. A square-head nail worked fine for the broken hinge. Harriett enjoyed the bigger surface to cook on. It put out a lot more heat, too, but they also had a bigger space to warm.

A gift of four laying hens and a rooster required a chicken house. Using the backside of the lean-to for one wall, Canady made a coop secure enough to keep varmints from making off with the hens during the night. The old ramshackle place was coming together. Next, Canady cut enough post oak to build a better lean-to and repair the corral. The formerly deserted homestead was becoming more and more hospitable as the months passed. Months grew into a year. That year grew into two years since the Holmes family called the river home.

Cold water from a nearby stream furnished water for the livestock, as well as a new cold box built in the stream closest to the house to store butter and milk. The latest addition, a half grown hog, was an exchange for chopping wood for an elderly neighbor.

"There's a mighty big difference a'livin on this farm where the boys can run energy off. I don't have to worry none about Haden a'goin' and drowning hisself on this farm like I did all the other younguns when we'se on that boat. Even sayin' this, I know I never worked so hard in my life since we'se been here, Canady. Are you sorry we come to this?"

"I reckon I don't rightly know, Harriett. I do know I miss movin' about. I knowed it's best for the younguns I s'pose, and it sure is a lot easier in some ways, but it is not to my likin' in others," he said pensively, after two years in back breaking effort to grow enough food to keep them going.

"Seems there's always somethin' needin' tendin' to around here—milkin', gatherin' eggs, pickin' poke and berries when we can and, of course, always there's work a'gittin' the ground ready for plantin' again. Ain't no end to it, Harriett, just ain't no end to it," he said wistfully.

"Canady, I am beginnin' to think the same thing. Ain't no end to it for me neither. We'se goin' to have us another youngun."

Mary Elizabeth Holmes

Chapter 13

LOST

The piney woods of Arkansas made it easy for the former boat people to forget a world that would inflict pain or judge them. Little associations outside the family availed themselves because of their self-imposed isolation. Hired scholarly tutors, as was the custom for early schooling, was out of the question and churches dotted throughout the mountains were gathering places shunned by the clannish people. Mr. Falkner's speech before supper reflected their only understanding of this matter and since speechifying wasn't a part of the clan's ability, church was unnecessary.

Most of the time, neighbors didn't have opportunity to mingle with the peculiar new people and so their isolation grew.

Interaction with the Floys was the closest association outside the family, and they were only friendly due to need. Harriett had need of help when she gave birth to her last baby, their first daughter, whom they named Mary Elizabeth, a good wholesome name. Just such a name should break the cycle forever from the stink that history had placed on them. It wasn't an Indian name. It was an accepted name.

Nearly thirteen years of memories made on rivers was something the family wanted to shut out of their present life. That past life emphasized a shame and disgrace of circumstance, giving them a background no one was willing to admit.

Lasting impressions made from floating bodies near Paducah, Kentucky, placed distrust in every witness. Because the boat people had no perceivable social redeeming attributes, according to the populace, their denial to step foot on land even to bury the dead at Paducah was a history no one wanted to carry into future generations. A standard of silence guarded these former boat people.

"Best not to mention this to nary a soul," was always the warning. It was ingrained into the boys. Without understanding the origin of their parents' warnings, the youngest sons accepted the coat of shame by their parents' voice inflections alone, which was further validated by the oldest siblings, who had experienced the story.

Canady was restless hoeing a garden and mending on things. He felt confined by stagnant scenery only changing when he hunted, but boomeranged to the familiar when the outing was finished. Trapping offered far more satisfaction than digging in dirt and chopping wood, since the older boys could do that, and listening to chatter from all the children. Fishing and trapping were far more appealing because he was a struggling soul seeking relief in any hidden outlet that could be out there somewhere. Closed off due to not finding kin, closed off because it was purposefully done, and closed off to other human communication, left Canady empty and crowded in by the piney mountains.

Quite by accident, an amusement did catch Canady's attention. When he discovered his mules could outpull any team in the logging camps, he quickly became addicted to a growing reputation and a little coin from betting. It had become a logging activity to break the monotony of land living. Those mules gave him a notoriety he never enjoyed before and he gravitated to the fame. Throughout the hidden populace in this forested area, Canady had garnered a reputation to be reckoned with when it came to his mules. His participation in the pulls first came about during times when trapping was weak, but then escalated on his priority list. Canady was hooked.

Wagers seemed an easy and a natural inclination at first, but mule pulls grew into newly established meets where competition was the soul purpose. They developed on a monthly basis making a draw throughout the mountains of Arkansas. Many wanted to see the reformed river man's team after hearing stories while others bet the farm their team could best the boatman's mules. Canady found something he had been missing all his life, some peer respect, and he would rather compete than trap. Even his moonshine sales excelled during times of competition and this peculiar boatman enjoyed a position of some notoriety. Being a topic of conversation for those placing bets and competitors alike lured him into new feelings of self-importance. As a young man he had experienced feelings of importance with women, but many bends in the rivers had come and gone since he had enjoyed his virile youth.

Canady's mules got more attention than Harriett, the kids, chores on the farm, or responsibilities of any kind. The mules became his lifeline from sinking and drowning. Temporary importance soothed the disappointment of never finding that special something he would know whenever he should come upon it. The cocky statement made to Harriett's uncle years earlier set a standard Canady never could meet, so riding the coattails of his mules' fame was as good as it was going to get.

Canady and his sons grubbed out stones from a new rocky field to plant more corn crop. His moonshine business was increasing and this gave him impetus to plant extra corn.

Harriett had arisen early to fry slab bacon and make grits for Canady before he left to check traps. She allowed the boys to relish the last few minutes in bed because as soon as their Pa came back such comfort would be something of the past. There was lots of work to do.

When she was in the process of cleaning up after Canady had eaten and gone, Harriett heard a terrible commotion coming from their yard. She ran out the door in time to see Canady kick the corral gate, cursing the irresponsibility of his sons. The gate was open and the mules were gone.

"Them boys is in for a whippin' of their lives!" he yelled. "Ain't I told them to make sure that gate is shut? Who fed them last night? Was it Shelby?" Canady was heading toward the house when Harriett caught his arm.

"Now, look here, Canady, them boys didn't put that tack on them mules and send them on their way! Where is your tack? It ain't here. How could the tack be a'missin' if it was just a corral gate let open?"

The whole household had been awakened from the racket outside and spilled out the door into the yard to see what was happening. They saw their Pa turn white and heard him mumble something about never finding them mules near their place.

"Who done this is goin' to wish they never messed with me," he said and walked past them toward the house.

"Don't talk to your Pa right now, William. He's pretty upset," Harriett said before following Canady into the house. "Somebody made off with his mules. I ain't never seen your Pa this mad before, so you younguns stay outta his way, you hear?"

Then everyone went back into the house in silence, but watching to see what Canady was about to do next. Nobody was thinking about planting a new corn patch any more—such a thought was foreign due to the disaster of the moment. A dire tragedy had overwhelmed Canady Holmes, a life-altering thing for their Pa. The boys quietly went to their pallets and waited to see what they were to do next. Chores, breakfast, the world was out of kilter. No one knew what to expect or what their part was in the doing of it.

"Ain't a galdurned thing I can do but track 'em down," he bellowed. "And, when I catch that son-of-a-bitch he'll wish he's never born! I gotta go whiles the tracks still fresh," he said, stuffing venison jerky and biscuits into his pouch. Canady turned to fetch his coat off a wall peg, added ammunition to his pouch, picked up his rifle, and sprang out the door.

Rage had consumed him so much he never bothered to say a fare-thee-well when he left. No words were spoken and the family watched Canady leave in a fast trot, following tracks made by his prized mule team. Then he disappeared.

Those intruders had left the door open to the corn bin looking for the tack. Canady kept the tack inside the bin hanging on the wall. The cow and pig ended up benefactors to family crises and shuffled around the dried ears of corn on the ground outside the door. Canady's curses had been so loud before he left that the yard had grown quiet, even the chickens. Since he left and took the new type of morning sounds with him, the pig was squealing and the cow's bell clanked as they enjoyed the unexpected bonus spread out on the ground.

Shelby grabbed the pig and pulled him out of the bin, then moved the cow. Jasper picked up the uneaten corn, put it back into the crib, then shut the door to the bin.

It had been a disturbing morning. Harriett did what she could to normalize things—she made the bed, cooked more grits, washed Mary's face, and told the boys they needed to tend to the corn planting. After breakfast she picked Mary Elizabeth up. *You're so tiny, can't fend for yourself none. You'se probly the last 'un, Mary. At least, I'm a'hopin' so. Can't never tell. I can manage chores for a spell without your Papa here, but havin' babies done took it out of me this time, youngun,* she said to herself, rocking Mary to her breast. Tears fell on the top of Mary Elizabeth's baby fine hair. *I'se just got to make the best of it. That's all I can do, make the best of it. Your Papa always said, 'You can do it Harriett, you can do it.' I hope that's so.*

"I'm hopin' your Pa finds them mules and stays out of trouble. I ain't never seen the likes of this before 'cept one time when he saw his aunt bein' drug by some Federals. If'n it weren't for me and you, Shelby, you'se a baby then, he might have let loose then too. I ain't a'goin' to think about it now. Chores has to be did, your Pa here or not," Harriett told her children. "The cow has to be milked, the chickens has to be fed. Somebody has to keep that ornery hog out of the corn crib."

"What are we a'goin' to do about the plowin'?" William asked.

"Don't rightly know what will happen just yet, William. I know we'll manage, you'll see. For right now, you boys grab you a grubbin' hoe and get after it. We can at least get some of that corn in the ground."

A week passed, then two weeks, since Canady left to track down the mule thieves. Those weeks grew into months and still no word came from Canady or anyone knowing his whereabouts.

Concern Harriett had for her husband had not reached the desperation level until she visited their neighbor and learned they hadn't heard anything about Canady either. *This ain't like Canady. He ain't never done such before. I know somethin' terrible has happened to him! Mules or no mules, he'd come home if somethin' hadn't happened to him.* "He must be laid up somewhere or worse," she told Nelda Floy. Nelda's husband was remarkably quiet during their conversation. He enjoyed the mule pulls too.

Seeing their Mama grieve made the children more upset than sorry after the long absence of their Pa. The boys were sympathetic at first and worried too. Some malfeasance happening to their Pa didn't ring true to the older boys. However, it was not like their Pa to not come home eventually. Anger at his disappearance began to replace any grief. If it hadn't been for seeing him making eyes at a pretty woman at one of the mule pulls, they might have been slower to skepticism. Not convinced something was detaining their Pa against his will, the sons thought some other reason instead of lost mules had kept their Pa from finding his way home.

"Yeah, he needed to look for them mules all right, but this here is over doin' it!" Shelby told Jasper, John and James. The workload had fallen on the oldest four and it was hard to work ground without a team to pull a plow. The boys tried to grub and plant with a hoe. They could hardly get the job done and were forced to find something else for income to make up for lost crops. Hiring out to the Wilsons, Partains and Finchers, piney woods neighbors, helped to put some extra food on the table. Several families felt sorry for the deserted clannish family, as rumor had been circulating that Canady had left his family. Several times, benevolent neighbors made the long trip to bring baskets of food and extra hand-me-down clothing to the abandoned woman who had a house full of children.

With each passing day, respect the children once had for the Papa mutated into resentment. Every time a neighbor gave them something, it became an embarrassment. If it weren't for the fact they had dire needs, the hospitality would have been rejected, but they had no choice and thanked the kindly neighbors. Every handout made Canady's memory become etched with no respect from his children.

Often times Harriett recalled the stories she had told her younguns before they ever came to this place, about how things would be when they got their farm in Arkansas, where land was plentiful and easy gittin'. She remembered the time rocking on the river water, how it was to be without a notion how things would actually turn out. *We wasn't rich folk, but we had our pride. We managed right well. We didn't have no neighbors a'livin' right by our side ever day a'feelin' sorry for us like we do here now. I didn't know back yonder how things was a'goin' to turn out.* A memory of river life once lived but hated while living it appeared softer when compared to life in Arkansas without Canady.

"Ma, I'm a'goin' over to the Partains after I milk this evenin'," Shelby said. "Lucinda says it's all right with her Pa for me to pay a visit."

Shelby had earned extra by working for Mr. Partain and an ensuing courtship with Mr. and Mrs. Partain's daughter, Lucinda, had mushroomed.

"I think Lucinda is a right nice girl, Shelby, even if I don't get to see much of you lately," Harriett teased her son. Such interaction was a distraction from her loss of Canady, as she refused to listen to rumors about her husband's disappearance. In her heart he was the trapping dandy of her youth and sweetheart until she died and that was that.

There were other rumors reaching out beyond those of Harriett's lost husband. Talk about war between the north and south back home was reaching tentacles as far west as Arkansas by now.

"Boys, they's trouble a'brewin'. Neighbors are a'takin sides agin one another, I heard from Nelda Floy," Harriett told her family around the supper table. She had paid Mrs. Floy a visit to swap some cornmeal for a couple of new laying hens.

"The family you never knowed back home is in the thick of it now. Most of them has joined up with the south, I 'magin, but I never figured out how some folks felt they had rights to own other people." Harriett remembered seeing the slave mother in a cotton field back in Alabama. *She's worried about her youngun' near the water close to folks like us, boat people. I wonder what she would be a'thinkin' now, knowin' boat people want her to be free?*

"That's what's a'happenin', they's tryin' to keep their slaves," she said. "Nelda figures like I do. I think my way a'thinkin' is what the north side thinks, the Union side from what she is a'tellin' me, ain't that right, Shelby?"

"Yeah, Ma, Mr. Partain is a might worried. Most of the neighbors is a leanin' to the south and trouble is a brewin' all around us here. Ain't all that many folks a'thinkin' like us. They is takin' over the country. Gray Coats is everywhere."

Shelby was fully aware of his world situation, but he was a man in love, living with possibility rather than negativity. Eyes for one person took up his thinking space and he refused to let loose the focus, talk of war or not. Working for Mr. Partain opened up opportunity to court Lucinda Partain. His love for Lucinda gave Shelby a resolve to start a new life, regardless of war threats. It must have been the same for Lucinda because with family present in the Partain's parlor on November 16, 1861, Shelby and Lucinda were married.

The first major vacancy in Harriett's family was Canady's absence but it had been filled somewhat by Shelby taking charge of the chores. Now he was a man in charge of his own life and could no longer fill his Papa's shoes. He was Lucinda's mainstay.

"Jasper, son, you is the manly head of this place now, it seems to me," Harriett told her son after Shelby and Lucinda's marriage. The last wedding Harriett had attended was her own. As her wedding had been performed in a parlor, so was Lucinda and Shelby's wedding ceremony. The Partain's parlor had decorations and more people in attendance then when she and Canady married. She also noted her son's marriage was one of want to, not need to. Nostalgically, she heard Rev. Goins' voice, instead of the preacher from the Methodist church outside Magazine, say the wedding vows for them to repeat. *It was a long time ago, but it was like yesterday too, Canady. You should'a been here 'specially for this 'un.*

"Jasper, you're more reliable than John. Girls is a'turnin' his head too much to depend on him. You stay closer to home then John does, even if twenty is old enough to be a'lookin,' I s'pose. John figures eighteen is right old enough and any need to care for his Ma won't be a'makin' no difference to him now. He's on his own and tends to do like your Pa done oncet." *John looks a lot like his Papa. That flashy smile melts all them young girls hearts. I'm sure he's got his pick, just like his Pa did oncet, but then I come along. There was some changin' done in him then. I reckon it will be the same for John some day.*

Harriett had a lot of things to think about, but it would have to be done during chore time. There was no time to idle away. Chores waited for no one, Shelby's wedding day or not. James and William picked up the slack made by their two older brothers' absences from home. One brother was permanently absent, understandably so, after being married. Their other brother was absent caterwauling.

William bonded closer with James as an apprentice learning how to work, hearing James explain how to do things. Since William had a sensitive spirit, he had an appetite to learn and sponged up new things quicker than the others. His active and imaginative stories told on many evenings were a favorite ritual for little Mary, Gus, and Haden. Being very careful to not appear interested, Jasper and James secretly got caught up in William's long yarns as well.

The country dried up along with Harriett's heart. The Civil War in the south was coming to Arkansas, making the world a place no one recognized any more. Harriett had lost her sure-footedness. The country lost its toehold too, as insanity broke loose in the fighting of kin against kin.

Harriett fussed about her hens starting to molt and the egg supply drying up. She rousted chickens in the wee hours of the morning in hopes that would help egg production, but lack of sleep posed further frustration when the exercise didn't work.

She had steeled herself to accept Canady wasn't coming back anyway soon. Knowing in her heart something had happened, her life lost its edge and she had no passion for it. She had numbed out without acute excitement for much of anything. Everything she did was by rote—chores, mouths to feed, and a growing daughter demanding maternal care, regardless of hardship. Mary gave a glimmer of joy, but was a challenge nevertheless, after rearing boys.

The corn was gone, the last of it used up. There was no more ability to plant, except to grub out a stony spot in unplowed ground and plant each kernel by hand. Gus and Haden pastured the cow on guinea grass. Great care to find pasture was given as they depended on their cow for milk and butter and thievery was a real possibility. It happened before to the mules. Noise from a crude bell and a rope trailing from her neck made her easier to find and catch when the boys fished at the nearby creek. Sometimes at days end, if they were lucky, one would carry a stringer of fish for their Mama to cook for supper, while the other led the cow to her corral. Both boys took turns milking before supper was eaten.

Gus could barely remember river life and his brother's fishing on the deck of their houseboat. His best recollections of life were formed in the piney woods of Arkansas. Haden knew no other kind of life except when his older brothers might mention a few things during the evening after chores. Their earlier life was a mystery to Haden, but the shame coming from it coated him anyway.

Mary Elizabeth passed time with a favorite doll made from gourds. Harriett replicated the doll she used to play with in Kentucky. Her aunt made dolls with gourd heads and bodies from sticks tied together with rags. Don't need that edgin' anyway, Harriett told herself, ripping frayed edging from her petticoat to make Mary's doll a dress. In petticoat finery, little Mary laid her doll in a very used and worn baby cradle. The cradle had begun service when Shelby was a baby, followed by the rest of Mary's brothers, ending cradle duty with Mary. Human duty days apparently over, this used, old wooden relic was the resting place for Mary's gourd doll.

"My cousin never will know how much that cradle was put to use over these years," Harriett told her daughter as she rocked her gourd baby. "Don't reckon there's ever goin' to be a need for that cradle again, 'ceptin' for your gourd baby doll, Mary," Harriett said.

"How could your Papa leave us? It's been so long now, I don't have much hopes of ever seein' my trappin' dandy again. Love is a strange bedfellow, my sweet little Mary. I loved your Papa the first time I come to know him, but I come to love him even more over these many years. Your Papa was a rare man, Mary Elizabeth. He filled my need to be part of a world that didn't want me. We had our own world, Canady and me. With your Papa he gave my life a bit of freedom I ain't never had before. That life stayed at least until all the younguns come along, but with your Pa, I was free no matter how many younguns they is."

"Mary, your great grandpa's compound was the closest place I ever come to feelin' at home, but that place or feelin' didn't last neither, not long if you look back'ards. I was only a girl then, just fifteen. I know there has to be someplace out there that will fit comfortable like his village, my Mama's village. I just have to find it, but how can I do it without your Papa? With all our years of troubles, many hard things to go through, I would give anything to go back just oncet so's I could be with your Papa one more time."

Harriett went to the washstand and pulled the bottom drawer out. She tenderly picked up a blackened silver concho belt and the useless tiara. Gently laying the ornamental finery atop the washstand she retrieved her keepsake wooden box tucked next to them. Tears streamed down Harriett's cheeks while her tiny daughter watched in puzzled silence. With trembling hands and with such care, she lifted the box out of the drawer. The very touch of the keepsake flooded her heart with the represented presence of her Canady. She opened the box and gently caressed pressed and faded blue flowers he had given her many years ago in her old Kentucky holler.

Oh, Canady, you is lost, I is lost, and I don't know what to do. I reckon the only thing I can do is go on. But, go on to what, where? How can I go on when I don't know where to go or how to get there? How can I do that without you, my sweet Canady?

The man without the Spirit does not accept the things that come from the Spirit of God, for they are foolishness to him, and he cannot understand them, because they are spiritually discerned.

1 Corinthians 2:14

Chapter 14
EXPANDED CIRCLE

"Ma, this war situation is a'gettin' real worrisome," Jasper said as soon as he had finished outside. "It 'peers to me, the predicament is more desperate than we first thought. Talk is the whole state is a'leanin' toward the south." Jasper got home before suppertime and had already milked the cow and slopped the hog.

Harriett dipped the last of her fried blackberry pies out of the grease. She had four sons in danger of getting caught up in a war that had no meaning to any of them. *Hadn't we kept to ourselves? Ain't our war.*

"It's a bed o'coals it is, it's, a real hot one! It ain't safe north of here. I come by the Floys on my way home from chorin' for Mr. Hammock. Mrs. Floy was sickly and didn't go with her husband to visit their boy this time. While's Mr. Floy was a'visitin', the Confederacy conscripted 'em right into the Confederate Booneville Rifles. She's left at home by herself. He ain't with her. Mrs. Floy is pretty upset, I'd say. The way things look, they ain't a'comin' back."

"My lands, Jasper, you mean to tell me she's over there without a bit of help? Her husband's older than your Pa. You meanin' to tell me they took him?"

"Yessum, that's it. Looks like it's done settled for Mr. Floy and Fred. We'se got it bad enough feedin' ourselves, but so far, ain't none of us is taken off and put in no army. And, if that ain't a sorry 'nuf state, I hear they lost one of the cows. There's a lot of pilferin' a'goin' on all around here, so we best keep a keen watch out. Mr. Hammock and his family is right nervous since two of their hogs was took. I don't reckon he knows about the Floys yet, but he will soon e'nuf."

"Ma, you watch yourself. It ain't safe no more, no matter how tucked away we is in these piney woods. When you least expect it, they's around. Mrs. Floy didn't know when their cow was took. When she went to milk this mornin' the cow was gone. She said they come in the night."

"I'm a'goin' to get that ham out of the smoke house and bring it inside right now," Harriett told her worried son. "The Floy farm ain't that far and if they's over yonder, they's apt to come here likely as not. I ain't a'goin' to wait 'til mornin'. I might be right sorry if I did."

"I think that is a right smart idee, but I will get if for you."

"Jasper, John keeps a'tellin' me even the rabbits is a'gettin' all hunted out. Do you reckon that's so? Them Confederates is scourin' the countryside for just about anything to eat, I s'pose. Tomorrow I'm a'goin' to have Gus and Haden stake the cow out away from the house. They can hobble her down by the canebrakes, near the creek, and keep a watch from there.

"Well, Ma, I hate to tell you this 'un, but it ain't just the Gray Coats a'takin things. I hear the Federals finally made it here and they's helpin' themselves to livestock too. If'n I had to choose sides I'se a'goin' to fight on, it'd be with the Union I reckon, but they ain't no need of it," he said, tearing one of the hot fried pies apart and shoving a wad into his mouth on his way out the door to the smoke house. Mary, Haden, Gus, and William passed him while they were coming in to supper in time to see Jasper sample the pie.

"You youngun's wash up now, so's you can eat your supper." William already had two dippers of water poured into the wash pan and was reaching for the lye soap when the other three did a u-turn toward the washstand. After Gus and Haden finished, William picked Mary up and held her over the wash pan for her turn. She splashed more than scrubbed. William wiped the wet grime off her hands with a towel, now dingy after the boys' use.

Arkansas was in the throes of war. Conscriptions by the Confederacy were pulling in Union sympathizers out of desperation to form a stronger militia to invade the occupying Union army at Fort Smith. Both Union and Confederate foraged from local farms to feed the moving men and depleted the people's food supply. Other factions of lawlessness prevailed, evil thugs called bushwhackers. Allegiance to anything mattered not a whit outside their maverick group. Nothing was sacred, no holds were barred from the Bushwhackers, be it thievery of livestock, chickens, hogs, or even rape and murder if they had a mind to.

More and more effort was required to save poultry and livestock in order to keep their families fed. Many hid out in the hills and made new secret cellars to store smoked ham, limed potatoes, and turnips. Small dirt hills with upside down cabbages inside protected and preserved one form of vegetable.

Harriett gave her two youngest sons, Gus and Haden, the responsibility to tend to the cow during the day. Instead of removing the cow's bell, the boys tightly packed leaves around the clapper when they thought they heard someone in the bush. Their bovine was saved, but a number of the chickens outside the dirt yard didn't fare as well. Once the hens were taken, the passing marauders never came back.

In time the family began to relax their guard somewhat, but, always, the possibility of losing their cow resonated a real concern. Innocent scenery of lacy pine boughs and curing grasses surrounding a secluded house in the quiet woods had a tendency to erode apprehension and make the family forget unless gunfire was heard echoing through the gaps.

Forever foraging for root foods, wild berries, and nuts had become an issue for every hiding family member. Harriett picked threads from worn cloths so she could mend lesser-worn apparel. All her sewing supplies were about gone. The needles were treasured for many reasons. Sanitized by fire, they were used to pick splinters and sew up bad cuts, as well as mend clothes with reused threads.

Harriett didn't like to take charge of family issues, to make the decisions. That was Canady's job. *But he ain't here. My spirit inside me is wore out. I can't quit now. I need to be a'makin' plans if we'se found out.*

But ain't nothin' a'comin' to me yet. I have to protect my younguns. Mary is so little, Haden ain't much bigger. Gus and William are a'carrin' more weight around here then younguns their age should. Can't be helped.

I hope John brings a rabbit home when he comes.

"Ma, what you want me to do with this here ham?" Jasper asked his mother.

"Sit it on the pie safe, Jasper. I'll take care of it later. James is bound to be in after a bit. You go ahead and eat. He can eat when he gets home, if you boys remember he hasn't et, Gus," she warned all of them, but looked directly to her bottomless pit.

"William, you is doin' a right nice job fillin' in for James on that wood pile. It will make your arms be like a man, won't it, son?" she teased.

William grinned, but didn't answer his mother. He had shot up in height and, at fifteen, was taller than James had been when he was that age. Lean and lanky, William secretly wished to have a filled-out manly body like his older brothers. He had hopes the woodpile could offer more than sore muscles, so he hadn't complained about his newly acquired position.

"How's things a'goin' over at the Hammock place, Jasper? Seems to me you always get home before John. What kinds of chores is he a'doin' that makes him so late comin' home?"

"Well, you might say it is a bit of my own doin' that he's always late. Old Mr. Hammock has a daughter that pesters the life out of me. Sis Hammock is all right, I reckon, but she's more to John's likin then to me, Ma. Leastwise, maybe I could get more food on our table if she would catch John's fancy, stead a'chasin' me. I reckon that is just what's happened," he said, shoving in a mouthful of fried potatoes. Jasper set a glass of clabber milk on the table after washing down potatoes, then wiped his face with his sleeve. "John's glad to catch any gal's fancy, but I want to do the pickin myself. She's been the one a'chasin me," he fussed.

As soon as Jasper gave reason for John always being tardy, the door flew open with an enthusiastic bang and startled everyone sitting around the table. John swaggered through the door with James following close behind.

"I nary saw a rabbit! I swear, Ma, they's just about hunted out," John said, sitting down to the table without stopping by the washstand. Jasper looked up knowingly. John continued to talk about the scarcity of game, but he couldn't fool anyone after what Jasper had shared.

"Oh, there's a scarcity indeed, John," James taunted. "How come I notice a'fore you leave each mornin' you take extra pains a'fixin' your hair? You think that's gonna help you catch a rabbit?"

James's chiding of John transported Harriett's thoughts back in time to when she witnessed Canady take extra pains with his hair before leaving their houseboat. *I remember a time you did such a thing, Canady. It weren't all that amusin' at the time neither. This is your son, Canady. This is your son! They's all yours, but this 'un is like an acorn a'fallin from the oak tree.*

Day's end would have been the best time of all if Harriett's tired parts would go to sleep too. Somehow aches and pains from grubbing with the hoe, grinding what few grains of corn were left, drawing water, and cooking and taking care of duties in the house, shouted their reminders during the night. Such time had come once again to replay the day's events. Supper was over, dishes done, and day mellowed with a sinking sunset to await an unknown God in heaven to insert another morning's lamp in a few hours.

"You is up and out first and most the times the last 'un in and you ain't brung home a rabbit in a spell. Why do you reckon that is?" Harriett asked John at the breakfast table the next morning. "You got a sparkle a'livin in your eye, John, any particular reason?"

Jasper stifled a laugh and choked on grits. John cut his breakfast short and was more fidgety to get out the door and be on his way after the comment. Before leaving, he tarried to comb some more on hair determined to flee fellowship with the rest of his tresses.

"Corrallin' you boys is more'n a woman need do," Harriett told the rest of the family after John left to wait for the others outside.

Oh, Canady, where in the world are you? Why didn't you come home? The same questions chewed on Harriett constantly because of perplexing responsibilities for growing son's behaviors. John's behavior was a new experience and she didn't know her place in it. *There ain't no comfort left in my bed, only memories of my dandy left in my mind. Maybe you'll show up tomorrow.*

Harriett followed Jasper and James out the door. She told her three sons goodbye when they left to hire out on neighbor's farms. Sun was coming up, no time to waste, she grabbed her hoe on the way to the garden patch to plant some crowder pea seeds she had saved from last year. It was doubtful they would make, but she had to chance it. *We'se a'needin' rain, drought will probably getcha before we do, I'm a'thinkin'.* She whacked the hard ground with her hoe. Spring is right hopeful for some rain. If it's a'gonna rain it'll be in the spring. Harriett dropped a couple of seeds into the hole then covered them up with powdery earth.

So went her day, grubbing out spots for crowder pea seeds, washing on a scrub board and hanging the clothes to dry on sand plum bushes, doctoring Mary's skinned knee with some coal oil compresses, and cooking supper for her family. Unexpectedly, suppertime was when it happened!

"Where's John," Harriett asked. Nobody said a word. Jasper cleared his throat. He looked nervous. Harriett could always depend on Jasper. One of the things he tried to do was shield his Mama from shenanigans John might pull. Jasper was old enough to remember times when his Ma had to swallow her pride along the rivers a few years ago. He understood her need for isolation in the piney woods, but her habit transformed their existence to have no other expectations other than isolation. Jasper wasn't comfortable being around outsiders either. However, she did expect her offspring home by suppertime.

"Do any of you boys know if somethin' has happened to John? You're pert near as quiet as I ever seen."

Jasper sighed and squirmed on his cane bottom chair. Finally he said, "Well, uh,   Ma, I think we ain't a'goin' to be able to count on John for much around here anymore. Leastwise, it 'peers to me that a'way." The normally even-tempered and unflustered son was fidgeting and seeking ways to speak to his mother, but really wanted to dodge the question all together. It wasn't like Jasper at all. He plainly was trying to sidestep an issue. Harriett knew something was up. Jasper carefully avoided eye contact with his Mama.

"Jasper, what in tarnation are you a'talkin' about? Has something" happened to your brother? Are you a'tellin' me he has gone off like his Pa? Has he deserted us too? Well, if this ain't a fine howdy-do!

Before Harriett could ask any more questions, Jasper's conscience got the better of him and he could hold his information back no longer.

"John has gone and got married, Ma!" he blurted out. "He married Sis Hammock today. I am sure he would have told you before they got married but he didn't want you to go a'causin' a fuss and all. He knowed you would try to talk him out of it," Jasper said, trying to smooth over a pretty lumpy situation. Jasper had figured the possible reception of his information right, but fell short of redeeming his brother, John.

Harriett wasn't happy. Stunned, she stared blankly back at Jasper. In barely audible words, she said after a long silence, "Times are different now I reckon, ain't nothin' like it ought to be anymore." Looking at Jasper and not expecting Jasper to have the answer any more than she did, she asked, "What are we a'goin' to live on without ever last one of us doin' our part?" Her words were really unnecessary. All the family knew if they were to survive, it was a joint effort for all of them. Certainly, there was no help outside each family member's contribution.

Hot tears filled Harriett's eyes when she looked at little Mary, Haden, Gus and her tender-hearted William. "You older ones can fend for yourselves. The youngun's still need carin' for. We all depend on you older ones to help out," she resignedly said.

After a few very quiet moments around the supper table Harriett said, "Well, I hope he knows what he's a'doin." Her words came out like a sigh of surrender.

As was the custom for Indians to find a lone, deserted spot to privately wail out their pain to spirits in the hills, Harriett's nature to find such release was denied. Her remaining family had to have someone to give them strength. *You can do it, Harriett, you can do it,* she remembered Canady telling her so many times as a young bride. *Just now, I ain't so sure, I ain't so sure.* Harriett struggled to hold the wail inside.

Stuffing more wood in the stove to break the chill had to suffice for any desolate spot on some hill that her heart craved. Biting her lip, she said, "He won't have to worry about all the mouths to feed by a'goin' off, if that's what he's a'wantin' to do.

Sobs refused to be held any longer and her body was wracked with grief. Everyone was miserable around the supper table. Mary was upset because she hadn't ever seen her Mama cry like this that she could remember.

Harriett left the house to go outside to find the empty solace she needed. It wasn't off in the hills someplace. She walked to the corral where some mules once stayed. The cow lowed when Harriett came near her. Their milk cow wasn't used to sharing her corral anymore since the hog got out and the lonely space belonged solely to her now. She mooed her greetings again as Harriett checked the corral gate by habit.

I have been in hard times before. You can do'er, Harriett, the voice said. Staring at the moon and the stars hanging in the same sky she watched as a girl, it shared an identical message in the heavens for her today as a woman. She needed something that didn't change. *Some things don't change or move,* she reminded herself, looking at the heavens. *But the things 'round me does,* she countered. Harriett wiped her eyes with her apron, blew her nose on a rag in her pocket and searched her soul for the extra strength she needed at this very moment. It was times like these she needed someone else to rely on, but who? *Ain't no family for me to lean on. My younguns need me for a'leanin', but where do I go? Ain't no Canady to handle things neither.*

Blowing her nose again, she turned toward the house after some soul searching. During the weakest times, she remembered Canady's words, but it was after those weak moments when she came to realize she had inherited grit from her grandpa, Chief Whitehorse. With genetic hope pulling her from the sinking waters of despair, she walked toward the house, opened the door and made her way to the supper table.

Gus Holmes was Gene Autry's grandfather.

Chapter 15
A REASON TO FIGHT

J asper and James were more sullen than usual when they left for work the next day before sunup. No one mentioned John but everyone gave the impression he had never been missed as they went about their business for the next two days. Work at home was accomplished in a ritualistic manner. Sunrise began with little enthusiasm. Each day's end reminded everyone that three members of the family no longer sat at the supper table. Casting family necessity aside, John's running off to an unexpected and early marriage subtly displayed on faces. The family, from the youngest to the mother, wore feelings of rejection, some warranted, some not. Changes had come to their security, but their structure had to be accepted anyway. About the time everyone started to get used to the idea that John was gone, John and Sis came home.

Sis stood in the doorway with John standing behind her. She was wearing a new calico dress. Mary had never seen new material before and it had been a long time since Harriett had seen crisp colors. *Her mama must a'stowed it away somewheres,* Harriett thought, eyeing her warily and resentfully before she spoke. Trying to hide feelings of desertion and nervousness she said in as calm a voice as she could muster, "Well, howdy. I'se wonderin' when we'd see the likes of you again, John." Grabbing the handle of the iron skillet with one hand, and a metal spatula to stir frying potatoes with the other, she faced the cook stove. Grounding herself by hanging onto objects kept her hands from trembling. If there were any wish she had at that moment it was to hide any indication her resolve had been affected by his irresponsibility and she was plainly upset with her son. Sis was a stranger and strangers don't get to know what types of feelings live inside the family.

Harriett eyed her new daughter-in-law standing in front of her son. *She's perty 'nuf, I suppose,* she had to admit, but resented Sis for taking her son in a very femininely calculating way. Jasper had already explained Sis's capabilities to the family before, *and I knowed the kind she is. John could have at least told me about her before he run off.*

"I want you to meet my wife, Ma, this is Sis," was all John said before he told Harriett they wanted to come home and live with the family. "You'se a'needin' all the help you can get here, I knowed it," John told his mother almost apologetically. "I ain't desertin' you and the kids but I had some business to take care of," he said smiling at Sis. "We'se needin' us a place and this is the most likely they is," he told his mother.

Harriett's first reaction was to not allow any other woman in her house, most especially Sis. This was her domain, fancy or not, and she was beholden to nobody, not even John! Before she answered her son, a normal, immediate reaction surrendered to their conditions at hand. Wasn't she just asking herself what in the world they were to do after she discovered John left? Desperate situations calls for desperate measures and she surprised even herself after she gave his question a minute to gel.

"Times are different now, ain't they son? *Oh, John, you ain't got any idee how different things is, you crazy youngun!* "I reckon I could use an extra pair of hands, son. I'm sure I can find plenty for Sis to do around here. If this is what you want to do, it'll be all right by me." Harriett reasoned. *With John back home helpin' it won't be no end to us leastways, married up or not.*

After a couple of weeks living with each other, happily, Harriett discovered Sis didn't have a lazy bone in her body. She was a hard worker. Because of these attributes, tension with another woman in her house subsided somewhat and became a tolerable acceptance, as Harriett described things. John, much like Canady, hunted and fished all the time to help out. Gus and Haden continued taking the cow to the canebrakes, and William hoed on the garden some of the time, besides chopping wood and mending broken things using other broken things to patch with. The neighbors didn't consistently hire Jasper and James to chore for them, but when there was a need the boys bartered labor for food supplies, a more valuable commodity than money.

Like John, Shelby was uncomfortable living with in-laws and he too had a desire to come back home to help his mother with the four remaining kids. Shelby had plans for his own future and he and his wife wouldn't be staying long, however. They had plans to build a house. Until it was built Shelby thought it best to come back home and do what he could do for his family.

Lucinda and Sis bonded and worked well together but they had known each other since they were girls. Time spent as kin increased their former friendship. Harriett silently accepted this arrangement but only out of necessity.

Early morning dew settled on the ground with hazy fog meandering throughout the pine trees, the yard, and encasing the lean-to. Tall grasses stood still as if nothing moved or if it did it was in slow motion since yardstick comparisons were shrouded in a milky veil. The four older boys already had arisen and walked through the fuzzy surroundings on their way to work. They had left early to hunt and clear a piece of farmland from heavy undergrowth that Mr. Partain had given Shelby and Lucinda for a wedding present. Their wives, Haden, Gus and Mary were still asleep on pallets, allowing Harriett more time to move at a slower pace before everyone got up.

William had roused before Harriett to gather more firewood, relieving his mother of the chore. This morning she had more time to slip into her dress and pull her worn, holey stockings up over her knees. She twisted the loose tops and tucked the ends under the twisted garter she had formed. This unusual leisure time made her feel a little guilty since William had already begun the day and she was not ready to feed her family yet.

William walked through the foggy yard over to the woodpile, picked up two logs and had reached for another when he heard a dry tree limb snap. He turned in the direction of the sound and visually checked out the corral to see if the pig had come home. William pretty well knew the answer to that before even looking. It would be more than a miracle to see the pig ever again. Next he looked for the cow but saw an open gate instead and a slight movement. Through the milky haze William saw a young Confederate soldier leading their cow away from the corral with a rope around her neck but no cowbell.

The two young men stared at each other. Both sets of eyes strained to see through the haze and connected in disbelief, one for seeing the deed and another for getting caught. The young soldier stood frozen, scared to move. Without thinking, William dropped the logs, grabbed the ax and swung it. End over end it flew through the air in a wide arc but missed the intruder by yards. Disgusted with himself for his clumsiness, desperate and unarmed, he started running toward the soldier. William hurled himself at the soldier, connecting his clenched fist to the side of the Reb's face.

Years of serious scuffling with his brothers, and more recently exercise from chopping wood, prepared William to match strength with anyone his age. But one fifteen year old boy was no match for the four rifles pointing at him from the plum thickets fringing their bare farmyard.

Unable to speak when William first discovered the thievery, he finally found his voice. "You ain't a'goin' make off with our cow without a fight first, you sorry son-of-a-bitch! Ma, get the rifle!" he yelled as loud as he could.

Harriett heard William holler and looked out the window. He was in trouble, that was plain for her to see, fog or not. Of course, William knew there wasn't any rifle in the house. "He wouldn't be a yellin' for me to get the gun if there wasn't a need to bluff," she said out loud.

"Get under the bed," Harriett called out to her sleeping children. Lucinda and Sis bolted upright and ran to the window. The kids scrambled from their pallets to squeeze under the bed frame while their mother ran out the door of the house. She grabbed the grubbing hoe hung just outside the door on her way out, taking long strides toward William.

William's bluff made no difference to the other Gray Coats controlling the business end of their rifles. Crack! Crack,crack! Sounds of rifles pierced the air. Before Harriett could see where the shots were coming from, she saw William go limp and sink to the ground. Taking advantage of the moment, the young Confederate soldier finished up what he came to do. He gave the cow a whack on her rump and she bolted toward the rest of the hidden Rebs deeper into the surrounding thicket.

"Hang on there, William! Oh, please don't die on me, son! William! William, don't you go and die on me son!" she screamed. "Oh, Canady, were are you?"

Blood was turning William's shirt red by the time Sis and Lucinda opened the door. Cradling her son's lifeless body, Harriett heard screams as she rocked him back and forth but wasn't aware she was the one making the sounds. Reeling with grief, she continued in shock to rock her son as William's life oozed crimson through her fingers. She called for help to get William inside the house as if that could make a difference and Lucinda and Sis helped her carry his dead weight to the bed.

Petrified with fear, Gus left the other two from under the bed to lock the door behind the women.

William's once expressive eyes no longer sparkled, but stared blankly into space reflecting a permanent vacancy. Harriett closed his eyelids and wiped her tears off his face with her apron while whispering his name repeatedly. "William, my son, oh, William." Nothing she did made any difference. He remained the same. Harriett's unbelief began to roost the reality. Her son was dead! The worst of all things that could happen, just did.

She laid his head on a pillow and bent down to straighten his legs as if the act would make her dead son more comfortable. Harriett untied her apron, folded it and placed it under his head to keep his blood from staining the bed covers. Mary and Haden crawled out from under the bed their dead brother lay on.

Both stared in tearful shock. Seeing William's shirt turning red told them he was dead without having to ask. Mary's outburst broke Haden's resolve to not cry. Brother and sister clung to one another unashamedly sobbing.

Gus forced himself to come away from the door to William's bedside with his eyes welling up too. There had always been a rivalry between the boys but death was so very final! So final it caused emotions he least expected to feel.

A built in competitiveness always picked at Gus to outdo his brother who had two years on him. Their fusses made up a great part of their relationship but that type of shared camaraderie certainly had no redeeming solace for Gus this morning. William's misfortune escalated far too far for such a notion. This morning Gus was vacuously empty and lost to his own inner feelings as he looked at William's blood soaked body.

Harriett motioned for Gus to get his sheet from his pallet. He welcomed the excuse to turn away without losing face or composure. Gus didn't want his mother to see him cry.

Sis had already left to go fetch the boys at the building site. The beautiful remote area had never been cleared before and was the very spot where she and John had camped out after they married. Shelby's cabin was growing out of the ground in the very place they had spent the night.

Nearly out of breath when she reached the cabin site, she tried to explain to Shelby and Jasper through gasps what had happened to William. After hearing enough of her story, enough to know something terrible happened, they left immediately before completely hearing her out.

The morning hunt for John and James had been uneventful. Bored with it, James decided to go back to the site to help his brothers instead of hunting. John's custom to hunt in this heavily wooded area where the new cabin was being erected would be changing with people inhabiting it and he was going to hunt it before it did change. James had arrived at the building site just as the others were leaving.

On John's return trip to help his brothers he sensed something wasn't right. He knew James had left earlier for the site but no one was at the cabin. Somethin' ain't right here, he thought, wondering where everyone was. John immediately left for home and arrived not long after the others.

Mary was by the corral crying uncontrollably when her brothers came home. With jerky sobs, she blurted out the awful tale but no one could make sense of her story. Jasper rushed past Mary to go into the house with Shelby close behind. William's body was the first thing they saw when they came to the door. Their dead brother was lying on the bed with an ashen face contrasted to a rivulet of blood staining the corner of his mouth. His once white shirt was mostly red and turning dark brown in places.

Each of the boys started asking questions all at once. Sis couldn't give them details, only that William had been shot and that they had carried him to the bed inside the house.

Harriett heard all the questions. She couldn't muster enough to answer just yet, but stared past every one of them.

Both wives tried to piece the puzzle together for their husbands between sobs. Sis was still out of breath from running to get them. She slid down on the floor in exhaustion and grief. John sank to his knees to hold her and tried to console her as best he could while choking back tears of his own.

All of the men looked at Harriett for information and instruction. She was incapable of making any sense as her life had gone blank. Questions kept pouring out of the young men, but all the questions in the world *won't make a whit of difference. Ain't it plain to see, William is dead?*

"Pa ain't here to make no decisions. I reckon it's up to us," Shelby told John, Jasper and James. Shelby knew his little brother would have to be buried and he didn't want the job all by himself so he motioned to them to go outside with him. When they got out of their mother's view, all four boys began crying and screaming their grief. They didn't need a private hill to hide in because their grief wouldn't wait.

Harriett's memory made from the hills of a Kentucky holler decades ago resonated with familiarity when she heard her son's gut-wrenching wails outside the house. She had heard plaintive cries like theirs before. *What in the world have we done to our younguns a'bringin' 'em here, Canady?*

"We have to do somethin' and I know you all know what it is we have to do," Shelby stammered after a while. " We can use some of the wood already cut for the cabin to make it if we plane it a bit. Each brother looked for assurances from the other, meeting gaze with gaze. They knew what they must do and each began gathering rough planks crudely cut by a cross cut for Shelby and Lucinda's new beginning.

Lucinda looked out the window to see the brothers carrying material to make a casket with. She went outside to the pile of wood, picked up a hammer and saw and handed them to Shelby.

Sounds of carpentry, sawing and hammering reached Harriett's ears while she bathed her brave young son's face and bloody arms. She unbuttoned his crimson shirt and saw the wound in his chest. *It is such a small hole to have took you from me, William.* When she turned William over to continue bathing his body she saw a gaping hole in his back. Harriett's moan could have been heard in the valley below and brought more sounds of grief to the casket builders outside. Wiping their eyes, they didn't interrupt their work except to pause for a moment to clear their own vision.

Haden and Mary wanted to find something useful they could participate in to honor their brother. Everyone was busy but them. They had to be busy too. Life demanded this pattern.

"Let's pick some flowers for William's grave," Haden told his little sister. Mary didn't know what that word, *grave*, meant, but if it was for William that would be a good thing to do. Running in the pasture in their search for wild flowers gave a four and six year old some release of anxiety.

Haden picked some fern and yellow daisies, making sure there were long stems, but broke the necks of several buds in the process. Mary found some fuzzy dried thistles, which left some of the stickers in her fingers. She fell down several times not watching where she was running before she made it back to the house. Her tear stained face was caked with dirt sticking to wet cheeks. The importance of doing something for William was worth stickers and a dirty face. She brushed her face with an arm, making the dirt smudge even more.

Gus' reaction to grief came in a different way. He looked for bigger and manlier tasks an almost eight year old could do rather than to forage for wild flowers for his brother's grave. He began to gather stones to be used as a marker.

Harriett's day had begun with an easy feeling, unrushed and aided by an early morning haze diluting any sharpness of nature when she looked outside her window. It had gone from the serene to the unimaginable. Now, a crude casket made out of rough- hewn boards originally intended for Shelby and Lucinda's new house was built instead. Time had come to lay her precious William in it.

Fighting waves of nausea and emotional exhaustion brought about by thoughts of putting her son in a cold hard ground instead of his bed was tormenting her to the breaking point. She heard a familiar voice inside, *'He's gone but you can do'er Harriett.'*

"No," she rebelled out loud, "I can't do it!"

Jasper and James moved their mother from William's side and gently picked up his body. They placed it atop corn shucks covered with a torn sheet. William had helped hew out some of the planks used to make the wooden box he now rested in.

Images of early morning when William faced the Rebs all by himself raced through the brothers' minds. Shelby walked over and peered down at his little brother's body, touching his cold face. He began to cry softly, unashamedly, in front of his other brothers and little sister. Probably, because he was the oldest of the brothers in his family, he was used to blazing trails for the rest to follow.

"Death belongs to the old, not the young. Fifteen years should be the beginnin' not the end," Shelby said through sobs.

"Do you reckon they is such a place called Heaven?" Shelby finally asked. "How'd a body ever know if they's dead and a body can't tell it? I wish William could say, if he knows anything," Shelby whispered out loud.

The night was quiet with only episodes of grief breaking the stillness. They sat for hours saying their goodbyes. Gus, Haden, and Mary had fallen asleep on the floor. Lucinda, who was seven and a half months pregnant, wearily leaned back against her grieving husband. Time, meaningless now, dictated no commitments to anyone. This void in all of them demanded no immediate chores, no cooking, no milking, and no feeding. Dread about moving the casket from inside the house climaxed when rising rays turned the morning sky pink announcing a new day.

"We better get this over with," John said. The sleeping three awakened hearing final farewells. Mary leaned next to Harriett and put her thistles near William's hands and next to Haden's wilted fern and crumpled yellow daisies. Haden reached into his pocket and pulled out a marble then placed it in his older brother's cold palm. Gus was fighting denied emotion. Gritting his teeth and flexing his jaw, he put a pocketknife next to Haden's marble. That pocketknife had been a source of many fusses and Gus had only borrowed it from William the night before the invasion of those Rebs.

Down deep, Gus was struggling with the question about taking that knife. Would it have made the difference if William had it to use against the soldier? Remorse and guilt surrounded the object secretly returned to the underside of the cold palm of his dead brother.

The first shovel of dirt hit the pine box with a thud. The four oldest boys took turns filling in the hole dug earlier in the south pasture. By sun up, William had been given to the earth.

Lucinda tried to console Mary and Haden as best she could because Harriett had become lost to priorities. Lucinda had heard her mother-in-law mention something about William not being at the breakfast table anymore or anywhere for the rest of their lives.

"I remember when William was born. It ain't been that long ago. He had a different spirit about 'em right after he went to that brush arbor meetin' along the river after we'se stopped permanent like," Harriett rambled on. Fred Floy just hired on at one of them loggers and he took to William even if William was a tad younger than Fred. We met up with Fred's Ma and Pa on account of William, I reckon. That's how we got us this place." Harriett continued to share with both young women who were tending to Haden and Mary.

"I find myself a'learnin' when I don't want to learn about things. I reckon death has lessons too but I ain't learned about that before. When such happens you learn more afterwards, I reckon. Only trouble is, it's too late. We live only one minute at a time. That's what my William did. Now, he ain't got no more time belongin' to him."

Everyone was attentive and listened to Harriett express herself in words, rather than just tears.

"I should have hugged 'em more, should have paid more 'tention to his a'wantin' to learn to read and all. He's right smart, he was. William kept a'sayin' if he could read, he could learn more things from books. Somehow, he hoped to get some of them books someday. I always thought there's more important things to do with a body's time. Lucinda, death makes you think about the important things," she told her when she and Sis nodded their agreement. "Maybe we ought to listen more with the minutes we have," Harriett added.

Shelby learned when he went to the Partain's farm to tell them about William's death and give a report on Lucinda, that there were several regiments of rebel troops running through the country conscripting people into the Confederacy. The same thing happened several months ago up north to Mr. Floy and his son Fred.

"I wouldn't be surprised if it wasn't the same bunch that come to our place," Shelby told his father-in-law. "Our new place is hid good 'nuf, I reckon, but Ma's house ain't. They know where's it is and will be back, that I'll guaruntee you!"

Two weeks later, Lucinda's father was caught in the field while plowing potatoes, Mrs. Partain reported to Shelby after he stopped by again to check on things once more. The same thing Shelby had reported earlier to Mr. Partain about Mr. Floy and his son, Fred, happened to him. He was taken right from the field by gunpoint.

"Ma, we boys is a'finishin up on our place, good 'nuf for you to go to it anyways. It ain't safe here now," he informed Harriett after a decision to leave had been made. "The boys and I are headin' for Fort Smith as soon as we get you moved in. None of us want to do no fightin' but they done brung it to us. They started it, we'se goin' to finish it," Shelby said defiantly. "We got to get shut of this situation once and for all! Ain't nobody goin' to have peace around here 'til we do."

Haden Holmes on a mule.

Chapter 16
CONSEQUENCES OF WAR

Harriett's esteem for Shelby's manhood was taking on new significance. She knew her son was an emancipated man with an heir on the way, but separating the man from the firstborn child in her heart had not always been so easy. He had taken the place of his Pa for the rest of the family. Maybe not so much for her as for the other children, but she relied on him far more now. Even after John married Sis and declared his own freedom from family attachment, he too heeded the pecking order and respected the counsel given by Shelby.

"We all decided we best move you to our new house, Ma. Lucinda and I feel this is the right thing because it ain't safe here now. We'se already found out what they can do and when the Rebs get through ransackin' this place, there won't nary be a thing left of it," he said. "You best not be here when they come back and they'se a'comin, you can count on it!"

"I need to ask, if you would take care of my Lucinda for me while I'm gone? I know I need to go to war, but I ain't contented to leave Lucinda 'til I know she'll be cared for when her time comes. Mrs. Partain is right poorly and ain't up to it since Mr. Partain was took."

"You knowed it son, without even askin' it," Harriett told him.

"Same goes for me too, Ma," John said. "We ain't havin' us a youngun but Sis would be a lot better off here than headin' back north where all them Rebs is at. That's where most of her kin is, north of us. I reckon the likelihood is great I might meet some of 'em at the other end of a gun," John ruefully said.

The place the family was to move to had been settled, but leaving the familiar things surrounding them were not. Trip after weary trip, their meager belongings were carried in the old mule cart to Shelby's cabin. Three boys pulled and two pushed the cart to move remnants of furniture that had seen years of river life. By the time the family had their cabin in order, more than half of September had come and gone.

It had been a cool September morning in 1863. That date would live forever in Harriett's memory, but her mind had reached an overload. Her four oldest sons were gone, with two of them leaving wives to carry on as best they could. Harriett's mind allowed this memory to exist but she tried to shut out the recent past. Time lived as a girl was easier to think about, but that had nightmares attached to it too.

Spiked emotional currents kept family members moving the morning the four had to say goodbye. Still numb from the loss of William, Harriett stayed outside after her sons left for Fort Smith. She kept looking at the pine trees they had disappeared through as if she'd lived this same scene at another place and at another time. The vista reminded her of Kentucky when she watched her grandpa leave. It was such a final goodbye.

This foreboding left questions about the importance of things happening in life—about the real meaning of life, if there was any, what she had come to, and what she and Canady had brought their children into. There were no answers.

But, it's the same everwheres, I reckon. I never worried about nobody a'shootin' me when I was a'growin' but my littlest youngun's hardly remembers nothin' else. My oldest 'uns knows about the river life, the shame and all we brought on 'em. None of 'em seen a four-poster bed before or any fineries. They sure don't know what a feather mattress is all about, just pallets. It ain't like it use to be.

It's durin' times like these when I know there's a hole inside me a'missin somethin'. It never gets filled in, it seems like. I felt it as a girl and I am still a'searchin', more than ever since William is gone. First it was Canady, next it's William, and if that ain't empty e'nuf, four more younguns is gone today.

Actively searching to feel rooted again somehow, Harriett experienced deja vu about her mother. Mental pictures she had formulated over the years in her fantasy world concerning her mother flashed before her. It was her history, but a starting point to think about to stabilize an erratic and crazy world she was now floundering in. Whether the memory was good or bad, it was her beginning and a building block for rejuvenation she desperately needed. Harriett allowed the memory, these thoughts she had concerning her mother, to escape its dark hiding place like experiencing an agony in common. They didn't have the same life story, but both shared a trauma just the same and in some sick way like water seeking its own level, made a connection to each another.

Patterns made by sunlight against fauna wiggled through the trees and rested on her body. Innocence and perceived seclusion engulfed her. White Dove was totally unaware of any observation while taking a morning bath. There were ferocious eyes eavesdropping from a hiding place and she unknowingly teased his appetite. White Dove shivered with water evaporating from her wet body and began to quickly dry off while evil personified watched for the right moment to spring on his prey.

She stepped away from the pool of spring- fed creek water as her singing escalated from a hum to words. Accompanying her song was rushing water over rocks, which camouflaged any noise the predator made when he moved closer. Several months of wilderness, with nothing but the birds and beasts of the forest to keep him company, added to his increased appetite for a woman. A beautiful woman in a private place was his for the taking. It was too opportune to resist. He flexed his muscles and was ready to spring.

A flutter of wings from cheewinks flying from the thicket caught her attention. Feeling a presence, she darted looks toward the very thicket responsible for her privacy to see a shadowy movement. Instantly, White Dove reached for her suede dress and was prepared to run naked to the safety of her compound a distance away. It was too far for anyone to hear her scream. She had to run.

Moving quicker then she, a sandy-haired, unshaven, human animal sprang from the bushes, grabbed her forearms and knocked her to the ground. Intent on pinning her to the bank, the trapper was not prepared for her instinctive recovery. White Dove clawed, bit, and fought with all the might her diminutive body was capable of.

"If'n I can trap me a critter, no little Cherokee mountain lion is a'goin' to get the better of me," he laughed.

Her wet skin worked to her advantage. But no more had she freed one arm before he recaptured it again. Each effort goaded his heated passion for her and it ate at his own determination to either rape or kill. The more she struggled, the more his evil hunger grew.

With defiant intensity, she freed an arm and clawed his face, leaving an erupting crimson streak across his cheek and nose. White Dove not only fought like a mountain lion, but she moved faster than lightning when the trapper yelled and grabbed his wounded face. This distraction was all she needed. Like a rock shot from a sling, she bolted.

A sharp pain from her ankle forced a sudden collision with the ground, knocking the breath from White Dove. She reeled from shock, pain, and the inability to get enough air. The underbrush at the spring that had concealed her bath now witnessed travesty. What once had been a haven containing peaceful scenery, became a vision corrupted by filthy, shed buckskins.

Unable to push the large, pulsating animal off her, she screamed with what little breath was left until he covered her mouth with his grimy hand.

Conquering nothing in his worthless life other than the helpless and never mastering anything of value, the vile forest tramp kept his hand over White Dove's mouth to muffle her cries. Grunting his war cry of completion he repeated the scene again and again. Leaving White Dove limp and bleeding on the ground, the monster picked up his buckskins and left the underbrush, the only witness to Harriett's beginning.

Reliving the horror of her imagined conception formulated from stories told her, Harriett once again was jarred into the present day reality of losses. The four sons leaving this morning then dominoed into the grief of William's loss.

"My William, I ain't never goin' to see you again. You was so full of life. Oh, my son, my son." Harriett grabbed her apron to her face and cried in the secrecy of scrub oaks sheltering her weakness from the knowledge of remaining family. Lost in grief and perceived hidden, she suddenly felt some little arms wrap around her legs.

Mary had heard her mother. Harriett dried her eyes and took Mary by the hand to a rocking chair on a small porch outside the new cabin. She pulled Mary up into her lap without saying anything to her. Mary put her little arms around her Mama's neck, then lay her head against her chest.

This is too hard for this youngun to understand. My mind is facin' confusion. My backbone used to be strong and I'm a'needin' to feel that way again.

"Why don't you come inside, Mary," Lucinda said. "I have made some real good butter bean soup, the kind you like, with a little wild onion in it," she told the little tyke.

The morning continued to slip by in reverie for Harriett, a highly unusual circumstance, which concerned both of her daughters-in-law. Clearly, Harriett hadn't been herself ever since William was shot. The past lured her sick mind backward rather than forward.

Harriett's world escaped to other times. "There he is!" Harriett told Aunt Nancy. Chief Whitehorse's visits were always an exciting time for his granddaughter. Like his name, he owned a white stallion and the chief was said to love the horse about as much as his family. His horse had filled up empty spaces after he lost his wife, Tuma, six years before White Dove died.

"Hello, Grandpa," Harriett called out. He sat ramrod straight atop his horse and, with a raised hand, acknowledged the greeting, but his face wore a stony expression rather than the smile she expected.

"Grandpa, are you all right? Somethin's the matter, I can see it. What's wrong?" There was no reply.

"Yes, something is plainly wrong, I can plainly see that!" Harriett said. The sentence was repeated in earshot of the worried family who knew she wasn't herself.

Mary cried each night when she went to her pallet. Her young years had seen too much already and she needed her mother, who was present but unattentive. Her storytelling brother, the one who showed affection, was buried in the ground with the thistles Mary had picked.

There ain't no cow left. Them Rebs is apt to come back and get my other younguns, but my boys outsmarted them Rebs. We ain't there anymore for 'em to come back to.

Chapter 17
NEW BLOOD

Busy hands, personal dependence, and growing hearts enlarged a common respect among each person living in this cabin secreted away among the pines and underbrush of Arkansas. Caring attention given to the children by the girls eased Harriett's responsibilities and from such compassion and work relief, a healing process began. A wee bit of hope for spiritual renewal in spite of war was evidenced each day.

Sis knew when it came time for Lucinda to have her baby that she needed Harriett. Assisting another woman in having a child was foreign to Sis and she wanted no part of such. Survival dictated the necessity for everyone to help the matriarch of the family recover her mental health. Lovingly, they grounded her wounded spirit by establishing as much normalcy as possible through daily routines. Through structure preset by others, Harriett's mind found succor for her grit to root.

War continued to move closer to their location but the family's hiding place had not been detected. With no other place to go, the family warily went through the motions of living, albeit heavy clouds of apprehension were gathering.

"You can't be sure of much anything or anyone outside family," Harriett warned her daughters-in-law when they were discussing gunfire in the distance. She had mentioned this not because they had much interaction with neighbors, but from the pure frustration of isolation during dangerous times. They understood those nearest neighbors were sympathetic with the north but they had no recent information about any of them. Cannon fire echoing in the valley mixed their booms with rifle cracks. Everyone's nerves were on edge dealing with fears beyond military discovery but, despite the nearing threat, Harriett appeared to be recovering emotionally from all her losses.

Fear of Bushwhackers ransacking farms closer to their vicinity was another evil presence for concern. These evildoers took advantage during times when battles raged the most in one particular location. Their mode of operation during such times was to choose an isolated and defenseless farmhouse to carry out their reign of terror.

Their closest neighbor, Mrs. Floy, had met such a fate. Gus reported he had seen the travesty when he wandered from home a couple of weeks ago looking for pecans. He had witnessed the Bushwhackers taking everything of value after they shot Mrs. Floy and burned the house with her inside before they rode off. Terrified and choking back tears, he was afraid he would be discovered and continued to hide in the tall grass and scrub oak, daring not to move until dark when the wanderlust came running out of the forest into the searching arms of his mother and Sis. He allowed his pent- up emotions to come tumbling out.

"I ain't never goin' to do that again, Ma, I promise. I ain't never goin' to get so far from home again," he sobbed.

Gus' disturbing news about the fate of Mrs. Floy warned the rest of them to take extra precautions concerning noise. No loud play. Mary Elizabeth had to stifle little girl screams. There could be none. This family knew what it was like to have their home invaded when William was killed and they also knew it could very well happen again.

No one in Arkansas wanted to share family members in this war. This former boat woman, who had endured restricted freedoms from those living along the banks in places they had come from, now demanded participation one way or another.

"I know the boys was ready to go," Harriett told the family as they were bedding down for the night. She blew out the lamp and crawled under her bed covers. "Leavin' was as hard on them as it was us, for sure, and it weren't no easy chore for them to get to Fort Smith, I don't reckon," she said in the dark. "But," she continued, "this war has to be stopped. We'se a' livin' right in a mess of Confederate families, and they ain't a soul you can trust. The boys had no choice." With that said, night sounds of winds rustling through the pines replaced echoes of gunfire. She turned over in her bed and went to sleep.

The food at Fort Smith, though simple, was more than enough. When the four brothers went to mess hall for the first time, the ample portions on their plates reminded them of food rationing back home where no one wasted a thing. They gratefully ate in silence. Training had begun the moment they arrived. Each was issued supplies and assigned a bunk, which would be claimed for only a short time. The boys' company was due to leave in the morning to fight their way to the Union camp at Duvall's Bluff.

If one were to judge by the sound of gunfire, Confederate soldiers were bringing the war closer to the family. Cannon fire and rifles once heard from a distance were louder, making confidence in the hidden cabin a thing of the past. Sis hurriedly came in from hanging laundry outside and told the children they better not go out this morning.

"Judging from the sound of things, the Rebs is probably less than a mile from here," Sis warned Harriett.

When Lucinda and Shelby's new cabin was built next to a hill, they took advantage of that hill for storage. A trap door leading down from inside the cabin floor back into a tiny cave on the side of the hill was planned for other purposes. Originally the small cave was built for a root cellar, but could be a possible hideaway, if need be. Potatoes, turnips and a few sacks of dried corn the boys had bartered their labor for, was stored with enough room for the family to squeeze inside. More and more, such necessity wore the cloak of reality.

"Lucinda, you best keep a closer look out this mornin'," Harriett warned Shelby's wife. Lucinda could do little since she was so large with child but this was a job she could accomplish. Harriett's former self, the decision- maker since Canady and the boys were gone, came to the fore.

"I am more feared of them renegades as the Confederate soldiers," she said. "None of this here war makes any sense to me. Neighbor agin neighbor, it ain't right. The best I figure, the Rebs could have a concience about 'em, but you know they will be a'takin' everythin' they can get their hands on when it comes to our food. Ain't much livestock left anywheres, I reckon," she told her family. "Everythin's about scoured clean."

Harriett remembered the lean days on the river where she experienced hatred plied on people who lived in boats. Being a recipient of hostile attitudes wasn't foreign to her but flip-flop alliances were out of character. Once these neighbors shared mule pull contests and fellow-shipped with one another. Now neighbors were ready to kill even those who had once shared the same church pew before the war. Eerily, former friends drew beads on the other. Any dependable foundation people had come to rely on evaporated with war. No one knew who to trust anymore, especially so for former boat people. One such person, a woman who had endured the harshness of river life, led the family in its decisions.

Lucinda knew neighbors living close to her family's farm but familiar relationships dissipated after Lucinda's father had been conscripted. Sis's relatives more than likely helped in the conscription. No world made sense anymore outside their immediate nucleus. Fear of unknowns lurked everywhere.

Mary and Haden rolled up pallets and stacked them in the corner of the cabin. Gus tried to chop wood but it was more than he could accomplish. He gathered dried limbs and sticks instead to use in the wood stove. When the seven year old came into the cabin with branches and kindling stacked nearly above his head, he noticed Lucinda bending over by the washstand and heard her cry out.

"Harriett, somethin' just happened!" Panic was Lucinda's first reaction until Harriett told her, "You sit a spell and save your energy. Don't worry, Lucinda, many a woman has gone through this and you can do it too. You will do just fine." Lucinda's labor came quickly with little warning. She remembered when she arose this morning a bit of dull cramping but put the inconvenience out of her mind. *You would think eight times would give a body enough smarts to help midwife. Now I know how Canady felt, but I ain't a'gonna let on to Lucinda.*

Lucinda could only gasp with her next pain. Little Mary was owl-eyed and puzzled at the circumstances. She came closer to see what was happening with her big brother's wife. Lots of unusual things were going on this morning.

"Can you handle things here, Harriett?" Sis asked her mother-in-law when she recognized the confusion and curiosity of the children.

Besides, she didn't really want to be around for this either. "If you don't need me, I think it would be best if the kids and I went out to get the rest of the turnips in the patch. Now, you holler at me if you have need, all right?" Sis got more flannel shirts to put on the children to ward off the cold.

Gus was disgusted with the fuss Sis made over him when she bundled them up to go out. On the way to the turnip patch, Gus and Haden fetched rough-looking grubbing hoes leaning against the cabin. All the turnip tops had been picked, boiled, and eaten but the turnips were still in the ground.

"See this here little hump and cracked place in the ground?" she asked the half- interested youngsters. Their minds were elsewhere beside turnips.

"You can tell where the turnip is by the bulge in the ground. Here, Mary, I got you a spoon so you can dig some of them too."

Sis made a game of digging turnips, to seek and find. Before long, each was trying to outdo the other seeking the find beneath the ground. Mary had a bit more difficulty than her older brothers by not fully understanding where to look. About the time she decided that a hump had a turnip in it, one of her brothers would edge her out.

"No, no, Gus, mine!" Squeals of frustration spewed from Mary's mouth each time one of her brothers pushed past to dig up her find. Sis tried to keep her shrill little voice down. Between rounding up children, keeping them quietly occupied, and the dreaded activity going on in the cabin, Sis wished she could be with John and forget all these hardships.

She knew the turnip chore diversion could only be counted on to last for a little while before something else would need to be figured out to keep the youngsters occupied. Before she could manufacture another interesting project, Harriett called from the doorway of the cabin.

"You all come on back in here. It's too cold to be out there. Everybody's bound to come down with the pneumonia. Baby coming or not, chores go on just the same. It's time to eat. The youngun's needs to eat," she told her daughter-in-law. Aroma from bowls of hot turnip and corn soup seasoned with a bit of fatback filled the air. The three children were so hungry they failed to notice the sheeting strung up hiding Lucinda's bed at one end of the cabin.

Her pains were coming fast. Sis had a hard time keeping the kids' attention off the commotion coming from behind the sheet and was hoping for each to take a nap. Mary was the only taker and fell asleep as soon as she lay down on her pallet.

Haden did dishes at the washstand but his attention was on Lucinda's complaint and not his job.

"Watch out where you are dripping all that water, Haden," Sis lightly scolded the six yearold. He had managed to slop water on the plank floor, making a puddle mixed with dirt brought in from the turnip patch. The muddy spot he made gave him something else to do when he finished drying the soup bowls.

"Did you hear that, Gus?" he said while on all fours smearing around the mud. Lucinda's groaning had been interrupted by a lusty wail. Then they heard their mother tell Lucinda, "Push again. You are just about through."

I did it many a time but it is still a mystery. Some of life's mystery was done told to my youngun's today, I reckon. They's so much more to learn, but today was a startin' place for 'em, I spect.

Nightfall was a welcome relief for new mother, midwife and spectators. *Arimenta would have been proud of me,* Harriett thought when her head touched the pillow. *This here is our first grandbaby, Canady. I wish you was here to see him.*

Days seemed to be eaten up during the learning process and care given to little Shelby Robert. An awe of the precious new life gave a diversion from the increasing gunfire around them, but made them more protectively aware of the new one's vulnerability.

Shelby Robert's name had already been decided upon before Shelby left for the war. It seemed the right thing to do to name the baby after his Papa, then Lucinda added her own dear father's name to bless the wee one.

Watching Lucinda work with her new baby was a joy for Harriett. The bonding was strong between mother and child.

"Oh, I felt that tug at my innards over each and every one of the younguns," she told Lucinda, "but, the first one is the memory makin' one you don't forget."

Harriett mused in her heart the first birth experience she had, little Shelby Robert's Pa. Now that first memory had another first added to it, the first grandbaby.

"Shelby Robert looks much like his Pa when he was born," she told her daughter-in-law. "I reckon Mary's doll is goin' to have to use another bed. This old cradle is bein' used again, after all." *Many a year of holdin' babies gives it a history worthy of my son's first youngun. That cradle first belonged to him.*

What Gus couldn't accomplish, Harriett and Sis did by cutting logs for their hearth. It was necessary to keep a bank log burning during the cold night. After hard labor to fell a big tree, then cut it, the struggle getting the big log in the house took group effort. They knew the smoke would give the site away to any scouts, should they be in their area, but it was a chance they had to take. The cold of winter dictated there was no other choice.

When Harriett went out to draw water early the next morning and check on what few remaining chickens they had, she noticed more smoke curling above the pines but it wasn't coming from their chimney.

"Sis, look here!" Harriett yelled at Sis to come outside. "That ain't no cook stove a'makin that much smoke!" Sis nodded without saying anything then went toward the backside of the cabin to the woodpile after seeing the alarming plumes in the sky. Chores had to be finished and there wasn't anything she could do about the alarming circumstance.

Harriett tossed a few remaining kernels of corn on the ground to the singing hens and clucking rooster, keeping an eye on the billowing smoke, trying to surmise what was happening but pretty well knowing what had.

From the direction of the woodpile came a shrill scream.

That sounds like Sis!

Without thought and purely by reaction, Harriett ran toward Sis in time to see two men dragging Sis from the stacked wood toward the cabin. Harriett's dishpan of corn flew out of her hands, spilling the rest of the corn everywhere. Gunfire split the air making her heart leap. Past memories of William's fate flashed in her mind. Before Harriett made it to the woodpile in defense of Sis, she was struck from behind on the top of her head.

Pain shot through her head, sending shockwaves of screaming agony downward while incapacitating her vision to a blur. When she was able to see, blood was on her collar with more of it oozing warm rivulets down her neck. Time had lost any accountability.

When Harriett could move again, she experienced waves of nausea and felt the cold ground solidly beneath her. She opened her eyes, only to fight vertigo. Direction refused to right itself as she dropped in and out of consciousness eating holes into time frames. When she was finally able to focus, Harriett saw smoke coming from their cabin but it wasn't from their chimney.

"Mary! Haden! Gus!" Harriett screamed while stumbling to her feet. Her legs refused to move and she crumpled to the ground. Harriett got up again out of pure will in spite of her head pounding and blood running down the side of her face. Reeling backwards, she struggled for balance, half walking and half crawling toward the cabin. Flames were licking the new pinewood by the time she got to the door.

"Mama!" She heard Gus scream for help. Stumbling over a chair, she reached for the washstand for support.

"Mama, we are in the root cellar," came Gus' muffled voice.

"Get out! Get out," she screamed to the children. Working her way into the smoky room, she gasped for air when she heard Mary crying. Turning toward the sound, she saw the trap door rise up with Gus emerging first, pushing open the door, while Mary and Haden rushed around him.

"Hurry, hurry up! Run," she ordered. All of them groped their way along the floor to escape the heavy smoke filling up the cabin. While gasping for breath and trying to see the door through murky smoke, Harriett stumbled across Sis and Lucinda lying on the floor.

"Haden, you and Mary get out as fast as you can," she yelled, then called Gus to help her get the girls out.

"Wake up, Sis! Lucinda, wake up!"

Both girls responded enough for Gus to pull on Sis while Harriett helped Lucinda move forward a few feet. A ceiling beam came crashing down behind them. Lucinda screamed. "My baby!"

Harriett grabbed Lucinda's arm when Lucinda tried to retreat into the burning inferno. Yanking her toward the door took all her might to move Lucinda away from the blazing beam. Gus turned back to rescue Shelby Robert before Harriett caught him and ordered him out of the cabin. Smoke had filled the house so that only a faint light spot hinted where the door was, and they pushed and stumbled over unidentified objects as they went with Lucinda rebelling all the way.

Fire was now raging where the beam had fallen and they felt their clothes scorching on their backs. Harriett knew it was an absolute certainty her grandchild could not have survived since the cradle holding Shelby Robert was directly beneath the falling beam.

After reaching a safer distance from the burning house, the blaze still scorched their faces while they stood watching in shock and grief. Through tears made from smoke and harsh reality, the family witnessed an unbelievable scene.

"Oh, God, my baby!" Lucinda's hysterical screams rose above the sounds of crackling fire eating up objects and heir alike. Moans of grief mingled with the sound of collapsing roof timbers. Screams coming from the witnesses flashed another place and time for Harriett. It was during a time she once heard moans coming from stockades years ago. *Canady, can you hear this? Do you know?*

The burning cabin warmed the frontside of the mourners and the January wind chilled the backside of them. Snapping sounds continued from burning timbers sizzling with turpentine oozing from the pine logs, but no sound coming from the disintegrating cabin could muffle the cries of their misery and helplessness.

What could have been the beginnin' of somethin' feelin' like home ain't to be. It's done gone and my grandbaby with it, she lamented to herself, not wanting to feel selfish needs when so much more had been lost.

Lucinda refused to recognize the inevitable, "No! I have to get Shelby Robert!" She clawed at Sis's restraining grasp. Folding like a limp rag and dropping out of Sis's arms to the ground, Lucinda let out a new wave of moans into the ear of the earth.

Two hours later, she sat in numbed silence with glazed over eyes. Her mind was too overloaded to grasp meaning. Mary finally broke the silence.

"What are we goin' to do now, Mama?"

Harriett looked at her broken daughter-in-law in a crumpled heap, and faced Mary to see her dirty tear-stained face with disturbed eyes asking for some sort of miracle. Harriett resignedly stoked Mary on her head and pulled her close to her chest. No words would come out to answer Mary's question. Only hugs were left to give. They would have to do.

Harriett's attention turned to her two remaining men in the family. They sat behind Sis with blackened faces. Like war paint, irregular patterns were etched by brine across their cheeks .

"Those Bushwhackers are animals!" Sis's grief had turned to rage. Fears for herself, trauma she had suffered, were vented in anger at the loss of Shelby Robert. She put her arms around Lucinda who was unable to respond in any way. Sis heard her only mumble to herself in unrecognizable utterances.

"It wasn't enough to rape us!" Sis screamed. "They had to kill us after they were through!"

Lucinda put her hands over her face after hearing Sis vent and began sobbing again. The disgrace of the ordeal she and Sis endured mattered nothing compared to the loss of her baby.

"Harriett, whatever will we do now?" Sis asked after spewing out her anger.

"The only thing we can do," Harriett replied quietly. "We are a'goin' to Fort Smith. We can't stay here. We'll either starve or freeze to death if we do. The house is gone, ain't nothin' left here to stay for."

Harriett slowly got up off the ground. Out of habit, she brushed dirt off the backside of her soot-covered dress. Ashes smeared on the front of her apron had turned it a dingy gray with black spots.

"I remember they's some empty corn sacks a'hangin' in the shed. We are a'goin' to need somethin' to break this cold or we will all die from it," she said. Harriett turned to her oldest son. "See if there's any sacks still hangin' there, Gus."

He ran to the cow shed with Sis right behind him as soon as Harriett gave them the idea about some meager protection from the cold. Gus grabbed the three hanging on the lower nail and Sis reached the others out of Gus' reach.

Each one had an old itchy sack to pull around their shoulders. Cold air still came through but the sacks helped break the solid blast seeking flesh to chill.

Before anyone could leave, they walked toward the smoldering cabin. The fire had been so hot, fed by turpentine in new logs, that the cradle was incinerated along with baby Shelby Robert. Lucinda pulled the sack close around her shoulders and went slowly away from the site. There was nothing left to bury. Sis put her arms around Lucinda and they both walked with Harriett and the youngsters toward the direction of Fort Smith.

Chapter 18

TOUCHSTONES IN CHAOS

Their desperate situation was uppermost in Harriett's mind and she tried to stay focused toward reaching their goal of Fort Smith before they all froze to death. She believed it would take several days at best.

After walking for the better part of an hour, they heard the sound of horses coming in their direction.

"Quick, get over yonder behind that big cedar," she coarsely whispered. Mary was having difficulty getting through the underbrush.

"Here, Mary," Harriett said ordering Mary to come. She picked her up and pulled back the brush while both young women and the two boys scurried past under a bough of the low-growing cedar. All of them hunkered down into the thicket, hardly daring to breathe for fear of giving away their hiding place to the approaching strangers. The hiding place seemed safe enough if the thump of the their hearts didn't betray them from beating so fast.

"It's Union soldiers!" Harriett recognized the blue uniform and without any word to the family, she got up and pushed the scratchy cedar branch away from her face. Bramble bushes snatched at her dress, entangling every effort to advance from the safe spot. Finally freed of the viney grasp, Harriett walked toward the approaching cavalry. It was risky, but less risky, she believed, than to not elicit any help she might find.

When she appeared from out of the underbrush, the lead horse shied. The startled rider grabbed the reins tighter and reached for his pistol, all the while looking in her direction.

To Harriett's surprise, she saw other women and children following behind the rider, with other soldiers walking behind them.

"Hey, what have we here?" the lead cavalryman asked, trying to calm his horse and holster his pistol.

Cannon and musket fire had spooked the lieutenant's horse enough without having an unexpected person pop up from the underbrush. The shelling they had come through had been heavy, from what they later told her. Images of smoke elsewhere began to make sense. More then Harriett's family had endured the same kind of treatment.

Maybe some of the bunch that attacked us could have attacked them too? She was relieved to see civilians but saddened to know the women and children had escaped a same experience life her own family.

"We'se burned out this mornin'," she told the lieutenant. "They burned us out completely and even killed my newborn grandbaby while doin' it," she told the cavalryman bitterly. She added, "I have four sons a'fightin' in the Union side somewheres. They joined up at Fort Smith in September." Harriett hoped by identifying her sons' position in this war, things would go better for them.

"There's nothin' left at home, no place to go to. Me and the family are headed for Fort Smith." Harriett motioned for the family to come out of hiding.

"Yes, ma'am," said the young man, still trying to control his fidgety horse. "I guess you can see you folks aren't the only ones that have had some trouble," he said, nodding his head toward the group of people on foot behind him. We are headed for Fort Smith ourselves and you folks are welcome to travel with us, if you like," he offered.

Mary was in such a hurry to get to her mother when she waved them to come, she stumbled and fell down a small gully after her dress snagged on the same bramble bush that had caught Harriett's dress earlier. Dusting herself off, she stopped and pulled the itchy sack back around her shoulders. Then Mary adjusted something in the skirt part of her dress before running to her mother's side.

With the offer made by the Union soldier to join their entourage, the group of people continued on their way toward Fort Smith in relative silence. No one had much to say.

At dark, the moving band stopped for the night and built a fire to ward off some of the January cold.

"Maybe my frozen toes can thaw out some," Harriett mentioned to the woman sitting next to her, whose feet also pointed toward the campfire. The woman looked pale.

"My name is Harriett Holmes," Harriett said after a long silence. The pale woman shook Harriett's hand. "My name is Jewel Simpson. I noticed you folks joined up with us a little while after I did."

When they shook hands, Harriett saw rope burns around her wrists. She rubbed them and winced when she did. Harriett figured her to be in her late twenties even if she did look a bit older. This war and hard times had a way of aging people. Her wheat-colored hair had streaks of gray, making a soft contrast around her brown eyes, which were filling with tears. It wasn't the cold in her face making them leak.

"My husband is gone off to war. I was left alone," Jewell said, after sitting a while warming by the fire and continuing to rub her wrists. "I ain't got no family outside my man. Ma died when I was a youngun and Pa had a heart attack. He lived with Merle and me. I thought maybe he would be too old to go to fight, but he needed to do his part, I reckon, so planned to join up too. He died before he could."

Harriett watched this once silent woman as she spoke. It was evident she had something inside her insisting on coming out. She patiently listened to her verbally relieve the pressure exploding inside of her.

"I reckon it was partly my fault he died." Jewell hid her face with swollen hands. Her body heaved convulsively with gutteral sobs. Others sitting around the campfire pretended to ignore something impossible to ignore, but out of needed and unobtainable privacy, they gave her space to vent without intrusion.

Harriett didn't know if she should ask her to tell what was bothering her or to just sit and put her arms around her pitiful frame. She, too, was at the bursting point over Shelby Robert but couldn't lay another thing on this poor woman by telling it. She kept her misery to herself.

Rubbing Mary's feet and telling Haden and Gus to do the same helped the children thaw out. After the children warmed themselves, they were off to seek out other children looking for diversions.

Finally, Jewel spoke up again. "They tied me up on our iron bed. Pa was tied to his chair. He couldn't take it. Before they shot him dead, the good Lord called him home and saved him any further pain." Jewel sobbed deeply then, after rubbing her eyes, apologized to Harriett for the emotional display.

Good Lord! What good Lord? What's she a'talkin' about? Where was this good Lord when William died? Where was He when my precious Shelby Robert died? Where was He when my boys' wives was defiled? Them's questions a body has to ask. Is there such a thing? Is there a good Lord? Good Lord, indeed! Jewel ain't a'thinkin' straight, is what I'm a'thinkin.' Ain't we all been through enough for none of us to think straight?

Children, as children do, found mirth regardless of life's situations.

Giggles and playfulness filled in gaps of silence plaguing adult conversations. Boys tried their luck at mumblypeg by light of the campfire. Those with marbles shared their treasures and took turns. Three little girls shared a china head doll, the first Mary ever saw and her eyes were glued to it, but she didn't join in the play. The sight was satisfying enough to give a diversion from losses.

"My poor younguns have been robbed of childhood," Harriett mumbled. Life in Kentucky when she was a child had been so different. "What will we ever do?" she said out loud. *Canady, what would you do? I know you'd tell me I could do it. I ain't a'gonna think about it now, it's too much to ponder on tonight.*

A young cavalry soldier heard her disparaging question. "Tomorrow we will be at Fort Smith and you ladies won't find it so hard then," he said. "We'll have to get an early start so you ladies need to get the children to rest as well as yourselves. It will be a rough day if we are to make it by nightfall. I don't need to tell you, the sooner we get there, the better it will be for all of us." He walked back to where his horse was tied and crawled into his bedroll.

The women huddled together around the campfire and shared what blankets were saved and brought by the other women. Then Harriett pulled one of those itchy old corn sacks across her shoulders once again.

Salt pork and pan bread from ground corn and wheat flour was the fare the next morning. No one person seemed any better off than another person and hungry people ate gratefully. The old houseboat had been a mansion of plenty in comparison. No worldly possessions were saved, not even the orphaned table scarred with age, that had served throughout the decades. Everything was either stolen or burned up, everything with one exception, which was unknown to Harriett.

Harriett's little treasure box she had saved through the passing years was outside the cabin when it was set on fire. Earlier in the day, Mary had pulled open the bottom drawer of the washstand, a sacred territory she was not to get into, and had pulled out Harriett's only keepsakes: her tiara, concho and box of dried flowers. She couldn't resist temptation to take one more look at the little box after her mother had gone outside to tend to the chickens early that morning. She had been playing with Harriett's treasures before the family was attacked. Mary had gone to the outhouse where she took all the treasures with her, hidden under her dress in her pantaloons. On the return trip to the cabin, she became startled when she saw her mother closer to the house than she expected and in her haste to make it inside, the box had come tumbling out from under her dress. It rolled under the cabin steps without Harriett's notice. Mary wasn't able to retrieve the box at the time without a severe scolding, and she wasn't willing to attempt it then.

Shortly afterward, Gus had pulled Mary into the tiny cave after hearing Sis's shrill scream. It was with great difficulty she tried to keep her hidden articles hidden. When Gus clamped his hand over his little sister's mouth to silence her fussing with him, she realized this was serious, not rough brother's play. They were saved from the Rebs, but that box still lay under the cabin steps. Mary had a lot of things to worry about.

The three remembered what had happened to their older brother, William. They had learned children were not immune to disaster. They were afraid. Mary also knew that the treasures she had secreted away under her clothes caused her guilt. But, guilt or not, she also knew brothers tattled. It would be best to suffer guilt pangs she decided, then to reap justice from her Mama.

When Harriett had ordered her emerging children coming from the turnip cellar to get out of the house, no one noticed when Mary stopped to reach under the step and pick the box up. It too had been put under Mary's skirt.

Harriett noticed Mary was having difficulty walking from their house when they left to go to Fort Smith but since her head throbbed so, she didn't think much of it. Several times Mary stopped along the way after joining up with the others. Her lagging behind didn't concern Harriett too much since she would always catch up.

About then, Harriett noted Mary's difficulty appeared to be coming from foreign articles moving about in her bloomers. Unable to keep the concho in place, it managed to wiggle out her pantleg and dragged in the dirt as she walked.

"Mary Elizabeth! What is that under your skirt?" Harriett demanded her little girl to confess what she was hiding and Mary's expression conveyed, I'm caught, bound up, and ready for the kill!

She fully expected a whack on the backside but, instead of being chastised, she found herself in a bear hug with tears of joy coming from her Mama. Harriett hugged her so hard Mary could no longer conceal all the hidden secrets. They came tumbling out.

"Oh, Mary! You little imp!" She got hugged more. "I never thought I'd see the likes of these again!"

Mary got a puzzling kiss on the cheek instead of expected punishment for disobedience, further solidifying her wonderment about adults ever making sense. Children have trouble figuring out grownup's actions. This morning completely baffled Mary, but her mother's grin was a relief for many reasons. She missed her mother's smile. Mary and her Mama shared warm hearts surrounded by itchy corn sacks and walked with renewed determination on this cold morning. It was the first evidence that her Mama had returned from bounding seas of overtaxed emotions.

The rest of the group had continued to move toward the west while the discovery took place, causing Harriett to hurry by carrying Mary so they could catch up.

The sounds of three horses, women, children, and seven soldiers mingled with the chirps of cardinals feeling confident enough to sing again. No rounds of gunfire were heard. Cardinal's innocent songs lifted spirits.

Oh, Canady, where in the world are you now? Just holdin' these keepsakes you give me renews my soul. I can't think of you a'bein' dead like William. You are alive in my heart. Here I am, your princess of our rivers, makin' our way to some strange fort with part of our younguns, but only part. Part of our flesh is a'layin' beneath the ground where we once lived, another part is burned to ashes that's a'cryin' for a restin' place of remembrance. Your memory is with me all the time but memory ain't got no warm arms, Canady. That's all I have left of us, our memory. You and William is gone, the boys are gone off to war, and our grandbaby was killed a'fore he even knowed a thing about livin'. Here I am, as lost as you, leadin' what's left of our family to a place I don't know. Touchin' my keepsakes reminds me of promises. It reminds me of losses, too.

Harriett cleared her voice and quickly turned her head away from others' view. It had been too happy a moment to ruin. *You have to take the happy times and forget them bad times that tags along. If a body looks, he can always find them tag along things. I don't want to do that. Maybe, someday, there will be a spot that finally suits us, where we belong. I am goin' to look for that spot, Canady. Maybe we will find it.*

The group continued to trudge onward with little talk but lots of time to think. Harriett thought about her trappin' dandy, not knowing but always hoping.

Canady Holmes lay shivering on his bunk of raw wood, clutching his tender belly. His mind drifted to a houseboat many years ago, to a black haired, spunky woman with grit of her own to match his. A shadow crossed the memory with another one of stolen mules, which opened up a road he wished he had never taken.

His wild-haired notion to look for something younger and better after following the mule thieves to the east side of Arkansas was a regret he would never be able to make up for. Getting on a boat, he had paddled up the Mississippi River and back to his old haunts where he used to trap. All had changed. It wasn't anything like he remembered. Just a little farther, get close to home, and things will be more familiar, was the excuse at first. Then, lots of commotion began about the south coming together to do some fighting, but he didn't travel all this way to do some fighting.

Killing those mule thieves was all the fighting he ever wanted to do in his life again. After the fight, he discovered his mules were lame. *Too many rocks and bad care had wasted the best mules in the country,* he conceded, before he shot them too, right next to the fellows who took them.

Too far from home, sick about his mules, he moved farther east for another pair of mules. While searching, he continued to go eastward and ended up being conscripted into the Confederacy as soon as he got to Tennessee.

Life wasn't supposed to be this way. He certainly hadn't planned to be captured by Union soldiers either. Months had grown into years. All he had to lay his head on was a wood cot in a stinking Union prison in Chicago. *This is a far cry from where I belong!*

No water bucket was allowed in the prisoner's barracks and he was too weak to even whisper for someone to bring him a drink. *Just a swallow of water would be enough to quiet his thirst, just a swallow.*

Bud crouched beside his buddy anxiously. "Gonna make it, fella?"

Canady groaned. When he first took sick, he had feared the smallpox, but before long it was plain he had dysentery. He could only see a face if it stayed directly in front of his by this time. Black spots raced eerily across Bud's face as it veered too far to the side. Burning pain fanned out from the pit of Canady's stomach.

"Hang on!" Bud patted his shoulder and got up. Canady thought in reply to his remark, *I have been a'hangin' on for several days, I reckon.*

When Canady was marched off the packet boat and through the arched wooden gateway into this Yankee prison, it looked like someone had pulled open an old, dead stump. Every nasty, crawling thing on earth was here. Everything moved. Prison guards postured and yelled at prisoners who slumped along before them. Yankee ladies and gentlemen on the observation platform high above leaned forward to watch what was transpiring with the captured enemy. Four high walls closed off Canady's view and the only animals in this place, other than the amiable, goodly-sized rats, were animals with two legs. *Ain't this a fine fix for a trapper to be in.* He grew weaker and his breathing grew shallow—then he closed his eyes.

"Would you like to chew on some of this, ma'am?" A young soldier tapped Harriett on the shoulder. He was passing out jerky from his knapsack.

"It ain't much, ma'am, but maybe it will tide you folks over until we get to Fort Smith. It won't be much longer if we just keep moving along. We've already sent word ahead and they will be expectin' you folks," he said.

The jerky teased hungry stomachs for the possibility of more to come but then stopped short of satisfying everyone's complaining innards for the rest of the three hours journey. Gus became more edgy toward Mary and Haden. His stomach was making noise and he took offense to his siblings making mention of it. He felt totally empty. It was getting late and he was thirsty too. The blister on the back of his heel was causing him the most misery.

William's boots were still too big for Gus, but on the morning of the fire Gus had tried William's boots on, just to see how they would fit. So much commotion took place he didn't have time to make a change before heading for the root cellar.

"There she is!" A private just behind Harriett called out.

"Won't be long now, folks," the young lieutenant said.

Fort Smith could be seen when the group rounded the bend clearing the view from the side of the steep hill they were coming down. The fort wasn't much further than a quarter of a mile more to walk.

Gus took heart. Blister or not, he quickened his pace. Tired and footsore, they continued on with renewed hope until they finally passed through the massive gates opened to receive them.

"This here's a sight for sore eyes," Sis said. "I thought we would never see the likes of civilization again," she muttered as they walked into the courtyard of the fortress.

Chapter 19
FORT SMITH

Due to grief and shock from the past events, Lucinda had been quiet most of the trip to Fort Smith. Too much had happened too fast. Now that they had arrived to the safety of the fort, just thoughts of Shelby maybe still being here opened up floodgates of grief again. Looking around for someone recognizable, she noticed a number of civilians, all of whom were unfamiliar. Desperate to find Shelby, Lucinda began walking toward the building in the middle of the courtyard when a young lieutenant emerged from the doorway and announced to the newcomers, "You ladies will find quarters in the building to my left. It's not fancy, but there are plenty of tubs and cots waitin' for you. We were notified of your coming a few hours ago and are fully prepared for you. After a bath and some hot food, you will feel more refreshed, I am sure," said the young soldier.

"Mama, where's the boys? Are Shelby and them here, Mama?" Mary asked, pulling at Harriett's skirt to get her attention.

One of the women who had found safety at Fort Smith earlier made her way toward the scraggly- looking family.

"My name is Amy," she said holding out her hand. "Amy Flurry. We came in last week. Our place was burned to the ground. Nobody was hurt and we are thankful for that," she said.

Amy was a jolly sort for someone having to come to a fort for safety. She was a bit talkative to suit Harriett but appeared to be sincere enough. *Maybe the problem with me is I just can't get used to strangers and this 'un will take some gettin'used to.*

"Are you folks all right?" Amy asked. Immediately Lucinda started to cry again and Sis winced at the inquisitive woman. They gave her a puzzled look for even asking such a question.

Who in their right mind could ask if everyone was all right when they had to come to Fort Smith? Sis thought.

Tears for Lucinda seemed to have a bottomless reservoir and the notion of safety within the fort walls allowed her to let go again. She didn't have to be strong any more to make it here. They were already here. The insult done to her by the Bushwhackers had pushed sane reason somewhere in the back of her mind permitting only one reality at a time. She wasn't doing well with that one. The defilement was the least of her concerns when it came to the loss of her child.

Perspectives were different with Sis, however. She was not ready to forget the rape. Her anger continued to smolder but, being prideful, she wouldn't let anyone know she suffered.

Not wanting to add to Lucinda's grief, Harriett took Amy by the elbow and nudged her toward the building they were to stay in.

"We are a might tired," Harriett told Amy, trying to make excuses for Lucinda's disheveled behavior. "We lost everything we owned, including one of our family. Lucinda's baby was burned up when our cabin was burned. He was my first grandbaby," Harriett said, choking the words out.

Horror crossed Amy's face when she heard the story. Harriett had left out the indignities done to her daughters-in law, but she knew Amy probably figured that out too. What had happened to the girls wasn't the first time such had occurred lately. This was private business and Harriett wasn't ready to divulge any more than need be said to any stranger.

The two girls caught up with Amy and Harriett. Mary walked next to Sis and the boys followed the tired women who were being escorted by a private to their quarters.

Amy picked up the conversation where Harriett left off. Harriett had so hoped she wouldn't, but the chatty woman didn't notice Harriett was through with conversation.

"Our son enlisted here but they are all gone," she said. We thought we might get to see him, but there was little time for training the boys before they left. I understand there's lots of fighting not too far away from the fort."

Amy was wringing her hands nervously while she continued to talk about their situation.

"I believe those men were fighting their way to Duvall's Bluff. Probably was a tussle to get there," she continued. "But, if your boys are like our Raymond, they don't really need all that much training in fighting," she laughed at the small brag. "He's always been a scrapper," she chuckled.

Not able to let socializing be, the friendly Amy continued to acquaint the newest homeless arrivals by pointing out fort facilities.

"Over there is one." She pointed to a latrine. "And, you couldn't help miss that wood pile when you came in, so if you run out, there's plenty. Then," she continued, "in case you get turned around, the command headquarters sits in the center of things and you can find the mess hall to the left of it, but we won't be using it. Food is in our quarters. I told you where it was so you could get your bearings from it."

"That's why there's more quarters here than need be, a lot of the men are out. Most of them had to leave since there was a Reb build-up not too far from here," she repeated herself. Amy continued to chatter in non-stop fashion, "Anyway, the young soldier who helped us out when we got here said the possibility of having to leave this place wouldn't be too far-fetched a notion. Now, that wasn't a thing a body would like to hear after having a time of it!"

Amy was talking far too much for the weary travelers, but she was sure they needed this bit of information before settling down for the night. She continued to prattle.

"The Confederates might have a go at this fort and if they do, we will have to leave. I sure hope that doesn't happen, don't you?" Amy didn't expect a reply because she continued her nervous chatter without pause.

"It's scary prospects if you ask me!"

The talking woman and Harriett followed the girls and children as they had moved ahead of them toward their quarters. Amy continued her helpfulness even when they got inside the building.

It was time for some private place but none was seen.

"You ladies best get your baths first and we'll get some food for the youngsters while you bathe," Amy benevolently ordered. She took charge whether it was her duty or not.

"There's plenty of cornbread and beans with some molasses to go with it, if you eat all your supper," she told the children before she took them to the men's mess hall.

Well, if that ain't a fine howdy do, Harriett thought after hearing Amy's remark to her children. *Those are mighty strange-soundin' words said to my younguns! Why wouldn't they eat all their supper? Seems foolish talk to me.*

Sheeting strung by cords made screens in the corners of the barrack for bathing in tubs of warmed water. No coaxing was necessary. Harriett was glad to take Amy's offer to tend to her children's meal while the dirty and tired women bathed.

Personal time was a rarity. With Amy's help, Harriett had time alone allowing self-indulgence to examine the bruising across her shoulders and head. Large blue marks were coming to the surface of her skin, drawing attention to the tender places.

The girls had bruises of their own, blaring messages of abuse. Water provided solace for a moment as each took turns removing the soot from the nightmare they had suffered. Reflection of the miracle to be alive became more evident when they had the luxury to contemplate it. Lucinda tried to hold back her tears once again but she couldn't.

"Get in the water, honey, it will help," Harriett told her.

Next Sis slipped into the warm bath water. She managed to push her emotions into a hole somewhere and cover them up.

"I'm a'movin' on. There ain't nothin' else to do but that," she said before ducking under the water in the elongated tub. Sis was a survivor. Lucinda's resolve was not a settled issue, however.

Children had been fed and bathed before their clothes were washed in the used tub water. Amy had borrowed clothes from some of the earlier arrivals for the newcomers to wear until their things could dry by the large fireplace. *Maybe this will help these itchy things to soften up a bit,* Harriett thought, scrubbing on the sacks along with dirty clothes.

Mary and her brothers didn't need to be told it was bedtime. With full tummies, they were asleep as soon as their heads hit the cots.

"I don't know how I can return your help, Amy," Harriett admitted to this chatty benefactor. It was difficult for Harriett to be beholden to anyone, but this woman deserved this uncomfortable compensation if anyone ever did. That very fact was a disturbance sometimes for the former boat lady. Amy's presence had been annoying, yet welcome at the same time, not an easy issue for Harriett to digest.

"Well, Harriett, I was glad to be of some help," she said patting Harriett's hand. "Do get some rest now, dear. We could be facing some very trying times ahead if the threat of Confederate attack comes to be. This whole place has gone crazy," she whispered, trying to protect the ears of children. "I've never seen the likes of what is going on! What do you think the good Lord thinks of His creation now?" she asked turning to leave, not really expecting an answer from Harriett.

In amazement, Harriett watched Amy walking toward her own cot. Troubled and puzzled in spirit about the possibility of a Higher Being, she questioned how any good Lord would let some crazed person kill her William. *How could any good Lord let an innocent baby die like her Shelby Robert? Why don't the good Lord send back my Canady?*

Dragging her weary body to her cot, she could find no answer to these questions but found temporary relief in blessed sleep.

Chapter 20
SLIPPERY ESCAPE

Mary awoke early to the crowing of a rooster. Being groggy from sleep, she was disoriented, because the last time she heard a rooster crow, she was in familiar surroundings. There was nothing familiar here! It was confusion. Grabbing for her cover to stave off the January cold, Mary tried to get comfort the best way she knew how, by curling up under blankets. This new morning brought with it a pressing problem she needed to solve. Mary didn't know where to find the chamber pot or the outhouse. Finally, slipping off her cot with her bed cover partially wrapped around her shoulders and trailing behind, she tried to awaken Harriett from a sound sleep.

No time to waste, Mary knew she had an accident on its way and became more aggressive about waking her mother.

Harriett felt pain coming from her sore head and shoulders, the best place Mary found to nudge. Her first tap was gentle but urgency translated further announcements with harder jabs to sore spots after Mary got no response.

Harriett opened her eyes and readily understood what was bothering her daughter. Slipping her drying dress over the borrowed clothing, she reached for one of the washed feed sacks and threw it over her shoulder as she gathered Mary in her arms and headed for the door. Such a time as now, Harriett realized what a treasure Amy had been, chatty or not. She hadn't forgotten a thing, even the locations of the outhouses.

This morning it would be little Mary who would take advantage of the four-holer before her brothers. Normally Gus and Haden were always up before Mary. Both boys were stirring from a dead sleep when Harriett and Mary returned.

Sis had added more wood to the fireplace from the wood box by the time they got back and the bunkhouse chill was dissipating. Soldiers had already put a wood allotment for the barracks in the quarters before their arrival. Harriett and Mary came toward the fireplace, consuming new logs to warm themselves after their morning run. Gus and Haden pulled on washed and dried britches, followed by boots and were out the door retracing their sister and mother's steps to the outhouse as soon as they returned.

"Ain't it a relief not to have to chop wood ourselves or to go outside in the cold to get it?" Sis said in a muffled yawn, not expecting Harriett to answer. Such small luxuries had become magnified after harsh times and hard work. Sis wasn't afraid of work, she worked hard most her life, but she had never experienced a continued diet of hardship before she married John, either. The stack of wood inside was savored.

Mary got her face washed after her mother discovered all the places she had missed when she took her bath last night. After the face-washing, Harriett went to the porch to throw out the water and that's when she saw some commotion coming from the very outhouse they had returned from.

About the time the boys thought relief was just a step away, but before they had time to grab the door pull, another boy about Gus's age shot in front of them. He seemed to have come from nowhere. The young lad had his own problems and mischievously whisked past Gus and Haden and locked the door to the four-holer as soon as he entered.

Gus looked at Haden and began to get red in the face, partly because of the cold, but mostly because his temper had gotten the better of him. Gus knew full well the interloper had orchestrated this fast entry on purpose!

Thinking he was out of his mother's hearing, he let out an oath at the boy, whose only comment was a low snicker heard from inside the outhouse.

"You sorry shit-ass! You gotta come outta there sometime!"

Anxiously Haden turned around to see if his mother was in earshot of his brother's profanity. Gus couldn't have cared less by this time if his mother had heard him and was about to make a dash to the huge woodpile by the fort gates when the outhouse door flew open. The menacing intruder streaked past both boys.

Picking up a rock, Gus threw it as hard as he could while making strides for the blessed contraption in front of him. There weren't any trees inside this fort, no other place to go, and no time to wait!

Haden had sense enough to drop the latch after they entered, which made no difference to Gus. He didn't care.

"He'll wish he never saw the likes of me when I get through with him!" Gus snarled through his teeth while jumping up and down. Gus was in no condition to follow through with his threat. By the time the boy's business was completed, there wasn't a sign of the agitator to be seen. Augustus Burton Holmes was content to wait him out, however, to when the time would be right.

"Come on, Haden. I'll get that coward when he is least expectin' it!" he vowed to his little brother on their way back to the quarters. It was time to put something into his equally quarrelsome stomach so future plans for retaliation could fall in behind that number one category.

Haden could smell the coffee perking before they came inside. Breakfast smells blended with the aroma of hot coffee tempted both boys to hurry for the head table by the fireplace.

Slab bacon sizzled in an iron skillet resting on a grill inside the fireplace of the women's quarters. The camp mess hall was full of soldiers this morning. That hall had only been used for the weary travelers last night but it was not the place camp refugees were to eat their meals. Provisions had been put in the barracks for the women and children to prepare their own food. Grits, biscuits and molasses washed down with hot coffee renewed spirits of the refugees. Unexpectedly, a loud knock at the door interrupted their morning meal. A private walked in before anyone could respond to his knock. It was apparent this was a rap to signify his presence and his intention to enter was without doubt, invited or not, when he boldly stepped into the barracks and stood near the door with a piece of paper in his hand.

"Is there a Harriett Holmes in here?" he asked.

"I reckon that would be me," Harriett said, while gingerly moving toward the young man.

"The captain asked me to give this to you, ma'am," he said handing the note to Harriett.

She thanked the young soldier who turned quickly to leave and firmly closed the door without any wasted moves in his leaving.

"Sis, you better come here," Harriett motioned to her daughter-in-law. "What in the tarnation am I to do with this?"

Not wanting to admit she could read hen scratch better than writing, she indignantly asked Sis if she would mind reading the note to see what the captain had to say in writing "that he couldn't talk about in person!"

Sis looked puzzled with questioning eyes saying, why don't you read it yourself?

Harriett felt the note must be important for it to come in writing, but who in the world would be sending somethin' to me in writin'?

"It appears the captain wants to speak to you personally, Harriett. He wants you to come to his office as soon as possible. That's all there is in the note. Must be important or he could have sent word without you a'goin, don't you think?"

Harriett reached for one of the feed sacks for the second time this morning. It was still scratchy but not as much as it had been before it was washed. Grateful for it, nevertheless, she put the sack around her shoulders and headed for the fort headquarters.

The air was sharper than it had been earlier. Blasts of wind had quit toying with threats to move and had escalated from small breezes to blowing gusts. Harriett pulled the sack tighter around her shoulders as she left the barracks and walked up the two steps onto the captain's front porch.

"Come in, Mrs. Holmes," said the fort commander through the door, not waiting for her to knock since he had seen her approach from the window. Harriett pushed open the heavy log door to enter the room while quizzically looking directly in the man's eyes for signs of his reason for summoning her.

"It's always nice to have something good to report and I believe I have some good news for you," he said after closing the door behind Harriett quickly to shut out the sharp air.

"Won't you sit down?" he offered, pointing to the chair next to his desk.

"Our dispatcher arrived last night from duty at Duvall's Bluff. He reported to me there was a Jasper Newton Holmes registered in our cavalry at the camp there. It seems this Private Jasper Holmes sent his first pay by the way of my dispatcher back to this fort in hopes you might be here. Apparently word has reached vDuvall's Bluff already about Logan County being overrun by the Confederates and he believed his family would end up here. At least, that was his hopes since he also heard others were finding refuge here."

Harriett sat dumbfounded with this news. *How in the world can Jasper afford to do such a thing?*

"According to our dispatcher, Private Holmes had gotten word from some of his former neighbors that there wasn't a house left standing where you folks came from," the captain said.

Lost for words, Harriett finally stated, "I know we lost ours and our closest neighbor, the Floys, lost theirs too. Mrs. Floy is dead, got burned up in her house after she's shot. But, captain," Harriett interjected from her reporting, " how in the world can Jasper afford to live without his pay?"

"You need not worry about your son, ma'am. There's no doubt in my mind he has made provisions for himself. It is highly unusual for any courier to make a personal delivery to a civilian, but I understand there were extenuating circumstances," he said. "Your son is a friend of Corporal Dean and, as a special favor for Private Holmes, the dispatcher unofficially brought Jasper's rations and pay to this fort since he had business here anyway. It goes without saying that Corporal Dean didn't want to get himself in any compromising situation so he reported here first his intent and the request your son had made of him."

Unable to find anything to say about Jasper's sacrifice for her and the family, Harriett sat quietly soaking up the meaning of his gift. *Jasper, you always tried to fill in for your Pa. My son, oh, my son,* she thought, touched by Jasper's caring. Harriett fought hard to compose herself, thinking of her son's selflessness.

"Oh course, Mrs. Holmes," the captain continued, "I am aware of the awful hardships that the general populace has suffered and I am only too glad to help out with this one kind son's solution for his family's need. You must indeed have a very fine son, madam. A caring and fine son I am sure you are most proud of."

The fort commander handed Harriett the leather pouch when a bugle alarm interrupted their closing conversation amid sounds made from men moving about in the courtyard. A troubled expression crossed the captain's face and he jumped up from behind his desk and rushed to the door.

"I'm sorry, madam, you need to get your family out of here! We are being invaded by the Confederates!"

The dispatcher who had delivered Jasper's pouch to headquarters was accompanied by another private making reports on the invasion. They hadn't finished their report before the captain put his rifle in the holster on Goldie, Corporal Dean's horse, tied at the front of the fort headquarters. Since the captain had no time to get his own mount, Corporal Dean's horse would do. The young private gave the reins to the captain and the officer goosed the horse, pulling at his saber.

Harriett began running back to the barracks to get her family. Someone must have notified the civilians as she met them running toward her in panic. Sis and Lucinda had taken time to get the corn sacks and clutched them tightly around their shoulders with one hand, while helping crying children with the other. The only possessions besides the corn sacks were Harriett's treasures Sis had thoughtfully taken before leaving. She was struggling to keep from dropping them when she screamed and pointed to the gate.

Next to the gigantic woodpile they went past the night before, were Confederates pouring up over the wall and onto the pile of wood. The family stood frozen with fear, not knowing which way to run.

Corporal Dean and the other young private followed Harriett to warn the women, but it was obvious they already had received word of the take-over. Corporal Dean pulled Harriett's arm instead and began leading them back toward the headquarters building.

Mary was running so fast she could hardly keep up and only managed to stay upright because Sis held her hand pulling her along.

Frenzy! Screaming children! Sounds of gunfire! Running scared! Lost with no inkling of direction! The only thing to do, trust the corporal.

The dispatcher continued to lead Harriett and her family into a building connected to the backside of the headquarters. They were running down a hallway in the direction toward the fort wall. Corporal Dean pushed on a rough timber post on the side of the hallway. It didn't budge. He gave it another push with his shoulder, and a large gaping hole opened up and he shoved the young women into the void. The boys and Harriett followed. Corporal Dean and the private pushed the massive log door back and the unfamiliar abyss became pitch black!

Corporal Dean groped in the darkness for Harriett's hand and ordered for each to hold hands and walk as fast as they could. Harriett took Mary's hand and Sis took her other one, followed by the rest feeling for hands to hold. Mary's feet sometimes didn't touch the ground with Sis and her mother lifting her when she couldn't walk fast enough. No one could see anything, but they heard Gus stumble. He gave himself away in the dark when he practiced a word he normally would have gotten smacked for saying. No one paid any attention to him. It was time for survival and there were more things to consider than the little boy's cuss words. All they knew for the moment was that the corporal was leading and the private was following behind them in this dark tunnel leading to unknown places.

"There it is," Corporal Dean said. Everyone wondered what "it" was when they began to notice a faint light. The escapees pushed through a brush opening and spilled out the dark cave onto the bank of the Arkansas River.

"You must be quiet now," Corporal Dean warned sternly. He pushed aside the scratchy brush and saw what he was looking for.

"We are lucky today! They haven't discovered it yet!" he said excitedly to the private.

On the bank, camouflaged by natural brush with some extra added to it for safekeeping, was a log raft tied to a stump. Two long poles were attached to it.

Harriett needed no further coaxing and led her family onto the raft once it was in the water. Corporal Dean boarded after untying it from a stump. In concert, he and the private gave the raft a good shove, pushing away from the shore with both feet.

A swift current caught the raft and spun it around several times. Lucinda and Sis had to stifle their cries of terror from the unexpected and swift movement. Mary hid her face in her mother's lap, clinging to her like second skin. Haden and Gus scooted their hands into the joints of the logs and had a death grip on the ropes binding the logs together.

Both warring sides, the north and the south, would be watching shorelines of the river for the enemy. Because of that, any escapee seeking refuge had to find it in overhanging bushes and tree limbs along the banks, and so the raft was moved as close to cover as possible.

To protect the fleeing family was not the primary purpose of the young soldiers. It was imperative to flee the best way they could to Duvall's Bluff and make a report about the Confederate attack on the fort. The dispatcher and the private tried to hide their escape with the help of low undergrowth extending into the river. Whenever possible, Sis assisted their maneuvers by pulling on overhanging limbs, aiding the young men to pole when necessary. Swift-moving water was a bonus.

After drifting past the fort the men decided they better pole, if possible, across the river to the north side for further protection. They gave a shove and the raft moved against the current causing it to spin quickly. Not expecting the sudden movement, Haden had loosed his grip on the rope. Suddenly the jolt made by pushing water sent the youngster sliding past Sis and his mother off the edge of the raft into the river. Corporal Dean grabbed Haden's arm just as he hit the water and with Sis pulling on the other arm, the water soaked boy was pulled back onto the raft.

Midmorning January weather was cold enough without water evaporating.

Haden shivered between his two sisters-in-law hiding under the folds of their skirts.

"Haden," Gus chided, "you pick the galdurndest times to go swimmin'!" It really wasn't a humorous situation but the absurdity of it all made the rafters giggle. They weren't out of harm's way by any means, but the slight snicker gave release from tension and a bit of renewed hope their escape could be achieved.

Time was kind and passed quickly for everyone but Haden. He continued to shiver in the cold while the rest did their best to stay upright and out of sight.

"It's starting to get dark and it will be better to travel at night to keep from being discovered. There could be a problem with that plan since you got yourself so wet, young fella," the corporal added.

"If we can get to Shoal Creek, I know some people, the Whitecottons, and I know they would help us," Harriett told the corporal. "They would, if they's still there. It was Mr. Whitecotton who talked my boys into enlistin' into the government army after my William was killed," she said. "He told them how serious things was and they would be a'fightin' for one side of the other. If they's a'goin' to choose, they had to join."

Haden's teeth were chattering and shaking so much Harriett put her skirt over him to make more windbreak.

"Well, that will work out just about right if we are lucky," the corporal said under his breath. "The trick is to get out of this area without Johnny Reb drawing a bead on us. From what I can gather, and from what came in that front gate, most of the invasion was bunched up in front. Looked like hundreds of 'em were pouring in that front gate." Corporal Dean cleared his throat after a few seconds of silence while his words soaked in to the adult passengers. "There weren't enough of us to give 'em a tussle," he concluded.

Harriett looked at the corporal when he said that and detected there was more he hadn't said. For the first time, she had begun to realize the unusual situation and the horrible thought crossed Harriett's mind relating to her chatty benefactor, Amy Flurry. *She might not be nothin' more than a casualty of war by now. Ain't no way she could have been as lucky as us. She might a knowed a lot about that fort and all, a'tellin' me where things is, but she ain't had no chance for somebody to lead her out, I'm a'feared.*

Thinking about Amy and the kindness given her and the family as the last act she probably did on earth, Amy's words flooded back to Harriett in a clear and resounding memory. *I wonder what the Good Lord thinks of His creation now?* A puzzling thought.

Chapter 21
FLIGHT BY NIGHT

"I figure we best take you folks along with us to vDuvall's Bluff where your sons are, Mrs. Holmes. It isn't safe here anymore. This whole county is fighting each other and there's nothing left anywhere for a person to survive on. If those friends of yours still have anything it will be a miracle. It will be a miracle if they haven't been killed themselves," he finished his discouraging discourse.

Minutes grew into an hour and the hour into three more hours. Lack of moonlight was not much help but it was a mixed blessing. Nighttime gave enough cover to conceal the escapees on the river raft,but it also posed a challenge to negotiate travel along a brushy bank.

The permeating atmosphere was as if dark specters peered through the chaos of earthly humanity and enjoyed the confusion and disaster they had perpetrated everywhere. One thing the evil spirits could not control was the weather—they just rattled men's souls. Apparently another source existed who had rights to ultimate decisions. A higher being appointed the river water not to freeze and for that the rafting captains were grateful.

Everyone listened for sounds other than the ones they were trying not to make. Straining their eyes in the darkness to see anything visible on shore kept them occupied and sharpened them mentally, helping them to somewhat disregard the cold, all but Haden.

"Well, folks, we are in Shoal Creek," Corporal Dean said under his breath.

Harriett had a hard time recognizing the place. Dark as it was, she could still see the landscape was a heap of rubble. Houses were tumbled and burned with some gutted houses still standing over the remains like skeletal spectators. Any familiar landmarks she had known when they first docked several years ago were unrecognizable or gone. Yards were bare of dormant winter grasses, replaced by broken fences and pieces of debris no one could describe. *It looks like some ragin' whirlwind punished things to pieces that wasn't capable to takin' sides to war.*

Struggling to get her bearings, she knew finding the Whitecottons wouldn't be easy. Without the chaos, the passing years and ensuing changes contributed to her disorientation. *All my landmarks is gone. How am I a'goin' to lead people to a place when I don't know where it is?*

"I believe the Whitecottons lived pert near five blocks from the dock", she finally told the dispatcher. "Now, how do we find the dock?" she asked.

"I know where the main dock is located," Corporal Dean said, and began poling the raft away from the shore.

"It'd be better to go to it by raft rather than make it afoot, that way we can keep tabs on the raft," he said. "We can't take any chances with this raft. There's plenty roaming around out there lookin' for something like this, you can believe that."

"That's it!" After what seemed like an eternity and a couple of bends, the captain poled the raft to the shore once more. He maneuvered to a ghostly dock sympathetically leaning with boards missing from a broken support pole.

Both men sought a sturdier spot and secured the raft to what was left of the pier while occupants scrambled for shore without instruction to do so. Haden's teeth could be heard chattering by now after losing his warm spot. He had kept the cold warded off under the girls' billowy skirts. Peeling away from his warm comfort sent shock waves from winter's chill tormenting him to the bone.

"Let's keep moving," the corporal said, "but keep your voices down."

Harriett timidly led the way since she was the one who was supposed to know where the Whitecotton's house was located. Nothing looked familiar. It was next to impossible to try to pick out anything recognizable. But, wait!

Something caught Harriett's eye. Directly in front of her was the moment's greatest dread! There was Henry and Molly Whitecotton's house, a pile of charred timbers. "Whatever will we do?" she asked softly.

Corporal Dean heard a noise about the time she asked the question. He reached for his holstered gun. Frozen in place, they heard a voice boom out in the darkness.

"Who goes there?"

No one could see a thing, but the corporal pointed his gun in the direction he had heard the voice and answered back.

"We are looking for the Whitecottons. Can you help us out?"

The voice once again broke the silence of the night. "Who is looking for the Whitecottons?"

Harriett recognized the voice to be that of Grandpa Whitecotton and before the Corporal could reply, she called out.

"Harriett Holmes is a'lookin' for the Whitecottons."

"Mrs. Holmes, is that you?" the voice said.

"It sure 'nuf is. Where are you Mr. Whitecotton? I can't see a thing," she called out to the voice.

"Wait right there. Wait where you are," he said. In a few minutes they saw a flash of light, then a mellow glow of lamplight in the dark. The glowing lamp came wobbling toward them like some eerie hobgoblin before the silhouette of Grandpa Whitecotton came into view.

"Well, Mrs. Holmes! If this isn't one kind of surprise!" he greeted her by stretching out his hand.

"I can't tell you what a sight you are yourself, Mr. Whitecotton. I want you to meet up with these folks. Mr. Whitecotton, this here is Corporal Dean. Thanks to him and to private—? For the first time, Harriett realized there was no name attached to the young man assisting them and the corporal. They were too busy trying to save themselves to consider social graces. Too much had been at stake to take note of handles.

"Private Davis, Jim Davis it is, sir, and I am real glad to meet you too sir," the young private said, shaking his hand.

Elderly Mr. Whitecotton's frame was no match for the strong youthful private's firm handshake and he caught himself losing balance. Embarrassed, Private Jim Davis steadied Henry before turning loose his lingering handshake.

"These here young ladies is my sons' wives," Harriett told the elderly man who was still working at rebalancing. Mr. Whitecotton nodded to the young women and asked the party to follow him without offering them his hand.

The air was sharp, making the night travelers miserable. Mary began whimpering until Harriett picked her up. Rubble was everywhere. It would be hard to walk during the day, let alone at night, especially for a child. Mary kept falling over unknown things.

Mr. Whitecotton led the group through debris from what used to be a fascinating river town. They had gone several blocks when the elderly leader stopped in front of what once had been a magnificent building made from native stone, now standing gutted and roofless.

"Be careful how you walk," he instructed, going through the stone archway of the bank's front door. After moving the pieces of ceiling tin aside, a small light could be seen meandering up from a stairwell hidden by the metal ceiling tile. The soft light at the bottom had a voice rising with it. "Is that you, Henry?"

"Yes, Molly, and Mrs. Canady Holmes and her family are with me, and a couple of young men," he told his wife.

"Corporal Dean and Private Davis have been helping Harriett," he told his wife when all but Henry began to descend into the basement room.

Haden felt blessed relief from the cold at the bottom of the steps. He was out of the wintry night breezes into the warmer room where the new light came from. Corporal Dean and Private Davis eyed the close quarters to see where they had been taken.

"You folks come on in here," the cheerful Molly invited. Henry Whitecotton busied himself at the top of the stairs putting the tin ceiling squares back over the opening, arranging and rearranging them until he was satisfied their dugout had been concealed satisfactorily. He was a gentle, meticulous man, never in a hurry, but he always seemed to accomplish as much as those who were in a rush. When he finished the chore to his satisfaction, he came down to join the rest.

"If this isn't a fine howdy-you-do!" Molly laughed. "Harriett Holmes, I thought the day you folks traded for those mules would be the last time we would ever see each other again. What in the world has happened to your folks?"

The question was a stumper. It had been a long time since she had seen the Whitecottons and, if it hadn't been for buying their mules, she would have known no one in this area to attach a name to.

Maybe if it hadn't been for them mules, Canady might still be here. Maybe still, he might'a been caught off guard, and sent off to war like Mr. Partain.

"So much I really don't know where to begin to tell it. Before we visit, Molly, I need to ask if you could spare some warm clothes for Haden until his own dries out? He fell off the raft and got soaked to the bone."

While the women took care of Haden, Private Davis and Corporal Dean went back up the steps to retrace their tracks to the river. Carefully removing the meticulously-placed tin, they put the pieces back as they were leaving, but not with the same care Henry Whitecotton had given earlier.

The only hope for them to reach vDuvall's Bluff was their raft. It was important to make sure it was hidden well and to check out the territory. Their trip to Duvall's Bluff would require the raft to get them to Conway Holler, where the raft would have to be pulled overland to White River. They knew this was the only chance they had to reach the Union camp. The journey would be a hard one with the worrisome land travel ahead of them. A decision was made to go by night, tugging that heavy raft overland and resting during the day.

Their hope at present rested on a possibility that the Whitecottons might share some provisions to take with them. It would be a lot to ask and Harriett hated to do it, but she had to do lots of things now she normally wouldn't have done.

Both soldiers picked their way to the river without conversation. The night was still since the earlier breezes had finally died down. Night birds had hushed their song, normal river sounds were absent, and no movement outside their own were heard. It was eerily quiet. Jim stopped and grabbed Ted Dean's arm.

"Listen!" he whispered.

Audible conversation drew their attention to the place where they had docked. Different voice inflections identified at least two men were out there somewhere in the dark. Ted and Jim darted behind some rubble near the water's edge and looked in the direction the male voices had come from. Their voices began fading, evidencing the men were moving further away.

Easing along the brush toward the raft, Ted and Jim were relieved it hadn't been discovered. They dragged it further back under a tree and camouflaged it with more debris after the men's voices had grown too faint to detect their maneuvering the raft to a more secure spot.

Retracing their steps to the cellar, they once again removed the ceiling pieces then drug them back behind them once they were in the stairwell. It didn't take the corporal and the private as long to achieve replacement of the tin as it did Henry Whitecotton. They felt their way toward a dark basement.

It was pitch black with no light coming from the basement and no one said a word until the men identified themselves.

"We were gettin' a bit worried," Sis told the young men. "Did you run into any trouble?" Lamps were once again relit. Molly and Henry had blown them out as soon as they heard steps above ground.

"Had to scout things out to make sure we didn't have any surprises in the morning," Corporal Dean, said omitting telling about the voices they heard. "We'll be traveling at night and resting during the day from here on out. Only problem we might have is keeping watch for anyone else doing the same. I don't need to tell you, I'm sure, but we must take every precaution. I believe we will make it fine," he added, after telling them in this indirect way he was in command.

Haden's teeth finally stopped reverberating but he felt a little flushed with fever. Mrs. Whitecotton's hot tea with a pinch of sugar helped warm his insides. The only inclination he had after thawing out was sleep. Haden found a corner and pulled a blanket over his head. Not even conversation from Corporal Dean and the others disturbed the relief he found in sleep. Mary and Gus found the same solace after eating some pan bread with their tea.

It was time Molly could ask questions of Harriett's circumstances and it was time Harriett needed to answer some of them. Canady was never an easy topic for her since his disappearance. William's death had been another trauma, but the latest one with Shelby Robert was still very raw. Waves of bitterness and lack of personal control over her life and circumstances were beginning to build evidences of resentment inside Harriett, who normally was a soft creature endowed with a granite core.

"I suppose you ain't heard nothin' about Canady since the time we bought them mules, have you, Molly?" Harriett knew her question would be a fruitless one, but she had to ask it anyway.

"Why, no, Harriett. We haven't seen him since you folks bought the mules. We heard about him using them in the mule pull contests, but my Henry never had any interest in such and didn't ever go to them. No, we haven't seen him at all."

"I know he has run into somethin' and I'm a'feered he's got himself killed somewhere without any of us a'knowin' it," she explained.

While Harriett was making her explanations about Canady, Sis's and Lucinda's eyes echoed volumes from one another without words conveying what they thought. They had difficulty understanding Harriett's feelings about her lost husband since listening to talk from their husbands about Canady's disappearance.

The account they heard wasn't the same as Harriett perceived it to be.

No matter how much the family tried to shield Harriett, she was not fooled, she instinctively knew how they felt. In Harriett's heart, she believed it possible some things in the world could look one way, but inside she knew it to be another. She didn't fault her sons for their opinions. *I have knowed their Pa longer than they have,* she always said to herself whenever she overheard disparaging remarks. *There's just some things I know. Maybe nobody else knows, but I know.*

In a short time after Molly and Harriett's visit, sounds of sleep were coming from everywhere in the cozy dugout. Some of the people sleeping were exhausted from a trying time. Then, there were two people there who were weary from time alone, too much of it. Those two had made everyone welcome regardless of their age and being feeble and war torn.

No sunrises could be seen in the dugout and only when Corporal Dean pushed back the ceiling tin did light break the darkness drowning vision in the hideaway. Molly lit the kerosene lamp and Harriett nudged Haden then handed her son his clothes. They were dry enough for him to make an early morning trip outside. Possibly he could catch up with Ted and Jim if he hurried.

"Get up, Gus. Go with Haden. Maybe you boys can catch up with Corporal Dean if you move along," she told her sleepy sons. Neither needed prodding. Mary's morning solution stood in the corner, compliments of Molly Whitecotton.

Molly and Henry had gotten up before everyone. It was their leaving that woke Corporal Dean. Henry had put logs in a wood stove outside the bank building earlier so Molly could cook the hungry people some food. Meals were always cooked outside.

No one was safe anymore. Bushwhackers were mean and thrill-killed. A woman wasn't safe, no matter her age, and Molly was cautious about being discovered. She tried to take extra precaution each time she went up to cook. Both she and Henry were getting feeble and had no family to defend them. Their only protection was the ability to live by their wits and outsmart any adversary. But, then again, there was their faith in God who they relied upon the most. He watches over sparrows. He will watch over us, they always told each other.

They had managed to save a salted-pork at the time of the invasion when their home was set on fire. Molly told about the miracle and that God had made this provision, they were sure. Listening intently to her stories, the Whitecottons shared with Harriett more than one so-called miracle they had experienced before sleep had overtaken her last night.

Fried slab bacon and cooked pan bread slithered their aromas down the stairwell under the girls' noses. The tantalizing odor intensified when the shivering boys took the ceiling tin off the staircase again. Gus and Haden ran to their borrowed corner and quickly slid under the quilt.

Private Davis and Corporal Dean were nowhere to be seen when the family breakfasted on the Whitecotton's generosity. A portion was put aside for the young soldiers, wrapped in some newspaper for them to take with them. Henry Whitecotton carefully put the fire out in the cook stove, throwing sand inside the stove to smother the cinders. A rain barrel caught water from the eave of the gutted bank and Molly dipped out enough for clean-up. Even if the domestic habits of the Whitecottons had been interrupted by a horrible war, they managed to restore some sanity to living. Both were able to create new ways to get the necessities of life and to live more comfortably, in spite of their circumstances.

Harriett made a mental note of their willingness to share with her family, an act most gratefully received, but not fully understood. They could ill-afford to part with their provisions since they had no family to look after them. They were old. *Who's gonna take care of them when it's all gone,* she wondered? *They hardly know who we are, and they took such good care a body would 'a thought we come from some fine place.*

Such behavior made no sense at all to her, especially since the only connection they ever had was when Canady bought the mules from them several years ago.

Something else didn't fly right in Harriett's thinking if she were to use memories from her childhood home for a yardstick. A quaint habit before they ate breakfast really caught Harriett's attention this morning. Before they ate, Molly grabbed Harriett's hand and motioned for the rest to follow suit. Gus and Haden looked quizzically at Mrs. Whitecotton when she asked them to hold hands. They were hungry and certainly couldn't eat much with someone holding on to their hands. Molly looked at Mr. Whitecotton and simply and expectantly said, "Daddy."

At that very minute, Henry Whitecotton and his wife bowed their heads and prayed, giving thanks to God for the food they were about to share and for the fine friends He had sent their way to partake of this meal.

Most the folks I know puts things back for a rainy day and can't afford to give it away. They appear happy to give it away and thanked God for the opportunity! I must say it's a bit peculiar!

Chapter 22

DUVALL'S BLUFF

"**H**as there been any word from Fort Smith?" Jasper asked Shelby. "I sent money with Ted Dean, the dispatcher, to take to the folks before he left. Just like we talked about, I know that's where they're at after hearin' what's takin' place back home. Fightin's been so bad, I don't know if Ted could have made it or not ," Jasper mumbled after not getting any response from Shelby.

"Nothin' ain't for sure, but word is the cabins all around the place was burned to the ground," Shelby finally said. The last bit of information gave Jasper reason for both hope and fear for the family's safety. It was the not knowing about them that was eating at all four of the boys. They knew there was one place left to seek shelter and that was at Fort Smith. The only thought they could live with was the possibility that the family had made it to the safety of the fort.

Jasper's and dispatcher Corporal Ted Dean's connection began with a favor Ted owed Jasper. Private Jasper Holmes had helped Ted out with one of the young girls living on the outskirts of the camp. Tina was the daughter of one of the camp cooks. Her mother got rations and a safe place to stay for her family in return for cooking and cleaning.

John had spotted Tina first, but Jasper thought he needed to do something to get her off his younger brother's mind or John would end up in a lot of trouble. After all, John was a married man and, indirectly, Jasper felt a bit responsible to help keep John faithful to Sis. It was he who had introduced John to Sis in the first place.

Jasper liked his sister-in-law well enough when they first met while working for her relatives up north of their place. She was interested in getting married but Jasper had no such inclination. Knowing his brother John was more at ease with women, he knew he could take Sis in tow but, much to his surprise, he married her instead. Nobody could have been more unprepared for this than Jasper. He felt responsible for getting them together in the first place, and that same feeling of responsibility reached out to help keep them that way.

Tina was a tad more temptation than John needed in his life. He was looking trouble straight in the face, taking no backward steps when it came to Tina and Jasper was worried. As Jasper knew and John should have known, John was in no position to continue on this path with this little vixen.

"There's enough trouble a'lookin' for a place to roost without this," he told John after seeing them together. "What in tarnation are you a'thinkin' about, John," he scolded him at the time. Tina quickly left when Jasper happened in on them before things got uncomfortable. John and Tina didn't see each other again the rest of the day until suppertime.

Jasper couldn't help but notice Tina's eyes leaving John and following the handsome Corporal Dean when he walked into the mess tent and sat down next to him.

Ted Dean could be the perfect solution without much trouble, Jasper thought as he watched the sixteen year old keep glancing in the corporal's direction. Jasper knew she was young but she appeared to have the notions of someone a lot older and she was trouble. *Well, it ain't the first time for her,* he consoled his conscience for what he was about to do.

"Hey, Ted, wouldn't you like to meet up with that for a little while?" Jasper pointed Tina out.

"I can help you out if you are a mind to see what could come of it," he badgered the dispatcher.

Ted looked directly at Tina. She lifted her eyes again to meet his and returned his smile. Such a small token, but it was enough.

"Don't mind if you do, Jasper," he said grinning, then turned to look at the girl's mother.

It was all her mother could do to keep food available for her family and a place to sleep. There were two other daughters depending on her besides Tina.

Word was, the mother had been known to be easy too, *but you could hear a lot of stuff around the camp at night,* Jasper thought, while waiting for a time to make introductions. *You don't rightly know if it's true or not, but it didn't really matter anyway. Who would want the mother when there was somethin' like Tina available? John's interest is caught, I gotta do somethin',* Jasper told himself to ease his conscience for what he was about to do.

Ted was tired from the past few days of travel. He made his way to his quarters to lie down to rest and kill a little time before he was to meet up with Jasper en route to Tina. As soon as his head hit the cot, Corporal Dean drifted off in a troublesome sleep.

Scenes of Paul Keefer popped into his fitful dreams, taking him back several months earlier.

Ted stooped to enter the stifling hot tent of Brigadier General John W. Davidson.

General Davidson was using the weathered tree stump that his tent had been erected over for a footstool, while wiping down his razor with a bit of cheesecloth. Dean straightened once inside the tent and brought his hand up in a spiky salute.

"Dispatches, sir, from General Steele."

Davidson glanced up, laid the blade on the brim of his hat, and held out his hand for the packet. "Thank you, corporal. Have a difficult ride?"

Dean was embarrassed by the question. He did not like to have the commander's attention on him.

"No, sir, thank you, sir, no more than usual in this heat."

The general opened the sealed dispatch and scanned its message. "True's Brigade is coming to add their strength to ours." Carson's eyes fell wearily.

"There is a supply train waiting at Helena for an escort, and some of the supplies belong to this division. We'll engage Marmaduke's outfit before we get to Little Rock, but our victory has been forecast. Look at this."

Davidson tossed Ted Dean a crumpled, water-marred copy of the "Arkansas Patriot". A few lines of an editorial had been circled which read: "Any head with a thimbleful of brains ought to know that, should their city be captured"—tears in the paper had stolen away some of the words—"the state of Arkansas falls an easy prey necessarily to the combined and various columns of the enemy. The fate of Arkansas rests intimately upon that of Vicksburg."

"It was a favorable sign when Vicksburg fell on July 4th." Davidson glanced away, deep in thought. "Did you ever think this was an interpersonal business, corporal?"

"No, sir."

"Well, it is. You'll come to know that for yourself." His eyes focused on Ted once more. "Remain with my division tonight. I'll want you to take a report back to General Steel at Duvall's Bluff tomorrow."

"We haven't much meat to offer at mess, corporal, but I believe some of the men are cooking johnny cakes on tin," he said with a mockingly imperial air. "Tell them you want some supper and to see to your horse."

"Thank you, sir." Dean saluted again, and backed out of the general's tent just as the cook entered with a plate of water dumplings.

Dean saw a soldier bound to an upright wagon tongue, stripped to the waist and gagged with his own belt. Inhabitants of the hastily thrown-together camp thumped him or ruffled his hair as they passed by. Dean thought the poor bloke must have been a prisoner until he noticed his Union-blue pants.

"What has this man done? Dean asked.

"Let his horse's back rub raw under a saddle blanket with holes in it," answered the sergeant. "We'll take him down at sunset. Next time he'll treat his horse right."

"Good lookin' mount you've got," the sergeant said.

"Goldie's one of General Steel's own horses," Dean grinned. "His orderly came bringing her to me last week."

"Don't say? She looks fast."

"She can pick her feet up when needs be."

"I wish you would look," came a voice from behind Dean. He wheeled around to meet a familiar face.

"Paul Keefer! What are you doing here?"

"Well, I was going to run for Congress, but—." Keefer laughed, shaking Dean's hand eagerly.

"Hey! They call this place Greasy Valley because there'so many hogs running around. Still got your bean shooter?"

"It's the same place your sling shot is. Daddy threw them both down the well! Keefer, your putting those broken pieces of iron stove in for shot was the cause of it!

The day Keefer had hit Ted Dean Senior's prize yearling smack between the eyes, they both knew they were in trouble.

"I remember she dropped down and we knew she's dead right off!" Ted chuckled to the sergeant standing by them.

"We ran 'til our bellies ached. I don't guess we went home that day or the next!" Keefer laughed.

"You best let me get your fancy horse cooled down and watered, corporal," the sergeant said. "Keefer will get you some grub."

"I'll do 'er, sergeant," Keefer said. "Come on, Ted."

The next day, Davidson's cavalry moved out at sunup down Wire Road with Ted Dean cantering beside the column. Ted pulled Goldie up so he could take one last look at his friend. Keefer marched along, powdery dust making a cream-colored vapor around his boots, and gave his buddy a grin.

Ted stuffed a quid of tobacco in his mouth and wiped his chin with his knuckle in one familiar motion. Keefer will never change, he thought, stopping to draw the strap of his dispatch bag over his head.

Then, from the corner of his eye, he saw a movement in the underbrush just inside the line of trees. A Rebel sharpshooter stood with his rifle steadied on the fork of a redbud tree, aiming at the exposed column. Ted heard the rifle fire. A shot ripped into Keefer, liberating a cascade of blood spurting in front of him.

The Rebel worked the hammer of his carbine clumsily with his left hand. Ted held Goldie's reins, drew his pistol, and squeezed the trigger. Goldie flinched and the Rebel wobbled forward, shot through the head. Ted jumped down and ran to Keefer. His shirt was sopping with blood. The sharpshooter's bullet had caught him in the heart.

"Corporal! Get the hell out of here!" roared General Davidson, trotting into view on the other side of the column. Blood gurgled through Keefer's parted lips, no life stirred in his buddy's eyes.

Ted grabbed Goldie's reins and jumped back into the saddle. Rifles popped behind him as he spurred her sides.

Davidson's division drove Marmaduke's Rebels forward to Bayou Meto where the enemy had set the bridge on fire. Ted's eyes smarted and watered from smoke. Goldie whinnied in fear as they rushed toward the blazing bridge.

"We'll never cross if the bridge goes. It's too deep. Try to put out that fire," the general ordered his men.

Ted looked at his hands. Keefer's blood had run between his fingers and had dried there. Dead, browning blood that only moments ago had been red and living in his buddy.

Psst, Corporal Dean, wake up. Wake up, corporal."

After the campfires had grown to embers and the rest of the soldiers settled in for the night, Jasper had made his way to Ted's tent.

"Psst," he motioned to Ted. Corporal Dean jolted upright, not knowing where he was. Images of a repeated nightmare mixed with the vision of Jasper standing nearby motioning him to come gave way to reality. Ted got off his cot, picking up his boots on the way out, following Jasper. Still a bit stupefied from images of the battlefield, he managed to get his boots on by half hopping and walking at the same time. Corporal Dean followed Jasper to the horse stables.

The horses were the only creatures with a permanent structure amid the tents at Duvall's Bluff. Jasper already had told Tina to meet them there at the stables after she finished up her chores when the men had gone to quarters for the night.

Adjusting their eyes in the dark barn, Jasper saw Tina move in the corner. He motioned to Ted to follow him.

"This here's Corporal Dean, the Fort Smith dispatcher," Jasper said to the young girl. At best, it was an awkward moment. Jasper wasn't very smooth talking with women like John was.

Tina's eyes danced with excitement and met Corporal Dean with expectancy, but the twenty year old soldier became noticeably unnerved by the intensity of her stare.

"I'm glad to meet your acquaintance," she said in a whispery voice that matched the message in her eyes.

"Would you like to rest yourself here besides me on this nice clean hay? We can get to know each other," she brazenly said to the dumbfounded corporal. He lost his voice. In the process of trying to retrieve it, he plopped down beside her without saying anything and looking for Jasper. Ted saw Jasper going out the barn door when Tina brought his wandering eyes back into her control by unexpectedly putting her soft hand inside his shirt. Giggling, she pulled her hand out and commented what a manly chest he had.

Shafts of pale moonlight fell on the front of her dress where Tina's roving hand unbuttoned the buttons of the bodice. The little hussy never said a word to him, but continued to stare into his eyes, fixing her gaze like a cobra hypnotizing its prey. Tina's parted full lips curled at the corners when she felt confident she had him in her power. Cupping her own body with both hands, she seductively looked at the desire forming on Ted's face.

"Doesn't this feel good to you?"

Dumbfounded, but easily led, he released his maneuvered hand and grabbed at her waist, lowering his head to introduce some seduction of his own. He found the sensation pleasurable and saw she was easy taking. Her offer invited intensifying and corresponding responses. No more invitation was needed and the dallying advanced to escalating passion and the shedding of clothes in the cold January night, with only heat radiating from their bodies to keep them warm.

Ted's lust for Tina wasn't wasted and it grew more intense for an object of pleasure only. After she screamed and begged for more from the dispatcher, they lay in total exhaustion until resuming the fulfillment of desire before the previous memory faded. So it was, until daybreak. War and lovemaking were strange partners. Both passions coming from different natures shared the same intensity as if there were no tomorrow. One moment the mutilated body of Keefer selflessly given in war and the stench of battlefield came into Dean's nostrils, destroying anything he ever thought to be good or holy. And the next minute his carnal appetite mesmerized him in another way with only selfish satisfaction being paramount. Strange feelings emerge during war.

Totally sated and carnal senses spent, it was time to leave. Corporal Dean knew he had better get back to his tent while dark enough to slip in undetected. He bid the young girl farewell and left the stables.

At breakfast, seeing Tina's mother cooking, Corporal Dean's face flushed when he passed by her. *Do you suppose she knows?* There was no doubt in Dean's mind this wasn't the first experience for Tina. It had become an expected pattern in this camp for other soldiers that Ted Dean knew all too well. Nevertheless, he owed Jasper one!

Jasper found Ted after breakfast and asked if he would mind taking money and some of his supplies to the family at Fort Smith. At least, he thought they probably were there.

"It's the least I can do for you, buddy," he said with a grin. "I'm obliged to you Jasper! Man! Am I obliged," he said.

I'm the one who's obliged, thought Jasper. *That girl is trouble and John is just ripe enough to find a heap of it with her. At least John was staved off last night.*

"Glad you can do this for me, Ted. I know there ain't no other place for them to be," he added. "Be careful, my friend, and my thanks to you for helpin' my family," Jasper told the dispatcher.

After bidding each other goodbye, the corporal swung up on Goldie and rode off. Jasper hadn't heard from him or anyone else from Fort Smith since that day.

Chapter 23
TEMPTATION'S OPPORTUNITY

Mrs. Whitecotton packed some food for their journey to Duvall's Bluff. The promise of darkness was upon them when warm friendship coming from virtual strangers was capped off with hugs.

"I'll never forget you, Molly," Harriett had said before they left because she really never expected to see her again. As the fleeing people departed for the hidden raft they marveled at the honest and giving natures of such feeble and vulnerable people.

Evening air was getting colder, encouraging them to step lively toward the brush by the riverbank. Walking left them open to the elements. On the raft they could huddle together. It was still light enough to see but darkness would overtake them, making the way not so surefooted.

Both of Harriett's arms were loaded with cloth sacks full of provisions. By the time she made it to the raft, Corporal Dean and Private Davis already had it in the water. She handed the bundles to Sis and Lucinda who had boarded with Private Davis's help.

The men poled from the shore as soon as Harriett got on where the raft could get caught in the river's current. After a hard shove, the raft once again spun out of control, catching the girls off guard. They let out a gasp and Haden hung on for dear life, hoping not to repeat a former experience.

The comfort of the Whitecotton's hideaway had allowed them to put aside their first cold river experience, forgetting how miserable it was. Memory of that first cold night came flooding back again as a yardstick to measure against their present discomfort. Bodies huddled together on the raft moving slowly down the Arkansas River. Sis sat next to Corporal Dean. She could feel his nearness but was afraid to make any conversation with him for fear the thoughts slipping in and out of her head could betray her wild imaginings. When she thought she detected Ted breathing heavier, Sis had a rush. Her husband had been gone a long time and she missed his arms about her, but she was also contending with a brutal act which had conflicted her emotions.

He don't know what I'm a'thinkin', she excused herself, daring to toy with dangerous ideas made from murmurs inside from the innocent nearness of her benefactor. *There's no harm in thinkin'*, she told herself, hoping to erase a horrible attack haunting her. Sis was a fighter.

Corporal Dean remembered a former romp in a stable, which was brought to mind by the nearness of Sis. Just thinking about a former time made him see the flirtatious eyes of a camp vixen teasing notions into his head. Closeness to one of Jasper's relatives was torment. He knew full well the futility of ever trying to get satisfaction from her. *After all, Jasper's my friend. He would kill me for such a thing,* Ted scolded himself when he weakened to think of any such possibility.

Travel time grew into a week since the party left Shoal Creek. Hiding out and resting during the day and going on the river by night was their pattern. Each day and every night, temptation provoked illicit thoughts between Corporal Dean and Sis. First it was a look, escalating to one catching the other in an act of looking. Nothing was said, but curiosity grew more bold, revealing a blush flushing across feminine cheeks and at times giving away the tell-tale thought each had when eyes made contact.

Rafting was uneventful and no Rebs were seen. If they were in the area, the Confederates must have been traveling during the day as Ted expected they would. Efforts to get to Conway Holler were cut short a day earlier due to steady movement down river. There were little rations and future need for sustenance gave them reason to keep moving toward safety at journey's end. The hard part lay ahead. Going overland would be exhausting, the most difficult part of their journey to get to White River.

Gus helped Ted and Jim drag the raft with ropes across the wooded terrain. They sledded the raft until trees were too dense, at which time they had to cartwheel it between the difficult spots. Haden tried to help, but proved to be more in the way than of help. Sis and Lucinda tugged on the burdensome thing when it was particularly brushy. Tired and physically exhausted, it was during such moments of difficulty everyone but the soldiers were ready to leave the raft where it lay.

Sis had shown an urgency to get to Duvall's Bluff to be with John at the beginning of the trip, but her hurry to get there was waning. She never tried to cover up her streak of wild oats. Her restless spirit was a part of her personality that matched that of her husband, John. Both owned the same characteristics which had been a major attraction enticing mutual interests prior to their involvement with this war. This wily streak is what bothered Jasper when he first met Sis. Right away, he knew she was more John's type than his. Sis's anxiety to get to Duvall's Bluff was being replaced with more regret the closer they got to White River.

Corporal Dean's bravery in assisting helpless souls to find refuge, and, at the same time, carrying out his own responsibilities to report episodes of the war, increased the vulnerable woman's interest. He was a take-charge type of man with impeccable manners.

Ted had found little ways to make the overland trip to White River full of expectations rather than one of dread. The dispatcher was a likeable sort with a ready smile, always pointing out something that took minds off misery. His smile lured Sis like bait to fish. So went the trip—sleep during the day, travel during the night. The closer their overland trip was coming to an end, the less complaint was heard from Sis.

Mary and Haden kept Harriett busy trying to console hungry tummies with only a stipend of food. She half-carried both of them from time to time when they stumbled over limbs and rocks embedded in the forest floor. One of Harriett's biggest concerns was Gus slipping off by himself during the day when he was supposed to be resting. Haden had already caused grave concern with possibilities of getting pneumonia when he fell into the river that first day. Mary was constantly falling down when Harriett wasn't carrying her. The weather was getting colder. Many times, Harriett thought if the enemy were out there somewhere, they could hear the complaints before they saw their party. She knew Corporal Dean had to have been a very patient young man to deal with these hardships and the likes of them.

Closer to Duvall's Bluff, Corporal Dean estimated one more day and night before they would arrive. Stamina was becoming a thing of the past. Pecans missed by squirrels were eaten when they could find them but rations had been spent. Weak from malnutrition and physical exhaustion, everyone was worrying if they could manage that burdensome raft any longer, but Dean encouraged them by saying they would only be a quarter of a mile from camp once they get that raft to White River where they were to cross over. He knew when they reached the river the misery of pulling the log raft would make sense to the weary travelers.

I'll be glad to be shut of this thing once and for all! River life ain't never been so hard as this, I know that for sure, Harriett told herself.

Thoughts of unrequited dalliance weighed heavily on Sis's and Corporal Dean's imaginations. Impossibility for any privacy with time running out for opportunity made interest for each other grow like yeast in dough. Sis's vows to John somehow lost significance in her consuming lust for a moment's pleasure in her lonely life. The last manly touch hadn't been from John, but from rape.

Corporal Dean's masterful way of taking charge and leading this family to shelter was a very attractive trait to Sis. This same trait birthed a beginning comparison of her marital union with a former boatperson. John always acted like he knew things, whether he did or not. It was obvious Ted always knew what he was talking about.

She had seen a tender and caring look in Ted Dean's eyes. It had driven Sis to investigate since the last image of intimacy was mistreatment from a two-legged animal. She desperately needed a concept replacement since her passionate nature conflicted with horrors of rape. Sis believed Ted to be the person who could trigger a healing solution.

Night travel didn't offer anything but the main objective, to get to White River without getting killed by Confederates or more Bushwhackers. Once she arrived to the camp at Duvall's Bluff, Sis knew she would have a husband to tend to. Would he be caring? Could he be tender? John was indeed a ladies' man, but he also needed to control his woman, which was done with less finesse than that of Ted Dean. That was quite all right by Sis until she met up with murderers and rapists. Somehow the relationship she had with John before he left felt tarnished and he bore no part in it.

Corporal Dean's gentlemanly ways, illusive but polite, teased her mentally. Some questions she feared would never be answered threatened louder as time ticked away. Sis felt sure John's first encounter with her when they got to the camp would bring home more of the same bitter anger growing inside since being raped. He wouldn't understand in a way she desperately needed, a tender way, making her feel important, helping her forget savagery. She knew her husband. If they had another week before they reached camp maybe things would be different, but physical stamina wouldn't allow that. Maybe she needed a rectified experience before meeting up with John? Confusion aided paths she knew were wrong to take, but she still chose to ignore an inner voice trying to reach reason. Sis was seeking her own solution and reason where reason shouldn't go.

After an hour into their last day's journey before reaching White River, Ted called Jim Davis over for a private conversation.

"I expect to reach the river by morning, Jim. There haven't been a sign of a Reb in this area."

"More than likely, it's due to the camp being so close," Jim said. "Probably have routed all of them out."

"I wager you're right on that one. Everyone is worn out and we are going to have a tussle on the river tomorrow," Ted admitted. "I'm thinking we best rest for the night and make it by daylight instead of night travel."

Underbrush had grown thicker the closer to the river they got. Dragging the raft was getting increasingly harder, partly due to the thickets and partly due to exhaustion and lack of food.

"Folks, we are going to rest for the night here. We are too close to camp for the likelihood any Gray Coats are in the area. The toughest part is behind us but tomorrow we don't want to lose any of you when we raft the river. You need to build your strength by resting as much as you can now."

It was settled. There was no complaint from anyone. Mary had cried more than usual but that was not surprising since she was hungry. Haden had been quiet and had run a fever. There was little worry about Gus running off now. He was too tired to check things out.

"We've been lucky so far, but we have been pushing our luck. Tomorrow is the day we reach the river. We aren't far from camp now," Corporal Dean told Harriett, trying to cheer her up. He then glanced briefly at Sis before giving orders to Private Davis.

"Private Davis, we need to get shelter erected for the night. Push that raft up and secure it to the pine there. Then, you take the south side and I will go to the north to look for loose limbs to secure shelter on the sides and top. That will at least break the wind during the night."

"It shouldn't take too long, Mrs. Holmes. You and the kids stay put. I don't want to have any of them get lost on me out here."

When the raft was secured in an upright position, it already gave a windbreak Harriett took advantage of. The children were glad to stop and were ready to sleep. Lucinda's frail and thin-looking frame was a worry to Harriett. *She's been through too much for her young age,* she determined after Lucinda plopped down next to her near the campfire Private Davis had started. The boys curled up next to her. Harriett had experienced hardships in life, but she hadn't had the kind of physical abuse Lucinda received and it was plain to see what wasn't said was physically showing on Lucinda.

It ain't so far-fetched to think we still could all die of the pneumonia, Harriett thought. Haden was too quiet to suit her.

"It won't be long now until we reach camp," Private Davis said to the women before he left to look for dead limbs. "There's a hot meal waiting!" With a cheerful note for the women to think on, he started scouting for shelter material.

Ted was already in pursuit of some small trees lying on Mother Earth's dark floor. After hearing several sneezes from the kids, Sis jumped up and offered help in gathering extra wood needed for their shelter.

"Three could do a better job faster," she told the worn-out family. She ran in the direction Corporal Dean had taken.

Shadows cast by a dim campfire mixed with look-alike branches moving about on the trees in the night air posed a problem to navigate through. Sis saw Ted just ahead of her. Groping a few more yards through the trees, she called out, "I can help get some wood too, if you hold up a minute."

"I know you could use another set of hands and arms to carry branches back." The offer was innocent enough, but both sensed an intimate opportunity hidden by the darkness.

"That's all right with me, but be sure to keep close or you could get lost out here," he half-jested.

"Bad enough trying to keep tabs on Gus, I don't want to have to go looking for you," he laughed. As soon as he finished giving Sis a warning, she tripped over some wiry native-ivy. Grabbing for anything to stabilize herself, she caught Ted's arm with both hands.

Corporal Dean swung around to break Sis's fall with one arm around her waist. Her weight from the momentum of her fall pulled Ted forward and they both crashed to the ground. He quickly got up and assisted Sis, miscalculating his movement and ending up closer than he had intended. Silence between them was as embarrassing as their position. Neither wanted to say anything, but neither of them wanted to be the first to step back either.

Ever so gently, he increased the tension of his arm about her waist, nudging her even closer to see what reaction he would get. Sis let go of his arm to reach up and stroke the side of his face, gently caressing him. After long gazes, silently looking, with his other hand he took her fingers to his lips and kissed her hand softly. Still looking for reactions from the shadowy face before him, her eyes were veiled in darkness. Good sense was replaced with naked emotion each had desperately fought to rein in during the trip. Opportunistic moments presently teased both of them. Neither felt hobbled any longer by propriety demanded from the eyes of others or from their own weakened dictates. They carelessly abandoned all at this moment.

It was dark. They were alone. Who would know? Who would it hurt if they didn't know? The inky black prevented discovery and both were keenly aware moments such as this would never come again. They gave themselves permission to proceed.

Ted removed his arm from around her waist and cupped her face with both his hands. Aided by muted moonlight, he saw her wanting eyes dimly yearning for satisfaction.

A replacement of Sis's past memory was an unknown and not anything he could fathom. After what seemed an eternity, each could feel the other's heart beating as he moved slowly toward her face touching his lips to hers. His kiss was tender, warm and had been given with an eager promise. There was no concept of retreat for him at this point.

She melded responsively to his embrace as he gently laid Sis on the cold ground without uttering a word. Voices would interfere and could support sinking consciences. Pushing every ethic aside, neither of them felt anything but the heat of passion for the other, for the moment.

When the lovemaking had come to an end, Ted helped Sis up and both started to catch up to the task they were there to do in the first place. Awkwardly, both were lost for words. Actions had been indelibly recorded. Nothing could erase them. They did silent duty, both reeling with disbelief at what had just happened! Each mind replayed the searing memory while they busied themselves picking up felled tree branches. This moment had come and gone so quickly. A one-time thing, only one time, but the ramifications it could bring began to mentally seat for a much longer period. Enough chance had been taken that no more could be dared again. The risk was too great. It was a one-time thing.

Jim had returned with an armful of long branches denuded by winter. Ted brought his bundle in and laid it down while Sis trailed after him carrying her load. She also carried guilt along with the wood for the three-sided shelter. John's image hung in a heavy cloud before her intensifying guilt feelings.

No matter the commotion the adults made by weaving branches and leaning them next to the raft for shelter, the children were lost in sleep huddled together to aid in the warmth the little campfire provided. Scratchy corn sacks were overlapped to mimic a burlap coverlet. Lastly, Jim and Ted made their way into the shelter's protection. Body heat helped spread warmth by their closeness but memories belonging to two people in the crude shelter helped expand more heat than their share.

John and Mattie Holmes. John was said to have a bad temper.

Chapter 24
BORROWED TROUBLE

Ever since Jasper sent his rations with Corporal Dean for the family at Fort Smith, he began helping himself to John's clothing, whether John approved of it or not. John found no humor when his socks were missing, or a shirt, from his brother's continual mooching. Repeatedly he was told to let well enough alone, to do extra duty for somebody to get what he needed. The trouble with that was, nobody had any extras.

"Do, what you have to do, Jasper, just stay outta my duds! I can't never find a thing and I don't have to think twice to figure where it's gone to," he scolded his older brother.

Ingrate, Jasper thought. He was totally disgusted by trying to help John out. He knew his younger brother would have been in a heap of trouble with that girl. But no sooner had the dispatcher left camp for Fort Smith did John hoof it to Tina's side.

It always was a mystery to Jasper why John was so selfish. As his big brother, he had done what he thought was in John's best interest by getting that camp whore off his back. What was more disgusting to him, his mother happened to be John's mother, too. *And there ain't been a thing a'comin' from you for the folks.* John's continual self-centeredness and lack of concern for anybody else galled Jasper. John owed him one, the way he figured it.

"John might be the best looker of us boys but he sure ain't got it where it counts!" Jasper lamented out loud after John left him from another scolding.

James and Shelby were bunking in quarters across the big camp away from John and Jasper. They were on reconnaissance most of the time. Both of them had added a little to the pouch of things sent to the family, but John never had any money left after giving it to Tina for certain favors.

Jasper was stripped. He had given until it literally hurt. His cold feet had no socks. "After all I done for you, John. We are brothers, you know," he had told him when he got caught pilfering John's trunk. John ignored him.

195

Instead of borrowing a pair of socks from John without asking this time, Jasper decided he was going to ask for a change. His boots were rubbing blisters on his sockless feet but the winter cold made his toes numb. When Jasper went into his barracks to ask John about the loan, only snickers came from his tentmates after inquiring where his absented brother was.

Finding no satisfaction from anyone about John's whereabouts, Jasper went looking for him. He checked the stables first, but no one was there other than the horses bedded down for the night. Then he went in an opposite direction over the hill back of the stables. That's when he heard it.

Tina giggled from inside the rations shed across from the wagon yard. Jasper had no doubt it was Tina and there was no doubt what was causing her to giggle either. No one had rights into that shed but Tina's Ma and it was too late for her to be in there for foodstuff.

Standing outside the shed was another man eavesdropping on those inside. Jasper stopped to see what was going on when the shed door opened and the soldier with Tina came out. From the reaction of the eavesdropper, fury must have consumed him due to the force of his attack against the emerging soldier. *I swear he fights like John!* Then he heard John's voice.

"Can't that little tramp stay true to nobody?" John blurted out before lighting into Tina's new interest. John apparently had ignored his own personal obligations to remain faithful.

When Jasper questioned John about Sis, after the first time he had been with Tina, he swore a reply. "Hell, who knows if I will even be here tomorrow, let alone be able to be a husband again?"

"Sis is at Fort Smith, I reckon. Tina, you are here at DuVall's Bluff," he had once reasoned in the beginning with a lost waif who had not much interest in explanations anyway. Wife or not, the thoughts of Sis were not on his mind when he had the temptation with Tina available.

"Yeah, this camp-trouble is with every tomcat and now she's added Owen Leaven to the list," Jasper whispered. Then Jasper watched John beat the daylights out of Owen after Tina had led him out of the shed, continuing to flirt with him while tucking her blouse back in her skirt. It was at that precise moment John chose to land one on Owen, taking him completely by surprise.

"When I get through with you," John grunted, after connecting to Owen Leaven's glass jaw, "you will ask permission the next time a urge hits ya!" John began to pummel Owen's face, rendering him harmless in short order.

Tina screamed and ran toward the tent quarters. The duty-guards heard the fracas and came running toward the ration shed. Jasper started to join them but thought better of it when he saw the guards grab John and march him toward the stockades.

Owen Leaven lay on the ground unconscious. Blood was dripping from his mouth and nose when he was lifted onto a stretcher en route for the infirmary tent.

Tina, in the meantime, was delivered to her mother's tent with reports of her involvement in the fracas.

After Tina's mother had been told of the fight, she promptly slapped Tina in the face.

"Don't you know, Tina, your sisters and me depend on my cookin' job? You are a'goin' to ruin it for the whole lot of us!" She slapped her again. Tina's mother knew things had gotten completely out of hand with her daughter. She had tried to ignore her fiascos but the possibility they would have to leave the camp due to Tina's escapades was a stark reality now, she feared.

After John had been arrested and Owen carried off on a stretcher, Jasper finally got up enough courage to go to one of the guards in charge of the stockade to ask permission to speak to John.

"No, private. Move out!" the guard ordered.

Without much luck there, Jasper decided he needed to see if Shelby and James were back from reconnaissance duty. He hadn't talked with either of them for several days. Jasper knew they wouldn't be happy with the news he was bringing them, but it would only be a little time before they heard about it anyway. News of the hot dispute over Tina was already buzzing in camp and the incident hadn't had time to get cold yet.

Shelby and James were not in their quarters. They hadn't returned, according to some of the men in the next tent. Not having any luck finding help, Jasper decided to try once more to see if he could talk the guard into letting him visit John. He needed to know what was going to happen to his brother and felt pretty sure John already knew.

Jasper was glad John hadn't killed Owen. He certainly was mad enough to have killed him. Thoughts of a firing squad taking care of Army justice if Owen should die infringed on Jasper's common sense. *He only gave 'em a good lickin',* Jasper told himself.

The guard had just sat down to roll a smoke when Jasper came up. It wasn't the same person who had been there earlier. Apparently, the first guard in charge had turned over the duty to this soldier and then left. After rolling his cigarette and lighting it, the guard looked up at Jasper approaching. He eyed Jasper keenly to see if he were reason enough for concern, if it would be necessary to get to his feet. The assessment made, he determined Jasper to be harmless and continued blowing lazy smoke rings from the big drag he had taken into his lungs.

Reaching out in a handshake, Jasper said, "Looks like we had a bit of excitement here tonight, didn't we?"

Before the guard had time to respond to his question, Jasper sat down on his heels to be eye level with the guard so as not to appear to be menacing or threatening in any way. The guard relaxed his stare and sucked on his cigarette before he spoke from the opposite side of his mouth.

"Damned near killed Owen Leaven. I've heard John Holmes had a temper, all right, but, man, I hear this was the beatenest thing you ever saw! They tell me Owen was out cold and was being beaten to a pulp even in his unconscious state," the guard continued. Guess this ole boy is headed for the prison in Little Rock in the morning. We sure can't keep him in the stockade here. What did you say your name was?"

Jasper shifted his weight to the other leg in his squatting position. "I am John Holmes' brother, Jasper Holmes," he said with an outstretched hand. Jasper didn't know what to expect from the guard but he was prepared to leave again.

"Well, if you ask me," the guard said shaking Jasper's hand, "I think that little trollop has caused enough trouble in this here camp. We need our fightin' men but, with the likes of her, we are fightin' the wrong enemy. This wasn't the first fight that has happened since she came."

Jasper was not expecting his remark. Taking advantage of the guard's mindset, he asked if he could please visit with his brother for only a few minutes. He then reminded the guard it would be impossible to see him in the morning.

"You got anything on ya?"

"No, sir, not even a pocket knife."

"You look harmless enough to me, Private Homes," he said nodding his head to enter the tent.

Jasper got up quickly and went in the stockade tent before the guard had a chance to change his mind or for anyone else to come by that could counter this opportunity.

John was sitting on the ground with his feet hobbled in a wooden stocks. When he looked up at his brother it was obvious by the look on his face Jasper was the last person he expected to see.

"Well, bud, now you went and really done it!" Jasper greeted.

"You can bet that son-of-a-bitch really deserved what he got," John snapped defensively. The stocks hadn't improved John's temper. In fact, the miserable stocks confining John made him even madder, he just was unable to do much of anything about it. What might be in store for him hadn't really jelled yet. He was still fuming over Owen Leaven beating his time with Tina.

John's early beginnings on a houseboat hadn't done a whole lot for his social skills. Even though he was the dandy of the family, John hadn't been exposed to interactions with others outside family and he tended to think on his own terms.

"I hear you are a'goin' to be taken to Little Rock in the mornin'. Guess you are headed for the prison there until they can decide what to do with you, John. You'se apt to be court-martialed."

For the first time, John gave notice to what his brother was telling him. It didn't seem right that he should have to be in such trouble for taking care of his own honor and for that thief, Owen Leaven to get off free. Still feeling more belligerent and stuck, John responded, "Oh, hell, who cares!"

"Well, it don't appear you are too concerned, John. Maybe you oughtta be?" John didn't answer his brother. He sat bolted in his confinement and stonily stared into space.

"James and Shelby ain't back yet from the field," Jasper finally said. "When they get back, we'se a'goin' to have to get together to see if there's somethin' we can do to get you out of this mess. We will do our best to come up with somethin', John, but for the likes of me, I don't know what in tarnation that will be right off hand. I ain't a'goin to be able to see you tomorrow. We'll see what we need to do to get them charges reduced so's you can get back here."

"Do what you can, Jasper."

"John, just between you and me, I feel a little like you do about Owen Leaven. He has rubbed me wrong ever since he got here. I might'a thought a'doin' what you did if I could conjure up a cause."

Just the mere mention of Owen's name made John draw a fist and pound the ground as if reliving the episode responsible for this mess.

"John, I don't know where in the world you have been but don't you know that Tina is used by everybody around?" Jasper's question provoked a red-faced John to look at him but before he could make any comment, Jasper continued what he wanted to say.

"Now, you get holt of yourself, settle down and listen for once. You need to control yourself or you are never a'goin to get out of that prison in Little Rock. It would be right smart to apologize for your actions, no matter how much it eats at your craw. I know the officers know that these things happen and if you play along with a cool and level head, you might just save yourself some real big worries down the road. That road starts tomorrow, by the way. They will probably dock you some pay and that will be the end of it if you don't go and get yourself into more trouble. The guard told me you weren't the first person that got into it over that tramp."

The tent flap opened and the guard motioned for Jasper to leave. He got up and headed for the exit.

"Remember what I told you, John, When James and Shelby get in we will do what we can. In the meantime, whatever you do, just get along with the folks in charge. If you don't, I doubt if we'll ever see you again." With that last remark, Jasper left the stockade tent and headed for his own quarters.

Early morning began with John shackled and set astride a horse with three soldiers accompanying him to Little Rock. Jasper watched as they rode out. Watching them ride out of sight, frustration overtook Jasper and he kicked the ground with his boot, which still housed a sockless foot. The more he thought about his brother going to Little Rock for discipline, the more he thought about retaliation. He never liked Owen Leaven in the first place. It seemed to Jasper, Owen must have come from some money and he had lorded it over the rest of them from the very first day he came into Duvall's Bluff. Jasper could remember as a child the time the townspeople ordered his family to move on down the river. He saw his independent Pa do what they said to do, move on down the river. Owen brought to mind a former time. It left a bad taste in Jasper's mouth.

It's that fancy carpet sack he carried into the quarters a'givin' him comeuppance over everybody, most especially me. Owen Leaven ate at Jasper. All Jasper could think of was a pair of socks and here he had a carpet sack filled to the brim with things. What those things were, Jasper wasn't quite sure, but the carpet sack added to his snobbish ways and rubbed the former river brat wrong. It rubbed him as raw as that blister growing on his heel.

When John rode off to Little Rock, an empty spot was left in his place as far as the older brother was concerned. *Maybe some more behind-the-barn tricks might be the thing to teach Owen Leaven not to mess with the Holmes brothers, John,* he secretly promised his shackled brother.

All day, the more he thought about what could happen to his brother, the hotter Jasper got. He was mad at Tina too. However, his mad at her was being satisfied as news was circulating, Tina had to go. She was too young to take out on her own so that meant her mother, the camp cook, would have to leave too. Tina and her mother had come of their own free will. It was to their benefit as well as to the camp's to have Tina's mother cook. But, Tina had come with the package along with two younger sisters too young to get into mischief like Tina had from the first day they came. The camp commander had his fill of the trouble she had caused his men. Time was up. Tina had to leave.

Now, as for Owen Leaven, he left the infirmary the next morning after John had been taken to Little Rock. His face was the worst for wear, causing embarrassment over the beating he took. It didn't do a lot for the image he wanted portrayed. He managed a way to overcome talk. Arrogantly, more obnoxious than he had been before his sound beating, he strutted around as if a medal hung on a wounded hero rather than a defeated foe. After all, it was John who was incarcerated, exonerating him from smear or talk of his sleazy trip with Tina to the rations shed. It was hard enough for Jasper to take Owen's inflated importance, but this masquerader was pushing it too far now!

John had hardly been gone two weeks when Jasper had an accident and needed to change his shirt. Carelessly, he had caught his shirt on fire helping cook since Tina's mother had left. He got burned a little and left for the infirmary first to get ointment for his chest before going back to his quarters to change into the one other issue left. No one was in the quarters when he got there.

Jasper opened the trunk at the foot of his cot and pulled out a wrinkled shirt. He looked at the relatively empty compartment, which contained no socks. "How foolish I was to send all of 'em!"

After buttoning the last button of his wrinkled shirt, he looked to see if his cot would pass inspection by visually comparing his to the rest in the quarters. Satisfied, he casually glanced toward Owen's cot and saw the carpet sack tucked beneath it.

Temptation overtook Jasper to just take a peek inside to see what that rich boy had in it. After all, what could it hurt to look?

Quickly pulling it from beneath the cot, he unlatched the latch and opened it up. Jasper's eyes fell on a wonder: a beautiful gold watch, a Hunter's case watch atop neatly folded shirts, three of them. He moved the shirts ever so slightly to see a pair of long underwear, then, there they were! He saw two pairs of socks on top of some handkerchiefs stacked on a portfolio. While reaching into the bag to touch the watch, Jasper decided to pull things out onto the cot to get a better look. About the time he did, he heard voices of two men walking toward the tent. There wasn't time to stuff everything back into the carpet sack and retreat. He grabbed all the contents and threw them into his opened locker shutting the lid, then stood beside his cot just as Owen and Private Router walked in.

Bruised and arrogant, Private Leaven went to his cot and bent over to retrieve a fresh shirt himself from his carpet sack. He looked to see if he had the right cot. Could he be disoriented beside bruised? A monotonous row of cots can fool you, he thought consoling himself. But it was only his face messed up, not his orientation. There was no carpet sack under his cot! He called out to Frank Router, his companion, and asked him if he had seen his carpet sack. Router gave Owen a negative reply. Jasper busied himself by smoothing out his blanket atop his cot. After he had finished he started to leave. Owen, by this time, was pretty agitated and had yelled something about a thief having been in their tent.

Jasper knew it was too late to return that carpet sack. No one would ever believe it wasn't an intentional thing to throw it into his locker. His brother had rearranged Owen Leaven's face and if John was capable of that and ended up incarcerated, who would believe Jasper had no ill intent? Too many people were gathering in their tent trying to see what Owen was yelling about for him to leave. Jasper was stuck.

I'll have to wait it out until everybody gets out of here before I can put that stuff back. All I need now is for Owen Leaven to have his revenge on John by gettin' me into trouble.

Sergeant Brock came for inspection immediately after someone reported thievery. All the footlockers were opened up including Jasper's. Owen's shirts had been thrown on top of Jasper's meager contents but nothing was detected unusual until Sergeant Brock saw the corner of a red carpet sack sticking out from under the sleeve of a government-issued shirt in Jasper's locker.

"What have we here?" he questioned. The sergeant reached down and pulled the carpet sack out.

"This look familiar, Private Leaven?"

"Damned sure does! I had a Hunter's case watch too, couple pairs of socks, some underwear, and a handkerchief my mother gave me laying on top of my portfolio," he told the sergeant.

"Looks like some of what you said is here, but I see only one pair of socks in the whole locker. Are you sure there were two pairs?"

Jasper knew his red face was going to give him away. *I've had it! Ain't no gettin' out of this! There the stuff is, everybody is a'gawkin'!*

The former river brat turned soldier was blocked from leaving the tent when Sergeant Blocker and other bunkmates came into the quarters and stood by the tent flap. He couldn't leave now.

"Holmes, isn't this your trunk?" Jasper was ordered to take a look. Jasper knew it was hopeless since he had shoved a pair of Owen's socks into his pocket—the pair that was missing.

Why did I stick 'em in my pocket? Ain't the smartest thing to do, I reckon, gonna convict me on the spot! Maybe the sergeant won't notice. If he didn't see me put Owen's stuff in my trunk, maybe he will figure there's a chance somebody else did it? Jasper tried not to break a guilt sweat and use the circumstantial evidence ploy. Conviction for theft would have to have factual evidence. About the time Jasper began to think his way out, the sergeant said, "Holmes, what's that in your pants pocket? Empty your pockets for me, private," he ordered.

Jasper reached inside his pocket, retrieved the pair of socks and tossed them on his cot. Owen identified them as his and Jasper found himself in the same position John had been several weeks ago. Circumstantial evidence had become factual, laying right there on Jasper's cot. He too became a detainee at the stockade tent. Jasper had been caught red-handed.

"Some help you are a'gettin' John out of the brig," Shelby said. He and James were able to visit their brother when they heard serious charges about court-martial pending for Jasper. They were told he would be leaving with an entourage for Little Rock in the morning.

"Now that this here war is about done over with, you and John go and get yourselves in a heap!" James fussed at Jasper. Jasper was the last person they expected to be in such a fix.

"What are we a'goin' to do, Shelby?" James asked.

He hung his head resignedly while speaking slowly. "Damned if I know."

"Jasper, why in the world did you mess with Owen Leaven? John got into enough trouble with that worthless sorry excuse of a man and now you have somethin' worse agin' you. Ain't no doubt about it, you'se a'goin' to get yourself court-martialed. The evidence was right in your pocket!" Shelby scolded his brother, in awe of his stupidity.

"No doubt it weren't too smart, Shelby, but I really hadn't meant to do what I did, if that makes any difference. I just took a look at that smart aleck's carpet sack and meant to put everything back. No one was around. I really just took a look, Shelby. But, then those guys started a'comin' in the tent and I knowed they'd be a'thinkin' what wasn't so, that' I was a'stealin' and not a'lookin'. I just grabbed the stuff and threw it in my open locker and closed it quick-like, before

I had to do some explainin'. I didn't have no chance to put it back. Who in the world would believe me if I told them what was really a'takin' place?"

Shelby put his arms around his younger brother. "Bud, you and me has seen some hard times. I think you are a'goin' to see more of 'em. I will do what I can, Jasper, but just like you told me what you said to John, I dunno what in the world it is a'goin' to be. There was four of us when he came in here and now there's only me and James left. You gotta take what's a'comin' to you, Jasper. It appears you done got caught red-handed, no matter what your story is. Ain't nothin' I can do for you right now. I don't believe that sorry Leaven is a'goin' to let you go until somebody pays dear for what John done to him. You are just as likely to catch his mad as John. You got yourself a double load, Bud."

The brothers shook hands and, with those last prophetic words Shelby had told his younger brother, the boys bade each other farewell.

Jasper left much like John had early the next morning for Little Rock Union Prison. It was like a scene played once before, only the main character was Jasper this time, not John. Jasper's humiliation was visible when he saw the guard who was on duty the night he visited John look his way. Jasper dropped his head and refused to look at him any more as they rode out.

Chapter 25
DESTINATION, DUTY, DISINTEGRATION

T ed was up first. Then Private Davis and Harriett emerged from the raft and tree-limb shelter. The older girls following close behind. Three kids cuddled closer together after the adults left.

"We are going to get started early," Corporal Dean said, while kicking dirt and snuffing out embers left from the campfire.

"Come on, children, we have to leave," Harriett called to her cold and hungry family. She reached for Mary limp with sleep. Gus and Haden sat upright and stared blankly for a minute before getting to their feet.

"Mama, I'm hungry. We ain't eat nothin' for a long time but that old jerky and I'm all out hungry," Gus complained. Both Mary and Haden looked at Harriett as if their looks would repeat what their older brother had said.

"I know, son, it's been lean. Just think, we'se a'goin' to be in camp later on today and you will get somethin' to eat. It won't be no jerky neither! Come on, we need to get a'goin'."

"But, Mama, Mama," Mary cried.

Harriett took Mary by the hand and led her through a thicket behind the makeshift shelter. The boys managed their own pressing solution, each pulling their corn sack around them tighter as they walked. Mary's sack barely caught around one shoulder and dragged the ground behind her.

Lucinda and Sis helped the soldiers untangle and dismantle the raft shelter. As soon as Harriett and the children returned from the thicket the four of them started dragging it in the direction of White River.

Ted and Jim's fortitude was wearing thin. With energy all but spent, the only hope was to keep moving before they froze to death or died of starvation. Knowing soothing relief was on the other end encouraged their overtaxed stamina to move yet a little further.

If they didn't, they'd probably die.

Most of the morning slipped away as they pulled and tugged to get the raft past stumps, bushes, and trees growing too close together in places, causing detours and using up precious energy they could ill-afford to spare.

First sighting of the river was a welcome relief, slightly altered with dread. This river water looked swifter than the water moving in the Arkansas River. Fast-moving water would be more challenging and more risky to ford in a raft for able-bodied people. This party was physically weak but mentally determined.

Harriett assessed that her childrens' little hands would have to search for spots between log joints to grasp a bit of leverage if they were to keep from slipping off. If the raft spun out of control in the swift current it would not be inconceivable they could all be dumped and drowned. Pneumonia was calling each person's name, should they survive such an ordeal. Mary started whimpering.

"Whatcha fussin' for, Mary, it's Haden that likes to swim in the river," Gus teased his little sister and brother.

"It'll be easy, don't you worry none," he tried to console her, but Gus was whistling in the dark himself. His eyes were wide, not missing a thing, peering at each of the men working with the raft,. Gus calculated his elder brother status made him the man of the family. Bravery was expected and he made a stab at it. Wouldn't his older brothers do the same?

Ted and Jim roped two ends of the raft to the trunks of a couple of oak trees before attempting to put it into the water. After securing it with ropes, they pushed it into the river, cinching it back to butt against the bank so the women and children could get on. As soon as Sis boarded, Ted and Jim loosened the ropes and hopped onto the raft, pushing against the bank with both their feet while the rushing water twirled it into a spin with the long ropes dragging in the turbulence. Retrieving the cold and wet trailing ends, the men stretched the ropes to the opposite side of the raft, hitching them securely around the ends of logs so the occupants would have a better hand hold. It was a good idea but with wet and numb hands, the task was difficult. If the alternative weren't so frightening, the children would have declined to touch it.

Fear overrode misery and they clung on for dear life.

Sick from hunger and cold, they clung to the safety of the bobbing raft for about three hours judging by the sun. No one talked above a whisper in case there could be Confederate scouts snooping around back in the underbrush along the riverbanks.

Ted and Jim loosed the poles tied to the raft and pushed them away from low-hanging branches sweeping over the river like fingers ready to pluck the hapless crew off.

"We need to head for the south side, Jim," Ted told Private Davis. White

River had narrowed, with shallow spots allowing the men to pole from the bottom. Both soldiers used one pole to nudge closer to the bank, then pulled the pole back quickly before the current sucked it away from them. Repeated maneuvers finally got them to their destination of disembarkation.

Being as close to shore as they dared be, the men jumped with the loosened ropes. Left with out their safety rope, the rafter's hands sought handholds between water-soaked logs. Scrambling up the low bank, the men tied off the raft around two tree trunks and cinched it as close to shore as they could. To depart was all that was left to do to be rid of this heavy misery they had dealt with ever since leaving Fort Smith. None thought this day would ever come, but it had and now they were petrified as waves hit against the cinched and resistant raft.

Ted yelled, "Now!"

Gus, Haden and Mary scrambled off with the adults' help to steady them. Next came the girls, then Harriett. The old raft had been their lifesaver, miserable as it was, but for all the miles they had to drag it complaining about the impossible thing, they were most grateful these complaints belonged to the past. The corporal was right all along. They could never have reached Duvall's Bluff without it.

"Camp isn't too far, now, folks," Corporal Dean said. "We gotta keep moving." Both men were soaked from securing the raft and helping get the family members off.

Sis caught a glance from Corporal Dean, but that was all. He had lost the earlier, warm transparency often apparent during the difficult trip and had become the professional soldier once again. Corporal Ted Dean was the camp dispatcher now, back on duty, doing what he was sent to do in the first place when he left for Fort Smith. The corporal had a report to give. In the process, he also had saved some civilians in the line of duty during the awful overthrow. The former bargain he had made with Jasper had been a bit overextended. No one could have foreseen such. The possibility of getting Jasper's family to Duvall's Bluff would have been the last thing anyone would have thought about. Strange things happen in war.

Sis's guilt was mounting the closer she came to seeing John again. If it had been any other time, she never would have been deceitful to her marriage, she knew. Or, would she? She tried to tell herself it was the personal violation from the Bushwhackers that had left her feeling no man had value. At least, that was her thought until she saw Corporal Ted Dean and his manly and genteel ways gave rise to interest again. She had never been around a man with as much culture or one who knew how to treat a woman, giving her feelings of true value. Or, at least that is the way she had interpreted it at the beginning. If anyone ever needed uplifting, it was a violated woman who swore to have nothing to do with men again, husband or not. Where were those feelings now? What happened to that tender and caring touch, that personal touch saying things she needed to hear?

Something was lost in the corporal's unattached glance. New rivers of guilt thrashing around more than the watery challenge they just left were eating away with each step she took. One traveler going to the Union camp at Duvall's Bluff was trying to erase a memory while the other toyed with that memory, seeing it as an opportunity that could have only come once, and who was left surprised it had come to fruition.

Wayfarers sick with hunger, cold, and fatigue. God's heaven was sympathetically reluctant to gobble up the light of day before they reached camp. Harriett felt a lump coming in her throat and desperately fought tears at the first sight of it. Emotion refused to be constrained when she secretly allowed her resolve to surrender when they entered the grounds. She turned her head and wiped her face with her torn, dirty apron.

I'm right grateful to be here. I need to tell it to any spirit that's out there. I don't know if they really is such a thing, but somethin' must be. There's been plenty of times I could just as well been killed like my William. Why am I still here? It don't make no sense to me. I'se been brought by somethin' to my boys. I'm bound to see my boys soon. I thank ye, whoever you are.

Corporal Dean led the group to General Steel's headquarters to make his report about the seizure of Fort Smith before he introduced the civilians seeking shelter. The general ordered quarters for the civilians and assigned some provisions to replace their wet clothes.

Corporal Dean showed them their tent and left.

"Ma'am," a soldier called from outside their tent.

Harriett pulled the flap to the tent back, allowing more cold air to whip in the cloth shelter.

"I was asked to see to it you had some food for your family. Harriett took the pans of warmed-over gravy and cold biscuits from the soldier, thanking him for his kindness.

"You are welcome, ma'am, it was General Steele's orders, ma'am." The soldier informed Harriett.

Mary was so tired she almost forgot she was hungry, but she ate before flopping on the cot with many blankets covering her. The corn sack had been retired for the night.

Haden and Gus ate, but not as much as Harriett thought they would. Sleep had been more important even than food. Harriett knew her children had pushed as far as they could. After getting the boys settled, Harriett told Sis and Lucinda she couldn't retire just yet. "Girls, I have got somethin' I need to do. I will be back directly," she said and left the tent, pulling the corn sack back across her shoulders.

She saw the man responsible for their safety sitting around a campfire and made her way toward him. The men took notice of a woman and silenced their conversation.

"Hello again, Mrs. Holmes. Is there something I can do for you?"

"How can we ever thank you, Corporal Dean? I can't turn in until I tell you we are more than beholden to you. We thank you for the pains you took to get us here."

"I was only glad I could help you, ma'am. You people try to get some rest and we will get word to your sons about your arrival."

Not knowing who else to say her thank you to, she left the group of men. On her way back to her quarters, Harriett saw a messenger running toward the tired dispatcher. She overheard the messenger say, "Corporal Dean, sir, General Steele has fresh orders for you, sir. I believe you will be doing more duty in the morning, sir. He said you best get some rest so you can leave early." The private saluted and left Ted opening up the envelope to see his new assignment.

It was late. Getting to Duvall's Bluff had been so overwhelming that Harriett barely touched her cot before she fell into a deep sleep comforted by warm blankets. Lucinda was desperate to see Shelby but she too closed her eyes as soon as her frail body crawled under the covers. She could go no further.

Shelby and James pulled on their boots after being awakened with word of the family's arrival. Each grabbed their coat running out of the tent. Shelby had been crazy with worry over Lucinda and their new baby. Ted told him there had been no baby with them so Shelby was anxious to learn what happened to their baby, to his wife. Both men raced across camp. When they went into the tent, they found their motley-looking family in deep sleep. Harriett felt Shelby touch her on his way to Lucinda's cot.

Darkness made it difficult for him to see his wife's face but he could see her thin frame. Lucinda had lost so much weight he hardly recognized her. Tears stung his eyes thinking of the hardships responsible for his wife's condition but his imagination wasn't prepared to see what the ravages of hard times had done to her. Gently stroking Lucinda's hair he bent down and softly kissed her cheek. She never stirred. Shelby slid down on the ground next to his wife, leaned back against her cot and was determined to stay there until morning.

"Go on back and get some sleep, James. I think I'll stay here," he whispered to his brother. "I'll take care of the family and get them situated in the morning. You cover for me, will ya?"

James tiptoed out of the tent after making the rounds and kissing everyone there, even his sleeping sisters-in-law. He acknowledged little Mary had grown. So had Gus. He was sprawled out across his cot almost as big as a half-grown man now.

The night passed quickly for everyone but Shelby. He agonized over the suffering his family had gone through as he endured the sleepless night. He had too many questions haunting him to sleep. *What had happened to the baby?*

Mary sat upright on her cot when the bugler announced the morning roll call. It was still dark out. She rubbed her eyes and tried to make sense of her surroundings.

Harriett heard the trumpet but couldn't make herself open her eyes or move from the warmth of her cot. Necessity dictated bathing but that could wait. Clothes needed to be washed. That too could wait. Sleep, on the other hand, couldn't. Her body wasn't numb from cold anymore. It was warm, a small thing most took for granted, but it was something she relished.

Slit-type openings from her eyelids allowed a slight vision into the darkened tent. She knew Mary would be wanting to make it for relief as soon as she awoke, but Harriett thought if she could only keep her eyes shut for a little while longer, that too could be put off. The sneak preview of the morning through tiny openings rested upon the form of Shelby sitting next to Lucinda's cot. Harriett could tell even in the dimly lit tent made by an outside campfire blazing, her oldest son had a puzzled and worried look on his face. Lucinda was still sleeping. He sat patiently by her.

Since Mary was awake, Harriett knew she better take care of her morning need or she would wake everyone.

What in the world am I a'goin' to do with her now? The question hit her for the first time. She didn't know where the outhouse was. *Well, it's still dark enough, best look for a bush.* Grabbing for the wretched sacks again after hugging Shelby, she put one around Mary's shoulders and one around herself before they left to find bushes.

"It'll do for you, Mary, I'll wait til a privy is pointed out to me," she told her daughter on the way."

On their return, James had come into the tent. His entry woke the rest of the family. Lucinda saw Shelby and began to cry. They held each other close and the morbid tale of Shelby Robert's fate was told. Nothing else was said, only tender comfort pats mixed with sobs coming from both parents. The-gut wrenching loss damped their reunion.

James hugged everyone and, due to Lucinda's need of Shelby's comfort, James felt it was his job to report about John and Jasper. He dreaded doing so but he knew the family would be asking about the missing pair.

Sis was shocked to learn her husband had beaten a man so badly he was arrested. Anger expanded when she learned why it had happened—another woman! *And, to think I'se a'dreadin' to see him because I have a secret of my own! He's been havin' a time of it all along and hadn't bothered to wait for me neither!* Sis was not prepared to hear the news that James brought.

"I don't care if I never see him again anyway if that's what he did," she told James, feeling embarrassed that her husband had found a trollop to his liking. "I'm glad he ain't here!"

Then James told everyone about Jasper. This family knew it wasn't in Jasper's character to end up like this. Harriett couldn't understand but she knew there had to be more to the story then the one everybody was hearing. Prospects for their safekeeping in the camp were uncertain when she found out two of her four sons here were imprisoned at Little Rock. Harriett's heart sank. She knew she must talk with the General that Corporal Dean had introduced her to last night. *Oh, Canady,* she moaned inside.

The decision to speak to the camp commander was set. Harriett was disoriented in the maze of tents but determination forced her to retrace steps she barely remembered. She recognized General Steele's headquarters and, surprisingly, found that General Steele was most receptive to her visit.

"Actually, Mrs. Holmes, our cook will be leaving us and we will be in need of another. Do you suppose you might be interested in this position?"

The commander needed a camp cook. Harriett Holmes and her family needed shelter and there were two more able-bodied cooks that came with this woman. Boys in prison or not, she may be what he needed for the moment.

After saying little about the questions she had about her sons, General Steele continued in his vein of thought. "You and your children are welcome if you are interested in filling in, Mrs. Holmes. We need a cook, but we do have rules here. However, we're more flexible with civilians."

"You understand, Shelby and James may see you on their own time but duties are spelled out and there will be precious little of free time. We are in war, even if it appears it is about to conclude. I can't allow fraternizations or make exceptions," the commander said.

"We are awaiting official confirmation that this hellish war is over, but in the meantime there will be much clean-up need for a while. We need a cook, if you are interested?"

"I would be much obliged, General Steele. We will do the best we can if somebody can show us what is expected. My son's wives are as good a cook as me and you can count on us to do the job and thank ye for it," Harriett said sitting in front of an immaculately dressed general. Her dirty clothes and countenance resembled what people thought of boat people. That connection Harriett kept to herself but she wondered what her contribution had been in both her son's troubles.

General Steele reached across the desk and shook Harriett's hand in agreement. "Well, the job is filled as far as I am concerned, Mrs. Holmes. I'll have Private Woodard take you to the facilities and show you what you have to work with. He will give you the lowdown on supplies and so forth and what our procedures are. A supply shed houses all the foodstuffs and you will be the only person privy with that key. It is your responsibility to care for this key and for the inventory of the supply in the ration shed. Intruders won't be tolerated. We have a lot of men to feed, but you will have some help from those on duty to keep clean up a minimum for yourself."

With these instructions, General Steele stood and pulled back the tent flap for Harriett to leave with Private Woodard waiting outside. The general managed to sidestep her questions about her two sons.

Seeing she was not going to get any information concerning Jasper and

John, Harriett left the tent.

It's done settled. I'm the camp cook and the kids won't be a 'eatin' anymore of that jerky. They's a 'gettin' warm victuals from here on out, Harriett tried to convince herself while being taken to the rations shed and given the instructions for time frames needed to get the meals started. Thoughts of being among so many people were overwhelming, not to mention the work involved. If it weren't for necessity, Harriett knew she would never consider doing it. *There ain't no choice, I will just do it,* she finally convinced herself when they reached the rations shed.

Harriett was almost ready to run to the river again to escape the mess she had gotten herself into when she began the monumental job of cooking. She had never seen so much food to cook in her life. After several weeks, the tremors from stresses she carried to bed and got up with began to subside. She learned more what was expected of her and set her own patterns in order to achieve the expected duties.

Lucinda was getting some strength back. The kitchen chores were doing her good to ease her mind of the loss of Shelby Robert. That fateful episode had been told to her husband. There was another part that wasn't told and Lucinda continued to live with nightmares where monster Bushwhackers waited for her. Time was a good healer even if some changes remained ever permanent with no hope of recovery.

Sis, on the other hand, was sullen with a smolder beneath the surface for the three weeks since arriving. Her temperamental changes had begun just as Lucinda's did initially. Only Sis had some extra fuel for her emotional turmoil. For that she had no one to blame but herself. Her discontent festered to discover John's unfaithfulness, but her own dalliance gave her no right to be indignant over his philandering. It was a combustionable situation and Sis could see no way out of it.

During clean-up times, after the men had eaten, Harriett noticed Sis rarely talked. She had been the forward young woman of the two. *Ain't no doubt about it, John has a lot of mendin' to do with Sis and nobody can do it for him.*

After slab bacon had been cut and put on the hot griddle and both girls busied themselves setting up for the breakfast, Private Evan Jones approached Harriett.

"Ma'am, a dispatcher from Little Rock came in last night accompanied by a John Holmes. Isn't that your son, ma'am? Which one of these ladies is his wife?" he asked, looking at the women setting up for the line to come through.

"For some reason he wanted me to contact you to let you know he arrived in camp last night. He has some paperwork he needs to get cleared up at headquarters, but asked me if I could tell you of his arrival since I was coming this way."

Sis overheard the news after seeing the bacon needed turning when Harriett was occupied in conversation. She kept her hands moving as if they had minds of their own and needed personal attention. It helped to stay busy so the shake wouldn't be seen and she gripped the turning fork tighter.

Everyone knew Sis was "the wife of that guy who beat the living daylights out of Owen Leaven." There was also speculation about what might happen when John came back to camp. Some even had pending wagers about one expected turn of events or another.

"I guess you heard the private, didn't you Sis?" Harriett asked her sullen daughter-in-law. Sis didn't utter a word to answer Harriett's question. Her eyes spoke. They flashed loud and clear that she had overheard the message about her husband being back in camp. After the angry look, her eyes welled up and spilled over. She turned her back to conceal her emotion from Harriett.

"Sis, I don't rightly know what to say to you." Harriett put her arms around the troubled young woman.

"I done felt such a sting inside as you do right now from John's Pa and I ain't never told this to nobody before," she said. "You are the first 'un I ever told this to. Maybe it won't help much to tell it. I can tell you for sure, you can still make up and it will get better after a time."

Sis excused herself and ran to the edge of the camp not far from the grill they were cooking on. The camp had evidently been cleared right in the middle of a forest, making the periphery densely forested. Sis ran into the wooded area and let go of the acid in her stomach working its way out. She had been doing a lot of this lately. Looking a bit pale, she returned to the hot grill and continued to tend to the bacon, but the acrid smoke made her repeat the trip. She ran back into the forest.

Harriett turned the bacon before it burned with the turning folk Sis had thrown on the grill when she left. She was pushed for time to put biscuits on and to make pots of gravy from the bacon drippings. Lucinda hurried to help Harriett so breakfast would be ready when the men assembled for mess. While it was cooking, gathering men formed in lines while Lucinda and four other men assisted her, ladling out food.

"Sorry, Harriett," Sis said coming back to the cooking area. "I am upset at my stomach. Must have caught the flu. I think I need to lie down a bit or I will keep throwing up."

Sis headed for the quarters without saying anything else.

Harriett resolved she could clean up without Sis. It would take longer but it could be done. The fire in the stove needed stoking up for the dishwater and she reached for some more logs.

"It's a good thing you younguns is keepin' this wood bin full," Harriett told Gus when he came with a couple of short pieces. Haden and little Mary were trailing Gus. It was time for breakfast but this was their job and they could eat after the men did.

Big heavy pots of water were starting to heat up on the stove and Harriett fed two other logs Gus was carrying into the big iron cook stove. The last thing she and Lucinda had to do after cooking was to slick up the grill after washing tin plates and cups.

"Howdy," came a voice behind her. "Ma, it's me," John said before she could turn around.

All the disappointment and anger Harriett had dealt with earlier melted when she saw her son's face. Their hugs overcame frailty issues and the shameful news of John's dallying was lost to his mother for the time being. *He's alive. It could be worse. At least, this 'un is here. Canady, William and baby Shelby Robert ain't.* Harriett couldn't stay mad at her son for long because she had been forced to learn life was too uncertain. She had learned over the years how uncertain her life could be and when you are dead and gone it's over, she was sure. What a lost and empty thought!

"Where's Sis?" he asked.

"She ain't feelin' too well, the flu I think. She's laying down for a spell in our quarters. We are next to the last tent on the edge of the clearin'," she told him.

He already knew where the quarters were. That was the same place Tina's family had stayed. He also learned after leaving General Steele's office that Tina and the others were sent packing right after he was sent to Little Rock.

"Think I'll go and check on her," John said to his mother. "I have lots to tell you about Jasper but I will do that later," he said, turning toward the quarters where Sis lay fighting with waves in her stomach determined to break free.

Chapter 26

PRELUDE

John wasn't quite sure what he needed to say to his wife. *I ain't no fool, I know she has already heard the scuttlebutt. Oh, well, I will take it as it comes,* he thought, opening up the tent flap and going inside.

Sis opened her eyes when she heard the flap move. She saw John close the flap and she quickly shut her eyes, hoping he didn't notice she had opened them momentarily.

John walked toward his wife and sat down on the cot next to her. *I can't pretend he ain't here,* she admitted to herself and stared blankly at her husband. He bent down and kissed her lips, but his kiss was one of passion meeting a response of stone, cold and unmoving.

It had been a long time since she and John first made love in the forest where Shelby later built his new cabin. As far as she was concerned, she wanted it to stay that way right now. She wasn't interested in John and the memory would have to do.

John became more assertive, overlooking the fact Sis was pale and not feeling well. He put his arms around her limp, unresponsive body and kissed her passionately again. Sis's stony demeanor began to thaw. She could never refuse John, no matter how sick she felt, and at this moment old familiar reasoning struggled to replace recent history haunting her. Sick or not, she allowed a thaw to welcome John a little whether it made any sense or not. Nothing made sense anymore anyway. It made no sense: certainly not the animal who raped her, the crazy war where no neighbor could be trusted anymore, the death of innocents, even recent indiscretions Sis wanted to forget with Corporal Dean. She had to put it out of her mind. John could never know. He wouldn't understand her chosen actions or any act perpetrated on her, she was sure.

John was surprised at her initial coldness at first but he grew more confident with the responses he was getting from his wife now. Determined to partake of what rightly belonged to him, John noticed Sis had lost weight in some places, but gained a bit of weight in others. Compared to Lucinda, who was frail all over from what little he could see, Sis had gained weight in her chest. Of all places!

John had his woman with little ado. Months of not seeing Sis were on John's mind and her nausea was disregarded. There was no brig time for this and it was his right.

"You are beautiful, Sis," he whispered in her ear.

Sis felt sick again and grit her teeth. The last month, her attention and dread had growing affirmation when buttons on her blouse were increasingly strained from her changing form. Sis's fears were validated when John noticed, leaving her no doubt to possibly cogitate over.

It's a relief John got back and we made love, she thought. It's good to be on the safe side. John might be a rogue but he sure wouldn't understand anyone messing with his woman, be it Bushwhacker or corporal. Sis was assured of that much about John's nature. This incident might allow her to sidestep an impending nightmare.

"We need to get back over yonder to talk with Mama. I need to tell her about Jasper."

"What about Jasper?"

"You need to come too, I ain't a'goin' to tell it twice," John said, getting up.

"Give me a minute, John," she told her husband, brushing her hair, after washing her face in a government-issued pan. She picked up the empty pitcher for a refill on their way out.

Little Mary struggled carrying her log and her brothers managed two apiece from the woodpile. They were stacking their contributions next to the cook stove at the time John and Sis appeared. All three ran to meet their big brother. John roughed up the boys a bit and picked up Mary.

"My, but you've growed, little lady! You boys have put on a foot yourselves," he told his younger siblings.

"Hey, I need you to run along now so I can talk with Mama about some grown-up talk, all right? I'll fetch you later and we will have our talk," John said, trying to shoo the kids out of earshot.

"Boys, go find Shelby for me, will you? Make sure you get Lucinda too, but take Mary with you and don't you run off leavin her neither, you hear? You can come back and stack some more wood when you tell them I'm a'lookin' for them," Harriett told the youngsters.

When the children were too far away to hear, John began telling his mother about his older brother, Jasper. The very circumstance of their incarceration was a touchy subject with Sis standing right next to him. Reporting the news brought up things John would just as soon not be talking about in front of the two people that meant the most. It was an uncomfortable position but he had no choice. Jasper's trouble had a connection to John's dalliance but the news about Jasper had more serious consequences then John's problems.

Sis stiffened once more because of the reason Jasper chose Owen Leaven in the first place. To think her husband thought he had dibs on the camp whore, that he had reason enough to beat Owen senseless, was overwhelming and she turned to leave. John grabbed her arm.

"You have to hear this, Sis," he said sternly. She looked pale and bit her lip.

Harriett knew Jasper sent some supplies by the dispatcher to them but she didn't know to what extent her second son had sacrificed. She didn't know her son thought he could spare those socks, thinking he probably would get more military issue, but that it didn't happen. The actuality was, if he really had meant to steal things, he wouldn't have gone about it the way he did. A fluke with extenuating circumstances was orchestrated by an evil spirit circulating that fateful morning. Jasper's family name was smeared. He lost status in all eyes but those of his family because the world perceived this giver had become a taker. Didn't he borrow money from Private Horn to send to the family once before? The family knew better. Jasper was no taker.

Now John was reporting something about Jasper that sent shockwaves through Shelby, Lucinda, Sis, James and Harriett as soon as he began his story.

"Jasper is in a bad shape," John began. He was pretty puny when we left for Little Rock but his run-down condition was all it took when he's put in the cell. Most of them Rebs is nigh unto death in there with the dysentery. That's what Jasper's got."

Gasps of alarm came from the women. Shelby shook his head and grimaced. James stared vacantly as if leaving embodiment to fly spiritually to be with Jasper, trying to imagine how it was. *Hang on, big Bud. Hang on.*

Harriett pretty well knew what her son had done regardless of the charges. Hearing it come from John's mouth amounted to an admission on his part with Tina. It wasn't easy for him to tell this in the presence of his mother and wife but tell it he did.

Sis turned to go back to her tent without saying anything to anyone. John watched her go but continued to tell the rest of the story.

"That's the stinkinest place you ever seen! There's Rebs in them cells everywhere and my brother is rotting away in there with them! And, to make matters worse, more'n half of 'em are sicker than a cow bloated from sour mash! Ma, Jasper is one of 'em like that too."

As self-centered as John had been, he was openly distraught about his older brother. "He needs a doctor bad. Either they just ain't enough of them doctors around, or they don't want doctors in that place at all. Whatever the case is, I saw him a'goin' downhill. He is so full of the dysentery he can't raise up his head, much less get up. I tried to help keep him as clean as I could while I was there since they let me stay with him. They let me stay with him probably because he's damned near dead."

Panic struck in the hearts of all who heard John's report but much more so in his mother's. She had to do something, but what? Her son was dying. She had to do something! *Jasper, I ain't kept you from a fallin' off that houseboat in the rivers all this time, and nursed you from the fever and chickenpox, to see you go an die on me! Son, don't die. You ain't lived yet!*

"If it wasn't for a Reb named Aaron McCoy, I think Jasper would be dead already," John continued after the news sunk in. "He took care of him with me and told me he would still do it until Jasper could get some help, which I was aimin' to get him."

Harriett knew something had to be done for Jasper if nobody there was seeing to it that he had a doctor.

"He ain't no thief. He ain't got no business a'bein' in there," she said. "I'm a'goin' to him and you are goin' to have to take care of the younguns while I'm gone. Ain't nobody free to go but me and I'm grounded to this cook stove. You girls are a'goin' to have to take over for me. Lucinda, you get Sis to help you out. She can do it, puny or not. This is our only keep. The younguns and you have to eat. I need you to look after things so I can go to Jasper because, I'm a'goin'."

"John, how long can we afford to depend on a Reb to take care of Jasper?"

John hung his head and shook it. "I don't rightly know."

"I'm' sorry, Ma. I hate like hell to have to tell you but you gotta know. I ain't goin' to have a thing to help pay anybody to take you to Little Rock neither. I been docked pay and I hear my muster a'comin' to me will be took up in fines. There won't be a coin to help me start up again after we'se mustered out. I came in with nothing, and I damned well am a'goin out with the same! I can't send you without any money."

"I can't lose another son! I won't! John, you'se the one that did your part to get us in this mess! Now, do you think you can behave yourself long enough to give me some peace of mind when I do what I have to do?" Harriett let her anger show to her number three son. She would have done the same for him if he had been the one in need and he knew it, whether he liked what she had to say to him or not.

John's handsome face reflected his inborn stubbornness. He ducked his head. What his mother said was true but he didn't want to be told that. Most especially, he didn't want to hear it from his Ma.

Harriett put feelers out to the soldiers that she was looking for a ride to Little Rock if she could go the next time anyone had a space for her. She was able to leave with a wagonload of supplies two weeks after learning of Jasper's condition. Keeping sanity during the long weeks was accomplished by hard work, but it was during the night hours that memories of Jasper from different ages played in her head and tormented her heart.

The camp commander allowed Harriett to ride on the supply wagon but with a warning that it would be a rough trip. "There will be no unnecessary stops." She would have to make do until they got there.

After hearing the warning, Harriett knew he was understating the conditions of the trip. To men, it is one thing to be called rough, but in a woman's talk it was more than he described. She told herself if she could endure such a trip as they had from Fort Smith to Duvall's Bluff, she could make it to Little Rock on the supply wagon. She had a habit of doing what she set her mind to do. The words, *You can do 'er, Harriett,* shouted in her heart. She had to do it. Jasper needed her.

The soldiers driving the supply wagon were given orders to take a special dispatch to the cook in charge of the mess at Little Rock. General Steele requested Harriett's keep, to see to it she had plenty of food and lodgings to sustain her while on her mission. It wasn't an official order, but it was one the cook would be glad to oblige. He did that and more—he provided her with his own small room off the kitchen with a cot.

Word had filtered into Duvall's Bluff that Private Jasper Holmes was in too bad a condition to withstand any sort of trial. Dysentery was taking its toll on many prisoners, Jasper being one of them. It was an epidemic, something of grave concern. So far, Jasper's name had not been listed among the dead. Only a miracle could change the likelihood.

Chapter 27
CONSEQUENCES

Lucinda and Sis spent a week doing the chores lined up for them while overseeing the whereabouts of the children. Caring for children had been an extra burden added to their complete responsibility of preparing food for the soldiers. Both girls had the youngsters doing errands, saving them some steps, but more often than not that ended up delaying processes more than helping. Wood for the stove they could handle, even if it took many trips. That served two purposes, keeping tabs and wood for the stove.

During off duty times, Shelby stayed with Lucinda. Sis often agreed to look after the kids to give them time together. Loss of Shelby Robert was still quite raw for Lucinda and she recounted the episode over and over to Shelby as if the repeating of it would remove it from being. The vision of flames licking around the fallen ceiling timber atop the cradle wouldn't go away, no matter how many times she shared the horror with her husband.

Shelby's time he had with his wife far outweighed John's and it wasn't to John's liking. It was okay with Sis. She lived with an upset stomach and would rather take care of the kids.

"Arent you puttin' on a little extra?" John made mention of Sis's weight gain after Lucinda had come back to the mess tent. She couldn't help overhearing what John said to his wife.

Sis didn't answer her husband.

"It 'pears to me the cook is takin' freedoms with the grub, Lucinda" he verbally poked again at his wife.

"At least you ain't a heavin' your heels like you done after you got here. Maybe you might ought to see to it them kids gets more to eat 'stead of thinkin' so much about yourself?" John was half serious but half curious too to see Sis's reaction. She had not been a bit responsive to much of anything he said lately.

Lucinda looked at her brother-in-law in disgust. She knew his poking barbs were generated by his own frustrations. Although Lucinda had not been privy to any of Sis's secrets with Corporal Dean, she had believed there was more than eye glancing between them on their trip from Fort Smith. For the likes of her, she couldn't imagine where or when anything could have possibly taken place, however.

Morning sickness was no stranger to Lucinda. She was positive Sis didn't have the flu. Sis had been acting poorly even before John came back from Little Rock. Sis was beginning to show.

John had suspicions something had taken place in his absence. How or who he wasn't so sure of. If he were wrong and misjudged her, he would only open up Sis's temper tantrums again about his dalliances. John was becoming a desperate man watching Shelby and Lucinda's life take up where it left off before they joined the cavalry at Fort Smith. He couldn't say the same for his and Sis's married life.

A few more days of the same daily routine dragged by. Lucinda was positive Sis was pregnant. Finally, she got the courage to ask her. "You are pregnant, aren't you Sis? I know the signs and I think John is beginnin' to suspect so too. How could you be showing so fast if it is John's?" she confronted her sister-in-law.

Sis began to cry. Lucinda tried to hush her up in case John happened by but Sis's tears wouldn't stay put.

"I'm three months pregnant as best I can tell," she blurted out. "Maybe more, I ain't sure." Sis's voice trailed off when she said, "It might be the Bushwhacker's, or—." Her words were interrupted with her apron pressed to hide her face in grief.

"I'se watchin' for signs myself too, Sis. I'se a'feared the same could happen to me too but, but I'm all right," Lucinda said. "Sis," she added, "you are a'dodgin' somethin', I can tell. It can't be anybody else's, could it? Who else could it be? When?"

There was no saving face now. Sis had no hopes of keeping her life going with John like Lucinda had with Shelby.

"It was something that just happened," she finally confessed. We'se caught off guard and before common sense got a holt of us it was too late. We ain't got nothin' in common ceptin' bein' lonely. It weren't nothin' to start with, just bein' kind like to one another and one thing led to another."

"Oh, my, Sis! John will kill you when he finds out! It will be hard for him to handle knowin' the Bushwhackers got at you, but this! This is somethin' else!" Lucinda was dumbfounded and after trying to soak in what Sis had told her she asked, "Have you told John what happened to us at home?"

"No." Sis did a double-take after feeling badly concerning her pregnancy. She spoke in her defense.

"He gets himself thrown in the brig for a'stompin a man to a pulp cuz that man beat him out with a whore and because of it all Jasper is a'dyin' in Little

Rock as I speak! I don't know how he can go a'judgin' me with that a'starin' him in the face! Sis, he ain't got a penny to leave out on because of his folly. He ain't got no right to go a'judgin' me," Sis said indignantly.

"I know, I know, Sis. Whatever will we do? John will not take this very calm. I know he won't no matter who he has slept with. Even Shelby might be a problem for me. I am afraid for him to find it out about them Bushwhackers too. He's dealin' with enough from losin' Shelby Robert."

"I'm afraid John will get shut of me. He is such a hot head. I would do anything if I could make it different, but it ain't gonna happen," Sis cried.

Unexpectedly John walked up behind Sis during her last sentence.

"What would you make different if you could?" he asked.

Sis started scraping on the griddle and refused to look at John. Before she had time to say anything, Lucinda spoke up.

"John, life has been pert near as hard as you can imagine since you boys left. It has been hard on women to carry on without their men folk around. That was hard enough but there's some things you and Shelby don't know," she said.

"What in tarnation you talkin' about woman? What things don't Shelby and I know?"

"You know about our Shelby Robert." Lucinda started crying before she finished telling John about their ordeal. Sis broke into the conversation when Lucinda couldn't get the words out just yet.

"Before the house was set on fire, John, those damned Bushwhackers had their fun with Lucinda and me. Now, I am pregnant!" Sis blurted out.

"That's why I have been growin out and it ain't been because I was takin' more'n my share of grub neither."

John looked stunned. He stared at his wife's face then looked at her growing middle. His expression went from stunned to red and then his forehead furrowed.

Sis and Lucinda watched John and said no more. They waited, expecting the worst from Sis's stinging confession. Sis saw her husband's eyes narrow. From the look on John's face, what Sis had told him was the last thing he expected to hear. This was the reason for her coldness. Or was it?

"I knowed you, Sis. You can't tell me you didn't ask for it a little bit!" A cold look and stony spirit drank in Sis's form standing in front of him. Piercing blue eyes sent a message designed to leave an imprint on Sis's heart. Compassion eluded John when he considered he was the husband of damaged goods. It was damaged because there was a calling card growing inside his wife, which would be a reminder to him for the rest of his days. He was incapable of feeling beyond himself so he turned and walked away.

"It's over," she said after John left.

Lucinda came closer to Sis and put her arms around her sister-in-law. She was worried herself.

"You can bet John won't let me tell Shelby my own way about what happened now," she told Sis. "I hope Shelby won't be as hard on me as John was you, Sis. I am so sorry."

By nightfall, all the anger Sis had about John's self-righteousness had about flared itself out and sorrow started to settle in its place. After he left she had scraped on the old grill until there was nothing left to scrape instead of going to her quarters.

Sis was a lost woman. It helped to stay busy. She wished for her mother-in-law, thinking she might talk some sense into her number three son. *No, it ain't goin' to do no good. I can see. She can't make a bit of difference now. John had that final look in his eye. I'se cut off.*

Chapter 28

LITTLE ROCK

Harriett was deposited at the prison as soon as the supply wagon made it into the command post. The private, with General Steele's memo, took her through the fenced yard, then through the tall front doors of the Union prison. He handed the memo to Lieutenant Wilkes, bid Harriett farewell and wished her luck as he saluted the lieutenant again before shutting the heavy door behind him.

Lieutenant Wilkes looked at the memo from General Steele then motioned for Harriett to follow him without saying anything. Sounds of their footsteps echoed through the native rock hallway. Strange, intensifying odors met them after the hallway changed directions. They turned left and continued on as the air became more tainted the closer they came to another heavy door. Lieutenant Wilkes pulled a massive collection of keys from his belt, inserted one, opened up the door, and motioned Harriett to continue following. Then the lieutenant looked at the memo again while Harriett stood aghast at the sight before her!

Steel-barred cages were on both sides of the room. As soon as they stepped onto the filthy stone floor, the stench overwhelmed even the lieutenant, who was prepared and should have been used to it. He wasn't. He grabbed his handkerchief from his back pocket and held it over his nose.

After stepping inside the insidious room, Harriett stepped in a muddy spot and learned to take care so that she didn't repeat treading in ooze. Her guide continued to lead her down the open space in the middle of cells flanking the walls. Harriett saw men jammed into quarters with hardly room enough to stand. Certainly, places to lie down in some of the cells were limited to nearly nothing.

As she made her way down the center, the sounds of men retching to the pits of their stomachs reverberated with the murmurs of men's voices in agony coming from the celled inhabitants. Many of the men, too sick to move, were laying in their own vomit on the filthy floor. Others were trying their best to give the sick room, but the helpless ones left vulnerable were trampled upon in the crowded prison until people came with a stretcher.

"Sorry you have to go through here, ma'am," the lieutenant finally said. "These are the Rebs we captured. They can't hurt you none, now. It won't be long and most of them will be free to leave. I hear the war is over. It is just the settling up of things that's going on, they tell me. He made a motion for Harriett to continue to follow adding, "We are just about there, ma'am. Just follow me.

"Here we are, ma'am," he said, taking his ring of keys to the lock on the cell in front of them.

As soon as they entered the next room Harriett saw Jasper immediately. His cell wasn't as crowded as the others had been.

"Now, gentlemen," the lieutenant said, "I expect you to be just that, do you hear? This is Private Jasper Holmes's mother." He opened up the cell door and Harriett gingerly walked toward her son.

"Mrs. Holmes, I am Aaron McCoy," said an unshaven man about Harriett's age coming toward her in a gray uniform.

"Jasper is real sick, ma'am. I've been a'tryin' to take care of him some, but he ought to be in the infirmary, ma'am," he continued. Harriett never would have believed the cruelty her Jasper must have suffered if she hadn't seen it for herself.

"I believe it was your son, John, that was in here with us before he went back to his camp. I told John I'd take as good care as I could of Jasper. It looks like no matter what I can do for him, though, it ain't enough."

Harriett looked at her son lying on the cot and saw his sunken eyes and cheeks. The men parted making an opening for her to go to Jasper. A covered bed pot was sitting next to Jasper's cot but it was evident by the looks of things that Jasper wouldn't be able to use it. He exemplified taut skin crowding a bony skeleton. He didn't look like the Jasper she always knew. Dehydrated from dysentery and unable to keep water down wasted her Jasper away. This strange gaunt man lay in his place.

"What have they done to my son?" she asked.

Leaning down to his cot, she stroked his matted hair and said, "Son, this is your Mama. I come to take care of you, son."

Jasper opened his eyes and blinked, trying to focus. Tears escaped from the corners of his eyes telling her he had heard her speak. In a whisper barely audible she saw his lips move to form the words, "Ma, is that you?"

"Yes, it is, Jasper. I'm a'goin' to get you some help, son, you'se goin' to the infirmary. I can't figure why they have waited to get you there. Don't worry none, I'm a'goin to get somethin' done for you, son."

Lieutenant Wilkes hadn't left yet. He watched the drama being played in the cell.

"Young man," Harriett addressed the lieutenant, "I need you to take me to your commandin' officer. My son is a'tryin' to die on me. He needs some help. I intend to get somethin' done for 'em, somethin' that should have already been done! Before it's too late, I want to see your commandin' officer," she said, hysterically turning back to Jasper and getting down next to him where he could hear her.

"Jasper, don't you worry none, son. I'se a'goin to get you a doctor and we will get you better in no time. You hear me now? I'll be back as soon as I can get you moved out of here. You hang in there, son. I'll be back shortly."

After assuring her son as best she could, she followed the apologetic officer out of the cell. Again they walked through the adjacent room with more cells full of wretched men watching the unusual circumstances. Some of them were in as bad a condition as Jasper or worse. Just ahead of Harriett and the lieutenant were two men carrying a stretcher, but it was plain to see the passenger wasn't going to the infirmary. It was too late for him.

Jasper had weakly nodded at Harriett when they left. Harriett wasn't sure he would even be alive by the time she got back, but she had no other recourse. She had to do something! There was no time to waste! She had to have an audience with General Marshall, head of all the facilities at Little Rock. Harriett insisted on seeing the main man in charge.

"John should have reported this to General Steele as soon as he got back to camp," Harriett told the young lieutenant as they were leaving.

"Yes, ma'am," he said. "Trouble is, there just isn't enough places to put the sick, ma'am. We are having at least six die every day from dysentery. The infirmary is full up as the prison is," he said.

"Full up or not, they's a'takin' one more! Jasper is a'dyin and nothin' is a'goin' to stop it if somethin' ain't done now!"

"Yes, ma'am, I understand, ma'am," was the weak reply from Lieutenant Wilkes.

"I know you say it's urgent, Lieutenant Wilkes. That's what they all say," said the private in front of General Marshall's office.

"With this war being over, there's a lot more folks than you that needs to see the General. He is up to his mustache in details and it is all happening at once. All I can do is tell him you are here to talk with him about one of the prisoners," he wearily said. "It won't do much good, I might as well tell you now, but I will approach him about it anyway. He is pretty unhappy about the death toll coming out of your prison and your wanting to talk to him will only remind him of it. I think he wants to forget about something he feels he can't do anything about. Don't say I didn't warn you."

When the young private got up to knock on General Marshall's door, something compelled Harriett to get up and run through the doorway. She surprised herself. Harriett pushed past the young soldier and into the startled general's office. Highly unaccustomed to such disorderly conduct, he abruptly looked up from his mounding paperwork with raised eyebrows.

"General, sir," Harriett said, feeling a bit lightheaded at her own brazenness.

"I need to tell you I have traveled from the camp at Duvall's Bluff to see my son being held here on charges a'waitin to go to trial. I got word that he was very sick, but it's far worse than I was told. I hope you 'scuse me for abustin' in like this, but desperation makes me behave like this. Please forgive me, but sir, I ain't got no other choice. My son's a'needin' a doctor. I fear he will die on me as we speak," she said, crying into her apron.

General Marshall asked Harriett to sit down in the chair directly in front of his big desk.

"What's your son's name, madam?" he said, astounded at the trim little woman's plea for her son.

Harriett could tell he was trying to decide if he should throw her out of his office or listen to what she had to say. Her mind raced for leverage where none existed.

"Sir, I'm the chief cook at Duvall's Bluff and I've been given leave to tend to my son, Jasper Newton Holmes. When I got here, I come here and I seen he was deathly sick with little hope unless somethin' is done quick. It's because of me he was arrested in the first place," she pleaded. "It's a long story to tell, sir, but one thing just led to another and Jasper ended up arrested. He was healthy a'fore he came here but the dysentery is a'killin him, sir," Harriett pleaded.

"And, what did you say your name was?"

"My name is Harriett Holmes, sir," she said with a glimmer of hope, thinking her position as camp cook at Duvall's Bluff helped get his attention.

General Marshall, not used to dealing with women, took pity on the frail little mother sitting in front of him pleading for her son's life. It was different business dealing with a woman than what he normally did in his line of duty.

Harriett sensed a bit of tension relax in the room and believed she wouldn't be asked to leave his office. Her fear upon entry for Jasper's life gave her the impetus to brave whatever this main man might confront her with. Jasper didn't have any time left for slow procedures taking up more precious time.

Lieutenant Wilkes was as pale as a ghost standing behind the young private who had knocked on the general's office door. Too many times stories had circulated about the hard line this general took when interrupted. They had even heard stories that he personally and bodily had thrown people from his office. The men looked as if they were prepared for the wrath of hell to break loose at any minute.

"Close the door, private," the general boomed.

The private quickly and quietly shut the general's office door, leaving the little woman sitting in front of his desk to his mercy, but she had subdued a general with the reputation of a Goliath who devours ants.

"Now, let me get this straight, Mrs. Holmes. Are you telling me that your son is a member of the Union army and he was arrested at Duvall's Bluff and sent here to await trial?"

"Yes, sir, that's zactly what I'm a'tellin' you." Harriett started to tell him that she had another son who had been arrested too, and it was he who had come home to tell about the bad shape his brother was in. She thought better of saying anything about John unless she just had to.

"I got word he was sick and I was able to get leave a'cookin', my son's wives is a'fillin' in for me, and I come here to take care of Jasper. I know he's a'goin' to have to go to trial but I found him much worse than I thought he was a'goin' to be. He's a'dyin', sir," Harriett cried. "He needs to go to the infirmary. He ain't even goin' to be here for no trial if he don't get some help in a hurry."

General Marshall looked at Harriett as if he were looking through her. He took a pen from his desk and dipped it into the inkwell to scribble something on a piece of paper, then handed it to Harriett.

"You take this to the lieutenant that brought you here and he will see to it your son is taken to the infirmary."

"I thank ye so much, sir," Harriett told the general, reaching for the signed order as he arose from his chair.

"Good luck to you, madam," Harriett heard him say as he reached for the doorknob. She generously thanked the general and moved as quickly as she could out of his office to find Lieutenant Wilkes.

He had left.

Harriett wasted no more time and rushed out of the headquarters building and across the large grounds to the fence around the huge rock prison. Breathless from her fast walk, she told the guard at the gate that she had a message from General Marshall for Lieutenant Wilkes. The prison guard called another guard to escort her to the locked prison door.

"Message for Lieutenant Wilkes," yelled the guard to the doorkeeper.

Harriett heard keys unlocking the heavy door that made squeaking sounds as it rotated on its hinges. After she entered, she handed the general's note to the doorkeeper and he ordered her to follow him up the stairs in the front of the building. It was cold on the bottom floor of the stone building, but the higher they climbed up the stairs, the more Harriett could feel a temperature change.

At the top of the stairs, on the landing, the doorkeeper knocked on a heavy plank door. Lieutenant Wilkes opened the door and grinned at Harriett when he saw her.

"Hello again, ma'am, what can I do for you?" At which time, the doorkeeper handed the lieutenant the message from General Marshall.

"Aha! I see the general gave you an audience after all, Mrs. Holmes. I wasn't sure just what would happen but I'm glad you got your affairs heard." He turned to the doorkeeper.

"We'll be needing a stretcher for Private Jasper Holmes and you are to take him to the infirmary right away." The doorkeeper saluted and retreated back down the stairs. Harriett shook the lieutenant's hand and thanked him, then wondered why she felt so grateful to this lieutenant. *Can't he plainly see my son is a Union soldier and he is a'dyin' in his filth?* Being grateful because he gave the order to release Jasper was determined reason enough to be grateful, maybe. *Ain't worth wastin' time thinkin' on things he should have done,* she thought.

"My men will bring Jasper up front so you can wait at the foot of the stairs for him, Mrs. Holmes," he said, leaving.

"It won't be necessary for you to go back there to get him, they will bring him out and then you may go with them to the infirmary." With that said, the lieutenant went back into his office.

When Harriett got to the bottom of the stairwell, she saw a couple of men with a stretcher. It was their duty to remove the dead, but this time the doorkeeper was instructing them differently.

"You are to take Private Jasper Newton Holmes to the infirmary." The surprised expressions on the stretcher carriers' faces demanded more explanation.

"He ain't dead yet and he's to go to the infirmary!" the doorkeeper ordered.

Harriett watched them go down the hall into the great room were all those wretched men were behind bars. Even the odor from the front of the prison was offensive. Harriett covered her nose with her apron. After having been kept waiting for nearly an hour,l she saw them coming toward her with Jasper on the stretcher. The rest of the trip to the infirmary was much quicker.

"Come this way," a nurse in the infirmary informed the men.

"Put Private Holmes on that cot over there," the nurse pointed to a cot in the corner. She barked to an orderly, "Get me some blankets, soldier."

Harriett watched her put a warmed cloth-covered rock at the foot of Jasper's cot. When she removed his boots she said, "This soldier has no socks! No wonder his feet are so cold."

Harriett's heart cracked open when she heard the nurse's exclamation.

"He loved his Mama and family more'n he did hisself. That's the reason he got into such a mess," she explained to the mystified nurse.

The nurse stood up from covering Jasper's feet and looked at this soldier's mother.

"How could loving your family more than yourself be a reason for being put into prison?"

Jasper Newton Holmes
(Picture of him in his casket, 1865)

Chapter 29
STOLEN LEGACY

"My name is Vera Adams," the nurse said with an outstretched hand. "My name is Harriett Holmes. The story is a long one, Miss Adams. I don't think it needs a'tellin' just right now. Do you have somethin' for my Jasper to eat? Maybe some hot tea or somethin'?"

"I know you have lots of things to be a doin' and I don't mind feedin' it to him. He looks so bad, I'm afraid," she started crying again in her dirty apron before finishing her sentence.

"Just a'lookin' at my son barely breathin' and motionless tells me somethin' needs to done in a hurry. I should have been here sooner," she told Vera, wringing her hands.

"Jasper, this here's your Ma. Can you hear me son? Try to open your eyes up. I want to feed you some hot tea. It will make you feel better."

Jasper cut his eyes toward the sound of Harriett's voice and started moving his lips.

"What you say, honey, I can't hear you?"

"That you, Ma?" he barely whispered.

"It sure is, son, what are you a'tryin' to tell me? Say it again." Harriett leaned close and heard the words, "Watch boot toe."

The nurse brought the hot tea and sat the cup on a table next to the wall near Jasper's head, then she allowed Harriett to give him what nourishment she could.

Harriett put a spoonful next to his lips after blowing on it.

"Watch boot toe," he whispered again, before she could put the tea in his mouth.

"Why in the world would I want to watch your boot toe, son?" Jasper's eye glazed over and the tea she was trying to feed him ran down the side of his mouth. He wasn't breathing. No one had to tell her Jasper had just died.

"Jasper, Jasper, no, please, no!" She put her hands under his head in desperation to see if he had just sunk into a coma. His ear lobes were turning blue and his eyes stared straight ahead. Jasper was no longer a part of the living world.

Guilt and sorrow tore at her insides. *Such helplessness. He's here then he's gone, He ain't no more.* "Oh, Jasper!" she moaned, collapsing across his lifeless body.

Vera came to Harriett's side without her noticing it. She put her arms around her and said, "I'm sorry, Mrs. Holmes. I know you loved your son very much. Ma'am, I am sure he knew that and he felt the same about you."

Harriett's tears flooded across Jasper's dirty face. She kissed his cheeks, cradled his head in her hands and tried to see if there was any evidence he could possibly still be here, but he really was gone.

"Why?" she asked out loud.

"Sorry, Mrs. Holmes," was all Vera could say.

"Mrs. Holmes, I would like to make a suggestion to you, if I may?" Vera said, helping Harriett get up from the cot. "I know your family isn't here. It is possible for me to call a photographer to make a remembrance of your son for your family, if you would like. This is done in some circumstances. I had it done of my husband and I have never regretted a day of it. All you have to do is tell me and I will make the arrangements with a photographer," she said and patted Harriett on the arm.

"Oh, yessum, please do. The last time the younguns seen their brother was in September over a year and a half ago. They lost another brother before the boys left. Now Jasper is dead. They ain't never a'goin' to see him again."

"Well, it's as good as done then. Now, Mrs. Holmes, why don't you go and rest yourself? I think you have a place to lie down, don't you?   I will see to Jasper for you. I'll also get the picture to you before you leave. I know you probably won't be leaving until you see your boy buried though, will you?"

Harriett assured Vera she wouldn't be leaving for Duvall's Bluff until proper burial arrangements were made for her son. Before Harriett left the infirmary she told the nurse she would leave word with the camp cooks if she were to be out and they would know where to find her, even though she didn't have any plans to leave the cook's room off the mess hall.

Nurse Vera picked up Jasper's boots and handed them to Harriett.

"He won't be needing these, Mrs. Holmes, you might as well take them."

Harriett looked at Jasper's worn boots and saw the imprint where his feet once were and said, "Thank you, ma'am," then left the infirmary.

She hugged her son's boots close to her breast as if to hug him by proxy, trying to feel her dead son through them. In the movement of walking she heard something rattle inside Jasper boot.

Walking in a fog of grief she arrived at the mess hall without noticing anything between it and the infirmary. Since the mess hall was only a few feet away she took advantage of the windbreak it made to stop and catch her breath for a minute. Before going any further, she squatted on the ground and turned

Jasper's boot upside down to see what was inside making the noise. A shiny object slipped from the toe of his boot onto the ground in front of her—a Hunter's gold pocket watch. Jasper's last words to his Ma were, "Watch boot toe!" Harriett remembered. His last thoughts were to give this to his mother. Even the last deed he could do was to help his mother out.

Harriett picked up the watch and stuck it into her apron pocket. *There's too much to think on now. I don't rightly know what I need to do first. Maybe I need to rest a spell. Maybe then, son, I might be strong enough to say my final goodbye to you.*

After allowing grief to empty itself, Harriett sank into her cot in the room off the kitchen of the mess hall and found sleep, her fingers folded around the hard circular object in her pocket.

Sis went to her cot as soon as she entered the tent. Little Mary was taking a nap on her bed so she held back venting her aching heart. Whatever will I do? Troublesome problems haunted her.

John won't have me, I'm stuck here with no one but Harriett, and she ain't here. I know she will stick by me, but how can I take such a reminder of her son by her bein' with me? As soon as Shelby finds out, he'll put his foot down for Lucinda havin' anything to do with me.

Sis started to cry. She was cornered in a tough spot and she could find no direction about her. She had to do something, but what? Sis couldn't help it so she buried her face in her pillow to crush the sound of her grief, Mary in the tent or not. Mary's questions of her sister-in-law would be too much to handle so she cried as silently as possible.

Lucinda hung the big stewer pan on the rack above the wood stove. She had to stretch to reach the highest rack, taking care not to get burned on a pot of simmering water. Hot dishwater steamed when Lucinda ladled it out of the simmering pan into a bucket. Walking a small way from the camp with the bucket of hot water, Lucinda began to dump it when Shelby came up behind her.

"Lucinda," he solemnly said, "where's Sis? Why ain't she helpin' you?"

Lucinda looked at her husband and she could see he was hiding something. She believed he had already been told about the rape by the Bushwhackers. This was something she wanted to take care of. It was her business to deal with in her own way but John had apparently shot his mouth off. She could tell, Shelby knew.

Not knowing how to approach her husband on this matter, now, she felt guilty as if she were partly to blame for something that was totally out of her control.

Shelby watched his wife struggle. What wasn't said was as vivid as what was. She struggled with the memory connected to the loss of her child. He grabbed her with both arms and pulled her to him in a compassionate hug. Shelby cried into her shoulder as he held her, venting his pain for her and for himself as well.

Lucinda was relieved but puzzled. The Holmes boys were not like this. Shelby was plainly heart-broken thinking of the indignities his wife had suffered. He was not the angry spouse like his brother. Maybe the difference between him and John was he knew he had found his life's partner. Shelby had no need to continue the search like John kept doing. This became a release and a renewing moment for Shelby and Lucinda, whereas John became more splintered.

"You feel warm to me, Lucinda, are you all right?" He felt her face with both his hands. Lucinda's cheeks were flushed red and her eyes were bloodshot.

"I'm all right. Oh, I might be a bit queasy at my stomach but, all right," she concluded. Then Lucinda shot a look at her husband as soon as she said what she did.

"Oh, Shelby, I'm not in the family way like Sis, so don't you get that look," she quickly added.

"I could plainly see if you were, Lucinda, it would be obvious by now and you couldn't hide it if you were. But, hon, maybe we are expecting again? Did you think of that?"

Lucinda never did, but now that Shelby mentioned it, she believed there could be a possibility.

Mary came out of the tent and toward Lucinda and Shelby in the mess tent. She was sleepy-looking after her nap.

"Sis is sayin' she is goin' back to where her Ma is as soon as the war is over. Are we goin back too?"

She had wrapped part of her blanket around her and dragged the rest as she walked. She rubbed her eyes still holding onto a corner of the blanket. Shelby picked his little sister up in his arms.

"We'll probably be a'leavin' in a few weeks, Mary. The war is over and we are waitin' to be mustered out."

"What's musserd out, Shelby?" She yawned, making her words mingle together.

"Well, little sis, it's the time the Army says, 'Farewell, boys!' And sends you home with a bit of money to start life over again. That is just what Lucinda and I are gonna do."

"Will Mama go home too? But, Shelby, our house is burned. We don't have a house. Where are we goin' Shelby? You don't have a house either, Shelby. Don't you remember?"

Both Shelby and Lucinda remembered all too well. It was far more loss than a house. "Well, little 'un, folks just have to start over and that's exactly what we are a'aimin' to do."

"Will we go back on that old raft, Shelby?"

"I don't think so, tadpole! How about catching a ride on a wagon headed back that a'way instead? Wouldn't you like that better? Now, don't you worry none about it, you hear? It won't be hard and you will like the wagon."

"Honey, I have to get back. James and I are shoeing this afternoon. James is spellin' me right now but I need to beat back or we will get behind."

Shelby held Lucinda in a warm hug, kissed her and left. The kiss was a reassuring one, putting her fearful heart to rest. She watched him walk out of sight amongst all the tents and men milling around going from one duty to another.

Lucinda took Mary's hand and walked back to their tent. When they got inside they saw Sis sitting on the cot.

"I've made up my mind, Lucinda. I am goin' back home as soon as I can. It ain't a'goin' to work with me and John," Sis said. "I ain't a'goin' to have anything to do with him if he's a'goin' to act this a'way."

Mary and Lucinda were quiet. They were afraid to say anything. Finally Lucinda asked, "How are you a'goin' back, Sis? We barely made it here with two soldiers' help, but how in the world are you a'goin' to make it back home by yourself?"

"Well, I've been a'figurin'. They's a bunch from our area a'goin' back as quick as they can and I aim to travel with them if they will have me. John sure ain't a'goin' to take care of me, that's for sure. I don't need him, neither. I can make it on my own just fine," she said.

While Sis was talking, Mary had crawled back onto her cot and covered up her head with her blanket. She didn't want to hear about the troubles her brother and Sis were having and hoped the troubles would go away with the blanket over her head.

Lucinda could see Sis had regained some of her spunk and had no intention of letting any man get her down. The grief she showed earlier had turned to anger. Sis continued making plans out loud for Lucinda to hear.

Sis continued to prattle about what her intensions were and in the process failed to notice Lucinda wincing in pain while she was talking.

Lucinda grabbed her stomach when the pain got so sharp she couldn't keep quiet. "Oh, Sis! Somethin' is bad wrong!" Lucinda lay back on her cot and doubled her knees up to her chest and cried out, "Oh, God, Sis, somebody, do somethin'!"

By the time Sis got up and over to her cot, blood was gushing out and soaking the blankets.

"Mary, stay with Lucinda, I'm' goin' to get some help!" she yelled, running out of the tent. Blood was everywhere. Lucinda was bleeding to death and no one could do a thing about it!

The next person Lucinda heard was Shelby. "Hold on there, Lucinda, we have the camp doctor on his way," he whispered, sitting on the ground next to his wife hemorrhaging her life's blood everywhere. Lucinda eerily looked at Shelby, then her eyes lost their expression. The light behind her pupils passed Shelby on the way to eternity.

"What's happenin' here?" Gus asked, swishing the entry flap into the tent, Haden's face following close behind him. Gus had a big catfish in one hand and a pole in the other when he came in. Both boys were home from fishing when they heard the commotion and saw people rushing to their tent. Among some of the spectators were fellow soldiers who slept in James's and Shelby's tent. They saw Shelby sitting on the ground next to Lucinda in a pool of blood on her cot. He was crying.

Sis picked Mary up and motioned to Gus and Haden to follow her outside. James stood up from sitting next to Shelby to whisper to one of the fellow soldiers outside the tent.

News had reached John, but only that something terrible had happened at the cook's quarters. He came in a dead run, not stopping until he pushed past some others congregating outside the tent.

"What's goin' on here?" he gruffly asked Sis as she was coming out of the tent with the children. All of the kids were crying.

"It's Lucinda, she's hemorrhaged to death. It was so quick!" Sis was in shock.

"She must have been in the family way too, John," she added.

John pushed past his wife and siblings to go inside. Shelby had Lucinda's blood on his clothes. John never saw so much blood in one spot in his life, not even during hog-killing time, or on the battlefield. Blood on the battlefield soaked into the hungry earth. Lucinda's blood had puddled on her cot and oozed around her clothing.

Last thing in the world I'd a thought. One minute alive, the next gone! John was lost for words. Hadn't he visited with her earlier?

Shelby looked up at John when he came in. "She's gone, Bud. She's gone. I think she was goin' to have another baby and somethin' must 'a went wrong," he said, crying.

Both brothers were aware someone else had entered the tent but didn't bother to look up to see who it was.

"What's going on here?" John recognized the doctor who had taken care of Owen Leaven after he gave him a good whipping.

"It's too late, doc, just lost my wife," Shelby said. "It all happened so fast, she just laid down and died," he cried.

"I'm indeed sorry, Private Holmes, indeed I am," he said, patting Shelby's shoulder after putting his stethoscope to Lucinda's chest and checking the pulse in her neck.

"We just don't understand why such as this happens, but it does sometimes, and there is really very little anyone can do, even me, when it does," he said.

"Well, young fella, I'll give you a few minutes, then someone will be here for her. I know you aren't ready to speak of such since she just died, but you need to know there's a civilian cemetery about a mile north of us and we will do what we can for you, sir. Again, I do give you my deepest sympathies," and with that the camp doctor took his leave.

James and Gus came back in when the doctor left. Both boys put their arms around their grieving brother and stared at Lucinda.

"Whatcha gonna do now, Shelby?" Gus asked. He knew all too well what it felt like to lose a love one and what had to be done from past experience with William.

"They'll come for her soon, Gus. She can't be left here. It's regulations for someone to be buried right away. Somethin' was said about a civilian cemetery about a mile north of here."

"Ma's gonna be plumb took back when she comes back. She went to take care of one sick 'un, only to come home to find one dead. Lucinda and Ma were good friends," Gus rambled, trying to comfort his big brother but not knowing how.

"I really liked her looks, Shelby." Gus began to cry softly when he heard his big brother bury his face in his dead wife's chest and cry out for her.

Two men entered the tent and waited patiently for Shelby to raise his head. After a bit, Shelby looked up and turned to see who was standing next to him.

"I'm sorry, sir, we have come for the body," said the short and stocky private. His partner was almost outside the tent holding the backside of the portable cot.

Shelby slowly got up from Lucinda's body now losing her warm life signs. She had a raging fever before she died, but that left with Lucinda too. Her body was turning cold.

The private motioned to his partner and they quickly loaded Lucinda, leaving the blood-soaked cot she was taken from.

Sis hurried back into the tent and took the bloody blankets out. She never said a word to anyone but did what she had to do, nauseated or not.

There you are, Mrs. Holmes," the cook called out. Harriett put the shawl Vera had given her around her shoulders. When she was at the infirmary Vera told Harriett to give her the corn sack and she replaced it with her woolen shawl, telling her at the time to not bend the tintype of Jasper. Harriett was touched by her generosity. She decided to roll up her apron and not wear it with the shawl. The round metal object was safely tucked inside many rolls of cloth with the sashes wrapped and tied together as was the likeness of Jasper.

"Thank you for the bed. It was mighty nice of you to give it up for me," Harriett told the cook when she was about to leave with the returning supply wagon. She had seen to Jasper's proper burial. He hadn't been sentenced for court-martial. Jasper died before such could take place so Jasper had a military burial in the Union Cemetery at Little Rock. Now that he was laid to rest, Harriett had others still living she must return to.

"It was my pleasure, ma'am. It gave me some special time with my old buddies in their quarters. You take good care of yourself, now, you hear?"

With quick steps Harriett started toward the supply wagon. The two soldiers sitting up front waved to her. What lay ahead of her was a dread. It would be a heavy thing indeed to tell her family about Jasper's death. All she could think about was Jasper in that wooden military casket. It was a comfort to know someone had furnished some decent burial clothes for her son. *Whoever did such a thing I'm greatly obliged to ye.*

"Lessgo," drawled the driver as he whacked the mules with the reins. The team of mules jumped and jerked the wagon into motion.

"Well, we should be there 'fore too long," the driver told Harriett.

"Right now, I could use the rest and I'm a'goin' to do a little of that while we go," she told the men. "There's a'goin' to be plenty of cookin' when I get back, and more dishes to do up than I care to think about right now."

"Yessum," he answered, "you best rest up."

The ride over rocks and ruts jarred and jostled with the hours passing uneventfully while Harriett lost her cares in sleep. When she finally woke, the daylight had turned to nighttime.

"I's gettin' a bit worried about you, ma'am," the sergeant said. "You were so sound asleep we were thinkin' you might have somethin' wrong with you. Private Gilley took a peek at you and said you were just sleepin' sound. You must have needed sleep to snooze through all these rocks."

Harriett stretched and pulled the shawl Vera Adams had given her more tightly around her shoulders. She put her rolled-up apron that had fallen off back on her lap. She felt stiff.

"Mrs. Holmes, we are goin' to take a rest stop for just a bit. These mules have been at it for quite a spell and we will be gettin' to camp soon enough. Shouldn't be much more than an hour from here."

Harriett thanked the sergeant and headed in the opposite direction from where the men went. They took time to build a small campfire to set a coffee pot on a grill atop some rocks. Perking coffee smelled good and buoyed the travelers' spirits.

"You know, ma'am, we will be musterin' out soon and I have give it some thought about goin' further south. I hear it is opening up with federal land grants to folks willin' to settle out there. Oh, it's wooly business, I reckon, and a tad bit dangerous with them Indians, but with this war business, I think I could handle a few Comanches or Kiowas anytime."

Private Gilly offered Harriett a tin of coffee and pulled out some cold biscuits the cook at Little Rock had sent along with them.

"What do you have to do to get one of them federal land grants?" Harriett asked the soldier.

"What I understand, you have to apply for it and you can do that right at

Little Rock. Somebody told me they have applications there. That don't mean this land is goin' to be yours if you get one of them grants, though, I understand. There's more to it than that."

"What does it mean? We just might be interested," Harriett answered the man. "There ain't a thing to go back to for us. The house we were a livin' in burned to the ground. I can't see a way in the world we can help ourselves one bit by a'goin' back. There's nothin' left in that country, not nary a rabbit for stew. My husband was a trapper and we are used to plenty of game, but there's nothin' left. We's liable to starve a'fore we can get somethin' planted and up out of the ground. And I have buried me some sons along the way. I need to find a place that is tolerable quiet."

"Ma'am, as I understand it, you have to live on the land and work it to make it a working farm for a period of time and then it becomes yours. It costs you nothin' but a good strong back to do the work. It is pretty hard work, bein' virgin land and all. But, hell, I've done hard work before," the sergeant said.

"Your sons will have a muster pay comin' to them at Little Rock and I'm sure General Steele has heard by now about when that time will be. He will be informin' the troops about the grants too, I 'spect. There's most a'wantin' to go home. They'll go back where they come from and the grants won't be a bit interestin' to 'em. I reckon that's why just about anybody can get a parcel of land down south. Ain't that many a'goin to take 'em up on it, probably. Hell, I'm ready to get me somethin' I can call my own and this here seems the best way to go about it. There sure ain't nothin' any place else."

Harriett listened intently to what the sergeant had to say. *Maybe this is the place we could find us some rootin' for ourselves? I ain't a'goin' back to Kentucky, that is for sure. Ain't no way I can do that with nobody to go back to. Maybe Texas is the place we ought to be.*

"I 'spect I'll talk to my boys when we get in about this," Harriett told the sergeant, but she didn't think he heard her because she heard him snoring. The private was not snoring, but was very quiet. He was still awake enough to rein mules, though.

Tomorrow is bout here. I ain't up to the tellin' about Jasper. Inside I still hear somethin' a sayin', 'You can do 'er, Harriett.' I ain't a givin' up just yet. Them younguns needs me and there's still somethin' I'm a lookin' for that I ain't never found. I might find it in Texas.

For we who are in this tent groan, being burdened, not because we want to be unclothed, but further clothed, that mortality may be swallowed up by life. Now He who has prepared us for this very thing is God, who also has given us the Spirit as a guarantee.

2 Corinthians 5:4-5

Chapter 30
DETERMINATION

*A*ustin State Gazette, June 1, 1864
Special Correspondence of Gazette
Tyler, May 16th, 1864

Editor Gazette.

Twelve hundred and thirty-three Yankee prisoners arrived here from Camden, Ark. yesterday—380 more are expected here tomorrow. They were taken at the fight at Marks' Mill. These, together with those already here, will make 4,500 free boarders, who are rather unwelcome visitors to the planters hereabouts, but certainly much more welcome as prisoners than as conquerors.

These planters, though willing to divide to the last with our own brave defenders, dislike to stint themselves to feed these despoilers of our country. Some of the prisoners were left at Shreveport; about 1,000 have been sent to Bonham, Fannin Co. Steele has lost upwards of 5,000 men in Arkansas. He went from Little Rock with about 15,000 men to overrun South Arkansas and invade Texas. He got back to Little Rock with from 3 to 5,000 armed men and a rabble of 2 or 3,000 unarmed ones (in their hasty flight, had thrown away their arms to increase their speed) without wagons, artillery or provisions.

The railroad from Little Rock to White River was torn up by McRae, who organized a brigade from men who had gone to the Yankees to keep out of the army and deserters from various brigades. The Yankees required them to take the oath, which they consented to, but when they were ordered into the ranks of their army it was more than they bargained for, so they left, and have been bushwhacking their Yankee friends ever since. He has about 1,500 with him now, who are redeeming themselves right well.

Many are returning to their commands, who have been shirking duty under various pretenses. Such are the fruits of the victory in Arkansas. I saw an officer who came to guard the prisoners, some of whom stood guard over him, when he was taken prisoner at Arkansas Post. He says that our soldiers are confident, and enthusiastic, and that the Yankees were "better whipped in Arkansas, than they were in Louisiana."

Steele is at Duvall's Bluff on White River, trying to get to the Mississippi River with the demoralized remnant of his army, harassed by our cavalry, who daily send to Camden squads of from 20 to 50 prisoners. Little Rock and Pine Bluff are evacuated by the enemy. Not having taken down at the time the number of wagons, pieces of artillery, arms, etc., which have been taken by our troops, I fear to trust my memory; but they were all his army had, except the few they carried with them back to Little Rock.

I understand from a gentleman just from Bonham that the crops of wheat in that region are not very good. The corn is late, and only tolerably good. The crops in this section of the country are tolerably fair, corn rather later, the fruit is all killed, I believe.

–Claude de Mogyns, Jr.

National Democrat, January 21, 1865
"An Urgent Appeal for Immediate Relief"

Within the past week some 300 refugees, women and children, have arrived here by the boats from up the river. Scarcely any men are with them, only those who, from sickness or old age, are unable to labor. There is one aged 83, and another 89. The husbands, sons and fathers of many of these people are in the service of the government, and where they can render them no assistance.

Their sufferings have been increased greatly by the attack made upon them on their way down, and by the plunder and burning of one of the boats, they are necessarily left in a most destitute condition. Contributions of second-hand clothing, or any material which can be made up for children, will be gladly received at the Room of the Relief Committee at the State-house. We trust that every one will do something in this direction at once.

National Democrat, Little Rock, Arkansas
February 25, 1865

The reception at the White House this evening was the most brilliant of the season. To interest your lady readers, I may state that Mrs. Lincoln wore a rich lilac-colored dress, trimmed with black velvet and narrow ribbon; the skirt being set with white satin and velvet formed in the shape of diamonds, a head dress of point lace and feathers; necklace of pearls; breast pin; white kid gloves and fan. Gen. Grant and lady, and Vice Admiral Farragut and lady, were among the distinguished guests.

National Democrat, March 11, 1865

We learn that the men of the second Brigade, 1st Division, captured at Marks' Mill, last summer, have all been exchanged.

National Democrat, March 25, 1865
Cairo

Five hundred more exchanged and paroled prisoners from Tyler, Texas, came up on the steamer Hannibal from New Orleans, about half belong to the 77th Ohio and the remainder to various other western regiments.

National Democrat, April 15, 1865

The Celebration Last Night. Pursuant to notice yesterday morning, the entire city was illuminated last night, and the most enthusiastic demonstrations of rejoicing made, in testimony of appreciation of the great victories recently achieved by the armies of the Union.

National Democrat, April 15, 1865
From the Memphis Argus
"Guerrilla Life in Arkansas"

We have authentic information of the following occurrences:
On Thursday of last week, Captain Brenker and eight men of Joe Shelby's guerrilla outlaws, who for some time past have been operating in Northern Arkansas, crossed White River below Carendon and entered Monroe County. They first proceeded to Mr. S. Peppers' plantation, near which they found a furloughed soldier named Keep, whom, without provocation, they murdered in cold blood. Keep was stripped, tied to a tree and made a target for their pistol balls. He received several shots, one of which took effect in his mouth and killed him. Mr. Peppers was taken out of his own house and killed, receiving a ball in his breast.

    Pink daylight sifted through huddled sweet gum, pine, and oak trees casting horizontal patterns of light and shadow across the dirt road. Sergeant Gilly's final snore bugled with such force it jarred him awake when they arrived at the outer edge of the Union camp.
    "Here, private, I'll take 'er on in," he said, taking the reins from the driver.
    Harriett watched the lazy sergeant's face saving effort and scorned the pretense of mankind. She was numb from losing another son. If there had ever been pretense in her makeup, no such trait could be counted on this morning.

Reality for her demanded nothing less than forthrightness. She had no substitute to tell the family about Jasper. It had been a solitary burden to watch him die in the infirmary and see to his burial the next day. Even now, events of the past two days seemed more like a nightmare than reality, but one she couldn't awaken from. Harriett was fully aware the nightmare would continue with the reporting of it to the family and that it would probably live on in her heart for the rest of her life. This prospect was too heavy for her to pretend this black voided spot was going to evaporate.

The creaky wagon flowed past camp tents as if in slow motion. Rotating wheels were inanimate, unfeeling objects pushing her toward the desperate need for family reunion, a dreaded moment nevertheless.

Jasper ain't never a'goin to be in one of them tents again, she thought, seeing men come from canvas shelters on their way to satisfy morning hunger.

He won't know anyone special in life or see any youngun of his own. Racing in her mind were past recollections of Jasper—times on the river, fishing with John, fussing with Shelby, chicken pox and the moment of his birth. Her family was scrappy, but tight. No outsider dared tread on anyone without righteous indignation retaliated from the rest. The caring for each person was a strong alliance no alien could break, regardless of inner circle disagreements. They had their own ways of doing things, their own understanding of survival.

Yet, in the known behavior patterns for emotional recovery, Harriett was increasingly aware of a nagging something else that was missing. Her fortress had a termite gnawing away its resilience, which increasingly left her knowing she owned no means of satisfactory resuscitation. A solution from outside sources for her empty spots inside never sated completely any more, be it necessities of life, passage of time or family fellowship. For a long while she attributed the slipping inability to the loss of Canady. He had always been her mainstay. That wasn't it. This vacancy was different. Harriett wasn't so positive anymore that if Canady were with her at this time the ache inside would find much lasting comfort from his presence. No, the emerging reminder about something else missing interjected a puzzling presence she was ill-equipped to understand.

Touching the only tangible thing left of her second son, his government issued boots, Harriett once again thought about the secret he had stored in the toe of one of them. The gold watch was safely placed in her rolled-up apron next to his tintype.

Thanks to Vera Adams, the younguns is a'goin' to get to see their brother, but it ain't a'goin' to be like any of 'em was a'figurin' on. How am I a'goin' to tell it? She was anxious to see them, but dread dampened the prospect at the same time.

When the wagon stopped, emotional currents scurried around inside her body seeking to magnetize to some miraculous strength for what she must do. *They ain't no easy way. How could there be? Jasper's gone,* she scolded herself for seeking ways to wimp out reporting. Harriett walked toward the cooking galley.

Only Sis, cooking grits in a big pot atop the wood stove, and a few men were moving about in the area. Several soldiers were invading the space where Lucinda normally would be, putting more firewood in the log bin, setting up utensils and bringing in buckets of water. It was far too early for Gus, Haden, and Mary to be up stacking split logs in the bin near the stove, one of their chores. Sis looked up when she heard Harriett coming her way.

"Harriett!" She ran to meet her mother-in-law, wiping her hands on her apron before hugging her.

"We've missed you, Harriett. How's Jasper?" she said, cutting short her first hug by wiping more water-soaked grits from her hands, then hugging her again. Sis knew Harriett couldn't possibly have known how much she had been missed. Austerity between them had melted from that first stiff encounter the two women had after John brought her to his mother's home to live with Harriett and the rest of the family. In the meantime, Sis had grown a respect for her mother-in-law and had hoped to be living near her after the war was over. She read Harriett's facial expression after getting no reply.

Frustrated and unable to speak, tears visually relayed what Harriett's mouth refused to utter. Her trembling hands clutched the rolled-up apron and Jasper's boots in a tighter grip, as if the touchstones would give her strength. Struggling to choke back her grief, she could only think, *I know I gotta tell but, the words don't want to come out!* Harriett's shoulders sagged and stress lines deepened across her brow in resignation to the bubbling turmoil from inner warfare.

"Oh! No! He didn't die? Tell me he didn't die!"

"He was so sick when I got there, Sis, there weren't nothin' that could be done for 'im," Harriett whispered.

"I hardly had time to get there before he died, and if it weren't for a Reb prisoner he wouldn't have lasted that long," were her unexpected explanations.

Like a small crack in a big dam, Harriett's words seeped out in whispers. "Aaron McCoy kept him a'livin', but Jasper couldn't hold out no longer. I'se able to get him to the infirmary, but he's so weak, nothin' mattered."

With remorse, Jasper's mother opened up another wound in her heart. "If he hadn't been a'tryin' to take care of us, he wouldn't have got in such a state. It was because he didn't have nothin' of his own. He done give it to us," she lamented. "Sis, he didn't have a pair of socks to cover his cold feet," Harriett added, reliving the despair, as if taking on the memory personally would lessen the pain of Jasper's reality.

"Poor Jasper," Sis replied, hugging Harriett again. The news about happenings at camp during Harriett's absence suddenly became secondary.

"He never had a chance at life, did he?" Sis asked softly, not expecting her bereaved relative to answer.

Comfort could only come in hugs. Sis stroked her head before her brave mother-in-law found a little of the gumption she was searching for. She pulled away from the temporary shelter of Sis's arms in order to compose herself. It was satisfying to be consoled by Sis, but not enough to remain in such a beholden position. *Maybe this here's my type of pretense,* she thought, thinking about the sergeant who took the team's reins on the outskirts of camp as if he were the one who drove during the early morning hours. *It ain't natural to be dependin' on a younger one. Grit is all they is.* Deep inside, Harriett questioned if grit was people's only sustenance? She had heard Jewel, Amy, and Molly talk about another form of support unknown and foreign to her. *Could there be somethin' else besides a 'growin' your own bedrock?*

"I can't believe what's happenin'," Sis said. Harriett's valiant struggle for composure argued the case for Sis to tell Harriett about other changes only because she believed Harriett would be more affected if she didn't. The breakfast cooking on the stove needed her to get back, urging Sis to take advantage of disclosure while she could without the ears of the orderlies hearing.

"I know you are goin' to hear so I might as well tell you. They ain't no good time to tell it and most especially now, I see. I need to tell you because you know I love you like my own blood, Harriett."

"Tell me what, Sis?"

"Since you left, John told me he don't want no part of me no more," she confessed. "And now, this about Jasper! The war has tore up folks ever which a'way."

Ill-timed or not, Sis knew Harriett would find out about the split and it best be from her. The other news about Lucinda was more than she could bring herself to share, however. Someone else would have to tell her about Lucinda. She could only report on her own situation.

"I'm pregnant, Harriett. I guess I'm about to have a youngun' from somebody I don't even know," she blurted out the explanation for her marriage break up.

"That renegade a'runnin' and killin' all over the countryside is the one ruinin' things for us," she said momentarily forgetting she had been one of the lucky ones who survived Shelby's guerila warfare. Most didn't. Harriett survived too, only because they thought the blow to her head had done her in. Baby Shelby Robert didn't.

"John can't handle it. I don't want to tell you this now but the kids will be a'tellin' it as soon as they get up. It's better you hear from me."

Sis wrestled with another secret complication muddying the waters to her confession. She wasn't all too sure about the truth of her explanation, only that the possibility was real enough. Somebody was responsible for the child she was carrying and it sure wasn't John. Bad as it was, her pregnancy would be better accepted if the baby were fathered from a known murdering guerila than from a fellow soldier and acquaintance. The Union camp dispatcher would be disaster from friendly fire. Disintegration would be better tolerated coming from an unacceptable stigma left by the marauding, detestable Bushwhacker.

Harriett was surprised by her confession and if she said anything to Sis, it wouldn't be the right thing. She needed to think and at this particular moment, Harriett didn't trust herself for any deductions. After miraculously living through that guerilla attack herself she knew Sis couldn't help being abused, any more than Lucinda could, by those cold-blooded murderers and rapists. But, a permanent reminder of family tragedy for the rest of their lives represented in an innocent child?

"What in the world is the matter with John?" she finally asked her red-eyed daughter-in-law, trying to rationalize.

After both women had confessed some of their consuming burdens, intervention of morning activity going on in the cooking area momentarily interrupted conversation. Lucinda's obvious absence led to the next question.

"Why ain't Lucinda out here a'helpin' you this mornin', Sis?" Harriett asked. From the surface, it appeared things had not gone well at home, or two daughters-in-law would be cooking this morning instead of one.

The mention of Lucinda created a new emotion for Sis. She was angry about John's leaving her. Lucinda was a different matter. She couldn't answer Harriett's question.

"Did you all go an have a fuss? That ain't like Lucinda to ever fuss with nobody."

After a few moments of silence, Sis cleared her throat and said they were behind schedule fixing breakfast for the troops. She knew this was a weasel way out but even Sis knew *now ain't the time.*

"We can talk later, men are a'comin' in now," she added, then left to tend to her grits boiled almost past stirring.

Harriett accepted the conversation's end but this strange behavior coming from Sis awakened invisible vibes. She could plainly see the need to finish cooking breakfast, but it was just as plain Sis didn't want to discuss the matter. Harriett would have insisted on some explanation if she were not so emotionally drained. *'Nuf is said for now,* she concluded, deciding her place was first in the galley with Sis. She would see the children later.

Unrolling her apron, she took special care that the two things concealed inside were tucked into the apron pocket before tying it around her waist. She stuffed a dry rag laying on a worktable on top of the contents for safekeeping. The decision not to reveal the hidden secret had been made on the trip home from Little Rock. If she were to return this pocket watch to the rightful owner, Owen Leaven, it would only heap more guilt upon her dead son. She fully believed Jasper had cared for his family more than himself and his sacrifice for them was the author of desperation. Her purposeful intention was for that pocket watch to never surface again in this camp. It would bring more disgrace on Jasper and her maternal protection for him in death was as strong, or more so, than it would have been in life. It was the least she could do for her dead son. The matter was settled.

Today is a 'goin' to be a soberin' time, a turnin' point for my younguns, she thought, sitting Jasper's boot down next to a work table before getting involved in the morning meal preparations. Harriett knew her youngest children managed to have childhood curiosities, even if they could only toy with such childish endearments in snitches here and there between adult expectations of them. They always seemed to find a way to make play in work. No matter what chore she jumped into she couldn't shake the dread that lay ahead. It would be a damaging report she could not shield them from and the result of it would dry up more of their childhood. Jasper had filled their Pa's shoes more than anyone since he left.

Necessity had it's own driving force, regardless of canyons from despair cracking through Harriett's only sacred reason for living, her family. So, with no further ado, she picked up her obligation. More than ever, her remaining children needed an umbrella of protection. A cooking job provided that.

Lucinda's absence required her help right then. It was a short-term relief which would prolong the agony of answering her children's questions until a later time. Harriett gave instructions to the arriving young orderlies to follow her to the rations shed for another large crock. She then handed a soldier slab bacon and a bucket filled with jars of honey to take back.

Relinquishing her position to Harriett as chief cook came easy and Sis was glad to do it. After telling her mother-in-law about the breakup, the normally free-spirited and headstrong take-charge attitudes weren't working well with breakfast making this morning. Orderlies set bowls of gravy out for biscuits and the grits Sis had been cooking when Harriett first arrived.

Now ain't the time for John to make more problems! Grief moved over to allow a smidgen bit of aggravation to emerge, released by pots getting put, pans getting slammed and bacon daring to not cook right!

Men made their way to the breakfast line as the last of the hot biscuits came from the oven. She set some jars of honey on the tables before taking the liberty to leave for the tent to see her children before clean up duty began.

Gus was sitting on the side of his cot. His hair, smashed upward, standing at attention on one side of his head, was complimented by a sleepy stupor masking his face.

"Hi, Ma. When did you get back?" he yawned.

Harriett hugged her amazingly impetuous and unpredictable Gus, then reached for Mary and Haden when they sat up.

"Just a while ago," she answered Gus. "I got here before Sis cooked breakfast and I had to help her out. She was short-handed. Where's Lucinda? She wasn't out there and it ain't like her. Ain't she feelin' good?"

"Oh! Mama, Lucinda died!" Mary burst out.

"What's that you say, Mary?"

"Yep, Mary's right," Gus said. "She died yesterday, Ma."

Haden grabbed Harriett's hand and blurted, "Ma, they's blood everywhere." All three youngsters mobbed their mother and sought comfort, trying to tell the story simultaneously about yesterday's account.

"What are you a'talkin' about, younguns? Tell me," she said, not being able to decipher all they were saying.

Gus squared his shoulders and cleared his throat. "Ma, she just bled to death. It was so quick the doctor couldn't do nothin'. I think Sis said she and Shelby was a'havin' a baby and somethin' went wrong." Gus had hardly finished telling his mother before he asked the question Harriett had been dreading to hear.

"How's Jasper?" Gus asked.

Her head reeled trying to take it all in. *No wonder Sis was cookin' alone. Lucinda would never leave it to Sis unless they's a reason. I should'a known.*

"I can't believe it!" Harriett said.

"It's true, Ma. She's gone and I heard Haden and Mary a'cryin' all night," Gus added, insinuating he was manly and didn't cry. "She died right here in this tent. They's goin' to bury Lucinda in the cemetery this mornin'," Gus finished telling his mother about Lucinda's passing, then repeated his question.

"Ma, how's Jasper?"

Lucinda's death has done cratered the children's hearts. Now I's got to dig the pit deeper! Time had come she could do nothing else. Harriett told of Jasper's death, then dug into her apron pocket for the tintype of him propped up in his coffin that Vera Adams had made.

Black days hovered. Wartime had been full of death and desecration. Occasions for mankind to reassess values and priorities with building blocks from shattered pieces were the norm. The pyre of broken bits from lost loved ones leaving empty spaces in hearts, shattered bodies from war injuries, cherished homes burned to rubble, loss of nature's game, of income and sustenance, affected everyone. Loose ends needed tying up and new ways had to be sought, especially for those whose roots had been plowed and busted up in Arkansas' populace, as it was across much of the country. America was a limping nation under unification wrought by victors of war and struggling for application of law. Through early stages of this unifying process some people in the ravaged south had enough ancestral foundation left to replenish emptiness, but only after a period of time. Some did not.

(Little Rock) Unconditional Union Newspaper, April 20, 1865
Meeting of Colored Schools

It may be that some residences of Arkansas, and even of Little Rock, have but a faint conception of change taking place in their midst with reference to the education of colored people. They may have heard that there are schools for that class, and teachers, but have ridiculed the whole thing, or passed it by in silent contempt. But had they attended a meeting of such schools held at the Clock Church on the 13th inst., they might have seen that this movement of the age is no more to be despised than the proclamations and armies of him whom they once laughed at as an ape.

For those who didn't have connection to kin, or prior scholarly knowledge and skills, a trade of some sort, or government program, as was the case of former boat people bearing their disadvantage silently, opportunities appeared to be miniscule. If life were to begin afresh in the war-torn land, those complexities continuing on from memories insisting on self-inflicting patterns had to be forgotten. But, how could they be at this point in time? Bound up in the stigma of emotional prisons as social outcasts, their secretly imposed inadequacies had to remain hidden. By this time, crippling infestations of perceived limitations was ripe enough to be projected onto succeeding generations. The Negro repatriation was being addressed, but no advocate existed for people like Harriett who hid a disgraceful heritage even some emancipated slaves referred to as being that of "white trash." Because survival came from lone family fortification and their own sense of pride, an unspoken resolve was for their lowly past to be incarcerated and entombed from this point on. Words once uttered a long time ago from Harriett's mainstay kept coming back to her empty circumstance.

"I never look backards, Harriett. Ain't no use in it. It's a waste to look backards. I just move on, just move on," her boatman had said.

But, where in the world am I to move on to? Always this nagging question was followed up with another remembrance that relentlessly invaded her times of despair, "You can do 'er, Harriett. You can do 'er," her sweetheart had encouraged. Harriett wasn't so sure anymore. She needed something more. From the passage of years the new message emerging suggested her grit was losing gumption.

Lucinda's ceremony had been simple and short. She was buried in the cemetery Gus told his mother about on her return to the camp. Jasper was gone and part of Shelby died with Lucinda. From the looks of things, it appeared her oldest son didn't care whether he lived or died either. *How many more's a 'goin' to leave? How many more's a 'goin' to die off or wishin' they had one?*

She tried to console herself by facing the fact they weren't the only people who had suffered in this awful war. The mourners were everywhere. "If a body took the time to look," she said, trying to buoy up her defeated family as well as herself.

"If you just look around you, younguns, they ain't much to steady your feet on for anybody, from what I can see," she had told Gus while forcing herself to overcome her own words. "But, we'se' got as good a chance as anybody," she added.

The level playing field was in word only. She was fully aware her family had known hard times, but so had many others according to the newspaper articles Vera Adams had read to her while she had been in Little Rock. She learned many other boat people had barely made it to shore and some of them hadn't at all.

At least Harriett had an emotional draw on a past when times were once different, giving an edge for the remainder of her grit to hone on. She remembered on one occasion seeing a pair of boots attached to her future, whatever it would be.

Canady, I gave you my heart once, intendin' to be with you forever. For your sake, wherever you are, I'll find determination for this day. But her vow had threats with cracks beginning to form. Harriett needed more than her own promise and grit if life continued in this vein. An erosion of spirit told her so.

Chapter 31
SEPARATION'S BIRTH

Little Rock National Democrat, April 1, 1865

Deserters from Texas. The number of refugees and deserters coming in from the state is very great. By all routes they come trooping; some float down Red River in dugouts, some walk across the country; some arrive crowded and jammed away by scores in the reeking holds of sail vessels. They burrow under guardhouses, they poison the blood-hounds, they wade through long bayous to throw them off the trail, they swim, they climb trees, they walk, they run, they lurk in swamps and bogs, whistled over by mosquitoes, which prevail there. Nor are they all of the meaner sort: two days ago there arrived here a Capt. Art Mead, formerly rebel Provost Marshal at Brownsville, Texas, and a Major Vandegraff, of some Texas regiment.

Many of these men are Germans from West Texas, who had been conscripted, and who hated the rebellion from the beginning, and fought against it from within it, and whom the rebels hate most cordially. It awakens by turns one's laughter and his righteous indignation to listen to the broken English of these deeply wronged men, relating the outrages they have seen and suffered.

(New Orleans, Cor., Cin.Com.)

Final weeks at the Union camp passed uneventfully after Lucinda was buried. Packing was a mental diversion while dealing with rational ideas for new beginnings somewhere. Most of the injured had already been taken to Little Rock, leaving able-bodied men to clean up and break down camp. Talk was cautiously shaded with renewed hope among people relieved to see a new day when no one had to report to someone in command of their lives. War was not over for everyone, however. Bushwhackers in Arkansas and bordering states either couldn't read or refused to listen. War for them continued.

Mustering out pay was speculation for hope. Many made plans to return to former homes or what was left of them. Some mentally searched for unknown destinations. Like the former boat people, they had nothing left to go back to. Much of the talk was about new frontiers in Texas and the roaming range cattle, Texas longhorns, waiting for the taking.

John was the first of the family to broach the subject of Texas. His interest first perked from scuttlebutt circulating throughout the Union prison at Little Rock when he was a "guest." Ironically, he had heard this from the imprisoned rebel who took care of his dying brother, Aaron McCoy. Aaron was going to take advantage of land compensation offered to Confederates in this frontier.

"Texas is a'givin' folks a chance to start over, if they's a mind to, I hear," Aaron had told John. "It's all a'goin' to happen down in Texas where there's land patents a'goin' to be handed out if you apply for 'em. My cotton patch in Alabama ain't where I'm goin' to go. I'm plannin' to go Texas way myself," he said.

"Ain't you got no family back home, Aaron?" John asked. "It was a long time ago, but I heard talk from the rest about my Papa workin' for some cotton man along the river. He needed to make us some money so we could come to Arkansas. They say Papa didn't like farmin' then and he never liked it when he got to Arkansas neither."

"No, John. They's nobody's left in Alabama. God's grace alone got 'em to Arkansas by boat last January, I hear. I only have a ten year old daughter, Cornelia, left. The boys are all grown and been caught up in the war. Don't 'spect to see 'em again. I have no idee where they's at. Tore up as it is, it's a big country, ain't it?"

"Angie and her youngun, Fannie, brung Cornelia here by boat from Alabam and they's at a refugee camp twelve miles south of Little Rock right now, they tell me."

"Angie used to be one of mine, but ain't that way no more, is it?" John never answered Aaron's question.

Decisions had to be made since the war's end and remembering what Aaron said about Texas was intriguing. Texas was the most likely place to go. It was far from Sis.

"Ma, you and the younguns need to come with me. Hell, we ain't got nothin' to lose. There ain't a damned thing left here in Arkansas," he told Harriett. He didn't consider he had any ties to Sis left. Hadn't he fought against the likes of that rebel guerilla running the countryside pretending the war wasn't over? One thing he knew for sure, he wasn't going to be reminded of it every day by the likes of a Bushwhacker's kid growing in his wife's belly. Harriett's handsome son planned to get as far away from Sis as possible.

"You and the kids can get a chance to own somethin' someday, Ma," John insisted. "Where in the world could you do such as that if it ain't there? We ain't got a thing here and there's cattle for the takin', railroads to be built, and whiskey to still and sell."

"I have to admit, John, you are right about nothin' here. Shelby's house is burned to the ground, and he ain't got Lucinda anymore to start up again. They's nothin' left here, John, I have to admit to that."

As disappointing as the poor farm she shared with Canady had been, it was the only life she had come to know in Arkansas. Harriett thought about die-hard rebs refusing to cede the war over in Arkansas and mentally compared it to reports of Indian massacres happening in Texas. She had experienced Shelby's guerilla warfare and was ready to take chances elsewhere. Indian threats got watered down when she remembered her grandpa's compound. *Texas might be a chance to do somethin' opposed to nothin',* she thought.

Moving on actually had become a second nature anyway. Life on a river was a good teacher for that. It wasn't like there were close friends and family she would be breaking ties with if they went to Texas. *I'm a 'thinkin' maybe it's time for me to move on too.* "We just might take John up on that trip to Texas," she told the family.

Hundreds of people were lining the streets of Little Rock when wagons arrived from Duvall's Bluff. Fine powder filled the air from horses hooves and rotating wheels grinding the road. Wind blew the gritty powder back onto the travelers and milling people.

"Corporal Dean? Is that you, corporal?" Harriett hailed a young man riding past her wagon stirring up more dust.

"Well, hello there, Mrs. Holmes! How in the world are you?" he said, reigning in Goldie.

"S'pose I'm all right considerin'." Harriett was surprised he was glad to see her after all the trouble her family had been to this dispatcher. "Never 'spected to see the likes of you again, Corporal Dean," she told him.

Dean shifted his look at Sis and Mary on the bench between her and Harriett. His expression had questions concerning the other daughter-in-law. The boys were in the back, but where was Lucinda?

"Reckon you heard about Jasper?" Harriett asked Corporal Dean.

In concert, Dean listened to the boys help their mother tell him about losing Jasper. Dean was stunned to learn of Jasper's death.

"I remember the day Jasper gave me the things to take to you folks, ma'am. He certainly was concerned about his family back home, all right. What a shame for such to happen to him. He deserved better," the corporal added, then changed the conversation.

"I'm headed back home as soon as I muster out. What's you folks plans? Where are you going now?"

Sis looked at her mother-in-law. Seeing words failed her, she struggled with an explanation.

"Well, I reckon I'll be heading back to Jenny Lind to find my Ma," Sis said apologetically. " There ain't no other place for me to go, if they is I don't know where it would be."

Dean couldn't help but notice Sis was in the family way and her explanation didn't fit her situation. Finally, after an awkward moment, Harriett spoke.

"We'd be much obliged if you'd allow Sis to travel with your group a'goin' home. It appears she will be a'goin' alone," Harriett admitted.

Sis reached across Mary and hugged Harriett. "It's ain't your fault. I'll be all right. John and I was havin' troubles and this was the excuse he needed. He didn't get thrown in the brig for bein' an upright soldier," she said, but was cut off by Harriett before she could say more.

"Sis, you need to be with your Mama right now. I wish I could help you like I did Lucinda. You'd be better off with your own Mama. I don't know what we'll find where we are a'headin' but I know I ain't a'goin' back where William and Shelby Robert's memory haunts me. It could be some of the folks a'livin' round us that has to take credit for their killin'."

"Right now, I'm thinkin' about trying for a piece of land down in Texas. We don't have anyone else left in Arkansas that I know of. The country is big down in Texas. Who'd care if we stopped on a piece of it and took in some of those free longhorns?"

"I understand, Harriett. It is unsettlin' times. Goin' back is different for me, I don't have to go back to that spot where it all took place. I'll stay with Ma, have my youngun and then move on, I 'spect."

"Sure, Sis, you can get back to your home place with some of us," Dean agreed. "We'll be glad to help you out," Dean said. "Let me help you down and I'll take you to where the others are joining up," Ted said getting down from Goldie.

Harriett was relieved Sis had a solution. Her mother would not take kindly about her pregnant daughter coming home without her man. She watched Ted Dean assist Sis while leading Goldie.

There's only so much I can do. He is past puttin' in a corner anymore. Life moves on.

"I s'pose we will be movin' on to Texas," Harriett told her children, watching Sis leave with Corporal Dean.

Fighting feelings of disintegration, Harriett reasoned inside, *the baby ain't John's. This youngun will be thought of as his, no doubt. It belongs to that renegade who killed my grandbaby!*

"Come on, kids, we are a'goin' to visit with a cook friend I met when I come to Little Rock. He let me sleep in the little room off the kitchen and I bet he would help us find somethin' for you to eat. Maybe we can talk him out of that little room again for just a night or two?"

Chapter 32

INTRODUCTIONS AND CALCULATIONS

Genaral Marshall's office, located in a big rock building, was alive with soldiers converging from different regiments leaving their signatures on paperwork. Shelby, James and John made their x's on the right line with witnesses. Quick physicals at the infirmary were the reason for additional paperwork requiring more marks.

"Pardon me, soldier, this is the line you need to get in," one of the orderlies said. Shelby had shuffled into the large room, appearing puzzled and disoriented. The orderly stationed outside the door directed men to lines, helping with entry and exit congestion.

"I thank ye," Shelby muttered, almost falling over his own feet and colliding with a nurse carrying an armload of paperwork. The collision sent papers tumbling to the floor. Embarrassed, Shelby quickly dropped to scoop up scattered documents for the flustered nurse attempting to do the same thing.

"I didn't see you, ma'am. Please forgive me," Shelby said.

The perplexed nurse pulled back and allowed Shelby to finish the job. When he handed back the bundle, no longer in alphabetical order, she stared at Shelby's face as if she recognized him.

"Thank you soldier, please don't worry. It was an accident," she said. Then, compelled she asked, "Excuse me, soldier, if I may be so bold, but, you look familiar to me," she said taking the stack of papers from Shelby's hands.

"You didn't have a brother named Jasper Holmes, did you?"

Shelby looked at the nurse and without speaking, just nodded his head. Grief had whittled Shelby into a changed man. Not much was left to cling to anymore.

"Well, sir, I think I know your mother. I helped her with your brother when she came several months ago. My name is Vera, Private Holmes, Vera Adams. I was the nurse on duty the day your mother brought in, it was Jasper, wasn't it?" Then she quickly added, "I'm sorry about his passing."

"I see you are next for your exam," Vera said turning to leave without getting any reply from Shelby. Clipped sounds coming from a stone floor as Vera walked away were covered over from laughs and camaraderie of a fresh wave of soldiers lining up behind Shelby.

Shelby finished with mounds of papers requiring his x then started to leave. He saw Nurse Adams across the room and decided to pay respects and apologies once again for earlier clumsy actions.

"You say you know my ma and you knew Jasper? I would like to talk to you more about my brother if you could spare a minute," he said to the auburn-headed nurse.

Obviously Vera was every bit the lady and it was well known nurses were properly chaperoned in the infirmary and on post. They were off limits to soldiers. Forewarnings about acceptable behavior toward the young women working were well ingrained. Nothing but utmost respect was expected.

Vera had a fresh and youthful honesty about her. She had been very kind yet reservedly proper at the same time while attending to business assignments. It was only a short duty time left before she would be off for the rest of the day.

"I didn't know Jasper very long," she said. "He was a very sick man when they carried him to the infirmary." Then, with compassion, she said, "You have a very strong and beautiful mother, Private Holmes. I tried to put myself in your mother's place, and to be honest with you I don't know if I could have handled the situation like she was able to. She made an impression on me, one that I don't think I will ever forget."

Shelby listened to this young woman tell him things about his mother he already knew. Vera Adams had to have a perceptive heart to recognize some of his mother's strengths, he believed. After all, Harriett showed little expression, but by her actions Vera must have noticed her beauty went deeper than skin. Shelby had heard challenging questions before about Harriett Holmes being old enough to be his mother.

"There's one thing I have learned over these past few years, Mr. Holmes, people have to do lots of things during war time and with some of us, it brings out the best. But, there's another side. I have seen persons completely destroyed by disasters of war," she told Shelby. "Your mother is a very strong woman. I don't mean just the willful type, but one who has a very big heart," Vera said.

Shelby noticed Vera's kind eyes and gentle spirit. "I thank ye for your kind words about the family, ma'am. I reckon I already know what you say is right, but this is the first time I ever heard a body say such. Ma is indeed a fine woman, and a brave 'un too. You don't know how brave Ma's had to be.

The twenty two year old nurse was attracted to this soldier's brown eyes and olive skin. Her own Oliver Adams had had a ruddy complexion with flaming red hair. Shelby's almost coal-colored hair was a striking contrast to the memory of Oliver.

"I understand probably more than you might know, Mr. Holmes. I lost my husband during the war," Vera told Shelby. "He was killed right at the beginning of it. My life was very empty after Oliver was killed and I had to make a decision myself. I could either fill life again with something or die myself. Nursing at this hospital seemed to be the best place I could find solutions for my own loss."

Shelby was quiet, without much to say. He nodded an understanding of her statements without comment.

"If you don't mind, I could use some help carrying these papers to the next office. It's on the way to the doctor's office where you have to go."

Shelby picked up the double stacks of paper without commenting and followed Vera down the hall toward another big room full of milling office help.

"When your brother, James, came in for his physical this morning, I noticed his resemblance to Jasper too. Then, when I overheard him give his name, I knew for sure it was another son of Harriett Holmes. A little while later, John came through.I could see the connection—the Holmes men resemble each other."

Vera saw sadness in Shelby's eyes not present in the other two. She had been with a number of young men in the dying process and recognized a hollow look each shared. For some reason, the same appeared in Shelby's eyes. He wasn't dying. Why did he look as if he were?

"All Harriett's boys look alike but I must say, you are the most handsome," Vera said, turning red at her own brazenness slipping out. "Oh! Excuse me, Mr. Holmes, I don't know what got into me!" she said, covering her face with her hands. The nurse's intention was to lift Shelby's spirits. That was part of her job. She was afraid she had overdone something and regretted her boldness as soon as she had said it.

Evidence of a smile forged across Shelby's sad countenance. He wasn't good with conversation like John. Shelby understood more than he could verbalize and struggled for his own composure.

"Vera, that's about the nicest thing I ever heard. No need to get embarrassed over it. I thank ye for tellin' me, whether it be true or not," he said timidly.

After finishing up business with the infirmary, Shelby gravitated back to Nurse Adams on his way out to ask to see her again. Accepting a time over coffee at the mess hall now before going separate ways seemed the best solution.

Nervous laughter filled the mess hall. An atmosphere of anticipation as well as dread for what might lay ahead instigated the mood of the men. Such was conducive to giving permission to the spiritually dead Shelby to feel more freedom to speak. Maybe it was the selfless woman sitting in front of him who gave him courage to speak more freely. Just the meeting and then the leaving soon after this visit made each keenly aware of the preciousness of time. Both understood this spiritual attachment, an instantaneous bond though they had only met. Sipping hot coffee loosed Shelby's tongue and shyness.

"I don't know what in the world I am a'goin' back to," he finally admitted. "I lost my baby, lost my wife, lost my cabin they tell me, and the only thing I have left is a piece of land without anything on it. Lucinda's folks give it to us. I don't feel right about a'goin' back without her. James and John are a'goin' with Ma and the kids to Texas," he told Vera. "I ain't too keen on it, myself. It ain't a easy life with all them Indians down there a givin' everybody trouble."

Shelby didn't intend to linger on the subject of Indians. He was old enough to remember all too well a time of leaving one place after another. It was suspected they were a bunch of shantyboat Indians on the run. He wasn't sure which was thought of as being worse—shantyboat people, Indians, or Melungeons. Problem was, they were all three. This was something Vera Adams need not know about.

"I don't rightly know what to do, to tell the truth of it," Shelby confessed.

Vera reached across the table and patted Shelby's hand when she deemed this man was perfectly harmless. Looking into his eyes, and he returning her gaze, she finally made comment.

"It always seemed right to me, when I didn't know what to do, it was best for me to do nothing. That has always been the safest answer for me," she said.

"Don't hardly see how I can do nothing," he said. "Times come to do somethin'."

"Well, I guess what I meant to say is don't do anything but what you normally do. Just take your time to make decisions. You could always work in Little Rock at the livery stable here. Didn't I hear James tell the private at the infirmary that you and he shoed horses in camp?"

"Yeah, that was our duty most of the time, we blacksmithed.It ain't too bad an idee, Vera, thanks. I think I'll hit James up to see if that's somethin' he would do. How'd you remember about shoein' and all with so many of us in and out of here?"

"Oh, I don't know, it was just easy to do because I got to know your mother. If you and James do stay, I wouldn't mind at all if you came to call," Vera suggested.

"I live at 110 Washington Street. It's a boarding house for seven of us working at the hospital. It's quite proper, I assure you. The boarding house belongs to Mr. and Mrs. Bowman. The war has been going on for so long, I wonder what there is left? I, too, have to think about building my life back again."

"There are patients who can't leave the infirmary for a while. My duty isn't finished here yet. It may be that I will continue to work here even after the war is phased out. God only knows I will need something to fill my time too," she admitted.

"You know, Vera, I think you have a fine idee about smithin'." Shelby got up from the table to go find James after their visit was over. On his way out, he turned back to ask Vera a question.

"If you don't mind, Vera, I might call on you when I get things settled," Shelby said, expectantly.

Vera's smile following Shelby out the door answered his question.

Weaving through the crowded grounds, Shelby noticed Sis standing with Corporal Dean about two hundred yards away from several wagons and four saddled horses tethered nearby. Facing Dean, she had her back toward him. Corporal Dean had one rein in one hand and Sis's hand in the other. They were oblivious to other people, deep in their own conversation. Not wanting to be noticed, Shelby moved past through the crowd. He knew Sis wouldn't be with the family any more, no matter where they went, and was saddened by it. From what Shelby could see, Sis didn't appear too worried. *I'm a wonderin' if they's somethin' to what John is a'sayin'?*

"Hey, James! Over here!"

James was surprised at Shelby's good spirits. Ever since Lucinda died, Shelby hadn't been himself. When his brother slapped him on the back upon greeting him, James knew something drastic must have happened to Shelby.

"If you ain't a sight for sore eyes, Shelby! What's goin' on?"

Shelby explained he had this new idea and wanted to ask him about what he thought of it. He went through all the reasons for not going back to Jenny Lind and every one of them were addressed to convince James to stay in Little Rock with him.

"Well, what you figure on doin' here in Little Rock, big brother? We ain't exactly rich, you know. You at least have a piece of land back in Jenny Lind and I ain't got a thing," James said.

Shelby pulled out his pipe from his hip pocket and slowly packed it with James hanging on to the suspense his brother was creating. He finally stuck the pipe between his teeth without lighting it and said, as if he had had the original thought himself, "Well, James, when you don't know what to do, the best thing is to do nothin'," he profoundly stated. Shelby lit his pipe and took a deep draw. James looked at his brother, dumbfounded!

"Well, ain't that just right smart?" James had been waiting to hear some great news. His comment was flat dumb and maybe he was not doing as well as thought. *Maybe losin' Lucinda has got to his brain?*

"How in the hell you a'goin' to eat when you do nothin'? Shelby, you'se behavin' strange like when I first seen ya, now, I'm sure of it. They's somethin' the matter with you. Have you taken leave of your senses? Are you a'sayin we are to make out like a pair of beggars? No, thanks, I think I will manage to find somethin' on my own, big brother."

Shelby hadn't figured on his borrowed words from Vera eliciting this reaction. After explaining how it had been their job to know how to work with horses and tack in camp, he stated, "Why, James, you and me was trained at it!"

"Shelby, you ain't makin' a bit of sense. Don't you know the war is over? We ain't at Duvall's Bluff anymore. This here's Little Rock!"

Frustrated from not being able to convey his concept, Shelby finally blurted out that the livery stables in Little Rock had need of blacksmiths too. "Somebody has to do this job, war or no war, and we'se trained how to smith."

James realized his big brother hadn't lost it all and possibly had a legitimate solution. At least it was worth listening to. The possibility always existed that, if the blacksmithing didn't pan out, they could traipse off to Texas like the rest of the family was planning to do.

At first thinking he had a deranged brother, James quickly changed his mind and believed Shelby had hit onto something solid for the first time in their lives. By living together, their keep financed by mustering out pay, they could make it until more money could be generated through blacksmithing.

Shelby's eyes danced with James's agreeing with the plan. It wasn't the time to reveal anything about Vera yet.

"I thought you'd come around oncet you heard me out," he told James. We best tell the rest what we'se a'goin' to do." It was time to share something else with James.

"When I went into Shoal Creek to look for Pa whiles back several years ago, I learned somethin' mighty interestin'. I learned the Land Office had patents for a piece of land and I signed my x for some of it back then. Well, things got unsettled with the war and all, and first one thing led to another. That was the end of it, I thought. Never heard no more. If folks are 'a'goin south to Texas for free property, then, maybe gettin' land around Fayetteville later on could be somethin' to think about. Whatcha' think of that idee, James?"

"It 'pears to me, you is a right bit smarter than I figured you for, Shelby," James said, but added no more. He didn't want his older brother getting any notion of lording life over him with his newly found intelligence.

Shelby added no more either about the possibility of finding someone to replace the loss of Lucinda. Maybe he might convince a beautiful woman named Vera to take a chance on him?

Chapter 33
TEXAS PLANS

John purposefully sidestepped all the places he thought Sis might be. He didn't know where she was and he didn't care either. His intentions were set in locating the six wagons going south to Texas in the morning. Several were riding single with the train Aaron McCoy had told him about. Not all of John's muster pay was taken up in fines from his entanglement with Owen Leaven like he thought it would be. He had enough to buy a horse and tack to make the trip with.

McCoy's former slave, Angie, who had barely made it to Arkansas' shores in January, was told by one of the supply wagon drivers that he had heard about Aaron helping out a sick Union soldier at Little Rock prison. Aaron's name elicited respect among the guards sifting to the chief cook. Picking up more supplies for the refugee camp had been opportunity for the cook to relate the most unusual story, which they shared with Angie. Relieved to know Cornelia's Papa was still alive, she hopped a wagon going for supplies in Little Rock, taking Cornelia and her daughter, Fannie. By leaving the refugee camp in early morning they expected to make their destination by evening time. Finding Aaron McCoy would be the next issue after they arrived.

It was a bittersweet day when two of Aaron's sons, George and Tom, came into Arkansas from their units in Missouri. Before leaving their units, they checked the prisoner lists, hoping their Papa was a prisoner and not listed among the recorded dead. Happily, they discovered their dad had been incarcerated at Little Rock. Soldier exchanges were being made all across the country and now was the time to find their Papa. The McCoy brothers made their trip in hopes to meet up with their Pa, but they met Angie, Fannie, and their little sister first. Both McCoy brothers couldn't believe it when they saw their Pa's black slave walking down the dusty street.

Angie told the McCoy boys that a mounted Union dispatcher revealed which way to go to find Aaron McCoy, after learning about Cornelia, the five year old white child she was leading. Their motherless sister had been put into Angie's care when the war started. The war was over now. Sympathies for the south remained inside the former Confederate soldiers, however, war's end or not. Angie Brown and her daughter, Fannie, had been Aaron McCoy's only hope for Cornelia's care after their house had been burned in Alabama.

"We'se barely made it out to the back cedar brake before the farm was run over with Union soldiers," Angie reported to George and Tom. "If it hadn't been for some shantyboat people, we'd never got out of there alive."

"Our boat joined others, pickin' up stragglers along the way, hopin' to find less war," Angie reported. After getting to the Mississippi River they found it was just as dangerous there as it was back home, forcing further evacuation and fighting off rebel forces belonging to no known regiment. So many women and children scrambled for safety on boats that the watery drifters' numbers grew to more than three hundred. The refugee camp south of Little Rock had been their place of safety until now.

After hearing Angie out, the McCoy brothers, their little sister, Angie and Fannie located the wagons readying for Texas. That's when they first saw Aaron McCoy. After initial greetings, he motioned to John passing by on his newly-acquired horse to come meet his family.

Aaron was a kind-hearted Reb and John liked him. That was the beginning of rebel friendship. Tom and George caught John off guard for a moment when the introductions were made. Being the loser of the war left a bitter attitude in the McCoy brothers and the message wasn't lost to John. Thoughts of sharing an adventure with them presented some possible conflicts without even trying and the trip hadn't even begun. They shook hands with noticeable reservations emitted from returned stares.

Aaron introduced Angie, Fannie and his five year old Cornelia, beaming with pride. He had hoped beyond hope for Angie to make it to Little Rock, not knowing how it could ever be possible. He knew it had to be a Higher Power than man who arranged such, and made mention of it, which triggered Cornelia's response.

Cornelia hugged her Papa's neck and said, "We said all the way a'comin', Papa, 'Lordy, please help us find safety.' I reckon the Lordy did," Cornelia giggled and hugged him again.

Angie was embarrassed by the formal introduction coming from a former "boss man", but Fannie's eyes lit up when she saw the roguish John. She grinned a big grin.

"Howdy, Mr. McCoy, I see your family has made it in," Harriett said, coming toward the group gathered about Aaron. It was time to settle who would be riding where. Harriett had her hands full trying to hold her energetic younger sons in check. Gus insisted on his own independence to explore without Haden. Everything Gus did, whether it be kick rocks, kick dirt or run, trying to jump high enough to touch the bottom of the big bell atop a pole on the street corner, Haden had to try it too. Contrasted to her brothers, Mary clung to her mother's skirt so tight it was difficult for Harriett to walk.

"Howdy," Aaron answered. Yes, ma'am, it does appear they did make it!" Aaron was beaming.

John's horse snorted out some excess dust from his nostrils, causing Gus to wipe his forearm on his britches after getting snorted on.

"John, I need to talk to you a minute," Harriett told her handsome son. The minute she said that, John grew a frown across his face. He knew what she wanted to talk to him about.

They walked out of earshot of the other and she asked, "What is this about Sis?"

John turned red, but it wasn't from embarrassment.

"You know, John, she couldn't help that attack back home and the youngun' a'growin' in her belly anymore'n I could've saved William, don't you?"

"Ma, there's stuff you don't know. I know I ain't no lily-white husband, but somethin' else happened beside that attack and I ain't so sure just whose baby she is a'carryin'. I heard things after you got to camp from Fort Smith, but I didn't want to believe in it. I ain't so sure now. She's set with Ted Dean to get back to her Ma, I hear. That's where she needs to be. It sure as hell ain't with me. I'm a'walkin'!"

"Well, folks, we need to get the rest of our things loaded. We're headin' out first thing in the mornin'," Aaron McCoy called out to the milling Texas-bound group planning to leave in his wagon train. He somehow became wagon master because he had been talking with people in Little Rock for opportunities down south for some time. Beside a scout who was going with them, he was the most informed.

At day's end, Harriett could tell it was going to be a long night in that little room off the mess kitchen. The boys were so full of excitement they couldn't find closure for the day without finding mischief to invest in first. *Since it's a'goin' to be me a'cookin' along this trip, them boys might not need to sleep, but I do! John always figures a way for things to happen. I just didn't know cookin' was part of the bargain to pay for the trip to Texas until you let it slip, John. We have need of a chance somewheres and this is it I reckon.*

"Hey, Ma!" Shelby and James waved at Harriett walking toward the little room off the mess kitchen. They told their disappointed mother of their plans to stay. It was their first separation. *But, they's grown men, what can I do about it now? Many things is uncertain. It's a long ways to Texas, how can we bear it? I must. At least they ain't dead like William and Jasper. They's still alive.* She didn't dare dampen her sons' spirits. Shelby was coming back to life since he lost his wife. *No more needs to be said.*

July 1, 1865 was a warm, if dusty, morning when the wagons pulled out. The group was a mishmash of people. Some were from Confederate sympathies coming from inside the Little Rock prison. Some were soldiers with loyalties to both sides. None of Harriett's boys wanted to go to war in the first place, but they had no choice. Now the war's over, it's over. It's a possibility John could have a different view of things if he had been on the losing side, but he felt right about moving on. Drifting was natural. John's daddy taught him how to move on.

George and Tom had other persuasions. Their countenance about moving on didn't come from a light heart that had no attachments to anything permanent. They had lost a family home in Alabama, lots of land now parceled out to some of those who once belonged to them. Moving on was more traumatic for the McCoy brothers.

"Maybe we can get us a piece of land and raise a cow or two," Harriett told her family. "Lands! That'd be more than I ever had in my whole life!"

Granted, the intention of everyone going south was to find a life, something new. Some men had wives with them and some did not. Maybe others were like John, a man with a wife he chose to ignore, but no one knew about it. Texas would be a good place to swallow up histories.

Silas Jones, Marty Shane, and Jacob Findley, single riders going with them, had met Aaron while in prison. Beside unmarried men making the trip, there were two unmarried women seeking independence too. Mary Jane Foreman and Monica Whitten wanted a new start. Life hadn't been satisfactory in Arkansas and change seemed in order for hopes of something better. Maybe there would be a good man somewhere in Texas waiting for them?

In the lead wagon were the Settles, Brian and Molly, with their daughter, Susan and son-in-law, Wilber Bergers. The Troutmans followed behind the Settles's wagon.

Mark Troutman was in his early forties and his wife, Nona, was very pregnant in her middle thirties. Minnie Felter, her sister, traveling with them, had never been involved in the birthing process. Nona was counting on Minnie after losing three babies before, or she wouldn't have agreed to travel this late in her pregnancy.

Next came the McCoy wagon with Angie, Fannie and Cornelia. Tom and George rode horses.

Two wagons pulled out at the last minute after hearing about a raiding party attacking a wagon train in north Texas from one lone rider who escaped the fracas. Unnerving as the account was, the thought of nothing left for them near Fort Smith was equally so. The rest were willing to chance it.

Felix and Julie Worthum drove the last wagon. The newlyweds had room for Harriett and the children since they owned little to set up housekeeping with. Harriett was reminded of another time in another world when she viewed the wagon's contents. *Oh, Canady, you need to be here. I'm a'goin' for a new beginnin', but it ain't fully satisfyin' without you.*

Chapter 34
LIFE'S NEW CHAPTER

Squeaks coming from wagon wheels invited memories of another sort made in Kentucky. Only the weather was cold then and not hot when those memories were made. Shelby was born in the dead of winter. Harriett's first long trip had been made while pregnant with him, much like Nona Troutman riding in the wagon following lead.

I could use some of that cool right now, Harriett thought, remembering how she had to pull the woolen shawl tighter around her shoulders many years ago. Even with the flaps of the Conestoga rolled up, the heat building inside the canvas covered wagons was sweltering.

Mary was lulled to sleep as if drugged from the rocking wagon going across rutted trails. It was a different situation with the boys. They couldn't stay confined for long stretches of time. Periodically, they climbed onto the back of the wagon to rest from running alongside after releasing pent-up energy.

"Move over, Haden," Gus ordered.

"Don't touch me," Haden answered. "I'se here first."

"It's too hot and I don't want you to touch me neither," Gus fussed. "It's too hot back here," Gus quarreled after crawling over Haden.

"Here, boys, we'll have none of that. Gus, you can put your head near the side and it'll be just the same as where Haden is," Harriett told her gangly son. Gus was beet red from running in the July heat. His fussy complaints made more discomfort for everyone who was searching for something cool to breathe. Stagnant air in the wagons added more difficulty to seven months pregnant Nona Troutman.

Horseback riders fared better from breezes blowing against escaping perspiration. Hot sun sinking further in the west offered precious little relief, as it threatened to become a fading ball of light. With less intensity, heat still saturated every blade of parched grass, regardless of the sun's illumination.

Toward day's close, horseback riders could be heard passing conversation between them. John had been a loner on the trip, but moved up closer to the other riders and tried to join in.

"Ma was the cook at Duvall's Bluff," he said. "She knows how to cook as good as any chuck hand. I sure could use some of her grub right about now, how about you boys?"

Tom and George openly agreed to the idea before George reported his trail observations.

"Been lookin' for game. Didn't see any tracks on the trail since we left."

"If it's anything like it was back home, it's done hunted out," John said, then added, "Sure hope it is better than this in Texas. It's gotta be better than this!"

George told the young women who rode closer, "We're headin' into Indian country. That part of this trip gives me pause to worry a bit. I don't think they's goin' to take too kindly to bein' crowded much, 'specially since some of 'em was ousted before."

John listened to George's comment. The rider's facial structure, narrow bridge and high cheekbones, looked pretty much like some of his own family, like kin. *Was George a 'puttin' space between him and his kin, too?*

"Oh, yeah, I heard me some of them stories. Don't rightly blame nobody though for gettin' sick and tired of folks pushin' 'em around. Don't cotton to it much myself," John said. He had no intention to reveal his biology and shantyboat connections. It wouldn't be profitable for anyone to take notice of his heritage. The least said, the best said, was the family understanding. It was enough to look suspiciously like the Indians from back east, but being Black Dutch was a more acceptable way of putting things to justify tanned skin.

"Cornelia's Ma was full blood Cherokee," George said. "Pliney was a good woman. She and Pa married after our Ma died. When Cornelia come along, Pliney didn't have no help and was too young for such a big 'un. Poor Pliney didn't make it," he said.

"I was meanin' to ask, but didn't know quite how to ask it, about Angie," John stammered. "Hell, the war is done over, what about her now?" The question popped out.

Tom darted a look at John and caught himself before he said what his look meant.

"Angie's like family. She's welcome to go with us anywheres and we'll always take care of her. If it wasn't for Angie, Cornelia probably wouldn't be here. She was her wet nurse after Pliney died," Tom said.

"Where in the world would Angie go? She ain't got no kin I know of since she brung Cornelia from Alabama. Well, she and that old Rufus got together at home. That's where Fannie come from. Rufus belonged to the neighbor who loaned 'em to plant our cotton. He's the Papa of little Railen, too, but that little fella got drown in the river," George added. "They say Rufus was the son of the plantation owner. Reckon that's why Fannie is so light."

"I think that Fannie is a looker, all right," John quickly inserted.

John's comment caused instant eye contact between the McCoy brothers and him.

"Ain't worth messin' with, John. Could be more trouble than it's worth," George said in a matter-of-fact way, fortified further by competitive stares from both McCoys.

John looked straight ahead, giving no satisfaction he had heard any of their warning, but switched subjects instead.

"There's the Sabine River! I thought she'd be low, but that sucker ain't as dry as I thought she'd be. Wonder what she'd be like when we ain't in a drought!"

"Don't 'pear to be a'movin' much," Tom said. "It ought to cool the team a'goin' through it, but I ain't so sure any of these teams ever forded water before. I 'spect we'll find out in the mornin' won't we?"

The wagons formed a tight circle before the horses were watered, hobbled and fed for the night. A campfire was grated for a big iron skillet. Mary Jane and Monica helped Harriett make tantalizing smells from slab bacon and jonnie cakes joined the sultry air in short order. Campfire coffee perked, teasing hungry stomachs all the more.

Aaron McCoy pulled his map after the meal. In the campfire light he scoured the yellowed map for what lay ahead. It appeared the morrow presented challenges of rivers and creeks.

"How in the world can we get those wagons across?" Nona Troutman asked Aaron.

She wasn't the only concerned person. Susan Bergers told of her fears about crossing as well. She and her new husband knew they had a world waiting for them on the other side, but getting to it was going to be scary.

Aaron said, "Ladies, all I can tell you is you will have to wait and you will see for yourself tomorrow. You'll be goin' on the ferry across the Sabine. The men will be drivin' teams. Hopefully, we can make passage where it ain't so deep and ain't no quick sand." Then he added confidently, "We men will make it across before you ladies do."

Fannie saw George, Tom and John on the other side of the circled wagons talking with Silas, Marty and Jacob. She grabbed the big coffee pot from off the coals and started toward the men.

"Yous gentlemens care for more coffee? We are 'goin to clean the pot and there's some left. Seems a shame to pour it all out," she said.

"Well, thank you, Fannie," Tom said, holding his tin cup out for her to fill it up. The rest held out their cups. George looked at John when it was time for Fannie to fill his cup.

"That's sure nice of you, Fannie," John said. It wasn't the words but the twinkle in his eyes that struck George while watching the interaction. It appeared the McCoy's warning concerning Fannie had been wasted effort.

"Yessir, Mr. John, it seems such a waste to toss it out. We have to be careful about throwin' away good food, now don't we, Mr. John?"

Fannie's eyes met John's twinkle with a twinkle of her own. Both had spoken to each other in an obvious enough way, but felt safe enough that George wouldn't have any right to confront anybody from such a subtle titillation. The message had to be seen, since it wasn't heard. Oh, but George was watching.

"Guess we'd better wash this old coffee pot up now," she said, turning to go back to where the women were cleaning up. Her frame was darkened on the backside bordered by campfire light as she walked away from the men. The men noticed the soft glow of light showed off Fannie's tiny waist and big bosom. John's appetite for a woman was whetted all the more just seeing her shapely form, even if she was only fourteen years old.

Morning brought much the same as any morning—hungry stomachs, women helping Harriett cook, cleaning up and putting away like they had their first night. Biscuits and bacon would tide them over until nightfall where the performance would be repeated. Men rounded up the horses, hitched them to the wagons and made their way toward the river and the ferryman. Their campfire and prospective business hadn't gone unnoticed by the boatman, who told them there had been several more wagons ahead of them. From the word he got, there could be lots more wagons to follow them too.

Molly Settles, her daughter, Susan, and Nona joined Harriett and Mary as they walked toward the ferry pier.

"You are a mighty brave young woman, Nona, takin' on this trip in your condition," Harriett told her.

"Oh, lands, I'll be fine, Mrs. Holmes. It isn't this baby that worries me, it's crossing that river."

Harriett refused to say anything about her experiences with rivers. No one knew of the Melungeon connection, nor did many know about shantyboat people. She sure wasn't going to say anything about her Indian heritage either, but some things didn't require explanations. Maybe if she glossed it over, if she acted like such didn't exist, it would disappear?

"My family come from Europe, Black Dutch, you know. This new country we're a'goin' to would've been quite adventuresome for them, I reckon," Harriett said with an air.

The women looked at her in awkward silence after questioning words that had just slipped from her mouth.

The least said is the best, she reminded herself.

Nona tried to break the silence. "The baby sure has been active lately. Mark thinks it's a boy. He could be right, but I guess we'll just have to wait and see, won't we?"

"What are you going to be doing in Texas, Harriett?" Molly asked, changing the subject. Before allowing Harriett to answer, she added, "We want to get us a place close to Susan and Wilber. Bryan wants to try his luck with those unbranded longhorns looking for a home if the grass is good. It would give us a start, he thinks."

Mary Jane and Monica rode up to the walking women on their way toward the river.

"Ladies, wish us luck! We are going to ford it ourselves. Old Bonnie is pretty goosey but I think we can make 'er," Monica said laughing.

"Let's hope she can," Mary Jane teasingly said, "or, I will have to take your patent too, missy, if you can't handle a little ole river!"

Both girls were in rare form. Prospects for meeting some rich Texas rancher or making it rich on their own were topics of their fantasies. These free-spirited women couldn't fit in Little Rock's society, but sought more rugged goals for their lives in Texas.

Angie, holding one of Cornelia's hands and Fannie holding the other to prevent her from falling in the dry grass, walked toward the talking women.

"Lands O'Goshen, I can remember a time when I thought life was a simple thing. It was just hard work, do the right thing and be good to each other. Funny how much you find this old world really is a troublesome place the older you gets," she said huffing.

The women laughed at Angie and agreed life had been a rude awakening for most of them. Molly looked at Mary Jane and Monica.

"Oh, to be that young again," she said about the single women.

"Don't you hope anymore, Molly?" Minnie Felter asked, after joining her sister and the rest.

"I have hope, and don't doubt most of us have. Jesus gives me hope. How about you, Molly?" Minnie asked her sister.

"I sure do, Miss Ladybug! It's just the older I get, the more that impossible dream I was counting on in my youth seems to lose ground. I guess what I was aiming to say is I'm going to see new things in Texas and have a new life raising cattle, but I don't know how my bones will cooperate. I have my doubts, but Bryan doesn't at all. You'd have thought he'd run cattle all his life after reading all those books."

Reading remained a mystery to Harriett. Letters with those marks made on them made no sense at all. *If you ain't never done it, you can't miss it.*

By the time they reached the water's edge, Fannie pointed out Julie Wortham watching her husband trying to drive their team across the Sabine.

"Water's up to the bottom of the wagon," Nona said excitedly as the ferryman motioned for the women to come. They hurried to the flat boat connected with ropes and large pulleys strung across the river.

Getting back on the trail after crossing the river was the first of many times this activity was repeated before getting to the Oklahoma and Texas border. Nothing major occurred other than Mary Jane's horse throwing a shoe, but it was replaced when they got to Caddo Valley. Silas and Marty helped put a wheel back on Felix Wortham's wagon at Arkadelphia on the fourth day of their journey. After finding the community of Antoine and fording the little Missouri River they made it into Washington before reaching Indian territory where the landscape undulated in more pronounced elevations rutted by rivers at their base.

The wagon train remained vigilant while going through the same place where the lone rider reported in Little Rock about the Indian war party attacking his wagon train. John rode ahead of the wagons. George and Tom flanked the first wagon with Mary Jane and Monica riding behind two wagon lengths. Silas Jones and Jacob Findley took the space between the third and fourth wagons with Marty Shane taking drag.

Everyone's nerves were on edge the first day into Indian territory. None slept well that night. If there had been a full moon, the temptation to move at night might have been acted upon, but it was not to be and gave the horses a much-needed rest.

"Best make sure you have your ammunition close if we should have any surprises in the night," Aaron McCoy cautioned the men at the end of the meal. They were camped west of Broken Bow, Indian territory, a hard day's drive from Arkansas.

"I would like to set and visit a spell fellas, but this ain't the time nor place for it. You boys put your bedrolls under them wagons and keep one eye open," he said to the single horsemen. "Those of us drivin' wagons all day will spell you about one in the mornin'," he said. Keeping wagons upright, and driving teams challenged drivers who were more than ready to find rest by nightfall.

"You younguns can't take care of personal business without an adult with you, do you hear me? Could be someone watchin' us and we ain't gonna take no chances," Aaron said to the boys.

Harriett knew there wouldn't be any problem with Mary running off and getting lost, but she knew her boys' tenacity and impish disdain for authority. "You younguns better listen to what he's a'sayin'," she told her children.

"But, Ma, I ain't gonna get lost," Gus complained. "I can take care of myself."

John heard Gus fussing with his mother and walked toward him with something heavy on his mind. He pointed his finger under Gus's nose, giving him fair warning.

"Don't let me hear no fussin' with Ma again when she tells you somethin', now, you hear?"

"Get your damned finger outta my face, John! You ain't my Pa," Gus warned his older brother.

He hardly had time to get his message out before he was eating dirt.

"Get off me, you, son-of-a-bitch!" Gus yelled and spit at the same time. John had his belt off in a flash and was sitting on Gus's shoulders whacking him with it on his behind.

Not being able to free himself before John's belt enforced his verbal warning, Gus's rebellion turned to cries begging his brother to stop.

"That's enough, John," Harriett said.

John got up off Gus and bent down to his meeker little brother, grabbing him under his armpits, and lifted him off the ground. Gus's face had mud where his tears mixed with dirt.

"Now, I don't want any argument out of you when Ma tells you somethin'. Do you hear me Gus?"

Gus kicked the dirt and wiped his face with his shirtsleeve. "Yeah, I hear you," he said softly.

"You ain't heard all that happened to the folks who came through here last time and I ain't gonna tell it now. Just don't you go off somewhere without some of us with you. You got that?"

Gus nodded his head without speaking, then retreated to the wagon he had been riding in. A wounded spirit needed a retreat.

"Ma, it ain't safe even if we haven't had any trouble yet. It could be a'waitin' just about anywhere before we get to the land office at Alvord. If he gives you any more trouble, you just let me know," he said before leaving to put his bedroll under the wagon.

Most didn't sleep except the team drivers. Those keeping watch knew their snores would give the location of the camp away if their campfire hadn't already done so. Change of guard was a welcome relief at one a.m. and only those now on duty could attest to snores coming from former guards.

Many found the night a long one. Molly Settles's caged rooster crowed before shades of darkness slipped away. Her four hens caged with him started clucking and making a racket when the fine-feathered alarmist announced it was a new day.

Everyone was anxious to get an early start and to not tarry long in the wilderness. Gentle hills as apposed to mountainous challenges thickly forested would offer more protection for the pursued. A more flattened and barren terrain could be safer in Texas.

Molly fed her chickens some corn and watered them. The chickens weren't happy having to stay in their cage and voiced disapproval each time their cage was jarred from deep ruts.

Morning turned to afternoon when the wagon train reached the first of a number of creeks they had to cross. The horses always drank their fill before moving on to the biggest challenge of all, Red River. A paddlewheel boat was moving west on Red River away from Davenport, the ferryboat town, by the time the wagons pulled in.

Women got onto the ferry to cross once again, all but Mary Jane and Monica, who forded their horses across without incident.

Aaron McCoy had plans to reach north of Paris, Texas before they camped for the night and they would have to keep moving if they were to make it.

"Move on, haw! Giddy-up!" Bryan Settles yelled, slapping the team's rumps with reins. They jumped and lunged into the river with Aaron's wagon following close behind. Red River churned with wagons and horses in the hot afternoon sun.

What a sight to see, Canady! It's been a terrible time, a horrible war. We'se lost our babes from one thing or another. Like you said, sweetheart, we can't look backwards now, it's a waste of time. We have to move on, just move on. Hopin' for somethin' better don't leave no room to pine on the past.

In the middle of the muddy river Harriett thought she saw Canady's face from the swirling red water. His face was circled with those faces of Jasper, William, Aunt Nancy, Uncle Will and her Kentucky cousins flocking around her grandpa. She saw Arimenta's face, and there was Lucinda's and Shelby Robert's reflection, but as quickly as they came, they vanished.

It's a crossroad, for sure. The past has to be left behind even if the future is a mystery and full of holes inside, vacancies that need fillin'. We's crossin to a new beginnin'. What's the purpose to it?

Chapter 35
SETTLING IN

H arriett knew cooking had been her calling whether she wanted to answer to it or not. She first opened the door to this job when she married Canady and began their big family. *Everyone came out hungry! Ain't no doubt if Canady had stayed, my complaint from the numbers of babes to feed would have growed more. It ain't been the cookin that's the problem. It has been the gettin' that's been the problem. Cookin' has bought our keep once again, and this time, it bought us a new beginnin'.*

Patents were had at Decatur and after two years of claiming their hundred-sixty acre farm, hope for the remaining five years of required occupation would be fortified with John's still and whiskey sales.

Even the Kiowas and Comanches learned where to get John's whiskey. He had made a deal with the Indians to swap for longhorns originally. No one knew where the cattle originated from, there were no brands before John and Gus burned the split arrow brand on them. No one asked any questions either.

Harriett still was in the cooking business. Slab bacon was in the skillet and about six eggs were slated to go in next, after forking bacon out of the grease. John already was up and out but for some reason Gus was sleeping in with the other two this morning. As Harriett busied about her early morning ritual, she recalled two years ago, when she'd almost lost Gus after they crossed Red River.

All the time they were traveling from Arkansas over the rutted trails into Indian territory, they never saw an Indian. They sharpened their lookout once they got on Decatur road. The children were complaining about being cooped up and, against Harriett's better judgment, she allowed the children to run alongside the wagon. Haden and Mary gave it up after a short while and got back into the wagon.

Gus ran past all the wagons ahead of them, even after John had given him warning not to do so.

It was when the wagons reached grasslands, belly high to a cow swishing underneath them, Harriett noticed Gus was missing. That was when it happened. Seven Kiowas on horseback popped out of blackjack trees bordering the grassland and met the wagon train with Gus held captive under a very stout-looking warrior's arm. He was suspended with his feet dangling by the horse's belly. The panic displayed across the gregarious lad's face implied he wished he had listened to John. Harriett's rowdy, hard-to-control son was unusually quiet and frantically helpless. Gus was scared to death and so was Harriett.

No one knew what to expect from these people, or how many more might be hidden behind the oaks. Caught unaware, confidences of supposed safety were shaken. They expected the worst, especially after the stories they heard before leaving Arkansas. The Kiowas knew exactly what they wanted and grinned, watching nervousness coming out the pores of the travelers. The Indian holding Gus made a gesture for a swap.

To Molly Settles's horror, the savages wanted her rooster and four hens in place of Gus. Getting that close horrified her for what else they might want. While the wagon train erroneously felt confident about traveling alone, the Kiowas had been watching and sizing the train up. The Indians were in mustang country herding horses back to their compounds across the river. In the process, unbeknown to the travelers, they had heard and watched the wagon train for miles while in search for mustangs. Gus was just too easy an opportunity to pass up.

Molly's plans for her transported seed flock of chickens she had hopes of prospering with in Texas evaporated with the swap. It was much to Gus's relief, but Molly cried. Instead of the plans Molly had to grow a brooder house full of chickens, the chickens became dinner for seven hungry Indians.

After living in Texas for the past two years and learning more about wild marauding men of the Texas countryside, Harriett believed they were more than fortunate the Indians had a hunger for chickens and nothing more that day. Many incidents since fortified a reason for thanksgiving then. Harriett had always wondered if the Indians noticed some of Gus's "Black Dutch" characteristics and if maybe that played a part in the non-violent swap.

It was also two years ago in the land office where Harriett saw someone she never dreamed of seeing again—James Holmes, the brother to Canady! He had stood surety for them when they married in Kentucky.

"Harriett, is that you?" James had been standing near the large counter with maps spread out over it. Two young men were with him.

"James? How in the world did you get here from Kentucky?" Harriett ran without thinking and gave James a big hug, feeling he was almost like a surrogate for her Canady at that very moment.

"After the war we needed to move on since there's nothin' left in Kentucky," he said. "Susan died soon after you and Canady married and I had to raise my younguns by myself. This here's Mayo and Robert," he said, introducing sons older than Shelby.

"Glad to meet you, ma'am," Robert said, removing his hat. Mayo just nodded and lightly tipped his broad brim.

"This here's your Aunt Harriett, Uncle Canady's wife, boys," James explained. "We lost count of you folks. Where's Canady? Never thought we would see the likes of you again 'specially with the war and all."

"I don't rightly know about Canady," Harriett finally admitted. "We made it to Shoal Creek in Arkansas then found a piece of land at Jenny Lind before the war got us. James, Canady bought the finest mules you ever did see and a body took 'em, I guess. I don't need to tell you how your brother is, he wasn't goin' to take that. We ain't seen or heard from him since."

Harriett had a lump she felt as big as a bowl of butter well up and dropped her eyes from James's look of disbelief.

"He never came back," she said, but quickly added, "somethin' must have happened to him or he'd come back to me and the younguns."

After telling each other some of their histories, they agreed to get land close to each other if they could.

"It might come in handy to have some kin close," he said. James looked at Harriett like it might be handy for him too. He saw her blush then she stated she hadn't given up on Canady yet. "Who knows, if you found your way here, maybe he can too."

It was James and his boys who helped with the dugout, and Gus and John helped him and their cousins with their set up in return. Evening time found all around Harriett's supper table until the soddy's were finished and John's still was completed and working. Swapping whiskey for necessities at the trading post in Alvord established a name for John, which reached beyond the pioneer population. Thirty head of longhorns from the Comanches over the past two years were traded for firewater.

Peace among pioneer and Indian alike lulled Harriett into a false sense of security. She knew, at least, it wasn't like she experienced in Arkansas where they never knew who or what renegade was going to kill you. On the plains, everybody was mostly viewed with suspicion until proven otherwise. But, no perpendicular rocky land, densely forested, camouflaged the view on the plains. You could at least see your enemy coming from the gun slots in the dugout. They named their place "Split Arrow Ranch." It still didn't feel like home after two years of effort, however.

Aaron McCoy settled a mile south of Split Arrow. Angie refused to live anywhere else but with the McCoy family and continued to mother Cornelia, teaching her how to read from The Good Book. Aaron hadn't been like most of the slave owners. He had taught Angie himself how to read. Now she was returning the favor for his child while he worked long hours establishing a working ranch.

It was dusty and hot. "Too hot for this time of year," Gus complained.

Beads of perspiration had already begun to run down the bridge of his nose when he raised off the cot on his elbow. Some of the salty stuff ended up on his lips, agitating an already quarrelsome mood starting off the morning.

"It's gonna be another one of those days again," he said out loud, making sure his mother heard.

Harriett knew what he had meant by it. If rotten moods were particles of dust then Gus was usually in the middle of a brewing dust storm. It was that way before he had even gotten out of bed. His growling stomach was teased by the aroma of bacon frying when he forced his eyelids open. If he didn't get out of bed soon, he knew any minute he would be rousted. Forcing his eyes open and adjusting to the light casting rays on him through an open door of the soddy, he managed to pull himself off his cot and into his britches.

"You know, Ma, you are still a looker," were the first unexpected words out of his mouth. You never knew what Gus was thinking and certainly she didn't think he had been thinking of her attributes after grousing this morning.

"Right nice of you to notice, son," she teased. "Now, do you think you can pull yourself together and get out there to help your brother? I have your breakfast ready."

Haden and Mary hadn't gotten up either. It was early. Mary usually slept later than the boys. Haden was ailing this morning and was stayed in bed longer than usual. Gus always tried to stretch a few extra winks if he could, but not Haden. Since John had already gone outside, Gus had taken advantage of a late start without his "overseer" hounding him.

Maybe I ain't lost all my looks, Harriett thought, if her budding young son took notice of his mother's appearance. *Reckon it all depends on who you is comparin' things with,* she reminded herself, knowing Split Arrow was remote, if not desolate.

Harriett's hair was black with streaks of white at the temples. Hard work kept her body lean and trim belying the fact of birthing eight children. *Maybe I can thank my kin for few wrinkles. Molly Settles already has the looks of an old woman. Too much work to do to grow flabby,* she thought. *Nobody in a right mind can believe things is like they was in my courtin' days, the "holler's songbird" they called me.*

"Mountain tall, sky so blue, birds do call to grass with dew.Make my day to spirit's plea, from work to play, earth's beauty see." Harriett, inspired by Gus' compliment, sang one of the songs that used to bounce off the mountain walls of her Kentucky holler a lifetime ago.

Gus had heard his mother's plaintive song over the years. It had Indian inflections in it. Puzzled, he said, "Them words don't make a whole lot of sense to me, Ma."

"I'm afraid you are right since you ain't never seen what I have, Gus. It's a regret, son."

Gus breathed deep while buttoning his britches. Searching for a cool patch of air he discovered was an act of futility. He shrugged his shoulders again, stretched and let out a small moan as he yawned.

Frustration once again overtook the kind words he complimented his mother with earlier. He discovered it was his own doing his shirt buttons didn't come out even with the right side being shorter than the left. "Damn, I hate mornin's like this," he swore. Mary and Haden were still getting to sleep, adding to his further resentment for not being able to do what he wanted to do. He had a job waiting for him and Haden got to stay home. *So what, if he's puking all night,* Gus thought.

The wood stove heated up the soddy quicker this morning. Normally chilly nights lingered in the mornings and heat from the stove was needed. This day had begun differently. Instinct told Gus this. He dug into his food and washed it down with a mouthful of coffee.

"Things is different than they used to be, ain't they, Ma? This here's the best thing that happened yet today," he said, taking another mouthful of breakfast and swallowing more coffee. "I can remember when we couldn't find a rabbit to cook, can't you, Ma?"

"Sure can, son. I think we have your brother's whiskey business to thank for the start we got here. I'm tolerable worried about them Comanches though, Gus. It could backfire on us, dealin' with them so much. They's a'comin round more and more."

Gus's conversation was cut short. The rest of the boys, cousins Robert and Mayo and the McCoy boys, Tom and George, were already saddled and waiting for the late riser still sitting at the breakfast table.

"Well, that was yesterday," Gus said, getting up from the table and referring to the lean times in Arkansas. "Yesterday don't need to butt into today's business, I reckon," he muttered while taking a bandana out of his hip pocket. Folding the cloth into tight folds, he shuffled to the opened door and put the band around his forehead to tie a knot in the back. Sweat had already started briny creeks toward the folded scarf. A few strands of sun-bleached hair insisting on freedom while he was trying to tie the knot got caught. Gus pulled on the ends. "Shit," he swore. Tying knots could be tricky if you were tender-headed and not too nimble fingered! With a few more words mumbled under his breath, Gus finally finished the job of creating a barrier for sweat running into his eyes.

The younger brother's distress lingered as he stumbled up two steps into the yard. His mood hadn't gone unnoticed by John. Everyone was waiting on Gus. Provoked by his brother's tardiness, John saw a wonderful opportunity to initiate a little brotherly ribbing. His weak spot about growing into manhood, but not actually being there, gave John a chance to crack the fortress Gus kept around that Achille's heel.

Harriett had seen this scene before. After listening to Angie read about stories in The Book when they occasionally visited, she related this morning's happenings to one such story. The account is about a fortress around a city called Jericho. Angie said Joshua merely walked around that walled city and blew a horn and the walls protecting the city tumbled down. This morning Harriett watched John prepare to tear down Gus's defenses, to watch him squirm just as sure as people in Joshua's day once did in Jericho. *Times ain't changed much,* she sighed.

Gus looked like a man, but it really was more of a promise of manhood than the real thing. At almost six feet tall, his strength was that of a young bull. He had to work like a man. There were times he could fool others into thinking he was a young man, until he opened his mouth to talk. At fifteen, Gus's tongue suffered the same unruly affliction as his hair. It just wouldn't stay put. At least, that was the case this morning.

"Kinda weighted down on the hind side this mornin', are ya' Gus," John taunted. Being eight years Gus's senior gave John just enough rope to let Gus hang himself with his hot temper and quick tongue. The sound of John's voice was full of meaning, even before listening to the words he spoke. Gus knew it well. Rivalry between brothers was common between these two.

It's like John is a watchin' competition a'growin' right under his nose. He acts like it just needs a'nippin' here and there from time to time to keep it tolerable, Harriett thought.

"Don't you go and fret yourself none about my hind side, big brother," snapped Gus. He looked up at his two cousins riding back toward the corral after scouting while waiting on him to get out of the dugout. Everyone was antsy about leaving, which didn't do a whole lot for a bad mood to start with. Tom and George turned to meet Robert and were having trouble concealing their amusement over John's needling, causing aggravation to escalate. Gus felt pressed to save face.

"What the hell is the all-fire hurry, anyhow?" he spat out, going to the corral to saddle up Buck. "Those damned Comanches will wait for us! They don't want to make their kill too much before we get there anyhow. Don't you know it's more irritatin' for the son-of-a-bitches to make a fresh kill on our stock so's we can see blood still oozing?" he barked at his grinning partners.

"Gettin' to you, is it, little brother?" John drawled out his needling. About that time, George interjected and cautioned with a bit of news of his own.

"Pa barely escaped from some wild Comanche's playin' war games last week. You better keep one eye draggin' tail with the other eye up front today. You can't never tell when they might want to play war again."

Aaron McCoy had run into the middle of a coup when he was scouting strays and barely escaped with his hair still on his head. The Comanches and ranchers had been living peacefully with only a cow or two coming up gone ever once in a while, but lately there had been some changes taking place.

"Pa thought they's liquored up," George said.

Gus thought his argument with John was gone too far to leave it alone now and this was a chance to get in a good one.

"Well, if you'd leave the firewater at home were it belonged, John, those half-crazed redskins wouldn't be so damned stirred up," he criticized self-righteously. The chip on Gus's shoulder was almost visible by now. Actually, Gus really didn't believe their homemade brew had anything to do with it, but it was a good comeback.

This argument was getting too heated for the cousins waiting on Gus to saddle up. George had thought a change of conversation about his Pa would do the trick, but confrontation wouldn't be denied.

Ah, too late! Gus's red flag did it! The blast of Joshua's trumpet cut loose with Gus's last remark. Before the youngest brother knew what happened, he found himself sitting on the ground, rubbing a stunned, throbbing jaw! Those walls came tumbling down!

"When you are big enough to piss for yourself, then maybe you can make some growed up decisions, but 'til then, you best leave the business to the men," John warned, standing over him, daring him to even try to retaliate.

Before Gus could pull himself together and confront John about his manhood, Harriett came flying out of the soddy. It was not time to mince words with her raw-boned, untamed Cherokee mixed-breeds! Her fury and tongue-lashing could match theirs, if need be, any day of the week, and she carried her broom to help her do it.

"John! Gus! I ain't come all this way out here to have you two kill each other! Save your energy to put food on the table. Didn't you boys get enough of that fightin' in the war, John? Can't you let your little brother get growed before you kill him? Gus, what's the matter with you this mornin'? You ain't gettin no chance to oversleep in the mornin' you can count on that, son! Do I have to remind you both the reason we come out here in the first place? You get on with it now, do you hear?" With that, Harriett turned to go back into the soddy.

Harriett's mumbling when she came into the house was heard by the other two, who couldn't help but overhear the commotion going on outside. "I swear, ever since Canady left, runnin' this family takes more'n a body can do at times. John's an immature ladies' man and Gus is a sprout! Chore of ridin' herd ain't easy."

Gus got up, dusted off and swung up on Buck almost in one effortless motion, saving as much face as he could. The rest had already left before Gus got out of the yard. He goosed his horse to catch up, leaving small puffs of dirt fogging behind him.

"Now, maybe Mary and I can get some work done," Harriett said in her daughter's earshot as she watched "Mr. Manhood" trail after the others.

Chapter 36
WESTERN COMPLICATION

"What's all the racket, Ma?" Mary asked. She carried a pan of dishwater and barely missed the old rooster when she tossed it out. His crowing protests and struts of lost dignity mimicked Gus's stance earlier. Harriett followed her back out into the yard.

"Men crow just like that old rooster when their feathers get ruffled, Mary," Harriett told her, pointing to the strutting fowl. "Lands! Your brothers were at it again. I swear! I don't think it will ever stop. Can't rightly tell which'un is worse, Gus or John. More'n likely, if your Pa was here, they wouldn't feel so free to smart off like they do."

Mary was mature for her twelve years. She always did chores and looked for more to do when they were completed. She was a hard worker and a blessed joy to her mother.

"Probably Haden wouldn't be so pesky either," Mary added. "Ma, are you sure he's too sick to go with the rest of the boys?"

Mary had hardly finished saying her sentence before Haden pushed the soddy door open after Harriett had closed it. His sister grabbed her throbbing behind after being whacked by the door and was prepared to swing the dishpan at her brother, but stopped short. He was waving the Winchester and yelling.

"Hurry up, Ma, get back in the soddy! Mary, get back in here!" Without saying any more, he pointed the rifle barrel toward the northern horizon. Puffs of dust could be seen, but it was too far away to see what was making it. The telltale signs of dust puffs in their area could mean a number of things, like bison or longhorns stampeding, a dust devil, a herd of wild mustangs, or a wagon moving fast and, if that were the reason, it would be bad news. It could mean a lone rider was moving fast too, but the same conclusion could be expected from riders moving fast, or a wagon, or an Indian war party.

Haden had been at his Uncle James's farm last night and learned of his recent narrow escape. He picked up food poisoning from leftovers when he ate supper with them and was too sick when he got home or he would have told everyone what he had heard. Likelihood of a visitor coming this way was not too realistic. It was by accident this morning when Haden ran for the chamber pot to throw up again that he happened to glance out the gun slot. Sick or not, it was time to take action, thinking this could be another Comanche coup.

Mary felt waves of guilt for earlier wishing her brother to be out of there. She suddenly was glad he stayed home.

"I don't believe it's any of the boys," Harriett said. "It's too far south for it to be them. Who in the world would be a'comin' out here unless it's Indians chasin' somebody this way?"

"The Comanches are tricky, Ma. This could be one of their tricks again," Haden told his mother. "'Bout the time you think you have met your end of torment and they won't be botherin' you again, they fool you," he said. Haden quickly tried to rectify his last bit of information. "Sometime all they want to do is look the place over," he tried to reassure Mary.

Mary stretched up from atop the bed to look out the gun slot after her brother tried to relieve her concerns. She got off the bed and walked over to the door, then pulled the heavy timber leaning against the wall across the latch and bolted the door. After finishing her task she replied, "Mud houses don't burn very good."

Harriett saw Haden start to say something, but he didn't get it out. She knew what he almost said to his sister and was glad he thought against saying it. She knew their log roof would burn real good. It had mud mixed with grass on top, but there was enough dried post oak to catch a good blaze.

Mary bounced back on the feather bed after she bolted the door to look out the gun hole once more. Patches of dust on the prairie were getting bigger.

Intuition told Harriett they had an edge on other settlers in their vacinity. She believed that from her experience with her grandpa in his Indian compound and from her own biology that they had an advantage. It was well-known among the Kiowas, Apaches, and Comanches that the Holmes family was Indian, but not like any Indian they had known before. *Guess they ain't never heard of Black Dutch,* Harriett had always said when discussing this topic. They lived like white settlers, in houses, and they didn't travel seasonally. They stayed put. *Our summer and winter place is right here and them Indians know it. Maybe them other settlers notice some differences too. No one has paid any visits since we staked our place. I do know our peculiarity is down-right puzzlin'.*

"Do you reckon we're gonna get another lookin' over by them redskins?" Haden asked, still straining to see what was happening on the mesa. Signs of the disturbance had grown into bigger dust puffs. A stampeding team of horses pulling a swaying Conestoga straining its construction to the breaking point was in the midst of the fog. "I never seen one lone wagon make so much dust in all my life," he told his mother, hoping for her comment.

"There!" Haden yelled. There they are! They's movin' faster'n lightin'. They's at least four of em!"

Their vision of the mesa, muted by dust, gradually revealed an awful truth to the three gun slot lookers inside the unfortified soddy. One woman, her twelve year old daughter, and her fourteen year old son hot with fever, watched the fate of another even more vulnerable than them.

Harriett rushed to the other side of the soddy and pulled back the curtain of their draped closet to get a ten gauge. Before she straightened up from stooping inside, she said, "This here will take out more than one if they are close enough," in a voice loud enough to reassure her children. Before she could turn around she heard the big timber at the door being slid back. Haden had gone past her when she fetched the gun, unbolted the door and ran out, yelling at his mother and sister, "Lock it!"

Mary jumped off the bed to do what her brother told her to do, but before she could slam the door shut, she saw Haden dash toward the corral, grabbing a bridle hanging on a post. He headed for the one horse remaining in the pen. Mole was the horse he normally rode when helping his brothers work cattle. After Mary saw Haden slip the bridle on Mole, to her horror she watched him ride bareback out of the opened corral gate toward the growing trail of dust on the mesa.

"There's too many!" Harriett screamed to her crazy son. "You can't do nothin', Haden! You're just a boy," she said, crumpling in the doorway in hysterics. The mother in her made her get up to see what may be the last thing her youngest son ever did in life. She slammed the door shut and bolted it before running to the gun slot. Her son was in full view of the Comanches wearing war paint and it was too late. "It won't help, Haden," she cried.

"We'll all be killed!" Mary screamed.

Both soddy dwellers watched in terror, helplessly frozen by an evil presence, as they watched one who was intensely committed to change the course of events ride into certain destruction.

"Haden, you foolish boy," Harriett moaned.

Mole's high-flying feet were moving so fast it appeared he made dust puffs fog without logical reason. Haden was the best horseman of all the boys and was sticking to Mole's bareback as close as any of the painted counterparts he was racing toward.

He ain't got a chance, the Comanche's outnumber him, they's got more experience, they are older, he ain't got a chance, were the thoughts screaming in Harriett's mind. Harriett knew her youngest boy well. He had witnessed the death of his older brother, William, by so-called civilized people. He was too little to do anything then. He believed he felt he wasn't too little now and that he could make a difference. *Haden's actin' out of emotion and sure not common sense.*

The closer Mole got to the commotion, the louder the noise of the horses' hooves and evil war-whoop screeches. Haden recognized two of the Comanches.

They had been to the soddy to look around a time or two. This bareback rider had lived long enough to have wisdom to know he was in the thick of danger but it was overridden by youthful zeal to make a difference. The sound of their war cries gave him a different understanding of the familiar faces now transformed by paint with bloodthirsty expressions. Flashes of earlier encounters had presented such a different story than the one being written at this moment. The only blind spot Haden had was the foreseeable outcome of his foolish actions. It never seemed to register. He charged ahead as if the possibility of his own defeat was simply unacceptable.

"I couldn't help William, but I can sure do somethin' now, and I ain't standin' by doin' nothin'," he screamed, mixing his words with those of Indian war cries.

Adrenaline flow of youth replaced sensible concern for his safety about the time he saw a man and woman clinging to the driver's bench, trying to drive the frenzied team. An arrow was already embedded into the man's thigh. The driver cracked the reins against the stampeding horses' backs, hoping against odds for more speed. Terror on his wife's face seemed to spur him to do more than man or horse was capable of doing.

Running Dog was catching up to the wagon as Haden flew past him, riding for a split second side by side. Each recognized the other. The four Comanches intended to finish their fight with these settlers. Much like a mountain lion focusing on its prey when running past many other potential meals, it was too late to divert his intensity to go after the passing Haden. Confusion seeing Haden's horsemanship slightly clouded Running Dog's mind when the wagon team made a sharp turn to the left and passed the wistful rescuer.

That was when Haden saw her. A young girl hung onto the back side of the wagon. A piercing scream came from the woman and instinctively he realized it was too late to do anything for her, so he focused on the lone person in the back of the wagon.

Mole, the best cutting horse of the lot, turned on a dime, nearly losing Haden even though he was expecting the abrupt change. Righting himself, he rode toward the back of the stricken wagon to the ashen-faced young girl looking at him. Haden had no plans laid out but only acted upon what he could see to do—pull that girl out of the back of that wagon.

The Comanches were going to take scalps and all the possessions these settlers owned. Crowding white eyes were taking too much hunting ground, killing off too many bison, rounding up the best of the wild horses, and building on migratory trails. With scalps first on their list, they were honed in on stopping the wagon and overlooked the firewater-maker's brother and the action in the back of the wagon. He was only a boy, what could he do?

Opportunity was now or never. Haden rode to the back of the wagon as fast as Mole had ever gone before, holding his Winchester and reins with one hand

and reaching for her with the other. Only because he wore clothes and not war paint did she respond, jumping from the wagon onto the back of the horse. The young girl clutched her arms around Haden's middle and hung tighter than a snapping turtle.

Wild yelps mingled with screams of those being murdered were occupying wild men's attention. The spectacle, dimmed with dust stirred by Indian horses, gave Haden a minuscule possibility to flee. Mole with his double load was directed toward the safety of the soddy.

Just a quarter of a mile, then you son-of-a-bitches won't feel so damned frisky.

Hot heat waves radiated across the mesa, eradicating what visual the blowing dust missed, making it difficult for Mary and Harriett to see what was happening. Both knew Haden had ridden into his certain and sure demise and were crying uncontrollably. No matter how friendly the Comanches had been when they came for John's whiskey, the interruption from Haden on their coup was enough for those savages to forget any friendly feelings ever shown in their yard. *Our fate is the same as what we are a'lookin' at,* Harriett thought, looking at her twelve year old daughter. She knew Mary understood this in her heart too.

"How could Haden have been so foolhardy? When William was killed it came as a surprise to him, he didn't know nobody was around. Haden ran right in the middle of his own death! Didn't the boys warn us about those Comanches this morning?" she scolded the empty space surrounding her and Mary without thinking. "He never stops to think about a thing! We'll all be killed in this desolate, forsaken, dustbowl," she cried, holding Mary close to her.

Mary pulled away from her mother to look again through the gun slot. She began to scream, "Indians are a'comin' toward the soddy!"

Both strained their eyes watching approaching death but fearful of making a sound now. Back flashes in time skipped through Harriett's memory. *Maybe Arkansas wasn't so bad after all. Time's been hard. A'comin' here was suppose to help us find some place, to find home. It ain't suppose to be this a'way. Ain't there no meanin' to life but misery? Ain't there more, somethin' better? Mary has got to feel some comfort and I am the only one she's got right now.* Harriett watched her beautiful young daughter tremble in fear. She knew it was time for life's receding grit to come to the fore.

Standing motionless and seeing the dust puffs growing larger by the second, Harriett put her arm around Mary.

"I heard Chief Nocona took a white woman for his wife oncest, Mary." She had to find some avenue of hope, black as it might be. "Mary, you are a looker, ain't do doubt you are bound to be wanted by some important chief some day. I spent a lot of time in my grandpa's compound in Kentucky and it was the best place ever," she said, trying to give Mary some false assurances.

"It ain't likely they's a'goin' to kill us, we's Indian ourselves. If Haden hadn't butted into their business, he wouldn't of been killed neither," she sobbed, stroking her little girl's hair, not believing a word she was telling her child.

In the process of trying to come up with some answer to what they could expect, lying to Mary calmed her down until they heard screams of agony shattering any hopeful expectations. Pleading cries heard coming from the wagon horrified them, knowing they were next.

"Mama! It's Haden," Mary cried, looking out the gun hole at the approaching rider.

Harriett pushed Mary aside to see. Haden was hugging Mole's back tighter than a tick. The horse's nostrils were flared and his mouth was open, sucking air in loud gasps. Mole was a strong little cow pony used to breakneck speeds in spurts, not prolonged periods. Mole was lathered and gasping. He had reached his limitations.

"He has somebody ridin' behind him," Mary shouted.

Harriett was suspicious, thinking it could be a trick of the Indians. Fear for Mary's protection forged adrenalin. *If we have to die, I'm a'gonna take some of them wild, yellin' Comanches with us!* The tale she told Mary about Chief Nocona and the possibilities for Mary to be saved for a chief's white wife was just that. She didn't believe for one minute there wouldn't be terrible things done to Mary before they finished her off. Lack of choice grew fight in place of fear.

The person behind Haden decidedly wasn't an Indian. Relieved it wasn't a Comanche, but a young girl clinging to the back of Haden, Harriett ran to the door and lifted the latch to open it before they rode into the yard. Mary ran past her mother to help them. She grabbed Mole's reins and looped them over the hitching post. Chore buckets rattled when Mole yanked his head back to see if he was free. After everyone bolted inside the soddy without saying anything, Mary immediately barricaded the door with the heavy beam once more.

Haden ran to the gun slot to peer out. He had complained a lot about those holes when they first lived in the soddy. The holes made it easy for slithering snakes looking for a cool spot to make their way inside. Scorpions and other pesky varmints found the holes accommodating too. Gus had threatened to chink up the holes when a scorpion had landed on his cot. To his way of thinking, the slots were more problem than problem-solver. After today, Haden believed there wouldn't ever be a complaint again, that is, if they made it though the day.

"So far," Haden announced in short, whispery gasps, "they's still at the wagon."

The young girl began to cry softly, burying her face into her hands. Harriett put her arm around her shoulders and tried to give comfort.

"I had a strange feelin' this day the minute I got up," she said to her children and guest. "It started off different than usual."

Haden didn't answer her, but nodded. His mother knew he couldn't have agreed more. It had only been a few minutes earlier that a slung tomahawk going end over end had barely missed his head. Running Dog intended to implant it between Haden's eyes, but Mole was running faster than Running Dog calculated. It fell past him when they rode off.

"Just a bit ago I'se where those folks are now, Ma," Haden said with boyish disbelief, still struggling to catch his breath from nervous fear. "I'm lucky, Ma! Those poor souls are a'dyin' if they ain't already dead!" Reality struck finally hit him and he shuddered.

Haden was a sapling wanting to grow. Sometimes he thought later rather than sooner and this had been one of those times.

Four people were mentally living the massacre happening no more than a quarter of mile away and didn't know if they were going to be next. Mary touched the distraught older girl's shoulder and feebly tried to give comfort. Mary had a problem. It was hard to comfort when she had trembles inside herself. Survival proved a powerful force for Mary and she still faced a threat. Twelve years wasn't old enough to develop courage to spare. The one she intended to comfort appeared to be about Haden's age, fourteen. The young girl cried silently and stared blankly.

Drops of perspiration flew every direction from Haden with any sharp movements. Harriett dipped some water into the pan on the washstand, grateful she had drawn early this morning, and handed Haden a wet rag to wipe his hot face with, then handed another to the young girl.

"Back when I was a girl, there's plenty of dangerous times, all right. Danger is danger I guess, no matter what time you live it," she nervously rattled, as if her reminiscence would make a difference to the hearers. "But," she continued, "times when Arimenta was taken by them soldiers, when grandpa had to leave, and when I had to be quiet on our houseboat so's no one could find me, all this has lost out to this here situation. I'm sure when the settlers come into Kentucky there's dangerous times with settlers takin' possession of places and my family a'fightin' back. That was generations ago. It all seems watered down compared to what we are a'dealin' with right now. What a strange world this is! I remember oncet people's word meant somethin'. Grandpa used to tell me, 'The white man will do what he said he'll do but only for a short time because he done lost his contentment.' He said, 'When you are out of harmony with nature, go against its intended purpose and don't respect nothin', your bed ain't got no contentment to lie upon.' Ain't it mystifyin' how some once crowded out my family and today the shoe is on the other foot? You reckon that's why them Comanche's is so savage?"

Driftin' all this time has showed me some mighty strange ways. Them folks in the wagon had some dreams, for sure. Tryin' to make themselves fit where they don't rightly belong has turned to a terrible fate. They's become another trophy scalp. Ain't there more to it then just a'takin' a chance a'driftin? Even their name will be lost after a spell. Lost and swallowed up like so many folks I know. Lost and swallowed up.

Homesickness hit like waves, as if only the day before these times were lived. Harriett pined for the familiar in the hot soddy, waiting out the impending doom that possibly would be their fate in a short while. Smells of damp earth, dew on grasses and trees came rolling back from the past to her present thoughts. *How I miss them smells. My younguns never knowed about it and I ain't a'goin' to be able to share it with 'em neither.*

"Yi yi yi yi yi yi-haw," screeched Running Dog. In his loud, high-pitched cry he rode toward the soddy with a tomahawk in one hand and something else in the other. Dust puffs once again began to fog up the air and grow larger as the Indian and his three companions joined him in riding toward the dugout.

"Here they come! Keep your eyes open, Ma!" Haden yelled at his mother in panic. "I'll cover the door if they try to take to the yard. Don't waste any of them bullets, Ma! We gotta make ever one count." The face of the young girl's mother kept tormenting his memory.

"Wait! Haden, wait! Don't shoot yet. They've stopped a ways out. Don't shoot whiles they've stopped," Harriett told her son. "Maybe they have changed their mind," she said hopefully.

"Yi yi yi yi yi yi yi yi-haw," Running Dog screamed again, then held up some long hair weighed down by skull bone attached to the bottom. "Yi yi yi yi yi yi yi-haw," the other three joined in. The Indians had items taken from the wagon draped around their bodies.

Jicara, the other Comanche Haden had recognized at the wagon, had a sack of flour draped across his horse's rump. In view of the gun slot holes, he dumped another bloody scalp into a pail hanging from his other arm, rendering the occupants in the dugout motionless. The Indians gloated and paraded around the soddy while their prey watched quietly through the narrow openings. They were prepared to shoot, but still held their fire.

As fast as they rode in, the Indians turned their horses toward the mesa and left in a flurry of war whoops. Haden noticed something before Running Dog left. He had a big grin on his face, a defiant grin. It was pleasurable for Running Dog to have Haden in his debt. Haden's interference had been temporarily given, but both Comanche and this Melungeon mixed Cherokee knew that Running Dog's benevolence would have a pay day some day!

"Thank God, they're gone!" Harriett had never used such an expression before. Wasn't it Angie who gave God credit for their safety when they finally reached Little Rock? She always heard Angie thanking God for something and if ever there was a need to thank somebody, Harriett deemed the time couldn't be better than right now!

"I hope so, I hope so," Haden repeated. I hope it ain't another game they's playin'. They are blood -thirsty sons-of-bitches!" he swore.

"Bless your heart," Harriett told the young girl, trying to comfort the lone survivor. The sight of her parents' scalps paraded around their dugout echoed screams of her mother for everyone. "You are safe here."

Mary dipped the washrag into the dishpan of water again, rung it out and handed it to Harriett to use on the distraught teen.

"What's your name, child?"

The young girl lifted her blue eyes up to meet Harriett's for the first time. "My name is Zella Barnard," she whispered.

"Do you have kin out here, Zella?"

"No, ma'am, we came from Kansas. My Papa has a brother living in Kansas, that's all the kin we have. My uncle works in the stockyard," she added. "Little Leroy, my little brother, died from the flu and there's nobody anymore."

Harriett assured the pitiful girl her folks would get a proper burial when her sons got home. Angie had read something from a book she called The Good Book about times for certain things. She remembered there was something she read about, a time for weepin', something she knew plenty about. She assured Zella that it was all right to weep. "It's a natural thing to do," she told her. Then Harriett shared something else she wasn't quite so sure of herself, but Angie had said it was in The Good Book and if anybody needed something good to hear, Zella did. Harriett knew Angie swore by what was written in that Good Book.

"Angie told me times comes for laughin' and healin' too and that will happen for you Zella, even if you don't believe it right now."

After trying to reassure Zella, something nagged at Harriett's spirit inside, suggesting there was more to Angie's story in The Good Book she needed to know. Angie had a peace inside her when she read this part, and Harriett wondered why she didn't share that same peace by repeating this comfort to Zella? She didn't. It was a growing curiosity to understand why not.

Haden left the soddy to take care of Mole. That little pony had never been worked so hard since he was broke. A greater respect was earned for his four-legged friend who was rewarded with extra feed after Haden washed him down. Mole was more needful for water and only after drinking his fill did he accept his reward.

Returning after a day of working cattle the boys inspected the carnage on the range but didn't tarry, not knowing what might have happened at home. Relieved to discover everyone was not harmed, the cousins and McCoys were uneasy and left soon after helping to bury Zella's parents. The Comanches might have continued their butchery and they needed to check on their own families.

"From the looks of things, this is probably all they did today," George McCoy said. "But I can't be satisfied until we check things out." The worried men rode off toward adjoining sections of land.

"Yes, sir, the day started out a bit different didn't it, Ma? I felt it when I got up. I know to listen to instincts better from here on out. One good thing, though, there wasn't any missin' cattle today," Gus said. He no more got the words out of his mouth when he realized why the cattle weren't bothered.

   Time had begun and come to a close. Shock was stuck in the middle of the beginning and ending of the day, making it a blur. Memories were so ugly it left time without meaning. All the family wanted to do was to shut out the horror, but they couldn't, the day had left a nightmare on their hands. When four people finally found sleep it was interrupted intermittently throughout the night with death screams ringing in their ears.

Chapter 37

THE BOOK

Zella had to make many adjustments living in a dugout and with strangers. Mourning for her parents interfered with being able to fit in anywhere. Grieving in surroundings she was unaccustomed to with foreign creature habits grappled with her emotions. Boiled prickly pear at first was a disgusting and fearful experience until she became brave enough, encouraged by hunger, to try it. Pork was a rarity as well, as they were used to eating beef in Kansas. Zella's uncle took beef for pay many times and every once in a while shared with the Barnards.

Living in a soddy reminded Zella of their root cellar. Houses she was used to living in were much different. Dodge, Kansas, had more of everything than the simple prairie, but she did her best to fit in and only lost ground when she was periodically sidetracked by grief.

John's whiskey business would bring first one, then another, Indian and settler alike to their yard for whiskey. During such visits, Zella found living there very hard and quietly hid in the house until the customers left.

Changes for Gus were hard to come by. With a new family member, a rivalry between him and Haden would have been unthinkable until Zella came. Gus always figured he was superior and had no competition with his younger brother, but Zella Barnard had eyes for Haden. Haden had made an indelible impression by saving her from certain death.

Mary enjoyed having a new "sister" in the house until she saw her position as the youngest sibling give way to her brother's attentions paid to this new sister. She had always been the recipient of their teases and pats. Then, when Haden stared at Zella moon-eyed it planted a bit of resentment. If Zella hadn't been in their soddy from a tragedy Mary had personally witnessed, her ire might have manifested more. As it was, she pouted silently.

The road between Aaron McCoy's ranch and Harriett's became smoother from John taking the girls by buckboard to visit with Cornelia after chores. Since the time Harriett and the girls were in Alvord for supplies, after being invited by Aaron McCoy, when Harriett made introductions to Zella, weekly visits became a ritual. During these visits, Angie would read from The Good Book, sharing reading time with Cornelia and Zella. Mary listened and secretly wished she could decipher the markings. Since she couldn't, it was entertaining to listen.

Harriett thought there was more to the story about John wanting to be the girls' protector and driver each week. It wasn't long before Mary told her she thought Fannie was pregnant.

Fannie caught the eyes of every single man around, and some not-so-single, like flowers attract bees. George and Tom found ranching kept them too busy working cattle to keep tabs on Fannie, leaving opportunity open. John's erratic absences left some to wonder about it when Fannie had need of Harriett's assistance to deliver Fannie's very light-skinned baby girl.

"I'se goin' to name my baby, Harriett, Miss Harriett. I like your name and you done help me get my babe here and all, Harriett will be her name."

After two years, John had worn his welcome out when another midwife call came to Harriett. Fannie named her baby son, John. John never owned up to anything, but he decided the girls were big enough to drive themselves for weekly visits with Cornelia and he never went back.

Two more years slipped by working the Split Arrow, picking up more cattle and trying to plant some corn to aid in John's other enterprise. John refused to go anywhere near Fannie.

"Aaron McCoy don't cotton much to John," Harriett explained to the girls when she accompanied them on one of their visits. Cornelia met the three at the door of their ranch house when they arrived. Aaron had replaced his soddy several years ago with a native rock house, transforming their soddy into a cellar that rattlesnakes found accommodating from time to time.

"Mornin' Miss Harriett, girls," Angie said. She always beamed when greeting the weekly guests. Angie never failed to have some sweet cakes to serve after their Good Book study. They began their study right away this morning.

"'For God so loved the world that He gave his only begotten Son, that whosoever believeth in Him should not perish, but have everlastin' life. For God sent not his Son into the world to condemn the world; but that the world through Him might be saved. He that believeth on Him is not condemned,'—" this is a real important part, Miss Harriett, listen to this,"—'but he that believeth not is condemned already, because he hath not believed in the name of the only begotten Son of God.'"

"I'm a'goin' to explain it like I sees it, Miss Harriett. You listen to what sweet Jesus wants me to tell you, Miss Harriett. We's all sinners, my Good Book says so. It tells me there's only one God in Heaven, but there's a mystery about it because He's three in One. That sounds confusin' but here's the way I understand it. Take me, for instance, I'm a Mama, I'm a grandma to little Harriett and John, and I done been a wet nurse for Miss Cornelia, but I ain't three people, but just one Angie all the same. They's God the Father, God the Son, and God the Holy Spirit and it is all One, even if it is three peoples. It is a mystery to it, but we's a'goin to understand it by 'n by."

"Lands alive, Angie, how could that be?"

"I don't rightly know, Miss Harriett. But that's the way it is and I done believe it. When I believed in it I learned more'n I ever thought I'd know from this here Good Book. That Holy Spirit done opened up my eyes to understand it more and more. I'm still a'learnin' at it too."

"Miss Harriett, the world is like little lost ducks a'needin' some Mama to show 'em the way to the pond. If they's hatched and don't know how to find the water to drink and live, they's all a'goin' to die. They get quarrelsome, the thirstier they gets, goin' and peckin' at each other and is a'goin' to die. Until somebody showed 'em the way to live, they's lost forever and ain't a'goin' to make it. Jesus is like that Mama, a'showin' the lost ones how to live and to be happy. He give 'em the everlastin' water so's they'd never be thirsty again."

As Angie spoke, scenes of leaving Kentucky on a houseboat in Harriett's youth flooded her mind, as she remembered her own effort trying to find ways to live. She and Canady had been like those lost little ducks in many ways, going from one place to another, searching for survival. Her history of emptiness, drifting through life and hard times during the war, met her face to face as Angie explained inner solutions to something she never knew about before. She remembered the young man with his dead wife in his arms on the river begging for someone to come save his Sophy. She also remembered she and Canady didn't help him. He needed to find help in life. So had she and Canady needed help, but they were afraid to help the young man.

This Jesus Angie was talking about helped people. "He came to earth to do that," she said. Angie explained that the sinful nature in people already exists from the time they can question. "We'se born that way." After having said this, she read some more passages that proved dying for people was the most important act ever done by Jesus when he died for all the sins of everybody in the world.

"'For the wages of sin is death; but the gift of God is eternal life through Jesus Christ our Lord.'"

Jesus died to pay for the sins like not helpin' that young man holding his dead wife and then doin' nothin' to comfort his pain when he had to dump Sophy in the river.

Harriett's heart felt a tug inside when she heard Angie tell her, "We have to ask God to forgive all the wrongs we have did in life. The Good Book tells us to ask God to make things right between us and Him. If we don't, when we leaves this here world, we ain't never goin' to have a home in Heaven." With tears showing in Angie's eyes, Harriett heard her say, "He already done took care of our wrongs by sendin' His Son to come live on Earth for a time and dyin' in our place to pay for them sin wages we can't pay for, Miss Harriett. Yessum, it's somethin' we owe, we just can't pay it."

"Miss Harriett, I done trusted Jesus to help me love folks the way He does. I had to love the folks that treated us bad back in the cotton patch in Alabama. That don't mean I had to love what they did. I just has to love 'em because they didn't know no better and because Jesus loves all us folks, black and white."

"In God's eyes, we'se all sinners and can't get past the gates a'goin' into Heaven when we leaves this ole world. If peoples don't believe in Jesus, they'se always a'goin' to be a'driftin' and a'searchin'. He paid the price and all 'cause we can't pay it for our unholy selves. No sir, not us."

"Now, Miss Harriett, my sweet Jesus wants me to ask you this mornin' if you want to try a'leanin' on Him the rest of your life, if you want Him to come live in your heart like Cornelia and her brothers and Mr. McCoy and I done a long time ago? If'n you do, here's all you have to do. Just follow, sayin' prayer words after me, but you have to mean it with all your heart. Do you suppose this would be something you'd like to do, Miss Harriett?"

"Angie," Mary interrupted, "do you suppose I could say them words too?"

"Me too, Angie, could I say them too?" Zella asked.

Harriett felt a longing growing inside her. The hole she had inside, the one she recognized being there as a young girl, was the same one she had tried to fill in many ways on her own with only partial satisfaction. The satisfaction never stayed. *Yes! I want to say them words, I want this Jesus to fill this emptiness up, the missin' part inside me.*

"I do, Angie, I want to ask Jesus to make me count for somethin'. I want Him to come live in my heart and I want to say them words," Harriett responded.

"Dear Jesus, I believe you is God's Son. I believe you died and paid them sin wages I couldn't pay. Jesus, I believe you's born of a virgin Mama, and when you died and was buried in the ground, you rose on the third day just like you said you would. Dear Jesus, I believe you's God's Son and I ask you to come live in my heart for evermore. Amen."

Harriett and the girls enjoyed Angie's sweet cakes and on the way home sang songs. There was something else Angie told them while eating their refreshment. She said The Good Book said you had to forgive folks who have hurt you before and the thought lingered in their minds.

That means I need to forgive them folks who killed my William and Shelby Robert. I can't rightly do it. I will ask Jesus to help me do it. She remembered Angie telling her that she could pray to God anywhere, at any time, and He hears, no matter what. *I'll have to ask Jesus how I can do this and pray that I can. I reckon Zella will have some askin' herself when it comes to Runnin' Dog and the rest. After all, them Comanche's don't know who the Holy Spirit is.*

Zella found no need to hide any more when the Comanches came to buy their firewater from John. Stories read from The Good Book each week gave the women much to talk about and, to their amazement, though the corral looked the same, the chores remained the same, and no other changes were made at the Split Arrow, the world took on a clearer horizon.

Haden also had lost any notion of brotherly love toward Zella. It had grown to something else, something deeper. Gus didn't have a chance winning Zella for himself now. Her heart belonged to Haden.

Chapter 38
TRAILS AND REVENGE

J ohn dropped his hat on a peg just inside the soddy door and plopped down on a bench next to the washstand. Gus and Haden were tending to the horses. Before they made it into the dugout John wanted to share something with his mother.

"I hear there's a cattle drive a'brewin around these parts. Mayo and Robert Holmes's ranch is plannin' on bein' a part of it. They's plannin' on goin' on Chisholm's Trail into Kansas. Some say it has natural gullies, makin' it easier to hole a herd up. Them longhorns oughtta make the drive without much trouble," he told Harriett. "McCoy's ranch has the most cattle herded up. The Settles, Troutmans, Shane and Wortham Ranches are all puttin' in some of their branded longhorns. All told, there's probably about two thousand head," he said. Then added, "I'm a'thinkin' on takin' a bunch of ours and give it a try."

Gus came into the dugout about the time he heard John tell his mother about plans for the roundup. Gus had made no headway with Zella. He had no prospects anywhere around as Cornelia wouldn't give him the time of day. She had turned out to be one of those foolish girls seeing more in Haden, totally annoying and obvious to Gus.

"I'm plannin' on a'goin myself," Gus told his mother. John looked at him with amazement. Gus hadn't shared any such intention with John at the time he told Robert and Mayo earlier he planned to hitch up with some cattle from Split Arrow. Apparently it appeared it would be up to Haden to tend to the ranch, most especially the whiskey business, while they were gone if Gus planned to go to.

After several weeks rounding up longhorns, the Split Ranch had forty branded head to add to the mix. Robert Holmes and Bryan Settles would be riding point, with Felix Wortham and Mark Troutman taking care of swing, leaving John and Marty Shane to herd riding flank. Gus and Will Berger got the worst job of all, that of drag, riding at the back of the herd. No matter what the weather would be, eating dirt on the trail would be their lot. One woman would be making the trip back to Dodge. Monica Whitten had enough of pioneer life and wanted to return to a more civilized Dodge. This would be her opportunity and the cowboys agreed to let her ride with them. She could help cook and spell-drive the chuck wagon.

"I figure Monica will have a time of it," Harriett told Mary and Zella. "She ain't a'goin' to fit into Dodge anymore'n she does out here. Them folks will be too high falooten for the likes of her after bein' out here on the range all this time. That girl ain't much to look at, but she has a good heart."

Zella jumped at the chance to get word about her parents to her Uncle Clifford in Dodge by way of John and Gus. She carefully composed a letter telling him of the ordeal over the years and that her parents had been killed before they even had a chance to start. She filled him in on what also had happened to her and of her intent to stay put in Texas.

"Uncle Clifford warned Papa about coming out here," Zella told Mary. "I know this will be a terrible shock. He and Papa were very close. It's bound to break his heart. Before we left Kansas, Uncle Clifford told him about stories he had heard from cowboys drifting into Dodge."

Zella looked at Haden. She saw a faint smile coming from him and eyes that told more than the smile. "I never would have found you if I hadn't come, would I, Haden?" she whispered to him in passing. "My Mama and Papa would have liked you, I know it."

She felt safe with Haden. He had earned her trust with the grit he showed in rescuing her from the Comanches. Zella had given her heart to him, not as a child, but as a young woman. The heart she gave had grown up purposes.

When the weather permitted, Mary, Zella, Gus, and Haden made it a practice to sit outside by the corral to talk during the evening hours. Some of Haden's tales about times lived during the Civil War sounded a bit long-winded. Mary was so young that her memory of it was not as keen as Gus's and Haden's. Counting stars became another occupation, like dreaming dreams out loud and sharing hopes for a future only the young have courage enough to dream about. Youthful memories that were to carry mature adults into future golden years embedded themselves around experiences and dreams by the old corral.

During these times of sharing, Gus and Mary suddenly acknowledged they were not included in the evening talk anymore. It had become private conversations between Haden and Zella.

"Ma, you mind if I sit outside with you this evenin'?" the fifteen year old Mary asked, while sitting on the left of her mother. Harriett gave her a hug.

"Is there a special reason you don't want to be with the others? I'm mighty glad to have your company," she told her daughter, holding her hand and patting and rubbing her back with nimble fingers from the other.

"I don't know nothin' special to talk about," Mary told her mother, removing her hand to pull her hair back out of her face. "'Cides, they are always making eyes at each other anyhow. Haven't you noticed how silly Haden is actin' lately, Ma? He even combs his hair before supper and scrubs his face so much it almost squeaks," Mary said disgustedly.

Harriett chuckled to herself. "Love must be in the air, Mary." She had noticed the fuss her boys had been making in trying to win Zella's attention. Gus had been strutting around like some proud bull, but Zella wasn't the least bit interested. She always found some excuse to talk to Haden. Mary was feeling like yesterday's clabber milk too.

John's absence had a lot to do with his whiskey business. It didn't sit well with Harriett for John to continue brewing after her understanding of Jesus, especially after seeing what the whiskey was doing to people, white and Indian alike. This was John's life, his decision. Now he was turning his business over to her youngest son in his absence on the cattle drive. That further didn't set well with Harriett when John carefully went over instructions. He didn't want to lose business while he would be away.

"Thank goodness for John!" Mary blurted out while sitting next to her mother. The two by the corral smitten with each other never heard a word Mary had said all evening. Gus had already taken his leave. The balm he relied on was John's story that they never could tell who they might meet at trail's end. Gus was eager to step into this man's world!

Robert and Mayo had been on a cattle drive before and had some experience under their belts. They had ridden point with Coy Bayfield a year ago. Greenhorns get the lowly position of drag. Gus wanted to go in the worst way, thinking the position of drag was nothing but nomenclature.

Haden left with John and Gus to round up the forty head and move them to the McCoy place. Moving cattle to congregate at the McCoys was happening at the Settle, Troutman and Wortham Ranches too, making it a sizeable herd to move. A growing sea of longhorns bellowing could be heard for miles around.

"You'll have until we reach Red River Station, Gus, to see if you will make the trail with us," warned Tom McCoy. "It's just like Bayfield warned us last year, you won't be cut any slack from us neither. He chopped quick and sure if he thought a body wouldn't make a good hand. I'll do the same. Nothin' personal, it just has to be that a'way," he warned. "Ridin' drag is the worst job a body can get on the drive, but it is a necessary one," Tom continued with his instructions. "Coy Bayfield wouldn't put up with a thing but gettin' the job done and I ain't aimin' to neither. There's too much at stake and it's a tough business. It'll tax you to the limit, Gus. Do you reckon you can take it?"

"I can stick no matter what. Ain't a problem, Tom. You can count on me." With that said, Gus milled with the rest of the hands anxious to get started to do some mighty hard work and, most likely, have some run-ins with Indians along the way.

"Better keep your nose covered good or you'll be sick the first week we're out," Tom warned Gus.

Advice stopped and the work began. With tearing eyes, Tom's words began to grow meaning while John's fanciful tales about the trail's end faded. Gus adjusted his bandana higher on his nose when the herd picked up their gait. Without notice, a steer peeled off toward the west. Something already had spooked the nervous herd and they were hardly started. A sea of bobbing horns now stabbed at space through clouds of chalky dust. Robert, riding point, rode fast to head the lead steer back, as Felix and Mark moved out, giving room for the herd to bend back in a counter-clockwise movement. Racing madly, the mass of horns and hooves circled, covering ground in jerky movements over ditches and uneven terrain for half a mile before the gait of the herd slowed. Tom and Bryan managed to turn the movement toward Red River.

Gus took off his hat and then placed it back firmly on his head. With clenched teeth full of gritty trail, he once again followed the northbound herd. As far as he was concerned, they couldn't get to something wet soon enough and the trip had just begun.

So began Gus's first cattle drive. If he were to survive the trip, which he was beginning to have doubts about already, it would be the biggest thing he ever accomplished. He was determined to see it to the end.

Haden had become the man of the house with Gus and John gone. He also was involved with taking care of his brother's still and selling John's moonshine to customers. It made money for staples—flour, sugar and other things at Alvord. Those known Comanches who had killed the Barnards felt no restraint to purchase the firewater from the very person who had cheated them out of one of their prey. They were regular visitors.

"Runnin' Dog, there ain't been no wampum for the last three times you'se here. We ain't had any barter of any kind," Haden told the menacing Indian. He had noticed Running Dog liked his whiskey more and more, but John would not be happy at all if Haden couldn't account for all the whiskey. Either it was whiskey or barter, they had to tally, and Haden felt responsible. The Indian trade had increased. While John was gone there were more and more Comanches coming into the yard for firewater, making it a habit of "pay next time" being said before they rode off with their refilled jugs. Running Dog kept pushing Haden.

"This could get serious, Ma. If I don't handle this situation now, it's only goin to get worse. John ain't a'gonna be one bit happy about this when he gets back."

There hadn't been any Indian uprising for a long time, only a missed longhorn from time to time, but the soddy dwellers agreed it was better the longhorn then them. The Comanches appeared peaceable as long as they could get their whiskey.

John and Gus had been gone a couple of months when Haden decided he needed to make an accounting for lost revenue on John's whiskey.

"I've come to see Runnin' Dog," he told an old woman after riding into the Indian campground. All the Indians knew Haden was their source for firewater and he was no stranger. A Comanche brave squatting on the ground near the old woman pointed to a tent near the center of the camp.

A woman was coming out of the tent. She took hold of the rope from a staked-out goat, went back inside the tent still holding onto the goat's rope, then came back out of the tent with a small child with her this time. Haden and she passed each other as she led the goat off to pasture.

Running Dog was not surprised at Haden's visit and met him in the doorway of the tent as he approached. While shaking hands, Haden heard a baby cry and saw it lying on the dirt floor wrapped in a cradleboard. The whimpers lasted for just a little while, then the baby dropped off to sleep.

Even with the gesture of shaking hands, the Comanche was not pleased to see Haden. He didn't like to be beholden to anyone and found Haden's visit irritating. There wasn't much honor between Comanche and white settlers, but Haden looked like he could be a blood brother. Confusion added to his dislike of Haden. So, Running Dog had two counts against Haden. One being he didn't know who Haden really was, and the other grievance was his long memory of Haden cheating him out of Zella's scalp. It was uncomfortable for Running Dog to rely on first John, and now Haden for his firewater. There was a war going on between his addictive desire for whiskey and dealing with someone he didn't like. The desire for whiskey won out.

The Comanche camp was quiet when Haden got there. Busy and silent women were actively scraping bison hides while most of the men were out looking for wild mustangs to add to their remuda. The woman who led the goat from Running Dog's tent had returned to help the other women scrape hides. A few children could be heard playing but mostly, the camp was quiet.

"Hello, Chief Running Dog," Haden greeted the disgruntled Comanche. The chief shook Haden's hand and immediately went back inside his dark tent. Haden followed him. It was spacious inside the tepee with the dirt floor covered over with a bison hide. Running Dog sat, making himself cross-legged at the back of the tent facing Haden.

It was always dangerous going into the camp of the Comanches. Their hatred for settlers taking away their prairie and killing their buffalo was the thing they thought about the most. As a precaution and for his own safety, Haden always took a skinning knife in a scabbard strapped to his calf whenever he had to come on collection visits. At seventeen he stood over six feet tall and had taken on the appearance of a man, but Haden was no match for Running Dog who was ten years his senior.

The Indian got up and moved to the side of the tent where the baby was sleeping in its cradleboard and pulled some moccasins and beads from a peg on one of the tent poles. He handed them to Haden without saying anything, as if that concluded the transaction Haden had come for.

Haden looked at the pittance for payment and argued with Running Dog. "This is fine but not enough," he said.

A scowl came across the chief's face. He hadn't slept off the results of the firewater from the night before and Haden's demand for more wampum was not what he wanted to hear.

"No more, is done!" Running Dog said sternly.

At that moment the agitated Indian grabbed Haden by the shirt collar and slung him to the other side of the tent, pulling a knife as he slung him. Trying to escape Running Dog's thrusts at him, Haden moved backward to where the baby was sleeping and pulled his skinning knife from the scabbard on his calf. Haden was more interested in missing Running Dog's stabbing blade than connecting in retaliation. The angry Indian lunged at Haden. Quickly Haden stepped back to miss the thrust and heard as well as felt a sickening crunch when his boot landed atop the sleeping baby's head. No sound came from the child other than that first impact and both of them knew it had been a fatal step. The little papoose never cried, but died instantly.

Haden dismissed the reason for ever coming to the Comanche camp in the first place and turned to flee out the tent door to escape death. As soon as he turned to go, "Yi yi yi yi-haw," came from Running Dog. A sharp pain in Haden's shoulder slanted across to his waist, oozing crimson from the gash made by Running Dog's knife. The force of lunging toward Haden unbalanced the Comanche and he fell, giving Haden time to get out and onto Mole's back.

Mole left in the direction of home, but Haden turned him toward the trees along a creek bank to the south of the direction of their soddy, hoping to lead Running Dog away from the house where his mother and the girls were.

After Haden left to make his collection that morning, Mary drove the buckboard to the McCoys on an errand for Harriett. They got word Cornelia had been quite sick from something she caught from Julia Wortham. Cornelia had stopped by to visit Julia after buying supplies at Alvord and now both women suffered the same malady,as well as Angie and Fannie. Harriett thought it might be neighborly when she heard Angie came down with it too for Mary to take them a big pot of stew Harriett had cooked. This would be a good time to pay back some of the kind deeds done for her over these years struggling on this dry mesa.

"We'll have these dried butter beans shelled by the time Mary gets back," Zella told Harriett. The women had waved Mary off and got to work hardly before the buckboard left the yard. Halfway through a bushel of the dried beans, the women heard a commotion outside the soddy. They had been so busy shelling and talking neither of them noticed the sounds of horses in the yard. Before they could get up to investigate, the door flew open and there stood Running Dog with a tomahawk in his hand and anger on his face.

Zella screamed, "Oh, God, help us!" The fear she had left behind, with the help of God and prayer, returned when she saw the evil written across the Indian's face and the two other braves pushing past him, taking hold of both her arms.

Harriett struggled to get off her stool, but Running Dog grabbed her with one hand and buried his tomahawk on the log stool Zella had been sitting on before putting a knife to Harriett's throat.

A fourth brave busted through the door with a rope and tied Harriett's forearms together in front of her, wrapping the rope down from her elbows to her wrists.

Zella was shoved on the bed by the first two Indians as Running Dog walked toward her. Her eyes were wide with horror. The Chief grabbed the material at her ankles and pulled it down and off. Then he jumped on top of her, forcing her legs apart, knowing his difficulty was due to her never having been with a man before. This gave even more cruel satisfaction to her tormentor. Zella's screams were incessant. It appeared her cries incited the Indians all the more. When the last of the four finished using her, they turned toward Harriett, leaving Zella bleeding and beaten. Zella watched in shock when Running Dog came with his tomahawk toward Harriett.

Grabbing Harriett's hands he held them flat on Zella's log stool and raised the tomahawk.

"Ugh," he grunted as he swung it down with a thud across Harrietts thumbs. Blood spurted as her thumbs shot off the bench from the force of the metal tool. With exaggerated swings, he uttered his gutteral sounds as he whacked a little finger and index finger off next.

"Oh, God, see what they do! Oh, God, come to me, help me," Harriett pleaded with God.

Running Dog stopped after he heard Harriett cry her prayer for help and walked toward Zella again. He grabbed her long, light brown hair with his left hand, all tousled and matted by now. Harriett heard a "crack" and the next thing she saw was Zella's hair in his hand. Zella's eyes were staring straight up. Blood gushed everywhere, soaking into the feather mattress as Zella's body jerked in spasms before she lay motionless.

Running Dog turned back to face Harriett. He lifted his tomahawk while staring into Harriett's pain-contorted face. Preparing herself for the same fate as Zella, Harriett shut her eyes before he hit. She heard the door open instead and the Indians going out, yelling war whoops as they went. Running Dog left carrying the scalp that was denied them years ago. Harriett heard their horses leave the yard and listened until their whoops grew faint.

Throbbing and gushing blood, Harriett's mangled hands could not free herself from the binding ropes. She cried in anguish for God to hear her prayer, to send help. It was too late for Zella and Harriett couldn't look any more at the blood-soaked bed with Zella's contorted body on it, missing the top of her head.

Several hours later Mary discovered the carnage. She fought hysterics when she saw her mother was still alive. She knew she had to get her to the McCoys for help, Cornelia sick or not. Before she could get her into the buckboard, Haden made it back, hoping to find help for the gash in his back.

"Oh, Haden, don't look," Mary screamed when she saw him open the soddy door. She had taken the rope off Harriett but hadn't had time to do anything for Zella. She wasn't sure she had the stomach to do anything, even if she knew what that was. Nothing could be done for Zella anyway. It was too late. Her mama was going to die if she didn't get help soon.

Mary saw Haden's back when he went towards the blood-soaked bed. His ashen face looked back toward his mother and she heard her brother cry out. "Oh, my God, what have I done?" He closed Zella's eyelids, heaving sobs. Mary ran to her brother after getting a bucket of kerosene for her mother to put her hands into to stop the bleeding and infection. "What are we goin' to do, Haden?"

Haden raised himself up from Zella's limp body. "Mary, we got to get some help. There ain't nothin' we can do for Zella now. Ma has to have some help to clean herself and get some laudanum. The whiskey will have to do until we can do the other. Can you take us to the McCoys?" he asked his sister, shifting, trying to stay conscious.

Mary knew Haden wouldn't remain conscious long. He had lost lots of blood from his own wound. She hitched up the team again and put quilts down on the buckboard for Haden and her mother to lie on.

"You better hurry up, Mary," Harriett told her daughter weakly. Before Mary drove the team out of the yard, Haden told her to go back for more whiskey in the closet to take with them. She climbed off the buckboard and back into the soddy, trying not to look in the direction of the bed, and retrieved two more jugs of whiskey from the curtained-off closet. Past thinking, she reacted. Grabbing the reins, she slapped the team and yelled, "Haw! .Haw! Giddy up there!"

Chapter 39

HOME

By the time John and Gus returned from Kansas, Harriett's hands had healed enough so there were no raw places, just misery. Haden's slashed back had mended too, but he was left with an outward reminder from his shoulder blade to his waist about an inward regret he would live with the rest of his life. Texas had left scarred minds and bodies. The major positive experience was learning about Jesus Christ from a former slave. Angie left this world's journey with the flu. Part of her stayed in Harriett's heart, however, with the hope that they would meet again someday.

Life's uncertainties for drifters like former boat people had a little anchor in the form of pensions being issued to Civil War soldiers. The son who had shared his worldly goods with his family was once again responsible for some form of easement to occur. Jasper's pension would be going to Harriett since he had never married, but it had to be addressed legally in Arkansas for her to receive it.

Gus left home in Texas before the family moved to Arkansas. He ran away at seventeen, almost eighteen, never to see his mother again.

John grew restless without his younger brother to help he and Haden do the work. His whiskey business would never be the same after what had happened to his family. It was time for him to move on, too. He had planned to go to Scott County in Arkansas but, *you never know about* John, his mother always said.

When Haden and Cornelia married, they lived at the old home place in the soddy for a while. Harriett had difficulty going back and was grateful that Cornelia had become a new member of the family, living in the soddy.

Evertime I look at that bed, I think of poor Zella. We need to get shut of this place, I'm a'thinkin'. Now'd be a good time since Cornelia is pregnant with her first youngun. Arkansas is where I can get Jasper's check. It will help out where I can't do much good anymore. Since Cornelia's Pa done passed on and her brothers has places and families of their own to tend to, I reckon, now's as good a time as any.

And, so it was. Drifting was a lifestyle known, but how to break it was unknown. Arkansas lasted until all the children from Haden and Cornelia were born, then speculation for buying a place sight unseen in Edwards County down in Texas once again challenged Haden to another change.

Lands! Where did all the time go? A tolerable amount of things has happened in my day, but there just ain't enough time to tell it, even if there was inclination to listen. Not many want to hear about it anyway. Most folks in Jacksboro are too busy to listen to old stories. Sure 'nuf, one thing's for certain, I knowed some things it's best unsaid.

Harriett heard Cornelia call, "Supper", but dimly noted through fading vision that Haden insisted on lighting and relighting his pipe anyway. *It's become a habit like your Pa had, son.*

This here rockin' chair feels like home to me. When I set I can take myself away from all the carryin' on them lively younguns do. Busy wears me out. I swear it's more a chore tryin' to understand what's happin' around here. It's easier to not think on it. Less tiring.

Losin' sight puts a halt to stayin' up with things. When I do recollect things my younguns used to do, I do get a chuckle over it. My family ain't aware of the things I can see. How can I explain it? I see things in my own world they have no notion of. I have secret talks with folks they never knew.

"Canady, can you hear me now? Do you remember that wild flower you gave me oncet? I nearly lost it durin' the war, but I still have it."

"Gus has a fine business head on his shoulders. A fine family too, I hear. There's a good need for Gus's moonshine, with ailments and all. Shelby and John are a'livin' in Arkansas, they tell me. Here we are in one place and they's in another! Same's with James. Mary is a'livin' in Point Cedar, married some kin of John's first wife, Canady. I hear she is took with the rhematiz pretty bad. I hope we don't have no more wars to deal with."

Haden's daughter, Sybil, passed by Harriett's rocking chair and patted her on the shoulder, after reaching down and kissing her on top of her head.

"That Sybil is such a sweet child. I helped ever one of them younguns get into this world. Cornelia lost the first two babies, Donnie and Newtie, then had two sets of twins after Wash was born. Maybe you seen Donnie and Newtie where you's at, Canady?"

"Harriett, it's time to eat a bite," Cornelia said. Harriett felt a gentle nudge and, with Haden's help, was seated at their long bench table.

"Boy, am I hungry!" Noel reached for a hot biscuit. Harriett heard Cornelia smack his hand, reminding him they had forgotten something. Haden led in prayer before their meal. *He sounded like Mr. Whitecotton, didn't he Canady?*

Harriett's appetite was minuscule anymore. A few bites and she was sated, then she asked her son to take her back to her rocking chair.

You know, Canady, it seem right strange, there ain't a drop of water in sight at Jacksboro, 'cept the pond. The nearest river is a ways off. I can almost feel the Tennessee River a'splashin on my feet and feel the cool breezes on my face." Harriett finished her thought out loud.

The house was beginning to heat up and Haden looked at his mother wondering, "How in the world can Ma feel cool breezes in this house?"

Ain't no use answerin' him. He can't see what I can see. Oh! Look over yonder on the bank. Ain't that the prettiest green you ever saw! Why, that grass is belly high. The oxen are fat this year, ain't they, grandpa? That is you, ain't it, grandpa? Listen! It's Suley Bluerain's pump organ and I hear lots of folks a'singin'. I see a pretty young woman who looks a lot like I did, Canady. You reckon it could be my Mama? Ever body is a'smilin and invitin' me to come on in and sit a spell. I can feel our houseboat a'rockin, gentle-like and see those blue flowers a'growin on the banks. Sweet smells of fresh earth a'birthin' mushrooms and a racket from a jay is a'callin me home as sure as Elizabeth's and my feather bed was a'callin at the end of the day. Canady, I can't stay here no longer. I need to move on. My journey has been long, Canady, my search has been longer. Home is a'waitin'. Can you see Haden and Cornelia a'standin' by my rockin' chair?

"There's no sparkle left in her eyes," Cornelia said. Moaning softly, she raised her apron up to cover her grief. The children gathered around the still woman sitting in the rocking chair.

"Maybe it ain't fittin, but Im a'goin' to leave you now, children. I can plainly see you are busy. There's somethin' a'drawin' me away. It's a'drawin' me to Someone Angie told me about in her book she gave you, Cornelia. You know, the book with the directions to home, the one a'holdin a special flower between its pages."

As for me, I will see Your face in righteousness;
I shall be satisfied when I awake in Your likeness.

Psalm 17:15